• BOOKS BY LOREN D. ESTLEMAN •

Kill Zone

Roses Are Dead

Any Man's Death

Motor City Blue

Angel Eyes

The Midnight Man

The Glass Highway

Sugartown

Every Brilliant Eye

Lady Yesterday

Downriver

Silent Thunder

Sweet Women Lie

Never Street

The Witchfinder

The Hours of the Virgin

A Smile on the Face of
  the Tiger

City of Widows*

The High Rocks*

Billy Gashade*

Stamping Ground*

Aces & Eights*

Journey of the Dead*

Jitterbug*

Thunder City*

The Rocky Mountain Moving
  Picture Association*

The Master Executioner*

Black Powder, White Smoke*

White Desert*

Sinister Heights

Something Borrowed,
  Something Black*

Port Hazard*

Poison Blonde*

Retro*

Little Black Dress*

Nicotine Kiss*

The Undertaker's Wife*

The Adventures of Johnny
  Vermillion*

American Detective*

Gas City*

Frames*

The Branch and the Scaffold*

Alone*

The Book of Murdock*

Roy & Lillie: A Love Story*

The Left-Handed Dollar*

Infernal Angels*

Burning Midnight*

Alive!*

The Confessions of
  Al Capone*

Don't Look for Me*

Ragtime Cowboys*

You Know Who Killed Me*

*A Forge Book

Journey of the Dead

≈ AND ≈

The Undertaker's Wife

· Loren D. Estleman ·

A Tom Doherty Associates Book / New York

JOURNEY OF THE DEAD AND THE UNDERTAKER'S WIFE

Journey of the Dead copyright © 1998 by Loren D. Estleman

The Undertaker's Wife copyright © 2005 by Loren D. Estleman

A Forge Book
Published by Tom Doherty Associates, LLC
175 Fifth Avenue
New York, NY 10010

www.tor-forge.com

Forge® is a registered trademark of Tom Doherty Associates, LLC.

ISBN 978-0-7653-8362-4

Our books may be purchased in bulk for promotional, educational, or business use. Please contact your local bookseller or the Macmillan Corporate and Premium Sales Department at 1-800-221-7945, extension 5442, or by e-mail at MacmillanSpecialMarkets@macmillan.com.

First Edition: May 2016

Printed in the United States of America

0 9 8 7 6 5 4 3 2 1

Contents

Journey
of the Dead

In Memoriam
Gordon D. Shirreffs
(1914–1996)
Más allá!

Pity for him who one day looks upon his inward sphinx and questions it. He is lost.

—RUBÉN DARÍO

• LEAD •

CHAPTER 1

The Coming of the Long Man

The desert is an amphitheater. Eternal in its architecture, infallible in its silence, it marks the disturbed pebble, the broken blade of feathergrass in never-decreasing reverberations to its outer edge. At a distance of fifty miles the click of an iron shoe against sandstone is as the scrape of one's own fork on the plate before him. This is how I became aware of the long man the moment he crossed into old Mexico.

The way along La Jornada del Muerto was hazardous and harsh, but the long man knew it like a lover. Peace after all was a fugitive concept. A war had torn him from his birthplace in Alabama, a different kind of war had transformed him from a hunter of buffalo into a hunter of men, and jeopardy was a state of being. He had a wife and a daughter, but they were aberrant to the Life, a respite rather than an addendum. Home was a place to gather strength and copulate and obtain fresh horses. It lacked the substance of heat and hardpack and the things with thorns and stings. He lived along the Journey of the Dead.

At night the day's heat drained away between the loose grains of sand that made up the desert floor. The long man's breath made jets of gray in the dry blood of dawn; those of the saddle horse and packhorse smoked thickly around their muzzles and condensed into drops that stung their eyes and made them blink. In the long shadows the long man wore a blanket of Hopi manufacture across his shoulders. As the sun grew yellow, the weight of the coarse weave lay heavily upon him, and he rolled it tight and lashed it behind his cantle. The sun's rays made blue pools atop distant rises, but he was not fooled by them, nor did they force him to drink from his canteen, although they made him thirst. He had more than water enough to reach his destination, but even a rich man did not spend his money promiscuously. He would drink when he rested.

In the stonehammer heat of midday he sat in the shade he created by stretching the Hopi blanket between a pair of boulders and two mesquite branches thrust into the sand. There he drank from his canteen, ate one of the pemmican cakes his wife had made for him, and dozed until the shadows stretched. Then he mounted and rode until darkness made the ground treacherous. He did not drink but that he fed water to the horses first from the cup of his hands. He did not make a fire lest the beacon attract the attention of Apaches. He lay wrapped in the Hopi with his hand around the oiled walnut handle of his big long-barreled Colt's revolver, and rose stiff and cold in the tarnished light reflected from below the horizon on the bellies of the clouds to resume his pilgrimage.

On the forenoon of the third day he entered the village.

He had found it more by instinct than direction, the instructions he received from farmers and beggars he had encountered along the road having been delivered in a mulch of bastard Spanish, Yaqui Indian, and fragments of the spoken language from the hieroglyphs in the ruins of Tenochtitlán; and what he had managed to understand was inaccurate. The four directions are as one to the snail who starts and finishes his existence within a handful of miles, yet he is either too polite or too fearful of the consequences of silence not to make some show of knowing the way for the turtle who pauses to inquire.

The village meant little more to him than the desert. Indeed, its features were more like the bleak memory one carried away from that country than the country itself, which seldom failed to surprise even the seasoned traveler with the variety of its shades of umber and saffron and terra-cotta, and after a brief rain with the glory of its blossoms. The squat earthen huts, the wrinkled brown men in their bleached cotton and the widows in their faded weeds, the flies humming soporifically around sides of meat slung from hooks in front of the butcher's like drunks singing, might have belonged to any of a hundred communities sprung up like cottonwoods wherever water trickled down from the yellow-ocher mountains. The desert hammered everything to sameness.

This village, at least, boasted a bath house, the only one between El Paso del Norte and Mexico City. The Aztec Baths shared a building with Juan Morales the barber, and after his haircut and shave the long man stripped to his red raw skin and soaked away the hard crust of sweat and sand like a salt rind while the old woman brushed his brown wool suit and boiled his white shirt in corn water and pressed it with a flatiron until it was as level and stiff as paper. When he emerged from the water, glowing all over and plum-colored in his armpits and private parts, he toweled off vigorously, put on clean long johns, dressed, and combed his thick black hair and smoothed his trailing moustaches before a mirror with an iron frame.

He smelled like a French king. The scent, heavy with crushed violets and lime water and oil of oleander, came from the bottles in Juan Morales' barbershop, where they had increased in potency from long disuse; but it could not entirely eradicate the long man's own smell, of woodsmoke and black powder and harnesses left out in the weather. It was his principal distinguishing feature after his great height, which in the time before he could afford tailoring had obliged him to stitch pieces of hide to the bottoms of his ready-made trousers to cover his long legs. He had never worn garters to gather the material of his shirtsleeves.

The path to the place he sought, and which had brought him all this way into a foreign country, was worn hollow and led through a stand of quaking aspen whose shade was as black and as cool as a subterranean lake. It ended at the base of a rock wall, natural and without features, with a ladder made from ironwood branches lashed together with sinew leaning against the face. This he climbed, the sun cruel upon his shoulders, the air parching his lungs, to the deep ledge at the ladder's summit. There the warm moist air struck his face like the breath of a large friendly dog.

The mirages of the desert could not deceive him, but the green grotto where stood my hut caused him to shut his eyes tight to clear his head of phantasms. Yet when he opened them again the grotto remained. Green in Durango is as gold in the cup of a blind beggar, and the story is yet told of the Spanish priest, his skull caved in and his hamstrings slashed by Apaches, who crawled upon the bloody stumps of his knees for thirty miles across that region that he might collapse and die with his face in the reeds that grew along the bank of the Rio Mezquital, in the time before the first Dutchman set buckled foot upon Manhattan. Had those yellow-green reeds ventured to show themselves upon my rock, I should have plucked them up and flung them over the ledge. Bushes of coriander, wandering vines of basil, forests of mariposa, rows of mandrake and ginseng, and half a hundred more varieties of herbs, spices, roots, and creeping ivy grew in profusion underfoot and wound up the aspen poles that supported the lattice overhead, from which hung black moss in bunches and chokecherry tendrils. Here was every shade and tint of green, from cerecloth black to fiery chartreuse, blinding bright; a botanical garden of wondrous diversity contained within a few square yards of weather-battered stone. There was not another like it between Tres Marias and the Gulf of Mexico. The air was drunken with leafy scent and as heavy as the atmosphere in a rain forest.

Opposite the ladder, nearly invisible in the deep shade, was the entrance to my workshop and home, a trapezoidal opening in an adobe hut of Pueblo Indian origin with walls three feet thick, which from a distance appeared as nothing more than a hollow in the rock scooped by eons of erosion. On his way there the long man trod upon the black soil that covered the rock, soft as pine needles, and ducked beneath a flowering bough that sagged from the lattice.

His stature compelled him to bow his head to clear the lintel and afterward stand with shoulders rounded and his hat off to avoid colliding with the objects that hung from the beams. He stood unspeaking while he waited for his eyes to adjust to the dimness within.

When they had, he still did not speak or look in my direction, but wandered the room, examining with a browser's interest the globes, astrolabes, books bound in decomposing calfskin, and apothecary jars crowding the plain table and shelves, the stuffed crow perched on the lintel over the doorway, the hard varnished shell of the armadillo suspended by rawhide from the center beam of the ceiling. He squinted at the calligraphy on the labels attached to the jars, trying to make out the foreign words, picked up the skull of a prairie dog, registering surprise that it weighed little more than air, smelled the unfamiliar odors that I myself had ceased to smell, of desiccated herbs and she-wolf urine and the exhalations of the athanor. He would know from instinct that these odors were as old as the building itself, permeating the adobe when the clay was yet damp, in the time of the trouble with the Indians up in New Mexico two hundred years before. Such things cannot be manufactured.

At last he came up to where I sat on my tall stool before the chimney, grinding yellow beetles in a mortar. His eyes took in the table in front of me with its litter of retorts, iron tongs, wooden scoops, clumps of borax, ampullae, and my grandfather's bellows, spliced and patched all over so that scarcely a square inch of the original apparatus survived. He cleared his throat loudly and shouted, in dreadful Spanish:

"You are the one the villagers call El Viejo?"

"I am," said I in English, without looking up from my pestle. "It is not necessary to raise your voice. I am not deaf. Merely old."

He hesitated, then dropped his tone. "You speak good American for a Mexican."

"I speak good English for an Englishman. And I am not Mexican. I am Spanish."

"I don't see the difference."

"You would if you came here from Castile with my great-grandfather in 1556."

"Sorry to give offense," he said. "I'm a stranger here. An old woman in Socorro told me you're the man to see when things need fixing that a doctor won't touch. I expected you'd be Indian."

His accent was gentle, dusted but lightly with the dry grit of the Southwest. There was nothing in it of the high honking bray of the Yankee. He had through all remained a Southerner, and he was genuinely apologetic. This too cannot be manufactured.

I laid aside my chore and studied him. The hat in his hand was a new Stetson, blocked into the Texas pinch, with a brown leather sweatband to which clung a number of cut hairs. His thinker's face was long with sorrow. To his vest was pinned a five-pointed star in a shield, nickel-plated, without engraving.

He was perhaps thirty, but his soul was older even than mine.

"What is the name of the old woman you spoke to in Socorro?" I asked.

"Epiphania Ruiz. She's a hunchback."

"I remember her. I treated her for epilepsy when she was a child. Her father was a stonecutter in this village."

"It wasn't her. She's eighty if she's a day."

"She is older than that. It was in the last year of the old century."

"That'd make you right around a hundred."

"It would. It does."

He said nothing, too polite to express disbelief.

"It is no great personal feat to live a long time," I said.

"It is in my work."

I folded my hands in the lap of my apron. "I am not a shaman, although I have learned much from their society that has helped me to subsist in this country. You saw my herb garden on your way to my door. Does it impress you that I have succeeded in making things grow on this bare rock where the rain comes once in three years?"

"I know a piece about growing things. I was raised on a plantation."

"For ten years I employed Yaquis to carry soil by the basket up the naked face of the rock. Nothing grew the first five years. During each of the next four, the plants reached a height of a sixteenth of an inch, then turned white and died. It was then that I sought out a shaman one-third my age and acquired the secret that has allowed me to harvest my own herbs for seventy-three years. I continue to employ a boy to bring water each day, and once each month to carry and spread horse manure, compost, and some other substance that he refuses to identify for anyone but another Yaqui. To know some things it is not enough even to be born in a place to generations born there. One must also share blood."

"Do you sell the herbs?"

"No. I am not a merchant."

"What do you pay the boy with?"

"Instruction works two ways."

He nodded, as if he understood. "You were born here?"

"It is the only home I have ever known. I have never traveled more than twenty miles from this spot."

"You missed a lot."

"Only things of small consequence. This village is the only source of water between Durango City and the Rio Nazas. Travelers stop here often, and they bring with them the news of the world. In time everything that matters finds its way to my rock."

"I didn't mean to say it's all bad. Missing things."

I saw then that the sorrow in his face came from behind it, and that his eyes were but the surface of a black pool whose depth was impossible to sound. They were the eyes of my grandfather in a painting made by my father from memory at my request, upon the occasion of my father's one hundredth birthday. My grandfather was slain in his ninety-seventh year by the Pueblo Indians in Santa Fe. They pierced his eyes with the lancet he used to bleed lizards and poured molten silver from his own athanor into the sockets, then threw him off a cliff. His third wife fled to this place with my father, who was then in swaddles. He was an alchemist, like his father and grandfather, who left Castile to avoid the inquisitors. We have all sought the secret of the Philosopher's Stone. What we have learned from our failures has been of greater value than what most seekers learn from their successes.

I asked the long man what had brought him so many days from Socorro.

"I ain't from Socorro. I was just riding through. I'm sheriff up in Lincoln County."

I had heard of this place, and of its troubles. Men who had no need of additional wealth had coveted the same piece of ground, and had employed other men to slay one another until one side or the other had lost too many men to defend their part of the ground. Both sides had claimed the protection of the laws they violated.

I said, "I cannot help you to apprehend fugitives from your justice. It is not the kind of knowledge I possess or pursue."

"I ain't looking to find anyone. I'm looking to get rid of something."

"A sickness?"

"Dreams." He circled the brim of his hat through his long nervous fingers. "I want you to give me something to stop the dreams."

CHAPTER 2

Badgers, Buffalo, and Bad Men

The long man's name was Pat Garrett. Born in Alabama, he had moved with his parents to an eighteen-hundred-acre plantation in Louisiana at the age of three, where he developed a man's hard muscles chopping apart the clods of red earth with a hoe and sharpened his eye plucking squirrels out of hickory trees with a boy's single-shot rifle. What reading and writing skills he ever had he acquired squirming on an axe-hewn bench in the single room of a log schoolhouse on the edge of a bayou alive with mosquitoes and cottonmouth snakes. Throughout his life he associated figures and words on paper with physical misery; his sheriff's account-books were a chaos, his stock tallies an affront to the rules of arithmetic. He acquired a reputation for not paying his debts because he couldn't be bothered to keep track of sums.

Religion he looked upon as scarcely less confounding. When he was ten, Pat put on a white sheet and allowed himself to be tipped backward into the spring behind the Baptist church by a minister who wore a plug hat with his gown to cover the scar from a scalp wound he received during the Seminole War. The veteran lost his grip and nearly drowned him in the roiling iceshard waters. Pat dated his lifelong agnosticism from the moment he was hauled spluttering from the ropy mud, his eyes and nostrils burning hotter than his faith. God was a hard old cob to work for if He existed, and although Pat had known some as hard, they paid better wages on the average and gave him Sunday.

That same summer, he set himself to rid the plantation of a badger that stole from its burrow in the black of night to carry off his mother's laying hens. After tracking the thief to its hole, Pat walked around spreading the tall grass with his boots until he found its hidden exit. This he plugged with a small boulder, then made himself comfortable a few yards from the remaining hole, intending to shoot the badger when it made its appearance under the half-moon. All night he waited, and at sunup went back to the house to learn that another hen had been taken. He returned to the burrow, but found the boulder undisturbed. For another hour he searched, finally discovering a third hole beneath a ledge of shale. He jammed another rock under the ledge, and that evening he again took up his vigil.

Past midnight a bank of clouds rolled in and erased the moon. Pat crept closer to the burrow, fixing his eyes upon the entrance while his pupils expanded, sorting the empty black of the hole from the shallow blackness that surrounded it. Things scurried through the grass, too small to be the badger. Crickets stitched. Somewhere off in the void, a pair of great wings pounded, followed by a short sharp squeal of pain and terror, then silence, filled quickly by the noise of the crickets.

At length something shifted in the blackness of the burrow. A pale muzzle emerged, paused, and lifted to sniff the air. Very slowly a shadowy bulk separated itself from the deeper darkness. A pair of tiny black eyes glittered in a shaft of starlight leaking through a hole in the clouds. Pat, who had applied whitewash to the front sight of his rifle, aimed at the center of the bulk and fired. The hen-stealing ceased.

The Civil War fell heavily upon Louisiana. Glowering, monkey-faced men in kepi caps rode through the cotton, their horses' iron shoes chopping the plants to pieces. In the winter they built fires to drive out the damp and left them smoldering when they broke camp, to flare up before the first wind and burn down the crop. Peace was worse. Conquered by Northern shot and steel, infested by small-eyed Yankees in derby hats and side-whiskers, ridden over by sour veterans with pillowcases on their heads and lynching ropes slung from the horns of their saddles, the land bled and mortified. Carpetbaggers confiscated Garrett cotton. Pat's father John, in debt and drinking, quarreled with a Union sympathizer on the courthouse steps, fumbled a ball-and-percussion Colt's revolver from under the waistband of his trousers, and discharged a chamber into the Yankee's belly. The muzzle flash caught the man's flannel shirt afire, and Pat, who witnessed the confrontation, would forever afterward associate the stench of burning cloth with violence.

The wound infected and the man died twenty-one days later raving of gangrene. John Garrett died soon after of drink and regret and self-loathing. The plantation was seized and sold. On a sodden January morning in 1869, Pat Garrett, aged eighteen, hauled his six feet and five inches into the saddle of a broken-down gray and rode to Texas.

He put in a season working a cotton field in Dallas County, then threw down his hoe forever to take up the reins of a cow pony. He helped drive a herd of longhorns from Eagle Lake to Denison, then signed on with another outfit to ride the line through the winter. There he rounded up strays that had drifted off the range ahead of the icy winds and shared the dugout line shack with a legion of field mice and a high-smelling cowpuncher named Doob. Doob spat tobacco into the stewpot as he stirred it over the fire and every three or four weeks put on a fresh shirt without removing the old one first. When Pat reflected aloud that he would never need a calendar so long as he could keep track of time by counting the shirts his partner was wearing, Doob came at him with a skillet. Pat unholstered his father's Colt from the nail in the wall where it hung and squeezed the trigger point-blank. It misfired, but Doob put the skillet away. They finished out the winter without further incident. However, Doob was a talker, and Pat Garrett became known as a man with his father's hot temper. This together with his great height marked him as someone to walk around.

In a saloon in Fort Worth hung with skins and a buffalo head the size of a cast-iron bathtub over the beer pulls, Pat got into his cups during poker and delivered a lecture to his fellow players on the various grades of cotton, and how a farmer not overburdened with scruples might deceive a potential buyer into paying a premium price for a substandard crop. Among his listeners was a rangy fellow three or four years Pat's senior, who spoke like a Georgia cracker and invited him for a drink at the bar when Pat went bust. The man's name was Skelton Glenn. He told Pat he had spent time in Louisiana himself, where he'd accumulated a knowledge of the cotton trade that had enabled him to establish a profitable plantation in Texas after he mustered out of the Confederacy, and to recognize another expert when he heard one.

"I'll spare you the rest," Pat said. "I've had my life's portion of farming. I'm a cowman and a first-class horse breaker."

"I guessed that from the look of you. I'm in cattle myself. Year before last I ran longhorns to Florida, then came back last year with a remuda. I cleared eight thousand."

Pat sipped at his whiskey carefully to avoid getting

drops in his beard. He'd grown a nice one since leaving Louisiana, full and black and stiff as quills. "You hiring?" he asked.

"No, I'm looking for a partner."

"Sorry, Mr. Skelton. I don't have a penny to invest in cattle or horses."

"Skelton's my Christian name. There's no mister about it. What's got you spooked, Indians or rustlers?"

"Neither. Both. My skin's mine to do with as I damn well please, but I don't favor letting my savings ride on critters so dumb they'll follow anybody anywhere, rustlers and Indians included."

Glenn grinned. "You had me going there. I was afraid you was smart."

"Well, I'm innocent of that." Pat's teeth showed briefly in his whiskers.

"I'm getting out of the cattle business, horses too. I could be a rich man if I stayed in, but that ain't why I come West."

Pat said nothing.

"Ever hunt buff?" Glenn asked.

"I never did."

"Money in it."

"I thought that wasn't why you come West."

"It ain't. That don't mean it's against my religion. It's something different is what it is. Buff's free for the taking, and you don't have to bring back nothing but the hides. They're fetching top dollar in Fort Griffin."

"I hear it's dirty work."

"None dirtier, nor hotter in summer nor colder in winter nor worse for bugs and rotten grub. I said it was different from cattle work, not better. I figure a man who'd trade cotton farming for fifteen and found and all the alkali he can swallow is a natural for buffalo hunting."

They had another drink apiece and shook hands on the deal. Pat and Glenn, a Kentucky friend of Glenn's named

Luther Duke, and Joe Briscoe, an affable youth Pat had
taken up with in Fort Worth, piloted a buckboard over
three hundred miles of Texas to Fort Griffin, where Pat
bought a '73 Winchester carbine with a brass receiver,
called the Yellow Boy, and the others selected big-bore
Sharps rifles. They bought a thousand cartridges, eight
hundred pounds of lead and six kegs of powder for reload-
ing, bacon, beans, coffee, tobacco, and liquor, and corn
for the horses. They picked up two saddle horses at thirty
apiece and a pair of skinners named Buck and Grundy for
wages and struck out for the buffalo range.

At first Pat took to the hunting. Reading the trail excited
him as nothing had since he'd staked out and shot the badger, and he was a crack shot and a natural stalker, who
with the wind in his face could down a hundred buffalo in
a stand before the herd caught on and stampeded. Soon,
however, the experience palled. There was little hunting
involved on a plain that was often black with their quarry,
and the shooting itself was little more than butchery. A parade of thunderheads marched down the Double Mountains
and across the tabletop land, saturating everything and
making campfires difficult. Everyone developed a rash.
Partners and employees sniped at one another. Fistfights
broke out.

Young Joe Briscoe was Irish Catholic and serious about
it; each night before retiring and each morning after rising, he kissed the tiny crucifix he wore on a chain around
his neck. Pat, who normally kept his lack of faith to himself, was wet and irritable, and his clammy underclothes
put him in mind of his near-drowning in the name of God's
mercy. One morning he muttered something about "that
damned dumb Irish Christer," and Briscoe charged. Pat,
who had nearly a foot on his attacker, merely knocked him
down. Briscoe sprang back up, only to be put down again.
Pat knocked him down twice more, and then Briscoe

scooped up the axe the party used to chop wood and split carcasses and swung it at Pat's head. Pat ducked and dived for his Winchester. It didn't misfire.

The authorities in Fort Griffin heard the facts and decided not to pursue charges. However, the incident soured Skelton Glenn's opinion of his partner, who had insisted upon bringing along the inexperienced Briscoe despite Glenn's objections. The party sold its hides in Fort Griffin, divided the proceeds, and went in five separate directions.

Pat lived for a time on his profits, then found work in Fort Sumner, New Mexico Territory, on a ranch owned by Pete Maxwell, the son of the late cattle baron Lucien Maxwell. There the vaqueros, thick-waisted and low to the ground, made jokes about the gringo's ridiculous height while their women admired his Southern good manners and custom-made clothes, an extravagance he allowed himself in an area where the trousers in the mercantiles ran out of material two inches above his boot-tops. In 1877 he met, courted, and married Juanita Gutiérrez, the daughter of a freighter. She quickly became pregnant and died of a hemorrhage. After the funeral, Pat strode away from his friends' soft words, mounted the tall bay he had asked Pete Maxwell for in lieu of his wages, and rode up into the bluffs of the Llano Estacado. What he did in that naked, wind-scraped country he never told anyone, but when he returned months later to Fort Sumner, he had shed his beard. His eyes were as hard as bedrock, and although his temper was noticeably under better control, in times of trial the muscles in his jaw were observed to stand out like train couplings. He was leaner than ever; his cheeks were gaunt, the joints of his arms and legs visible beneath his clothes. From any distance he looked like a prairie wolf strung from the overhang of a hider's cabin.

Cattle work no longer interested him. He took a room in Fort Sumner, his first home in any sort of town, and stepped behind the bar of Beaver Smith's saloon, where he kept track of territorial activities through information supplied by the thirsty transients shedding the dust from their clothes at the brass rail. There he refilled their glasses from a measured bottle, listened to their reports, and kept his opinions to himself.

Most of the news came drifting in from Lincoln County to the west, where an Irishman named Murphy, backed by Jim Dolan's political machine in Santa Fe, established a general store in the city of Lincoln. A lawyer named Mc-Sween then opened a competing enterprise with financial help from two ranchers, big-eared, whipsaw-lean John Chisum and John Henry Tunstall, a young Englishman. The tendency of Tunstall and Chisum cowhands to "throw a wide loop" around unbranded strays, a common practice and largely overlooked, enabled William Brady, the Lincoln County sheriff and a stolid Dolan man, to issue warrants. One was sworn out against a slight, garrulous, buck-toothed youth who worked for Tunstall. His wanted condition drove young Billy Bonney to do most of his drinking and gambling across the county line in Smith's saloon.

Pat, who liked poker almost as much as he favored tracking and shooting game, took time out from behind the bar frequently to sit at Bonney's table. The pair got on, and when they broke for drinks, the spectacle of long tall Pat and little Billy standing side by side at the rail, observed in the mirror behind the bottles, moved the smaller man to laughter. Billy's mirth was infectious; Pat, who had lived long enough with grief, joined in.

Billy Bonney loved cards. His hands were small and slender and he liked the feel of the waxed pasteboards between his fingers, the way they skidded off the sensitive tips. He took to calling Pat "Big Casino," one of his favorite poker terms. Pat in turn called Billy "Little Casino." Fort Sumner was Billy's vacation place. He kept company there with Paulita Maxwell, Pete's daughter, and visited the Mexican bordellos on the other side of the Pecos when Paulita had the curse. Whenever things in Lincoln became too lively even for Billy, he could always go to Fort Sumner to rest and drink and fornicate and gamble and share gossip. Billy loved a salty story about people he knew as much as any ranch wife, and he knew more about what went on behind the arched doors of the whitewashed adobes in Santa Fe and Albuquerque than anyone else in the territory.

Then in February 1878, deputies sworn in by Sheriff Brady ambushed and killed John Henry Tunstall on a canyon road, and Billy stopped coming to Fort Sumner. On April 1, six men crouching inside a corral fired rifles through holes drilled in the adobe wall and cut down Sheriff Brady and a deputy named Hindman on Lincoln's main street in naked daylight. Witnesses recognized Billy Bonney's Irish green hatband among the killers.

A murder warrant was issued from the governor's office for Billy's arrest. To serve it, a successor had to be chosen for Sheriff Brady. Pat listened to the political talk in Beaver Smith's saloon, then untied his apron, crossed the county line, and threw his Texas hat into the ring.

CHAPTER 3

Long John

In January 1880, Pat Garrett married Apolinaria Gutiérrez, the sister of his dead wife. A small, otter-eyed woman, she wore her blue-black hair in ebony combs atop her head during the ceremony to lessen the difference in their height, but at all other times allowed it to spill to her shoulders in a glittering fall. She had no English, and Pat's Spanish was bad; when they fought, she threw china and he slammed doors. They loved each other completely.

Her father, the freighter, bought them a small house in Lincoln. It was a pleasant adobe, built flush to the ground with the warm pinkish hue of the native clay showing through the whitewash in a way that pleased the new sheriff. Riding in the rain and the heat, he looked forward to settling his angular body into the depressions in the big horsehair chair by the kiva fireplace, when he wasn't attending a hanging or riding down yet another rumor about Billy Bonney's whereabouts. Apolinaria decorated the rooms with bright rugs and wooden crucifixes and embroidered the couple's initials in blue and silver thread on the fine linens in their bedroom. There was always a pot of strong Mexican coffee boiling on the stove in the kitchen.

The Mexicans in Lincoln enjoyed their sheriff. Like Pete Maxwell's vaqueros they coined rhymes about the way he towered over them in the street, looking like a great stoop-shouldered crane, and grinned when during their fandangos he could not keep his big feet from bouncing to the music of the drums and trumpets and tambourines even when he sat. They called him Juan Largo, Long John, and asked to see his big long-barreled Army Colt, which he had purchased from a gunsmith in Fort Sumner to replace his father's cumbersome ball-and-percussion Navy of Civil War manufacture. Pistols were expensive everywhere. The machete was the weapon of preference locally; many of the civil disturbances Pat was called upon to investigate involved beheadings.

Some of the crimes over which he had jurisdiction shocked him. The Mexican temperament was a bed of smoldering coals, fanned into white flames by a sudden crosswind or splash of the raw tequila that could not be drunk except through a crust of salt to cure the stomach lining. When the hot wind blew up from Chihuahua, withering the poor corn crop that supported them, the men drank, the women's tongues grew sharp, and the children whimpered and howled because their bellies were empty. One blistering July night, an unemployed ranch hand named Manuel hacked up his wife, his boy and girl and a neighbor boy who was visiting, and took off for the Sierra Capitan aboard a razor-backed burro without provisions or even a canteen of water. Pat examined the scene in the little adobe hut, went out to throw up his coffee and corn cakes, and mounted up to follow the unshod tracks. After two hours he spotted the burro grazing, and a few hundred yards away discovered Manuel's body, seated with his back against a piñon tree and his bowels in his lap. He had let open his belly with the machete he had used on the others. Because he could not be buried in the churchyard with his family and the neighbor boy, he was dumped into a hole in the desert. A few days later his body was dug up and devoured by scavengers. Some blamed the digging on coyotes, but Pat suspected Manuel's brother-in-law, a Yaqui who had fought for Juarez and fled Mexico when he had failed to foment another revolution against Porfirio Díaz. It was a harsh land, more brutal in its way on those who lived upon it than the war had been in Louisiana.

Pat was not often in Lincoln. When he was not dining with John Chisum, who complained between courses about the Mexican squatters he was obliged to burn out and run off his range, he was in Santa Fe discussing with Governor Wallace the wisdom of issuing pardons absolving the participants of all responsibility for crimes committed during the war in Lincoln County, and whether Bonney's shootout with federal troops during the siege on McSween's general store made him eligible for reprieve at the territorial level. The latter question went unresolved, condemning the Lincoln County sheriff to scour town and territory for Bonney.

The young hellion knew the country better than most natives. New Mexicans reveled in his audacity, distrusted authority, and delighted in sharing the details of his exploits, magnifying them for the sake of the story and shifting the locations to confound the law. Now he was in Las Cruces dealing three-card monte, bewildering even hardened gamblers with the swiftness of his slender hands and long, delicate fingers; two days later he was in Roswell, one hundred sixty miles away, shooting the epaulets off a cavalry lieutenant who favored luring outlaws to Santa Fe under the promise of pardon, then trying and hanging them. The same night he was in Fort Sumner, sharing a bottle of mescal with Pete Maxwell and galloping his daughter. Pat followed up the rumors that sounded most logical, and more often than not found himself sitting in a chair in some flyblown cantina still warm from Bonney. He had a sense for looking in the exact right place, and for being exactly twenty-four hours late each time. This stimulated rather than frustrated the long man. It excited him to come so close to the man he sought, and he knew Billy well enough to be certain that he would one day linger too long in one place.

That happened on a bitterly cold night in December, when word reached Pat in Puerto de Luna that Bonney and a group of his confederates, among them Charlie Bowdre and Tom O'Folliard, were camped outside nearby Fort Sumner. Pat, who disliked ambushes in open country, where there were as many escape routes as there were directions, apprehended a Mexican named Juan Gallegos, who was sympathetic to Bonney, and offered to blow his head out from under his sombrero if he did not agree to tell Bonney that Pat and his deputies were pulling out of Fort Sumner bound for Roswell. Gallegos, badly frightened by Pat's show of temper, carried the message, and came back to report that Bonney and his crew were on their way into town to celebrate.

On the east side of the plaza stood an adobe missionary hospital, abandoned for years, with its roof fallen in and holes in the walls big enough to sling an armadillo through. Charlie Bowdre's wife lived there, and Pat calculated it would be Bonney's first stop. He seized the building, locking up Señora Bowdre and a number of Mexicans who might warn Bonney in one of the rooms and stationing a guard with them to keep them quiet. Pat dispatched Barney Mason and others to block the most likely path of retreat, and with Lon Chambers took up a position in the darkness under the overhang of the front porch behind a tangle of hanging harnesses. As the moon rose round and white, glaring off the snow on the ground and turning the adobe bone-white against the hard machined edge of the shadows, Pat swore he caught a whiff of sorrel blossoms, which he had neither smelled nor seen since leaving Louisiana. He decided it was the memory of a scent. It had filled his nostrils when he'd waited out the badger that had stolen his mother's hens. Then as now he had crouched in darkness, gripping a rifle, while the minutes crept past like small creatures in the grass. His fingers stuck to the metal of the Winchester's receiver when he touched it, like that of an iron pump handle in the cold.

He sensed the sound before he heard it. He turned his right ear, numb now, crosswise to the wind that skinned around the edge of the building, squealing through the spaces between the roof and the posts that supported it. There was another high-pitched sound below it: someone whistling between his teeth. Pat knew the refrain. "Darling, we are growing older." Silver threads among the gold. Billy Bonney's favorite. He whistled it when he raked in his poker winnings, sang it when he was drunk, in a light, untrained tenor, as pure as any boy's in a church choir.

Now came a creak, as of stiff saddle leather or a hoof crushing untrod snow. Lon Chambers, invisible in the shadows at the opposite end of the porch, heard it, too; he hissed between his teeth. Pat made no noise in response. Bonney had ears like an owl.

Ghostly silent, like a line of ships against a foggy backdrop, six horses and riders slid from darkness into the moonlit ribbon of road, strung out, the men hunched in the thick vapor steaming from their mounts' nostrils, headed for the old hospital. Pat recognized Billy Bonney's green hatband on the sombrero of the man in front.

A dozen yards shy of the building, Bonney reined his horse's head around suddenly and trotted to the back of the line. Pat swore beneath his breath; the youth had seen or sensed something, and was conferring with one of his friends about fleeing.

"Halt!" barked Pat; and again, "alto!"

The rider who was now in front straightened up suddenly in his saddle. His horse's head was under the porch roof. Pat saw moonlight reflecting off its blaze face, felt the mist of its spent breath condensing on the back of his hand where it gripped the forepiece of his carbine; the tiny droplets twitched and crawled like ants. The man clawed at his bulky overcoat. Lon Chambers and Pat fired simultaneously, their muzzle flashes splintering the shadows. Afterward Pat would swear he'd heard the slugs striking the horseman, like meathooks chunking into a side of beef. That old homicidal stench of burning cloth shriveled the hairs inside Pat's nostrils. The horse spun, whether in its own panic or its rider's no one knew, and clattered back down the road. Now Pat and Chambers swung their guns on the others. Reports crackled and snapped in the frozen air; spurts of blue and orange flame destroyed Pat's night vision, yet he continued firing and levering fresh shells into the Yellow Boy's barrel. Barney Mason and the men Pat had stationed down the road joined in, catching the riders in a ferocious crossfire. Billows of pewter-colored smoke drifted across the road and collected under the porch roof. Sulphur stung Pat's eyes and scratched his throat.

The horsemen bolted from the road in two directions, shouting and quirting their reins across their mounts' withers. The night swallowed them. One rider remained, slumped in his saddle with his back to the hospital: the man Pat and Chambers had shot at point-blank range. Slowly, leaning far out to one side, he turned his horse in Pat's direction. One arm hung lifeless. The moonlight reflecting off the snow glittered on the fresh dark stains on his coat and shirt. Pat recognized the beardless face beneath the slouch hat. Tom O'Folliard had often accompanied Billy Bonney during his visits to Beaver Smith's saloon at the time of the war in Lincoln County.

"Don't shoot, Garrett," he called out. "I'm killed."

A figure came loping the rider's way from the shadows down the road, carrying a rifle. "Take your medicine, old boy." It was Barney Mason's voice. "Take your medicine."

Pat cupped a hand around his mouth and shouted. "Back off, Barney! He can pull a trigger yet." To O'Folliard: "Throw up your hands, Tom."

"Pat, I ain't got the sand to throw up breakfast." The words were slurred.

Pat and the others came forward then, helped O'Folliard out of his saddle, and carried him into the hospital, where he died forty-five minutes later, begging for someone to put a bullet through his head and finish the pain.

The tracking began. The sheriff, who never felt more alive than when he was on the scent, acknowledged neither fatigue nor the cold that froze his companions to the marrow. At times the hoofprints they followed were obliterated by the wind-driven snow; hours would be lost while they quartered the countryside trying to pick up the trail. At times Pat led by instinct alone. Then a freshly broken tree limb or a black hole in a frozen stream where a hoof had gone through would appear, and they picked up the pace. At Lake Ranch, acting upon a hunch, the posse surrounded a house, but it turned out to be empty. They pushed on.

After three miles they encountered a lone rider. Pat called for him to throw up his hands. When he obeyed, Pat rode up and recognized Emmanuel Brazil, an old friend who worked at the Wilcox Ranch nearby, a some-time stopping-place of Bonney's. Brazil reported that the gang had pulled out of the ranch several hours before, and with the posse retraced his steps to where a trail of fresh tracks led away from the road.

"What's that way?" Lon Chambers inquired.

Pat said, "Stinking Springs." To Brazil: "Alejandro Perea used to have a house there."

"It's still standing."

The riders came upon the old shack in the iron cold of predawn. A cramped, bare-bones structure built of native pine with a slant roof and no door, it stood against a backdrop of rolling foothills dotted with aspen. A thin curl of smoke twisted up from the stovepipe. Three horses were tethered to the roof-beams that projected from the front of the house.

"They've either lost two men or two horses," whispered Chambers.

Pat flicked frost from his moustaches. "They've not lost either. If I know Billy, he's got two horses inside."

"What do we do, start blasting?"

"Only if they start to leave. We'll surround the place, then wait for first light. Fire when I raise my gun."

"No call to surrender?"

"Billy ain't the surrendering kind. It's my intention to kill him the second he pokes out his head. The rest will throw down their arms then."

"I heard you was soft on Bonney. I reckon I heard wrong."

Pat swung down from his bay. "You might have noticed Bonney's friends don't fare much better than his enemies."

The posse fanned out, silently in the fluffy snow. Pat tethered his horse to an aspen rubbed raw by mule deer and cleared himself a resting place in the snow with a boot. Then he stretched out on his stomach. The ground sloped down to the shack from a treefall across which he rested the barrel of his Winchester. Before leaving Fort Sumner he had thought to dab whitewash on the front sight, but the snow gleamed with an illumination all its own. If Billy were to show his face at a window, Pat could have shot him between the eyes as easily as at noon.

The shadows east of the shack had begun to grow grainy before false dawn when someone stirred inside the doorless entrance. Pat worked the stiffness out of his fingers and drew a bead at doorknob level. A man in a loose canvas coat and broad-brimmed sombrero came out carrying a nosebag. Pat strained to make out the color of the man's hatband. It looked black. In daylight it might be green.

The long man rose to his knees, bringing the Yellow Boy to his shoulder. The chugging of shots from all sides drowned out the sound of his own. The tethered horses reared, squealed, and jerked at their reins, releasing a shower of dirt and dust from the projecting rafters. The man in the entrance stumbled, dropped the nosebag, and pitched backward into the shack. Slugs chopped at the boards on either side; one gonged off something made of iron inside, a stove or a skillet. The guns went silent then, as if a bell had been rung.

"Garrett, that you?"

Lon Chambers broke cover and duckwalked Pat's way. "Who's that, Bonney?"

Pat shook his head. He cupped a hand around his mouth. "Is that Billie Wilson?"

"It is. You sure killed Charlie."

"Charlie Bowdre?"

"None other, though he's breathing yet. You boys got him through the lungs and gut and I don't know what all. He's bleeding like a leaky bucket."

"Tell Charlie I'm sure sorry. I thought he was Bonney."

"Tell him yourself, Garrett. He's coming out."

There was a scuffle inside, and then the wounded man plunged out into the snow, hands out from his sides with a big pistol dangling by its trigger guard from his right forefinger. His canvas coat hung open, his shirt dark and drenched.

Chambers lifted his rifle. Pat laid a hand on the barrel, deflecting his aim. "Don't waste your shot, Lon."

The face beneath the big sombrero was young and pale

and glistened in the light reflecting off the snow. He spotted Pat at the top of the slope and lurched that way, sinking in up to his knees and gesturing with his free hand in the direction of the shack.

"I wish," he said. "I wish—Lord, Pat, I'm killed." He fell on his face in front of the treefall.

"Billy Bonney, you in there?" called the long man.

"Why don't you come down and take a look for yourself, Big Casino?"

"That's him," Chambers said. "Goddamn."

"How you fixed in there, Billy?"

"Pretty well, though we got no wood for breakfast."

"Come out and get some, then. Be a little sociable."

"Can't do it, Pat. Business is too confining. No time to run around."

While Bonney was speaking, an arm bent around the door frame. A hand closed around the reins of the horse tethered closest to the door.

"Sheriff," Chambers said.

"I see it." Pat drew a bead on the back of the horse's head and fired. The animal threw up its head and heeled over, blockading the entrance.

"Nice shooting, Sheriff."

Pat said nothing. He worked the lever twice and shot through the reins holding the other two horses. They reared and cantered away, slowing and stopping at the edge of the little clearing to nuzzle through the snow for grass.

That ended the conversation. Pat sent Chambers to the Wilcox Ranch for provisions and spread his blanket on the ground, settling in for a long siege. When the wagon came in the afternoon, the posse built a large fire and began cooking. The sharp smell of hot grease from the beef and chickens rode the smoke in the direction of the shack.

"God*damn,* don't that meat smell good," Chambers said. "I ain't et since Fort Sumner."

Pat said, "It ain't for us."

Twenty minutes later, a rifle barrel nudged out through a window with no glass in it. A dirty white handkerchief fluttered from the muzzle.

"Tell your boys to hold their fire, Pat. We're coming out."

Pat and the others disarmed Bonney, Wilson, Tom Pickett, and Charlie Rudabaugh; fed them, bound their wrists and ankles, and loaded them in the wagon with Charlie Bowdre's corpse wrapped in a blanket. Pat rode alongside on the way to Las Vegas.

Billy Bonney stared at the corpse. "I sure will miss old Charlie. We was fixing to homestead as soon as we stole enough cows."

"I heard that," said Pat.

"Tom O'Folliard's dead too, I guess."

"Dead as King George." The long man rode a little farther. "What spooked you outside the hospital? I was about to plug you when you turned around and rode back."

The young outlaw showed his big teeth. "I wanted a chew of tobacco bad. Wilson had some that was good, and he was in the rear. I went back after tobacco."

"Too bad for Tom."

"Tom didn't chew. I guess you could say it was tobacco killed old Tom."

"I mean, too bad he missed tomorrow. Charlie too."

"What's tomorrow?"

"Christmas Day."

"Well, well." Bonney stared down at his bound wrists. "I didn't have time to get them nothing anyways."

Barney Mason rode up from the rear. "I was you, Billy boy, I wouldn't shop for Easter, neither. You're fixed to hang in Lincoln for Brady and Hindman."

"Oh, I'll see Easter. Just like the Lord."

CHAPTER 4

Midnight in Fort Sumner

And did he see Easter?" I inquired.

The long man looked up quickly from the swept stone floor of my hut; not so much as if he'd forgotten I was there as in surprise to find he wasn't still on the road to Las Vegas, New Mexico Territory, talking with Billy Bonney.

"He saw it," he said then. "Independence Day, too, though not by much. He killed two of my best deputies in the Lincoln County courthouse, stole a horse, and rode away with about a hundred folks looking on. Coroner counted thirty-six buckshot holes in Bob Olinger's body."

Bonney's recapture became a condition of Pat's continued employment as sheriff.

Incredibly, or so it seemed to Governor Wallace, Pat's rivals for county office, and many of the outspoken citizens of Lincoln (some of whom had watched from windows and boardwalks while the territory's most notorious outlaw stepped calmly into leather and steered his pilfered horse around Deputy Olinger's butchered body in the street), the long man appeared to do nothing for nearly three months. He replaced the hinges on all the doors in his house, strung fence along his western property line, oiled all his harnesses, and whitewashed the barn. Apolinaria had recently given birth to his daughter, Ida, and he bought a goat for the milk, only to learn that it was a disagreeable animal that tried at every opportunity to disembowel him with its horns. After one particularly close incident, Pat went into the house, came out carrying his ten-gauge Stevens shotgun, and blasted the nanny as surely as Bonney had blasted Olinger. Since then he had entertained a hatred for all goats more intense than any he managed to work up for the slayer of his two most dependable men.

Meanwhile, newspapers and gossipmongers who at the end of 1880 had celebrated Pat Garrett's abilities as the most popular lawman on the great frontier had swung the light of their admiration to the audacious Billy Bonney, who as before was reported to be working his outlaw wizardry from Mexico City to the Panhandle of Texas. Sheriff Garrett's lackadaisical attitude toward his duties obliterated his former celebrity; rumor suggested Wallace was considering replacing him with John W. Poe, a stock regulator and sometime deputy U.S. marshal, or Charles Siringo, a cowboy up in White Oaks with law enforcement ambitions. Pat replaced some broken tiles on his roof and said nothing.

Frustrated with the sheriff's inaction, on April 30 the governor issued a proclamation:

BILLY THE KID
$500 REWARD

I will pay $500 to any person or persons who capture William Bonney, alias the Kid, and deliver him to any sheriff of New Mexico. Satisfactory proofs of identity will be required.

I read the notice, printed on brown newsprint disintegrating at the folds, which the long man produced from a soft stubbled cowhide wallet stitched with leather cord. He had cut it from the Lincoln newspaper and still carried it in hopes of collecting the reward.

"Billy the Kid?" said I.

"I don't know where Wallace got that." He refolded the cutting and returned it to its place as gently as if it were the five hundred itself. "I never heard no one call Billy that to his face, nor heard him referred to that way before the governor did. Now I almost never hear him called nothing else."

Since Bonney's escape, Pat had taken the single step of posting a letter to Emmanuel Brazil, his man in Fort Sumner. Early in July Brazil wrote back: While the governor, the newspapers, and those pundits who gathered in cantinas and found their opinions in glasses and bottles had been after Pat to scour Arizona and Texas and old Mexico, the fugitive had not left the territory. He had been seen coming and going in Fort Sumner, where blossomed Paulita Maxwell, the fairest flower of his young life.

This was the news the long man had been waiting for. He wrote again, asking Brazil to meet him and his party at the mouth of Tayban Arroyo, five miles south of Fort Sumner, one hour after sundown July 13.

In White Oaks, Pat met with John Poe across a linen-covered table in the dining room of the hotel where Poe was put up by the Canadian River Cattle Association. A thickset former cowboy with pomade in his hair and a weakness for Norfolk jackets and striped ascots, the young man had spent months tracking down and stringing up rustlers for the association, which had recommended him to the Lincoln County sheriff as a dependable detective and mankiller, who also held a commission as a deputy United States marshal. He had the cleanest fingernails Pat had ever seen; pared, pink, and polished, they flashed like pearls as he prised open an enormous pile of steaming clams on the plate in front of him.

"Bonney's gone from New Mexico," Poe said, chewing the rubbery meat. "Even he isn't reckless enough to hang back with a price on his head and every peace officer between Taos and the border carrying his reader in his vest pocket. But I'll ride with you to Tayban. Things have not been various enough around here to suit me."

In Lincoln, Pat and Poe collected Thomas K. "Tip" McKinney, short of stature, mild of feature, and the most amiable and obedient of Pat's deputies, who took off his hat, scratched his crown, said he doubted Bonney was anywhere within five hundred miles of the territory, and went to get his saddle. Since the deaths of deputies Olinger and J. W. Bell, Lincoln had gotten to be as quiet as White Oaks, and McKinney was inclined to fiddle-foot. The three set out for Tayban Arroyo.

When, two hours after dark on the night of July 13, Brazil had failed to show up, Pat asked Poe if he knew anyone in Fort Sumner.

The deputy marshal screwed a cheroot into the ground with the heel of his boot. "No, I'm a stranger in this country. Want me to ride in and sniff around?"

"Give it some slack. Fort Sumner's mostly Mexicans. They'd take the devil's side over the government's, and they're brought up to hate the devil."

Poe swung aboard his piebald. The moon shone on his pale barbered face. "You think Bonney got wind of what Brazil was about and killed him?"

"I doubt it. Billy don't kill in anger. Mostly it's for something to do."

"Them greasers don't know one date from another unless there's a fiesta attached." Tip McKinney grinned.

Pat slid a mesquite branch into the campfire. The flames gobbled the dry wood. "Showed the white feather, more than likely. You never can tell when Billy might get bored."

Poe returned the following night. His brow was

congested and the cords showed in his neck. "You called those Mexicans right," he said, spreading his palms in front of the fire. "They all forget their English when they see me coming."

"You didn't tip your hand?" Pat asked.

"Credit me for something better than a fool. I am just not Mexican enough for their high standards."

"Is he there?"

"If he's not, that's one suspicious son of a bitch of a town for no good purpose."

"You *are* a stranger here," Tip said.

Pat untethered the bay. "We'll go in and talk to Pete Maxwell. He never did make his peace with Billy sniffing around Paulita."

Tip said, "Pete's half Mexican."

"We'll just talk to the American half." He stepped into leather.

Pete Maxwell's house, modest for the dwelling of a successful rancher, was a single-story adobe, built in the territorial style over brick, with a gray puckered pine porch running its length. The three visitors dismounted, tied up at a log fence, and started across a green orchard separating them from the house. A sudden Gatling burst of laughter stopped Pat, who threw out a long arm to stay his companions. In a patch of mottled moonlight scattering through tree branches, a group of men in sombreros were seated on the ground a hundred yards distant, passing around a bottle and conversing in rapid Spanish. As the trio watched, one of them rose unsteadily, vaulted the fence near the house, and walked down the shallow slope to a smaller building nearby.

"Know him?" Poe asked Pat.

"Let's go in another way and avoid these fellows."

They retreated to where they had left the horses and walked around the orchard. In front of Maxwell's porch,

Pat said, "I'll go in and talk to Pete. You can watch out here."

Tip blew on his hands. "I wouldn't turn down a swallow or two of tequila. These summer desert nights are colder than Montana in winter."

"I'll bring you out a bottle. Pete ain't much for crowds."

A row of doors provided access to all the rooms from the outside, in the old Spanish style. Pat went to the one that led into Maxwell's bedroom and let himself in without knocking. A slab of icy blue moonlight lay like a stone on the floor by the bed. The sheets were humped and motionless in the reflected light. Pat crossed the room noiselessly and sat on the edge of the feather mattress near the head.

"Pete, it's Pat Garrett."

The man in the bed did not move or acknowledge that he'd heard. His breathing was shallow, and Pat saw the gleam of an open eye.

"Qué hora es?" said Maxwell then, and switched to English. "What's the time?"

"I don't know. Past midnight."

"You're too quiet, Pat. You always was too quiet for a cowhand, always slipping up behind folks. I near winged you once, just so's you'd drag a foot."

"Seen Billy, Pete?"

There was a long silence, as if Maxwell had drifted off to sleep. But Pat could see his eye gleaming. "Here and there," he said then.

"I ain't interested in there."

"He's been about, all right. I can't say if he's left yet."

"Can't or won't?"

"Don't ride me, Pat. I gave you work when no one else would."

"The work's different now."

"A whole heap's different."

"Quién es?"

The question was a hiss, louder than the footfalls of the man who had sprung through the open door from the porch outside. A slight figure, this, bareheaded and shirtless, with his galluses dangling and his feet clad in stockings only. Pat, whose instincts had not been blunted by life in civilization, looked quickly at the man's hands. He held a knife in his left. His right was empty.

The newcomer was blind in the darkness beyond the slab of moonlight. He crept toward the bed. "Who is it, Pete?"

Pete Maxwell sat up. "That's him!"

Here the long man fell silent.

I waited, seated upon my wooden stool, while the flames in the athanor lunged at the few crumbs of charcoal that remained. "And was it him?" I asked at length.

The long man nodded, not looking at me. "It was him, all right. Tip and Poe didn't know him, and when he asked them out front who they was in Mexican, they thought he was one of Pete's vaqueros and let him pass. Some folks claim now it wasn't him, but some imposter, and that Billy's raising hell down in Mexico or some such place. But I heard him, and I seen that long jaw and them big teeth clamping his bottom lip like a prairie dog's. When Pete said, 'That's him,' Billy come up from his crouch and pointed that Bowie square at me there in the darkness.

"'Quién es?' he said. 'Quién es?'"

"I swung up my Colt and shot him and rolled off the bed and shot again. I wasted that second ball."

"And the first?" I asked.

"It caught him just above the heart. He was dead as Pharaoh when he hit the floor."

"I have a question."

I waited until he looked at me. It took a long time, although not so long when measured against the hours I had lived.

"When Pete Maxwell said, 'That's him,' " I began.

He nodded, anticipating the rest but too polite not to let me finish.

"Was he talking to you or Bonney?"

The long man smoothed his moustaches. They were as even as the legs of a machine-made table. "I don't know," he said. "I don't reckon Billy knows neither."

" 'Knows'?" I asked.

CHAPTER 5

Phantasms of the Night

Billy Bonney had been dead one year. In the time between, his fame had spread like black Spanish moss beyond the boundaries of Lincoln County and the territory of New Mexico. He was written of as far east as New York City, where newspaper accounts of his youthful exploits (he was said to be but twenty-one at the time of his death) had inspired a number of fabulists to embellish upon that which had already been invented. Stamped in syrupy ink upon coarse brown paper, his edda whirled off steam-driven cylinders through carnivorous trimmers and piled page upon sawtooth page like igneous and aqueous; these were pressed between bright paper covers and shipped to train stations and mercantiles across the continent, whence they invaded the libraries of civilized homes on the Hudson River and the saddle pockets of cowboys not much older than Bonney. Lanky youths in chaparajos and hook-heeled boots mouthed the unfamiliar words by the light of campfires and lanterns from the grasslands of Nebraska, as flat as a scraping stone, to those same fluted canyons into which Bonney had fled to elude Pat Garrett along the Journey of the Dead. In death, Billy Bonney had acquired both a legend and a nombre de guerra that he had scarcely known in life. As Billy the Kid, his name was spoken in places whose very existence he himself had not suspected.

Pat Garrett acquired notoriety in equal measure. The body had scarcely begun to stiffen in its grave when Pat found himself writing a book.

His collaborator, Ash Upson, was thick-built and fifty, with fingers permanently stained purple, who bore a close, if debauched, resemblance to the novelist Alexandre Dumas. He was a former New York newspaperman who had come west to establish journals in Albuquerque, Las Vegas, and Mesilla. Weary of newspapers, he now ran the post office in Roswell and served as justice of the peace and notary public while selling desert acreage to gullible transplanted Easterners on the side. He drank pure grain alcohol when he could get it, trade whiskey when he could not, and while in his cups was given to questioning sacred beliefs with an edgy persistency that had cost him most of his friends. He wrote with the skill of Arthur Conan Doyle and possessed the poetic vision of Lord Byron, along with most of the latter's social indiscretions. Pat liked him on sight. He pistol-whipped red-faced saloon rats who proposed to string up the drunken journalist for smashing their icons in discourse, carried him home when he could no longer stand without the bar for support, and on whoozy mornings poured thick hot Spanish grind down his throat in time to open the post office lest Washington City move to revoke Roswell's charter. On his side, Upson paid no attention to Pat's needling humor and held his tongue and kept his distance when the sheriff's temper was short. They were fellow unbelievers, bonded by the common religion of their lack of faith.

Whose idea the book was, neither could say. Pat, whose first political campaign had taught him to track the course of popular opinion as surely as a fugitive's line of retreat, sensed early that Billy's posthumous reputation might surpass his own on this side of the pale, and chose to press the advantage of hindsight. Upson, who when he cut himself while trimming his goatee bled purple ink, was not so much the public servant and private pariah he had abandoned his instinct for a story with legs. They met through the summer in Pat's house, Upson's bottle-strewn room above J. C. Lea's general store in Roswell, and the Lincoln County courthouse where Billy had slipped his manacles and slaughtered Olinger and Bell, Pat reminiscing and at times rationalizing, while Upson scribbled with a chewed stub of yellow pencil on folds of tattered newsprint. They passed the bottle and suggested substitutions where Pat's memory failed him and Upson's knowledge stumbled into one of its alcohol-eroded holes. At length, when the manhunter had exhausted his investment capital, Upson locked himself away and under the influence of his hundred-proof inspiration weaved a scarlet tapestry of point-blank duels, harrowing escapes, and breath-snatching midnight rides on the backs of lathered steeds to fill in the blanks in Bonney's past. The physical manifestations of his muse included a chipped marble bust of Homer that had come with him all the way from New York and a greasy stack of paperbound Buffalo Bill novels written by Ned Buntline.

The book was published in April 1882 by the New Mexican Printing and Publishing Company. A tinted lithograph made from the only known photograph of Billy Bonney, standing with his Winchester propped on its buttstock at his side, decorated the paper wraps. The legend on the front read: *The Authentic Life of Billy, the Kid, the Noted Desperado of the Southwest, Whose Deeds of Daring Have Made His Name a Terror in New Mexico, Arizona, and Northern Mexico. A Faithful and Interesting Narrative by Pat F. Garrett, Sheriff of Lincoln County, New Mexico, by Whom He Was Finally Hunted Down & Captured by Killing Him.*

The slim volume sold for about as long as it took the average reader to digest the title.

Upson, publishing veteran that he was, sought refuge behind the writers' scarred but dependable breastwork of poor distribution and inadequate advertising. Pat, who assumed books were like harnesses and either walked out of the stores or grew cobwebs in the back room according to their merits and deficiencies, wondered if the book would have found more readers if the ending were different. Upson called him an ignorant heathen and started an angry letter to New Mexican Printing and Publishing, but got too drunk to finish it. Pat carried him home.

Restless, the long man decided not to seek reelection as sheriff. He endorsed John Poe for his successor. His former deputy's predilection for red-wheeled buggies over saddle horses and his ability with a ledger, whose narrow-ruled columns Pat just made a mess of with nicotine thumbprints and blobs of ink, seemed best suited to the clerkly duties that the office had begun to assume. The sheriffs of the future, he thought, would wear pinch-nose spectacles and only carry pistols on ceremonial occasions.

Despite the disappointing sales, the announcement that Sheriff Garrett had written a book increased his standing as Bonney's killer. When two vacancies appeared on the New Mexico Territorial Council, Pat made known his intention to run for one of them. If manhunters were obsolete, he proposed to lay down his cartridge belt and don a wing collar.

It was at about this time that the dreams began.

One night—one vaulted, star-scattered night in the endlessly turning wheel that is New Mexico in late summer—Pat Garrett arrived home stinking of horse from ten days of riding in search of votes, certain that his bones had torn loose from his tendons and that he was dragging them behind him like scrap iron in a gunnysack. His wife had retired hours before; not having left home on the best of marital terms, he was unwilling to wake her. He poured himself a tall whiskey and stretched his long legs toward the fire. The big shabby leather armchair was suited uniquely to his own physical imperfections, the piñon flames in the kiva fireplace were warm and danced mesmerically, like the Aurora Borealis atop the table rocks along the High Road to Taos, filled with fandango figures and visions from the pueblos in Socorro where the long man had chewed peyote and waited for news of Billy. Very soon he dozed.

His sleep, light in times of peace, was in periods of stress so close to waking that he could afterward recount everything that had happened in his presence when others had thought him safely under. Now he started awake at the squeak of a light footfall on the pine floor, or so he was certain at the time, so vivid were the details of the room and what he heard there.

"Apolinaria?" said he, raising his chin from his chest; for he thought that his wife had entered the room.

"Well, Big Casino," came a voice in response.

Pat was on his feet in an instant, clawing at his belt for the big Colt in its scabbard. He wore neither, as he had not thought he'd need a weapon to hunt for votes. For one terrible, sphincter-tightening moment, he felt as if he stood naked on a needle rock, a target in the moonlight. Only one person in this world had ever addressed him by the name he had just heard, and in his state of exhaustion the long man had forgotten that person was dead.

"Billy?"

This time there was no response. The room was filled with shadows, much like another room he remembered in another house, and though they stirred in the crawling light from the hearth they were empty. They moved in, enveloping him like a Navajo blanket and warming the blood in his veins.

He knew then he had dreamt. He did not suffer physical hardship so well in his thirties as he had when he was an overgrown boy in chaparajos, and the quest for political support in the bunkhouses and barrios of that vast territory had proven fully as frustrating as the hunt for Billy Bonney, with tracks harder to follow. Dissipation and strong spirits had made fissures in the walls that enclosed the present, allowing a shade from the past to slip through. To satisfy his manhunter's instincts he circled the room, poking at the dark corners with the toes of his boots and tapping at the panes in the windows to make sure none had fallen out. Then he undressed and went to bed, sliding carefully between the crisp linen sheets to avoid waking Apolinaria.

"Quién es?"

Now he sat up rifle-straight, and again reached for a phantom weapon. An exclamation escaped him, startling his wife awake, her hair in her eyes.

And for an instant he saw.

Saw a pale half-naked figure, translucent in the moonlight shining through the window upon the whitewashed wall facing the bed, approaching in leather breeches only; saw the hairless cylinder of his torso and the slack jaw beneath the band of shadow covering the top half of his face; saw the prominent front teeth, as large as dove's eggs, in the mouth that opened to repeat the question:

"Quién es?"

Who is it?

Saw the blade in the intruder's hand, shining like cold fire. . . .

And then the figure was gone, evaporated in midstride as completely as the stain of breath upon glass.

Pat did not tell his wife about the apparition. He explained merely that he had been awakened by a nightmare whose details he could not remember. Apolinaria was Mexican and superstitious. If he told her he had seen

Billy Bonney, she would insist upon bringing the local padre to the house to make the sign of the cross and pronounce
three long and tiresome exorcisms in border Latin, and
Pat could not abide this particular padre, who considered
him an infidel. He turned over, but he did not sleep for
hours. Bonney had looked exactly as he had that night in
Fort Sumner, and asked the very question he had had
upon his lips when he died. The scene had not been so real
even when the long man had set it down for publication.

It had seemed to him, too, that there had been an ele-
ment of threat in Billy's approach holding the big knife.
Paulita Maxwell had told Pat, among tears and wishes that
his soul would rot in hell, that Bonney had gone straight
from her bed to her father's house that night to carve a slab
from a side of beef Pete Maxwell kept in a cold box on the
porch; but upon the occasion of this dream, if dream it
was, Pat had felt that the blade was intended for him. If
so, this was a vindictive shade, more so even than the youth
who had lain in wait to slay the men who had butchered
John Tunstall.

Since that night, Pat Garrett had dreamt of Billy Bonney
dozens of times: at home, in the gaudy and flyblown hotel
rooms along the electioneering circuit, lying on the ground
beside a fire, sitting upright in a day coach on the A.T.&S.F.;
wherever bone-weariness overcame his fear of the phantasms of the night and he slid into slumber. Sometimes his
tormentor was fully dressed in the Spanish costumes he
favored, complete with the green band. More often he appeared as he had died, fresh from sex and holding a shaft
of moonlight in the shape of a bowie. On occasion he recognized Pat and addressed him as Big Casino, showing
his big front teeth in that idiot's grin that had finessed so
many into thinking him slow and weak, so many dead by his
hand. Other times he did not know him. Pat would start

awake with the smell of Billy's semen and his own sweat in his nostrils, chilled to the core.

The long man could not say which Bonney he found more unsettling, the swaggering dandy or the sleep-fuddled lamb trotting all unknowing to the slaughter. Chiefly he feared that if the dreams continued he would soon be as mad as those excursionists from Rhode Island and New Hampshire who struck out across the Jornada del Muerto with heads uncovered, their brains frying in the sun like tortillas.

I listened without interruption to the narrative of the man from New Mexico. He was an individual on the cusp: When his account touched upon his public life, he spoke in elongated, windy phrases, invoking politicians' fustian with the stiff, uncomfortable gait of a backwoodsman trying on his first tailcoat. Only when his subject became personal did he subside into the shambling speech and broken accents of the plantation youth, the western drifter, the laconic lawman. At these times I rather liked him.

Insofar as a man of my cloth could ever enjoy the person of a supplicant, and an Anglo-Saxon into the bargain.

At last he fell silent. Sunlight dappling through the leaves outside lay across his narrow face in the path from the window like patches on an adobe wall.

"No other words passed between you?" I asked.

He shook his head. "Just them. He calls to me, or he wants to know who I am. That's it."

"I don't suppose you've tried talking back."

"No. Maybe I'm loco, but I ain't so loco as to try talking to a dead man."

"And yet who among us possesses the wisdom of the dead?" I stepped down from the tall stool and crossed the room, aware that with each step I eradicated a measure of whatever polite belief he held that I had passed the century mark. It had only been since my ninetieth year that I had given up my daily climb down the ladder that led from my rock to the desert floor, leaving the harvest of toads to the boy who brought my water. From a high shelf I brought down an apothecary jar, ancient in the time of my grandfather, and removed its glass lid to sniff at its contents. They smelled of dust and putrefaction. I replaced the lid.

"Do you know grams?" said I.

"I sure don't."

"A teaspoon will answer, or a quarter of a jigger if you haven't a spoon. Heat that amount over a low flame until it liquefies. Swallow it then, just before retiring. The dreams should stop."

He peered at the label. "That Mexican?"

"Latin. You wouldn't understand it even if you could translate it. My people have used it as a nostrum against phantasms since before Christ."

"It smells it." He wrinkled his nose and clamped down the lid.

"Come back if the dreams continue."

"Ain't you got any more faith in your medicine than that?"

"One day it will be gone. The same is not always true of a ghost's patience."

"I don't believe in ghosts any more than I believe in God or the Devil," he said.

I folded my hands. "Perhaps if you live to be as old as I you will not be so certain about the Devil."

"How much?" He produced a drawstring pouch from the pocket of his trousers.

"I have no need of money. The villagers provide me with food and I have no reason to leave my rock."

"What, then?"

"Bring me wisdom."

He bounced the pouch on his palm. The coins shifted

and clanked like hollow bones. He smiled then, as slowly as shadows lengthening. "That's a stiff bargain, seeing as I got so little to spare."

"Your store is abysmal," I agreed. The smile withered. "Still, it is the medium of exchange here. I honor no other."

"Just what kind of wisdom are you wanting?"

"You will recognize it. When the dreams stop."

He put away the pouch and tugged on his big hat, growing with the gesture. At the door he looked back. His long solemn face clouded with thought. "I'm kind of a long time paying my debts. It's a failing."

"I shall be here," I said. "I am always here."

He left my shop. He remained in my thoughts.

The nostrum is but a sleeping draught, distilled from poppies and wormwood, with oil of creosote to bind. It was first composed by my great-great-grandfather, alchemical master to King Philip II, to send that ruler to the black depths below the level where dwelt the demons that gnawed at him in the dark. In return, my clever ancestor was granted the whole of Durango, of which the rock upon which stands my simple workshop is all that remains. My great-great-grandfather was a quack, a detestable puffer who worked his bellows to no good purpose but his own exalted station. He was drawn and quartered when his crystal failed to reveal the Armada's destruction. But his nostrum has its uses.

· IRON ·

CHAPTER 6

Generations

Clay to iron, iron to steel. All substances are transmutable to base metal, and all metals save one transmute to the stuff of which the earth was formed. Heat and corruption are the agents of change. Quicksilver is the first to liquefy, at minus thirty-nine degrees Fahrenheit. Tin, cadmium, bismuth, thallium, lead, and zinc melt at less than red heat; antimony, calcium, and aluminum, at more. Silver, copper, and gold—trackless gold, the blessed Mary of elements—require a cherry-red heat to alter their outward shape; iron, nickel, and cobalt a white flame. Platinum, iridium, rhodium, vanadium, ruthenium, and osmium are the most intractable, demanding the intense, world-generating heat of the oxyhydrogen blowpipe, the voltaic arc—indeed, the athanor, the alchemical furnace from which poured forth the stuff of life like milk from a pap. All these things I had transformed in the womb of the chimney upon my rock in the desert.

Iron to rust, rust to clay. Oxidation and time transmute as surely as heat. This process I had not the life to follow to its finish, nor had my father nor my grandfather nor my great-grandfather, nor all the chain completed. The passing down of notes from generation to generation did not answer, for the very corruption that was under observation destroyed the record, unless one squandered the little time he had transcribing what has already been written. Sulphuric acid hastened the timetable, but distorted the effect, like turning up the flame beneath a spitted hog to expedite dinner, incinerating the meat and making it inedible. A beast in a cage will not behave as it does in the wild. Time is the enemy as well as the agent.

Quicksilver to silver; elusive. Maddening. It is brittle, it is liquid. It is neither of these long enough to scrutinize and assign to a category. It is a woman in the prime of her beauty and treachery, glittering just within reach and then spinning upon its heel and fleeing before one's grasp, to turn again at the top of the next hill, flashing its eyes and laughing. It courses through the Devil's veins, it is the nimbus about the head of Christ. It may be the Philosopher's Stone. It may be fool's gold. It has consumed the lives and studies of more alchemists than all the other elements combined. We know nothing more of its true nature than we knew in the beginning. We bypass it in the service of time at the risk of losing our way forever.

Silver to gold; unlikely. Silver putrefies before the naked eye, turning black like a potato and then dissolving in a despicable foam, like hydrophobic spittle. It is a charlatan, like my great-great-grandfather, and its glory is brief. Its metamorphosis is in retreat from the blessed goal rather than toward it.

Lead is the basest of metals. It changes not, except to become even more like itself. It is an unwashed old man, malleable by force but resistant in its obese spirit. Its filth comes off upon one's hands. It knows no conscience and once smelted, will weight a fishhook or form the snout of a bullet. Moreover, it is poisonous. Its venom leeches forth to work slowly and undetectably, and by the time it is discovered it has blackened the blood and bagged in the liver, transmuted its victim to lead. It is a loathsome gray tongue in a dead mouth. It is to gold what the lowest pit-brained ape is to the dignity of man.

But if clay to iron and clay to gold, why not iron to gold? The orange cast iron assumes is encouraging, but then like all things it disintegrates short of the state, like Galahad in possession of the Grail. Its failure is noble, but in the end, it is no better than false silver or amoral lead.

Nor was I; nor am I yet. In the time after the departure of the long man, villagers and strangers came to my rock with their complaints, shouting at the top of their lungs to make themselves heard as my eardrums thickened with callus. I slept at a level close to waking, I shrank in stature, my joints swelled and pained me when the monsoons came. I lay round-eyed on my pallet, wondering (when I should have been reflecting upon the day's experiments) who was crueler, the Pueblo Indians who blinded and tortured my grandfather before they put an end to him or this eternal millstoning time, that ground a man small and smaller until he was fine enough to fall between the wheels. The son of the boy who carried water to my garden when I gave up that chore, a father now himself, assisted me when I could not apprentice myself, recording the lengthening list of failures in the yellow leaves of my notebook when I was unable to hold a pen, and gathering the coals to feed the athanor when my back would not bend. But my eyes were keen, and my mind was as a thing honed by the wisdom that came my way in small quantities, like grit on a whetstone. Tin to bronze, bronze to brass. The books I had read rotted on their shelves, like oranges that had surrendered their juices and whose seeds were barren. Increasingly I felt an urgency to uncover the secret of the stone. I had no grandchildren, no children. My wife and infant son had perished of a plague borne upon the wind from the field of the bloated dead of Chapultepec. Another

wife had flung herself from the rock upon being told that
she could never return to her ancestral home in Mexico
City. I had considered training the boy who brought water,
then rejected it. The mysticism was too deeply entrenched
in his people, he would never succeed in laying aside the
old gods in the service of pure reason.

The thick and braided vine with roots in the court of
Carolus Magnus ended with me. There would be none to
work the bellows when I relinquished the handles; no hand
would take up my pestle when I set it down at last. I who
sought to live in three centuries would close a way of life
that was already ancient when the pyramids of Egypt rose
from the quarries.

Antimony and arsenic. The first is medicinal, the other
deadly. It was an ancestor of mine who discovered the
health-preserving properties of antimony, by accident; for
all things not directly applicable to the production of gold
are serendipitous. How many of my forebears may have
found the opposite to be true of arsenic will never be known,
for they died before they could record the fact. We perish
in flame, we die from poison, we wear out our lives in the
quest. Like the metals themselves, rapid and slow oxidation
is our fate.

Iron to rust, rust to clay. Gold to gold. Not for personal
wealth, never that, but for the benefit of knowledge, and
of man's mastery of the natural world. Gold to gold. Gold
did not oxidize; of all the metals it was the only one to
break the circle. There was the lock that fit the key.

But where the key? Not in the red lead of cadmium, nor
patrician-white platinum, that self-deluded metal that thought
itself gold's superior. Not copper, nor zinc. Certainly not
molybdenum, forged in fire and generations removed from
the earth. Tungsten, manganese, palladium, the alloys and
amalgams—disappointments all. My notebook, my larder
filled, but it did not nourish.

In a seizure of pique I threw my grains of ore into the fire. They ignited, sending sparks up the flue. Their essence rode the smoke to freedom and then, heavier, settled to the desert surface, beginning the long slow return to the womb that bore them.

As would I.

These things I heard; for a lone village in a naked desert draws travelers as spring water draws the creatures that fly and the beasts that crawl, and wisdom is the coin of my tiny realm.

John W. Poe, Pat Garrett's friend and deputy during the final days of the hunt for Billy Bonney, swept Lincoln County in the sheriff's election, bringing eastern-style efficiency to the office. Pat's splotched, thumb-smeared entries in the ledger gave way to Poe's tidy, two-colored calligraphy between the columns. Instead of Pat's tall horse, the whirring red wheels of Poe's buggy announced that the sheriff was on his rounds. With oiled charm and blue-eyed promises he siphoned gold from the big ranchers and silver from merchants and pennies from beansnappers into a treasury that had rattled like a dry gourd before the hackle-raising efforts of his predecessor. There were those who said that Pat used the territorial cache as his personal bank account, drawing from it willy-nilly to buy supplies and fresh horses and pay his mercenaries as he scoured the country for Bonney. Others grumbled that much of the money never got to the treasury. Bonney himself had been overheard to say that if John Chisum would pay him what he was paying Pat to prevent Bonney from rustling cows and horses, he would leave off rustling cows and horses. Sic transit gloria.

None of this was lost on the newspapers. Ink and press oil and bales of newsprint are not bought with deeds of glory, but with advertising. Hordes of money in Santa Fe meant roads and reservoirs, and roads and reservoirs drew pilgrims, who bought lumber and farm implements and seed corn from general merchandisers, who bought quarter-pages and fillers to hawk their stock. Pat Garrett had no use for roads or reservoirs. Pat Garrett spent money on cartridges and scaffolds. Pat Garrett punched holes in bandits in the dark and crowed about it in books. A pilgrim with his nose buried in a nickel novel had no time to read a newspaper and learn of the many wonderful items that can be procured for a fraction at the Great Plains Emporium.

The editor of the *Rio Grande Republican* tagged Pat, who had declared his Democratic candidacy for membership in the New Mexico Territorial Council against D. M. Easton and John A. Miller—endorsers both of his campaign for sheriff—"Ungrateful Garrett," called him an "illiterate man," and opined that "the newspaper notoriety he received from his success in killing Billy the Kid has upset his brain." Many of the same sentiments appeared in a later issue in the form of a letter to the editor signed *X*.

Pat, trusting his reading skills hardly more than the opposition press, passed the letters column across the breakfast table to Apolinaria to read to him aloud. His brow darkened and the points of his moustaches met beneath his lower lip as she mouthed the difficult English words. Before she finished, he stood up from his chair, upsetting it, and reached for his cartridge belt and holster dangling from the coat peg beside the door.

His wife asked him what he was planning to do.

"I found Billy Bonney," he said. "I'll find *X*."

"Where will you look?"

"That pleader Roberts in Lincoln's had a hard-on against me ever since Billy jumped jail while I was out of town. I'll start there."

"You did not sleep last night."

This was the coded statement Apolinaria used whenever Pat was about to commit a foolhardy act. On this morning it was literally true; despite taking a double dose of the nostrum the night before, he had dreamt again of Billy, and awakened smelling the stench of spent powder. Unwilling to take up the dream where he had left off, he had stayed awake, reglazing a windowpane that had been threatening to fall out of its frame. This, and the fact that his wife had gone to their daughter's crib and unbuttoned her blouse to let the child feed, made him reach instead for his hat.

"I'll go see Ash."

"Buy flour." She sat down, cradling the infant to her breast.

Pat found Ash Upson sober behind the counter of the general store in Roswell. The journalist-merchant-realty salesman's hair was brushed back, his moustaches trimmed, and his chin scraped. As soon as he recognized Pat he said, "I read it. You on your way to blow a hole through the Republican son of a bitch, or are you on your way back?"

"I don't do that kind of thing any more, Ash. I'm running for office."

"You mean like Garfield."

"I got pigs to feed. You going to help me write a letter or not?"

Upson sat down at the rolltop in the back corner and opened a drawer. "Go feed your pigs. I'll bring it around for you to sign."

The letter, when it appeared in the *Republican* late in September, was a marvel of the ghostwriter's art, which was the ability to state a case with journalistic eloquence while preserving a sufficient imperfection of style to sustain the premise that it had been penned by the man whose signature appeared at the bottom. It continued for several columns, sniping at *X*'s accusations with the patience of young Pat waiting out the chicken-stealing badger on his father's plantation, laying out the planks in his political platform, and effectively transforming the opposition newspaper into a conduit for his campaign message. Upson even found opportunity to indulge his good-humored contempt for his friend's deficiency in letters: "If this be true, I claim that it is more my misfortune than my fault, and I must say it does not look very generous for *X* to blame me for faults over which I have no control." He was rather more satisfied with the result than he had been with *The Authentic Life of Billy the Kid*, in which he had had to put up with contributions from the man who was there. After posting it he celebrated by going on a bat, and found himself four days later in Toyah, a hide-smelling town with the bark still on it on the Texas Pacific right-of-way; a place he never visited when he was temperate. He knew he'd bought himself another week in Purgatory whenever he woke up in Toyah.

The *Republican* editor, an old campaigner with a taste for peppermints and snuff and an eye for a distinctive style, was not taken in by the letter. He had read the putative Garrett book and was familiar with Upson's New Mexico newspapers—a number of which he had occasionally pilfered items from to fill out his own columns, in a tradition that went back to the respective editors of the *Sodom Intelligencer* and the *Gomorrah Gazette*—and recognized the bibulous Easterner's pet phrases when they crossed his desk. Nor was he diverted by this bald attempt to use his journal for a Democratic shinplaster. He had voted with the Party of Lincoln since the beginning, supported abolition when Free Staters were strung from the trees like May ribbons, and had twice been forced to seek cover when some supporter of the old Confederacy fired a dissenting editorial through his plate-glass window. However, he was a newspaperman first, and not unaware of the fact that Pat Garrett's name sold papers. He typeset and printed the letter without comment or editing.

Ash Upson remained proud of the letter throughout the remainder of his days, quoting from it from memory long after it had been interred in the bound back numbers of the *Rio Grande Republican* and all who read it had forgotten it, along with everything else about Garrett save that he had killed Billy Bonney. Whenever he and Pat fell out, he would grumble over his cups that it might have influenced the election had Pat heeded his advice and gone down to old Mexico to hunt lions until after all the ballots were counted.

While the issue containing the letter was going to press, Pat encountered W. M. Roberts, whom he considered the man responsible for the *X* letter, in J. A. LaRue's dry goods store in Lincoln, where the attorney took delivery on his monthly shipment of General Gordon cigars from Denver. The long man inquired, with the kind of diplomacy more associated with a sheriff than a politician, if Roberts was *X*. Roberts denied the accusation vehemently, maintaining that he had better things to do with his time. Pat seemed satisfied, but when the two were out on the street in front of the store, Pat said that if he was not *X*, he certainly knew who was, and if he didn't come forward with the man's identity, Pat would know Roberts was in bed with Easton and Miller and the *Republican*.

"You have my answer," said the attorney. "If you try to make it anything else, I'll call you a goddamned liar."

Pat said nothing. At this point, Roberts selected a General Gordon from the box, snipped off the end with a clipper attached to his platinum watch chain, and struck a match on a porch post. The flame found twin reflections in the long man's dark eyes.

The former sheriff of Lincoln County unholstered the long-barreled Colt .45 he had used to subdue Billy Bonney and opened two deep gashes in Roberts' head with the heavy butt. The lawyer fell into a swoon. His cigar rolled to a stop in the thick dust on the street.

Later, Pat asked Ash Upson if he thought Roberts would prefer charges.

Upson, still recovering from Toyah, held up his coffee cup for Apolinaria to refill. "I wouldn't concern myself," he said. "They'll hang you in the *Republican*."

No legal action followed the incident. Pat carried Lincoln County in the election, thanks mainly to John Chisum and his ranch hands. He lost in all the rest.

CHAPTER 7

Texas Fever

The years passed, slowly in the desert, like gilas on their pale bellies, and for many of them I heard nothing of Pat Garrett. I concluded from this that his passage was quiet. It is the fate of the alchemist to be wrong more often than he is right.

Disgusted with politics, and surfeited with life in town, early in 1884 the long man brushed his Stetson, allowed Apolinaria to pluck the lint from his black suit, and met with an Englishman of dubious nobility named Harrison in the office of W. M. Roberts, where he exchanged a bank draft in the amount of five thousand dollars for a thousand acres of range land along Eagle Creek, a tributary of the Rio Hondo in Lincoln County. Hide-through lawyer that he was, Roberts made no mention of his pistol-whipping by Pat two years before as he added his florid signature to the witness blank on the bill of sale. Pat's backers included the Cattlemen's Bank of Lincoln and John Chisum.

From there, the former sheriff went to the Lincoln County Stock Growers Association to register his brand. For years afterward, rustlers who styled themselves after Billy the Kid took a signal delight in spiriting away Eagle Creek cattle with PAT burned in block letters on their hips. Regulators employed by the association dragged one such

miscreant from his home and shot him after he displayed
a hide with the brand prominent on the wall above his
fireplace.

Apolinaria took to the life with fervor. The ranch house,
abandoned for months, had become a shelter for every variety of Southwestern wildlife; with a broom she drove out
the porcupines and badgers, tied her hair up in a kerchief
and climbed into the rafters to poke the little brown bats
free of their inverted perches, then swept out the cobwebs
and dried dung and scoured the floors and whitewashed
the walls. She hung Indian rugs, blacked the stove, and embroidered new sheets for the master bedroom and the
guest room where John Chisum stayed when he came to
visit on his way back from decorating the cottonwoods in
old Mexico with rustlers from north of the border. Señora
Garrett was beginning to show with her second child and
disguised the evidence behind her prettiest apron when
people came to call. As the daughter of a rancher she
thought it a fine thing that her children should grow up like
desert flowers in the open air, away from the meanness of
crowds and the diseases of neighbors packed as closely as
blankets in a chest.

Pat envied his wife her complacence. He would not have
said it or even thought it, but he was secretly grateful for
the thefts from his stock, and for the necessity of ordering
his hands into saddle and tracking the path of the rustlers'
escape. Routine ranch work vexed him like a boil. He
could not comprehend those soft-bellied individuals he
met on trains who, in times of upheaval, said they longed
for a sameness to their days. The thought that when, exhausted to the soles of his feet from the sheer physical
labor of maintaining even such a moderate spread as his
ten hundred acres, he retired to his bed knowing that the
next day would be identical to the one he had just put
behind, filled him with dread. The buffalo were gone, Billy

Bonney was gone; sheriff's work had begun to resemble that of a store clerk. John Poe wore a green eyeshade and sleeve-protectors to the same office where Pat had cleaned and oiled his weapons and interrogated prisoners with his bony, knob-knuckled fists for news of Bonney's movements. If ranch work was all that remained, his life was over. More and more he found himself turning his daily management chores over to his segundo while he went hunting—ostensibly for antelope and boar—but hoping to catch some luckless night-herder in the act of cutting his line fence.

When he did not hunt alone, he was often accompanied by some officers whose acquaintance he'd made at Fort Stanton, where he picked up his mail. One, a straight-backed, stick-up-his-ass lieutenant two years out of West Point, with a puppy moustache, rode like an Apache. Pat considered this a sign of character, and was inclined to overlook a man's less attractive traits if he sat his horse well and took care of the animal. John Pershing had the bad habit of wearing his campaign hat parade-drill fashion, tilted so close to the bridge of his nose that he actually had to tip his head back in order to see game crossing directly in front of him; the long man broke him of it at length, but seeing photographs of him in later years accompanying General Miles on Geronimo's trail was dismayed to learn that he had sunk back into it.

Pershing, a Missourian, was a passing good marksman, but Pat thought his judgment faulty. He based this belief on an incident that took place late one afternoon as the pair were riding not far from the fort. The lieutenant dismounted suddenly, slid his Springfield carbine from its scabbard, and downed a running creature at forty paces with one shot.

"What you fixing to do with that?" asked Pat, when his companion grinned broadly in his direction.

"Make an ammo pouch out of the hide, I suppose. Sell the meat to Mrs. Lisnet at the inn."

"She won't thank you for it."

Pershing produced a skinning knife from his saddle pouch. "And why not?"

"Because that was one of her pigs you just shot." Pat gathered his reins. "Shove back that damn hat."

Later, when the lieutenant was placed in command of black cavalry during the Geronimo campaign, his former hunting companion said, "I knew Nigger Jack Pershing wouldn't amount to a heap of shit when he mistook a tame pig for wild game."

On a steel-cold day in January 1885, weary of shooting jackrabbits along his north fence, Pat crossed into Texas to accept an invitation to dine with the Panhandle Cattlemen's Association in Mobeetie. He was motivated less by the prospect of dinner than by Apolinaria's pregnancy. Mobeetie was near Tascosa, where in times past the Lincoln County sheriff had gone for word of Billy Bonney, and to scrub the crusted dirt from between his toes in a bathtub he shared with one of the city's celebrated whores in Hogtown, south of the tracks. Tascosa's chief exports were mellow cowboys and crabs the size of buffalo. On this occasion the long man separated himself reluctantly from a flat belly, put on his best shirt and the suit he had worn to ask Governor Wallace for his support in the sheriff's election, and feasted on the tenderest beef he had chewed since leaving Louisiana, cooked in champagne sauce and served with a smoky red wine, bottled in the time of Napoleon in a country he had never heard of. He felt out of place among the shirtboards and cutaway coats in the walnut-paneled private dining room on the second floor of Mobeetie's best hotel, and when the brandy came he jerked it down and waited for that old warm rush of confidence he got from tanglefoot.

He was relieved when the company adjourned to the club room, a high-ceilinged chamber with a Brussels carpet whose thickness Pat could feel through the high heels of his boots, scattered with deep leather chairs and sofas arranged in groups for private conversation. There were stacks of local newspapers and *Harper's Weekly,* well read, on tables, and ranks of law books bound in mustard-colored leather, unread, in a massive mahogany case with eagles carved in the corners. An oil painting in a gilt frame the size of a barn door leaned out from one wall, depicting a gaunt cowboy aboard a lathered sorrel chasing a calf down a switchback under a sky crowded with purple clouds. Pat didn't think much of it. The calf was scrawny and probably wouldn't have lived long enough to butcher even if it were captured, and anyway any cowhand with brains enough to move his foot when he was pissing on it would have abandoned a prize bull to run for cover with a storm approaching. He supposed someone had bought the picture to help out some stove-up old hand who could no longer hold anything more worthwhile than a brush, and was shocked when one of his hosts told him the association had commissioned the painting for two thousand dollars from an illustrator who worked for the New York *Herald.* Two thousand would have bought all the available grazing land in New Mexico Territory.

Upon taking his seat in a tall wingback that placed him in the unfamiliar position of feeling dwarfed, Pat was pleased to note the presence of a convenient cuspidor. While the two men who had joined him were snipping the ends off cigars, he used his pocketknife to carve two inches from a plug of Levi Garrett's, popped the length into his mouth, and sat back chewing loose the stubborn shreds of beef that clung between his molars. The moment had arrived for him to be told why he had been invited.

His companions were J. E. McAllister and W. M. D.

Lee. McAllister, whom Pat had met before during the spring roundup, managed the sprawling LS Ranch, smack dab in the middle of the Staked Plain. He was a short, wiry Irishman, burned red to within three inches of the crown of his round bald head, with black side-whiskers and a gold tooth in front. From any distance that white cupola of naked scalp, covered by a hat at all times when he was out of doors, looked like some kind of skullcap. Lee, a new acquaintance, was senior partner in the ranch. He was nearly as tall as Pat and terrifyingly thin, the bones of his face standing out like canyon rocks beneath the tight sallow skin. His eyes were sunk in deep hollows and his wing collar, thoroughly buttoned, lay loose around his neck like an open lariat. He seldom spoke, coughing quietly from time to time into a white lawn handkerchief he kept balled up in one bony fist. Pat suspected he was consumptive. His cigar smoked untasted between the first and second fingers of his other hand, moving only to drop ashes into the heavy bronze tray on the table at his elbow.

"How do you find our accommodations?" McAllister opened. "I don't mind telling you they're a far cry from the card room of the saloon where we used to meet. Back then it was buffalo steaks and raw whiskey."

"I like buffalo."

"That's right, you told me you used to hunt them. Not many of the brutes left."

"No, we knocked a hole in the population."

"Not that there was much sport in it. Not like hunting boar."

"Nor men," said Lee.

Pat leaned forward, shot a stream into the cuspidor, and sat back. They were getting to it now.

McAllister said, "I read your book. Splendid blood-and-thunder stuff. I liked it so much I lent it to Bill." He cocked his white-capped head toward Lee, who said nothing.

"That's one reason it didn't make any money. Nobody bought it. Everybody borrowed it from everybody else."

"You knew Billy the Kid."

"I played poker with him."

"I heard he was your friend."

"Bonney didn't have friends. He had men he rode with and men he shot. They wound up just as dead either way."

"You killed your share of the men he rode with," McAllister said.

"I was sheriff then."

"So you were. How do you find the cattle business now you're in it?"

"I like chasing strays over chasing votes."

"I should think it's dull work for a man with your background."

Pat made no answer to that. He wondered where McAllister got his information. The long man confided in no one, including Apolinaria, but he supposed his hands drew the obvious conclusion from his frequent absences. Dinner conversation had been mostly gossip about what the ranchers who weren't present were up to. He had a notion he'd been one of them. He spat again, just to make sure he was among men and hadn't stumbled into a quilting.

A look passed between the ranch manager and the ranch owner, who nodded behind the handkerchief he had pressed to his lips. McAllister settled back into the corner of the sofa and crossed his short bandy legs. "You're aware, no doubt, of our mavericking problem. Chances are you're suffering from some of it yourself."

"Mavericking's no problem. Everybody throws a wide loop one time or another. Herds don't start themselves."

"There's a difference between finding strays and making them. Some of the cowboys looking to start their own outfits have been fencing off unbranded calves belonging to the ranches they work for, separating them from the cows until they're weaned, then slapping their own brands on them. Last month I caught one of the mean bastards burning a calf's feet with a running iron so it couldn't follow its mother."

"What did you do to him?"

"I made him jerk off his boots and marched him sixty miles to the jail in Amarillo; let him feel what the calf felt. He spent the last ten miles begging to be strung up."

"Did you oblige him?"

"Five years ago I would have. I can't abide a man who's cruel to an animal, even one of those flea-bitten sons of bitches. He was just a small thief, though. We've got organized operations stealing whole herds and changing the brands, forged bills of sale, rustlers passing themselves off as officers of the court and confiscating cattle on the grounds they're infested with Texas fever. Last spring the LIT lost a thousand head in one lump. It's gotten out of hand."

"What's the law doing?"

"Oh, they're regular hounds. Whenever they pick up the scent they chase it hell for leather to the New Mexico line. Then they stop."

Pat nodded. "That's a problem."

Again the two Texans exchanged glances. Lee laid down his cigar and drew a long fold of paper from the inside pocket of his dress coat. McAllister took it and thrust it toward Pat.

He read the letter, holding it before his face so the others wouldn't see his lips forming the syllables. It bore an Austin return address and granted W. M. D. Lee permission to organize a *posse comitatus* to apprehend and deliver to justice any and all parties considered a threat to peace and property in the Panhandle region. It was signed by John Ireland, Governor of Texas.

Pat handed it back. "It's a big jurisdiction."

"Effectively, it has no boundaries," McAllister said. "As a private citizen, the leader of this band is at liberty to press pursuit across all state and territorial lines. The job's yours if you want it. You pick the men, you pay and supply them and provide the Panhandle Cattlemen's Association with a record of expenses. It pays five thousand a year. If you accept immediately, I'm authorized to offer you five hundred head of prime breeding stock at a quarter of the market value, to be bought back at full price should you decide to resign."

"Suppose I take it and quit next week?"

"We've agreed to take that chance. I don't think it's much of a gamble. Your honor is well known." The Irishman rotated his cigar. "Have we an arrangement?"

"I need three things."

"State them."

"The first is a free hand. I take the risks, I give the orders. I answer to no one, not you or the association or the governor or Chester-by-God-Arthur."

"I can promise most of that. Bill and I *are* the association, and President Arthur hasn't taken notice of what's been going on out here so far. Ireland may take some talking, but it shouldn't be necessary to remind him who put him in office. What's the second?"

"You can discuss it with the governor when you're getting my free hand. I want a proclamation against carrying six-shooters in this state."

"A handgun prohibition in Texas? You must think he's retiring after this term."

"I won't have my men shot in the belly. I'll take my chances in New Mexico, but I'm a sight less popular here. Bonney didn't raid into Texas."

"We'll convince him it's necessary to attract Eastern investments. Which brings us to the third condition."

"I won't make arrests without warrants. When the dust

settles it's always the bounty hunters that wind up on the wrong side of the law. If I didn't learn nothing else from the war in Lincoln County I learned that."

McAllister frowned at his boots. "That's a tall order. You need a judge to issue warrants, and a courthouse for him to sign them in. Tascosa has neither."

"Build one."

CHAPTER 8

The Home Rangers

On an unseasonably pleasant morning late in January 1885, the citizens of Tascosa, Texas, awoke to the clatter of a heavy wagon built sturdily of elm delivering a load of rocks smelling of moist earth—the best kind, freshly disinterred and not weakened by exposure to sun and rain and ice—to an empty lot on the respectable side of the tracks. There a crew of stonemasons working under the direction of a great slope-shouldered Greek named Venizelos, who had little English and communicated mainly with sweeping and stabbing motions of his thick arms burned dark as bricks, laid the foundation for the first stone building in the history of the clapboard town. The mayor, beaming as he picked eggs from his teeth at his customary table in the dining room of the railroad hotel, explained to his curious constituents that the philanthropic owners of the great LS Ranch had agreed to loan Oldham County the sum of twenty-five thousand dollars to construct a courthouse and jail.

"Well," said one of his listeners, "that will be the first thing that outfit ever gave us apart from shot-out windows every Saturday night."

The residents of Hogtown, across the tracks, were less easily impressed. Buffalo Lou, a whore of somewhat longer standing in the area than the ranch itself, paused in the

midst of soaping the genitals of a customer to wring out
her sponge and deliver her own assessment of the situation: "The only good business reason to build your own
jail is to be the one to decide who gets put in it."

As it happened, the owner of the genitals, a cowboy
named Bob Bassett, worked for the Tabletop Ranch, whose
owners, Bill Gatlin and Wade Woods, were identified in
the small leatherbound notebook J. E. McAllister carried
next to his ribs at all times. In it, written in the Gaelic dia-
lect he preferred to any code, was detailed information on
every rustler whose name he intended to appear in the first
flurry of warrants issued from the new courthouse. Bassett, who was unaware of the notebook's existence and
couldn't read it even if it were to come into his possession
and if it were written in English, nevertheless understood
the importance of what Buffalo Lou had told him. Upon
ejaculating, he went straight to Gatlin with the information. The pair held a brief conference with Wade Woods,
whose mouth, paralyzed on one side by a kick from a mule
that had knocked out half his bottom teeth, dropped into
a lopsided sneer.

"The Home Rangers, they call theirselves. As if Garrett and his pack don't wear the LS burn on both their ass
cheeks."

"Burn or no burn, he's the one kilt the Kid." Bassett had
read *Billy the Kid and the Preacher's Wife* until the book
fell apart in his hands.

The three agreed to transfer their operation to Red River
Springs on the great Canadian, where Woods knew of a
granite shack that could be defended in case of siege.
Gatlin, the only one present with a discernible sense of humor, commented dryly upon the irony of retreating to one
stone building to avoid incarceration in another. Woods
told him to get his truck together and stop talking Greek.
They pulled out under a February sky purple with snow.

"I never heard of an outfit called the Tabletop," Pat said. "It can't be big."

Jim East, Oldham County sheriff and an old acquaintance who had sided Pat in the fight at Stinking Springs, shifted his ubiquitous toothpick from one corner of his mouth to the other. He was a loose-boned former top hand with an uncombed pompadour like a roadrunner's and a sandpapery face that a man might have scratched a match on; but he'd have been stopped by East's ice-blue gaze. "No bigger'n Bill Gatlin's hat," he said. "That's the headquarters. The Tabletop brand's wide and thick enough to cover every other one in the valley except the XIT. I thought at first that's where the rustlers was operating, on account of they had the smallest losses. Then one of Jamie McAllister's boys skinned a winter-killed Tabletop cow on a hunch and came and showed me the inside of the hide. Someone had went and burned the new brand smack on top of one from the LS."

"I do loath and despise a sneaky thief."

"So do I. Bonney just up and shot you when you found him out. He was an honest crook."

Pat, who had dreamt of Bonney again the night before, sealed off that path of conversation. "In or out, Jim? I need ten good men."

"What are you paying?"

"You didn't ask that on the way to Stinking Springs."

"That was different. Times was different. This ain't about rustling, Pat; it's about squeezing out the small fry. The big outfits didn't have anywhere near these losses till the LIT squashed that cowboy strike two years back. All they wanted was fifty a month and the right to do a little mavericking on the side. They got blackballed instead. Couldn't get work shoveling shit anywhere in the Panhandle. That's when the rustling started."

"That why you draw rein at the state line?"

East studied the masticated end of his toothpick and flipped it into the wood box by his office stove. "Talk is you're getting five thousand from the association. How are you splitting it up?"

"Sixty a month and the use of a good horse."

"If they done what the strikers wanted in the first place, they'd have saved ten dollars a man and about five thousand head."

Pat's face grew dark. "If that's how you feel, why don't you unhook that star and haul your freight over to the other side?"

"I didn't say I wouldn't take the job. Who've you got so far?"

"You know them. Barney Mason and Lon Chambers."

"No other takers?"

"I just started looking."

"Come on, Pat. In Lincoln County you had to beat them off with a switch."

"Times was different. You said it yourself." The long man touched his moustaches. "I won't deny there's a deal of bad blood."

"Mason's a son of a bitch, meaner'n a shithouse rat. I don't want him standing over me telling me to take my medicine like he done poor Tom O'Folliard."

"I don't pick them for their character. He's a good shot and he'll grow roots at the backdoor if that's where you post him. You and Chambers get on," he added.

"I'd side Lon to hell and around. What about Poe?"

"John's a civilized man. He likes to scribble in his ledgers and ride around in that buggy of his and get home to his new wife by sundown. Those red wheels won't stand up where we're headed."

"I didn't know you fell out."

"I said he was civilized."

"It ain't a disease, Pat. Though it's spreading."

"In or out, Jim?"

East hesitated an instant; any longer and he'd have been considered a civilized man. Then he nodded. "Assuming we get your ten, where do we look first?"

"My sources claim Red River Springs is a good place to start."

"Yes, I get my best information from Hogtown as well." The sheriff glanced through the window, where a wet snow had begun to fall. The flakes were as large as twenty-dollar gold-pieces and thin as cobwebs. "I don't guess you care to wait for the thaw."

Pat shook his head. "Injuns and outlaws are alike, lazy as niggers. They'd rather sit around a fire than break up drifts and they think everyone else feels the same."

"Everyone else does. Except Pat Garrett."

"Evening, Barney. Shoot any kittens today?"

Barney Mason lifted his thick china mug for Sheriff East to fill from the steaming pot and said nothing. He sported a winter beard that served only to increase his resemblance to a nocturnal rodent of the large-eared, pop-eyed variety.

Most of the Home Rangers were seated around the table in East's big kitchen. Outside, grains of snow like hard dried peas rattled against the siding on the north wall in gusts that searched out the places where putty had fallen from the windowpanes and made the lamp on the table glow fiercely yellow. Coats, hats, and mufflers hung three deep on pegs by the stove, steaming and filling the room with the noxious stench of mothballs and unbathed flesh. The rest of the crew stood and sat about the adjoining small living room. They smoked, conversed in low voices, and stared at their reflections in the night-backed windows. Shotguns and rifles leaned in all the corners.

East returned the pot to the stove, where Pat Garrett stood poking cartridges into the loops on the belt around his waist from a deal box. "Christ, Pat, I've had half these men in my jail more than once."

"They all came recommended."

"Not by me. Those LS men are barroom gladiators. They drink too hard and they don't pick targets. Charlie Reason's as bad as any of the Tabletop outfit."

"I didn't pick them for a choir."

"I won't have nothing to do with them."

Pat looked at him. "Don't wobble on me, Jim. I've got a hundred and fifty-nine warrants and only one man in a position to serve them."

"The jail won't hold ten."

"We'll start with nine."

"Well, I'm riding in back. I'll take my chances with wolves and Comanches."

Lon Chambers, who at Stinking Springs had asked Pat about his friendship with Bonney, got up from the table and came over to refill his cup, using a spoon to hold back the grounds. "We waiting for this storm to let up?" he asked the sheriff.

"Pat's running the show."

"Get your gear." Pat dumped the remaining cartridges into the pocket of his hanging coat and took it off the peg.

"Shit." Chambers gulped down his coffee. "Someday you'll tell me why you got such a hard-on for blizzards."

"Kid Dobbs used to hunt buff in this country. If you lose sight of him, look for Albert Perry. I appointed him first sergeant. He's an old cattle detective."

"He knows the ropes, all right," East said. "He's stole his share."

They rode Indian file across the white plain, shoulders hunched and hats pulled down and secured with their mufflers tied beneath their chins. Snow blew into their faces, drawing them tight as masks. The snowfall gave off its own illumination independent of the skillet-black sky and sculpted the flat landscape into hills and hammocks like dunes. Clouting forward, the horses plunged into hidden hollows with grunts of shock and pain, blowing steam that condensed on the riders' faces and frosted their eyebrows and moustaches, turning them into old men. At Trujillo at two in the morning they fed the horses and kicked at the door of the cafe until the owner came down and built the stove back up and fed them tortillas and chiles and refried beans with scalding coffee and tequila to wash it down. Charlie Reason filled a canteen from the bottle. When Sheriff East protested, Pat drew him aside. "It's medicine for such as him."

The storm blew over at daybreak. Shortly afterward the rangers drew rein on a rise overlooking the Canadian River. All around them for miles were blue-shadowed drifts capped with reflected orange light, unbroken except for the angry puckered path they had made and the black thread of the river chuckling under the ice flocs piled like rocks in the bends. "How far's the shack?" Pat asked Dobbs. The words, the first spoken in hours, crackled in the brittle air.

"We'll have a dandy view from the top of the next hill. Trouble is, so will they."

"How far to circle back from upriver?"

"Couple of miles."

"Then put the steel to your horse and lead the way."

Half an hour later, approaching the top of a hill heading upriver, Pat smelled woodsmoke and passed the order along to dismount. They hitched their horses to cottonwoods and spread out, floundering on foot through waist-deep snow to the crest of the rise. There they assumed a semicircular formation with the shack at the base of the hill in the center of their field of fire. The building had been dug into the slope, reinforced with round stones pried from the riverbed and chinked with mud, and roofed with poles. Coming upon it from the side where the snow-covered poles slanted into the hillside, the rangers might have overlooked it but for the crooked stovepipe lisping smoke from the center of the roof.

A figure was moving around thirty yards from the entrance to the dugout, snapping dead branches from a tangle of fallen trees and laying them across the crook of his left arm. "Who's that?" Pat whispered to Jim East.

"Looks like Bob Bassett. He runs with that Tabletop bunch."

Someone said, "Shit!" loudly enough to make echoes. Every head in the vicinity, including Bassett's, swiveled upriver, where Charlie Reason sprawled on his face in the snow, the toe of one boot hooked on a snarled tree-root.

"Charlie and his medicine." East's whisper was savage.

Bassett dropped his armload of wood and sprinted toward the dugout, shouting, "It's the Pat Garrett Rangers!"

Pat sank into a crouch, raised his Winchester, and led the runner with the muzzle. Sheriff East closed his fingers around Pat's wrist.

"They're just cattle thieves," he said.

The long man lowered the carbine.

There followed a shouted dialogue between East and Bill Gatlin, who informed the sheriff that Wade Woods wasn't present. East promised Gatlin and Bassett a fair trial if they gave themselves up without gunplay. Gatlin offered to discuss it if East would come down in person. East hesitated, then unbuckled his cartridge belt. Pat, still in his crouch, leveled the Winchester at him across his thigh.

East looked at him. "You wouldn't shoot me, would you, Pat?"

"I won't have to if you start down that hill alone."

"I know those boys. They wouldn't shoot a calf with its leg broke."

"The calf wouldn't be fixing to hang them."

After a moment East grinned. "You want to set up another barbecue?"

"We ain't got the provisions, and town's too far." Pat signaled to Albert Perry, who duckwalked over from his position behind a treefall. The former cattle detective had a round soft face with sparse ginger moustaches and the dead eyes of a killer. Pat said, "Send a crew down to strip the poles off that roof."

The delegation mounted the roof from the hillside and got to work.

After three poles had been torn loose and flung to the ground, exposing the interior of the dugout to fire from above, the two men inside announced they were coming out. The rangers surrounded them, tied them up, and took them to Tascosa.

On their first night in jail, a former LIT striker poked a file between the bars.

"I hold Sheriff East responsible." J.E. McAllister dipped the end of his cigar into his glass of whiskey in the association club room. "He used to punch cows with those boys. I wouldn't be surprised if he took a walk while that file was going in."

"Jim's straight as a bull's dick." The long man spat into the cuspidor at his feet.

"Next time you have someone pinned down, go ahead and shoot. We only built that jail to go with the courthouse."

"They're just cattle thieves."

"So was Bonney, but you didn't say that in your book."

Pat said, "Send someone around for your cattle. I quit."

CHAPTER 9

Black Cattle

Well, Big Casino."

"Well what, Billy? You're dead."

Bonney showed his big front teeth in a grin, appreciating Pat's joke. He had on his favorite wide sombrero with the Irish green band, a bolero vest over a white linen shirt with the sleeves gathered by garters, tight black trousers split below the knees with tiny silver bells stitched along the vents, and boots with four-inch heels and Mexican spurs. He jingled when he walked and his erection was obvious where the trousers hugged his crotch. The Mexican girls in Fort Sumner and along the Journey of the Dead— the ones who spoke of such things—referred to Billy Bonney's impressive endowment as La Culebra: The Snake. Pat, with customary empirical reasoning, considered that it wasn't that big; it was just that the rest of Billy was that small.

"I hear you stepped out from behind Beaver Smith's bar," Bonney said. "Hooked on a star for Old Elephant Ears and General Wallace."

"For Lincoln County. Chisum don't pay me except in taxes, and Wallace can't vote."

"I never cast no ballot."

"That's because you move around too much. And besides, you're dead. I blowed you clean through the door of Pete Maxwell's bedroom."

Bonney appeared uncertain for the first time. Then he recovered. He reached inside his vest and Pat's hand went down to his belt, despite the fact he knew he was dreaming. But the weapon Bonney produced was only a deck of cards. He slid off the rubber band and shuffled, the waxed pasteboards hissing between his slim, supple fingers.

"I'm going on the scout," he said. "How about a few hands before I ride out?"

"Go down to old Mexico, Billy. Or up to Texas. Maybe I won't have to kill you this time."

"Straight stud, nothing wild. I'm the only wild card in this here deck."

"Not no more. You're part of the deadwood."

Bonney's hands slipped, an unprecedented event. The cards skidded free and fell to the floor in a slithering cascade. His expression became blank, then frightened. Then a shadow obliterated his features like a cloud sliding over.

"Quién es?" he demanded, from the darkness. "Quién es?"

Pat sat up straight, spilling the sheet from his naked chest. He felt not fear, but a terrible, burning sense of shame, as if he'd been caught masturbating with one of his mother's petticoats. He looked over to see if he'd awakened Apolinaria, but that side of the bed was empty. It wasn't even his bed, nor the room the bedroom they shared at Eagle Creek. The walls were not the familiar whitewashed adobe, but papered plaster, and the sun slanted in greasily through plain muslin curtains instead of the white lace his wife had made by hand. The woman standing by the window smoking a cheroot was thin and slack-breasted in a plain shift through which he could count her ribs. There were hollows beneath her eyes, like depressions in a clay head made by the sculptor's thumbs, and her hair, tinted red, dangled in sweaty strands to her thin shoulders.

"Bad dream, Long Tall?" Her voice was a raspy whisper.

Pat hawked, rolled over, and spat into the china thunder mug on the floor beside the bed. He was in Hogtown: the room smelled of rancid renderings, old semen, and the sweat that soaked the walls to the studs. "What's the damages?" He wiped his lips with the back of his hand.

"Two dollars. I took it out of your poke."

"What else did you take?"

"Go to hell. I could of slit your throat and sold your spurs. You sleep like a old boar."

"You know who I am?"

"Sure. You're P. T. Barnum. I seen your Tom Thumb." She skinned her lips back from a set of nicotine-stained horse teeth.

"You just fucked a famous man."

"They're all famous after I fuck 'em."

"I'm Pat Garrett."

She blew smoke at the curtains. "I knew a Garrity up in Denver."

"Garrett, not Garrity. You never heard of me?"

"You with the railroad?"

"I killed Billy the Kid."

"Who's that?"

"You're full of shit," he said.

She turned away from the window. Face on, she looked a little less emaciated. She was probably still in her twenties. "I hated to see him go."

"You knew him?"

"Never laid eyes on him. I never seen a Comanche, neither, but I miss them just the same. First you clear out the injuns, then you start on the outlaws. When they're all gone, who's left?" She thumped her chest. "That's why I left Denver. Christ knows what's waiting for me after Hogtown."

"You think too much for a whore."

"It's a failing," she agreed.

As was his habit when he was hung over, Pat dressed with particular care, inspecting his collar for smudges, brushing and picking lint from his lapels and trousers, and combing his hair and moustaches with clean water from the basin. When he entered the downstairs parlor on his way out, a man rose from the faded settee, swiftly enough for Pat to touch the pistol scabbard beneath his coat.

"Have I the honor of addressing Sheriff Pat Garrett?"

He took an instant dislike to the stranger. His accent was English, and the long man belonged to a generation that had not forgotten the burning of Washington City. Also his clothing beneath his open bearskin coat, too heavy for the Texas spring, was of a material and tailoring far beyond the budget of one such as Pat, who preferred to be the best-dressed man in any company. The fellow wore his fair hair long, brushed behind his ears, and his Vandyke beard received a great deal of attention with scissors and a comb. He was nearly as tall as Pat, and good-looking enough to have had to fight off two or three whores to have the parlor to himself. Pat didn't trust a man who had no weakness for women; it meant he was either a pansy or concerned with some worse vice.

"I'm Garrett. There hasn't been a sheriff in front of my name for a spell."

"Yet there are those of us for whom you will always bear the title to which you have brought so much glory, like Gordon of Khartoum." He smiled. He had good teeth for an Englishman, even and white. "Captain Brandon Kirby." He proffered a slim pale hand.

Pat took it, having first noted that the man's other hand

was occupied holding a pair of deerskin gloves; even an ex-Ranger had to look after his skin in Tascosa. "Where's your ship?"

"I was privileged to serve Her Majesty with the Army of Afghanistan." Kirby actually blushed as he said it. His new acquaintance decided that he was an inept liar. "They told me in Lincoln County I'd find you in Mobeetie. I was told there I'd find you here, and so I have." He looked around, at the parched furniture and dust that showed in the shafts of sunlight. "Are the women clean, by the way?"

"I wouldn't eat off them. What's your business, Captain? I quit the Association three days ago."

"So I was informed, and all the better for my mission. My employer is James Cree. Do you know the name?"

"Creek?"

"Cree. The name is Scottish, as indeed is the man himself. He's outgrown the Highlands and wishes to increase his considerable fortune by raising cattle in New Mexico Territory. I'm representing him in his quest for land."

"Tell him to invest in a whorehouse. Easy women are quicker to come by than cattle when your stock gets run off."

Kirby exposed some more of his teeth to show he was a man of the world. Pat was fascinated by the growing depth of his distaste. "Unfortunately, Mr. Cree is respectable. In any case, he's concocted a scheme that promises to make the practice of cattle rustling in the West as obsolete as piracy on the high seas."

The long man, intrigued despite himself, said he'd pay to hear it.

"You won't have to; rather the other way around. I would admire to discuss it with you, if it's not too early to drink."

"In England, maybe."

They walked to the first saloon on the Tascosa side of the tracks, where the bartender drew a beer for Pat, added bitters to a glass of gin for Kirby, and banged the drinks down on the bar. "I say," the Englishman complained, brushing drops of gin from his waistcoat. But the man had turned his back on him to wipe down the beer pulls.

Pat said, "Forget it. He punched cows for the LIT until the strike. A lot of these town boys are on the blacklist."

"I had nothing to do with that."

"You have now. You've been seen with me. From now on you want to watch to see your glass don't get pissed in." Pat carried his glass to a gaming table unoccupied at that hour of the morning and sat down. Kirby joined him.

"Mr. Cree began his search in Montana Territory, but found the climate too much like Scotland's for his taste. The Southwest is not so good for grazing, but the land is cheap. He hopes to control a million acres in New Mexico and the Panhandle."

"Nobody can afford to keep up a spread that size."

"But a very rich man can easily afford to acquire all the parcels in the region which contain water, granting him virtual ownership of an area as large as all of western Europe."

"He'd need ten million men to protect it."

"Hence the scheme." Kirby drew a flat wallet from inside his suitcoat and unfolded a rectangular scrap of newsprint containing a steelpoint engraving in profile of a heavy-shouldered bull. It was an advertisement for a stock auction cut from an Aberdeen newspaper.

Pat read the legend. "What's Black Angus?"

"A breed of cattle, far superior in meat production to any in this country. I attended this auction last month and bought one hundred and fifty bulls for breeding. They're not as hearty as the local red cattle, but by crossing the strains, Cree expects to create a supreme hybrid that will outproduce all the others in the world."

"Where are the bulls now?"

"They're currently in quarantine in Canada. I hope to arrange for their release in time for an autumn drive. By then we should have all the land we require."

"You better leave them where they are. The thieves in this country will steal everything but the hoofprints before they get ten miles."

Kirby drained his glass, bringing an orange flush to his face. Pat had never met an Englishman who could carry his liquor. "I understand you're a rancher, Mr. Garrett. How do you protect your stock from theft?"

"Burn them like everyone else. But any rustler with a running-iron can change a brand."

"Cree's idea will make branding a thing of the past." He thumped the clipping on the table with a forefinger. "These bulls are *black*. They sire black calves. Any man not connected with the Cree organization found running black cattle will be apprehended on the spot. I promise you that after the first round of trials and convictions, the remaining rustlers will seek elsewhere for their livelihoods."

"It makes too much sense," Pat said. "I'm suspicious of something nobody thought of before."

"It's in your nature to suspect. Surely everyone out here knows that. Which brings me to why I have come all this way to seek you out."

"I'm through regulating for Big Cattle, black calves or no. There's no satisfaction in it."

"You don't understand. It isn't Pat Garrett's gun I wish to hire. It's his regard."

"I wouldn't try living on it here in the Panhandle," Pat said.

"It's a different story in Lincoln County, where we intend to concentrate our efforts. The name Cree inspires either indifference or avarice there. When the landholders agree to discuss a transaction at all, they dictate terms more suitable to a Stuart king than a simple speculator in cattle. I hold the conviction that a union with the man who slew Billy the Kid would enable us to negotiate something far more to our advantage."

The long man swallowed the last of his beer. "Still thirsty, Captain?"

A glimmer of greed appeared in Kirby's eye, which he sought to dissemble by unpocketing a watch the size and thickness of a silver dollar. "I suppose I have time for another."

This time, when the bartender banged the glasses, Pat asked him in his quiet drawl if he wouldn't care to pick them up again and set them down gentle-like. The man tried to return his gaze, wavered. "Pardon." He reached for the glasses. Pat slapped down the exact change and whisked them away, leaving the bartender's hands cupping empty air.

"Supposing I agree to front for your Mr. Cree," Pat said, reclaiming his seat. "What's my end?"

The effort of not looking at the glass of gin still in the long man's grasp stiffened the muscles in Kirby's face. "I think I could persuade him to agree to a finder's fee of ten percent, with a substantial bonus should you succeed in delivering the deeds under the amount budgeted."

"How much is that?"

"I've been instructed not to go over three hundred thousand dollars."

"Done." Pat withdrew his hand. "We'll start the ball with my spread on Eagle Creek."

Camping out that night on the road back to Lincoln County, Pat drank the very last of the nostrum he had acquired from my hut in old Mexico. He awoke with the sun full in his face and no dreams in his memory.

CHAPTER 10

White Wind

T hey can't *walk?*" Pat was amused.

Kirby, perspiring freely in his tweeds on the verandah of the Angus Ranch headquarters (the role of English country gentleman had caught his fancy like the jaws of a gila monster, and he would no sooner surrender it than he would his North Country accent), shook his head in no particular response to Pat's question. "It seems the worst quality the indigenous red longhorn possesses is also its greatest strength. That tough stringiness diners complain of when they try to chew the meat is the very thing that allows the steers to cover so many miles in a day without dropping dead from exhaustion. I selected the black bulls for the succulence of their hams, never dreaming that they were simply too fat to waddle more than a hundred yards at a stretch. The cost of shipping them here by wagon from Canada will annihilate this year's profits."

Pat laughed. He felt he could afford to. He had sold James Cree his own ranch at a substantial profit, along with four hundred head of stock, and delivered a hundred thousand acres besides. The porch they were standing on was brand new, constructed along with the rest of the house on the site of John Poe's old house and barn, whose sale

Pat had negotiated on the strength of their past association. Privately, he thought it was to Poe's pure profit, since the current Lincoln County sheriff had grown too fat sitting behind his desk going over his highly regarded ledgers even to ride comfortably in his fancy buggy, let alone hoist himself into a saddle for the long trip to Lincoln from his ranch. In any case he enjoyed laughing at anything that caused Captain Kirby displeasure.

"I had hoped to fold the expense into the profits from last spring's calf crop, but the numbers are far below what I estimated." The Englishman steadfastly ignored his companion's mirth. "The local brigands appear to have wasted no time. Perhaps they hope to offset their losses when the cows begin throwing black calves."

"I wouldn't count too much on that." Pat wiped the tears from his eyes and lit a cheroot, striking the match on a freshly painted post and leaving a scar.

"Why not? What are they going to do, paint them?"

"All I'm saying is you're laying down a mighty lot on them bulls being around long enough to rut."

Kirby didn't appear to pay much attention to the answer. He was looking out across the scraped plain, where a wind had sprung up, pushing cottonwood leaves ahead of it and combing the short grass between the bulbs of mesquite, which had begun to turn color. "And now it's cold. A moment ago it was sweltering. I was told the winters were mild in this country."

"Depends on the winter. I hear the buff up north are putting on their woolies early. That's a sign, or maybe not. One thing you can count on about the weather here is you can't count on the weather."

"How very picturesque." Kirby went inside.

Pat remained on the verandah, smoking and watching the wind from the north grow horns.

* * *

Most of Lincoln turned out to see the first wagonload of Black Angus rattle down the same street Billy Bonney had taken out of town after gunning down deputies Bell and Olinger. Extensions had been built up on the sideboards, but the spaces between were wide, and everyone got a good look at the future of the American cattle industry. The bulls appeared not to belong to the same species as the red longhorn, wild-eyed, gaunt in the hips, their bones standing out like angle irons in a gunnysack: More fist-shaped than rangy, the Angus were rounded all over and stood low to the ground on legs as big around as telegraph poles and were shaggy all over like buffalo. Their coats were dead black, more charcoal than India ink, and the light of intelligence did not shine in their eyes. Their lowing had not the arrogant edge of the longhorn's bellow; one onlooker likened it to a fat woman's fart. Nobody was much impressed except the representatives Captain Kirby had invited from the meat-packing plants in Chicago, who informed him that if his first generation of cattle looked as good as their sires they would take them all off his hands. The owner of Lincoln's butcher shop confided to his customers that those loose-bellied Easterners wouldn't know a steak from a tin of sardines. "What's the point of eating meat you don't have to pound the hell out of to get it to lay down on your plate?"

When the first bull was found castrated, Captain Kirby's gentlemanly repose went up the chimney. He told Pat he wanted the culprit tracked down and hanged.

"Not without a warrant," Pat said. "Anyway, the tracks'd just lead to the bunkhouse."

"We're employing a traitor?" Aroused from bed, the Englishman had pulled on a soiled shirt without a collar. He was unshaven and his hair stood up on one side.

"Likely more'n one. There's a deal of bad blood around

since the strike. The way you treat the hands don't help the situation. This ain't Scotland, and they ain't tenant farmers."

"If they think I've been harsh before this, they have a surprise coming."

"Let it go, Captain. One bull's just a reminder. He could've went ahead and sliced the balls off the bunch."

"Only at the peril of his own. I'll not have these animals mutilated. My God! Do you know what it cost to bring them here?"

"A cowboy has to be plenty hot to choose such work. You got them out stringing wire now. Give them Saturday off if they string five miles by Friday. It's heaps better to offer them sugar than a singletree across the ass."

Kirby filled a tumbler with brandy from a cut-glass decanter bearing the Cree family crest. "Well, who the hell are they?"

"New Mexicans. They fought Maximilian and Geronimo and the whole Comanche nation. The rest of the time they fought each other. I wouldn't go so far as to say they look down on anybody, but they sure as hell don't look *up* to anybody this side of God Almighty."

"Tell them that until the man who castrated that bull comes forward they work Sundays."

"You tell them. I don't cherish getting shot out from under my hat."

"That's another thing. From now on the carrying of pistols on company property is prohibited. Violators will be dismissed immediately without pay."

"You'd best throw in their knives and rifles. Boots, too. They'll stomp you to death otherwise."

"I'll take that chance. Anyone who would take his revenge in this cowardly way will surely hesitate to face a man who can defend himself."

Pat, accompanied by a group of Cree employees who

had been with the outfit since Montana, enforced the anti-firearms regulation with dispatch. They surrounded lone hands along the fence line, disarmed them, and sent them on their way. When the hands caught on and began carrying their weapons inside their trousers and in shoulder rigs under their vests and coats, Pat moved in close and slammed the barrel of his big Colt across their skulls, apologizing curtly on those occasions when a subsequent search failed to turn up contraband. Whenever a running-iron came to light, proving the man a rustler, Pat took him into custody and delivered him to John Poe for prosecution. A second bull was found castrated, then a third. Kirby fired twenty men suspected of complicity in the mutilations. Still they continued: a dozen in a single night, sixty by the end of the first month.

The country through which the long man rode on his patrols became increasingly white and bare from drought. The water holes controlled by the Cree company were fenced in with barbed wire, and armed riders were stationed to prevent men employed by the surrounding ranches from cutting it. Where no riders were to be seen, there was a hole that had dried up. As the rainless weeks crawled past like thirsty vagabonds on their hands and knees, the abandoned stations multiplied. Dry rot consumed the fence posts. The wires drooped like neglected debutantes. Even the vultures deserted the holes for better pickings nearer the ranch buildings. The deep roots of the indestructible feathergrass drew up, the tufts fell over and blew away with the dust. The topsoil and then the subsoil dried out and was peeled aside, seeking shelter between jambs and sills and hammocking in the corners of interior cabinets. The land turned brown, fading like old cloth.

Then came the winter of 1886.

The last morning of 1885 was cloudless and balmy. In the forenoon the wind shifted toward the south, drawing a dirty gray veil across the sky from Canada. The air smelled of iron. The first long icy drops of an afternoon-long drizzle struck the pulverized earth, darkening it momentarily, then disappearing beneath it like burrowing insects. They froze on the blades of grass that remained, turning them into glass filaments. The wind steepened. By nightfall the rain had given way to a fine, powdery snow that clung to the cottonwoods, piled up on roofs, and snaked along the wind-scraped ground until it stacked up against the walls of barns and curled back on itself in the hollows of hills like a barber's last flourish with brush and pomade. The wind turned white. It shrieked around cornices, shook shutters in its teeth, and stung the eyes of beast and man, burning exposed flesh like sheets of flame. From northern Dakota to the belly of Texas, from Topeka to the Great Salt Lake, the storm bellowed. It continued without letup for three days and three nights. Eighteen inches of snow dropped like a great smothering mattress, obliterating roads and fences. The temperature plummeted to twenty below zero. Trains were held up in Kansas and Colorado. The mail stopped. Telegraph lines, embrittled with ice and whipped about like scourges, snapped, and where they did not part, the poles that held them leaned over and were buried beneath the drifts. By the end of the blow, the High Plains had been catapulted back forty years, to the time before the Transcontinental Railroad and Western Union. One-half of the United States was cut off from the rest.

Three hundred people lost their lives in the blizzard. They were found frozen in the snow near the remains of their blasted houses, huddled together stiff as cordwood in covered wagons whose teams stood frozen in their traces, curled into fetal positions in the dubious shelter of sheds and lean-tos forty yards from their own hearths. When the snow began to recede, seas of cattle dead from cold and starvation appeared in wallows and arroyos, driven there before the wind like debris. Bloated, sticklegged carcasses bobbed in the spring runoff. Faced with losses of eighty-five to a hundred percent of their stock, the buildings, fences, gates, and ledger books that encompassed the great beating heart of the great cattle ranches showed themselves to be mere shells. Correspondence from the eastern banks whose funds fueled the traffic in beef ceased to be cordial, then ceased altogether, replaced by the letterheads of collection agencies based in Chicago and St. Louis. When another drought came in the summer of 1886, killing the new grass and scraping away the bottomsoil, the smaller ranches dried up and blew away with it.

Prairie fires gorged themselves on the dead blades, naked branches, and empty line shacks, carving black swaths across the land. Range hands, Pat among them, pulled bandannas up over their faces, slapped out what flames they could with blankets doused with water, felled trees, and dragged burning bunches of mesquite across the brown hills to create firebreaks. The mountain ridges glowed red in the evenings. The sun came up behind a haze of smoke and floating ash. As the drought and fires spread eastward, destroying the wheat and corn crops of the Middle West, shipments of feed slowed to a trickle. Cattle grew hollow in the flanks and starved to death in the middle of the very grasslands that had fed the buffalo for ten thousand years.

Then came the winter of 1886-87.

Snow began to fall in October. By Christmas the mercury in the thermometers had dropped to forty below, and stayed there through February. In early January the sky turned black as a skillet and dumped sixteen inches of snow over most of North America in sixteen hours. From New York to Washington State, the continent was as a thing dead beneath a shroud of blinding white. The last of Cree's Black Angus bulls perished of thirst while standing up to its chin in snow, unaware that the stuff could be eaten. Pat and others donned two suits of underwear and as many flannel shirts as would allow them to move their arms in their fleece-lined coats, smeared lampblack beneath their eyes to forestall blindness, and waded through waist-deep drifts to extricate foundered cows and deliver fodder to herds stranded in ravines. The hearts of two of the older hands burst from the strain; their bodies were carried back and stored in a barn to await the thaw, when the ground would be soft enough to dig graves without breaking a spade. Two weeks later a chinook wind blew warm air across the plains, but before the snow finished melting, an icy blast issued from Alberta, freezing it into a crust as hard as iron. The cattle who had survived the blizzards could not break through it to forage for the grass beneath. Maddened, half-blind bulls, cows, and steers, their ribs standing out like umbrella staves, staggered into town, pushed down fences, and ate the tar paper off the sides of shacks. They heeled over in backyards and school playgrounds and putrefied when the thaw came. Teams and wagons were employed to drag the carcasses to a mass grave, where lime was shoveled over them to prevent plague.

Captain Brandon Kirby, looking nearly as gaunt as any of the remaining Cree cattle, counted banknotes out of the strongbox on his desk and pushed them across the blotter toward Pat. "You'll find it's all there, and you may count yourself fortunate for that. There won't be enough if all the hands ask for their time."

"I never did trust to luck." Pat counted the notes for himself and put them in his inside pocket. "I been waiting outside since before sunup."

Kirby was looking out the window of the ground-floor study he used as his office. "The Stock Growers Association has ordered a thousand rolls of barbed wire. They're going to fence in the open range, trim the herds. It's the only way to keep count and feed them in the event of drought and blizzards. I never thought I'd see the day."

"I seen my share. You get so you take what comes. What's next?"

"Mr. Cree sets sail for Scotland on the twelfth. I'm to sell off the rest and take my commission. After that, I don't know. California, perhaps."

"All the gold's dug out there."

"There's gold and gold. What about yourself? Back to sheriffing?"

"No, irrigation."

"You're starting a water company?"

"Yeah. Well, not exactly. I'm getting together an investment partnership to dam the Rio Hondo and flume it out across the desert. The territory's seen what drought can do. I figure to make something off the water rights."

"You'll lose your shirt. God doesn't want this country to have water. Snow, yes. Water, no. You'll be broke in a year."

"I'm broke now. Anyway it beats going to California without a plan."

"I didn't say I didn't have a plan." Kirby uncorked his pocket flask, swigged from it, and looked at the flask. "Maybe I'll try the liquor business. Make wine."

"Lose your shirt."

The Englishman found a glass in a drawer of the desk, blew dust out of it, and poured from the flask. He pushed the glass across the blotter and lifted the flask once again. "Here's to your water," he said.

Pat picked up the glass. "Here's to your wine." He drank.

· SILVER ·

CHAPTER 11

The Cyclone and the Peccary

In the autumn of my one hundred fifth year, the rain fell for three days in the desert in a month with a blue moon.

Three days of rain in the desert is a rarity during the monsoon season of spring; that it should happen in the time of the harvest was a thing unknown in my lifetime, nor could I find any reference to such an incident in the journals of my father and grandfather. That it should take place between two full moons appearing in the same month assigned it to a unique category, shared by the Immaculate Conception and the Detonation of the Godhead, and thus the creation of the universe. It was a time—if ever there was a time—to forage for the Black Maria.

La Maria Negrita is a desert mushroom, whose span is measured in hours. It grows in heavy moisture and dense shade—two things not to be found in that burning land except under the scarcest of circumstances—and sheer chance governs its discovery by one knowledgeable enough to recognize it and to harvest it immediately. It cannot be domesticated. I had never seen the Black Maria in nature, although I had searched for it when I thought the conditions friendly. My experience of it was confined to a single paragraph in my great-grandfather's journal and three desiccated specimens in the bottom of an apothecary jar labeled in his hand. It was said to cure the Plague, leprosy, and male-pattern baldness, to restore fecundity to the barren womb, and, when pulverized and mixed with the menstrual blood of a virgin, to rejuvenate the soil in a field exhausted by poor agricultural planning.

I had no interest in curatives and placed no faith in the last property, which smacked of quackery and even if true served only to sanction the farmer's incompetence. My keenness to secure a fresh specimen of La Maria Negrita was based entirely upon the results of experiments recorded by my great-grandfather, who claimed to have managed the transmutation of silver to quicksilver with the introduction of eighteen grains of new Maria to a forty percent solution of molten silver in purified water. His conviction that an additional eighteen grains would complete the transmutation from quicksilver to gold, was obstructed by the fugitive nature of the fungus, whose properties fled when it was exposed to the dry air. If his belief was correct, the spore of the Black Maria contained the secret of the Philosopher's Stone.

The blue moon doubles the force of lunar gravity. It steepens the tides, stimulates crop growth, and elevates all things created of nature to the second power. It increases the ability of the male sperm to impregnate the female egg, and of the egg to reproduce. Infants born between the pull of the two moons are wiser, healthier, and more fertile than others of their generation. That property of the cinchona bark that cures fever is pronounced when it is harvested and applied during that period, and the yarrow plant that blossoms then will cauterize and heal at an accelerated rate. It follows that the power of the Black Maria to alter the molecular structure of base metal will be heightened and its span of effectiveness will be extended.

This, at least, was the theory; and since a theory had driven all the males in my line to the last ounce of their life force before the earth was known to circumnavigate the sun, I prepared for my first journey in a decade from my rock to the desert floor with all the solemnity of a Christian priest assuming his vestments.

First, I filled a goatskin bag with water from the barrel the boy kept filled for me. Should my energy flag, I placed in a pouch seven pemmican cakes made from chokecherries and coca leaves, with animal lard as an adhesive. I removed my sandals, pulled on thick woolen stockings, and stamped my feet into a stout pair of infantry boots given to me by a Mexican Army deserter in return for a compass to find his way to the sea while avoiding contact with patrols. These were chosen not so much to protect the pickled and hardened soles of my feet as to shield my lower legs from snakebite. Over the tops I dropped the hem of my heaviest sackcloth, for my skin had grown too thin with age to withstand the scorching rays of the sun. Last I put on a broad-brimmed hat woven of soft straw, the gift of an itinerant missionary who had last been seen riding a burro south on his way to convert the pagan Indians residing below the ruins of Popocatepétl. (Nothing more was heard of him for six years. Then a Yaqui who stopped in the village to visit his sister and stayed to tell of his experiences as a slave to the people of Popocatepétl reported upon the missionary's fate. Remembering from the tales handed down by their ancestors that Spanish-speaking warriors valued gold above all else, a delegation of Indians had sought to please a company of federales who camped near their village by presenting them with the gift of seven gold teeth. They explained that the teeth had been torn from the head of the living missionary before he was split down the middle and roasted upon an altar for the pleasure of their omnipotent god. The outraged captain had the delegation seized and hanged and the village put to the torch, enabling the Yaqui to escape and relate his sad tale.) After forty years the hat the missionary had made was still supple, and resilient enough to roll into a cylinder and pass through a copper bracelet, resuming its original shape without a crease or a crumple. The shade of the brim was as cool as the patch beneath a plane tree, and the hat itself was as light as air.

I slung the water bag behind my back after the fashion of a quiver, appended an oilcloth pouch to my belt for the collection of specimens, took up my ironwood staff, and went out. The herb garden, moist in the early light, slumbered through my passage. I threw the staff to the desert floor to free my hands for the descent. Even at that tender hour I felt the sun heavy across my shoulders, the warmth of the weathered rungs as my hands gripped them. My exhilaration was complete. I felt as if I were ninety again.

The village was not yet awake. I had told no one of my plans, and as I walked down the deserted street behind my elongated shadow, the thump of my staff echoing off the adobe walls dozing on both sides, I felt a tug of apprehension. If the boy who brought my water should visit during my absence, he would surely raise the alarm. I had been a part of the village since before its oldest resident was born—indeed, since before the first course was laid to the first house—and even those whom I had not met held a proprietary interest in me. If I were to be returned under escort by a search party, would they understand the importance of my mission and that it must be solitary, or would they assume that my mind had begun to wander, and seek to confine me to my rock for my protection? If the excursion was successful I cared not to venture forth again, and yet that was not the same as being informed that I could not. Not at all the same. I was not, I am not a sorcerer, I cannot combat the determination of a whole village, not even a well-meaning one. Upon reflection, however, I was serene in my chosen course. It is always easier to ask forgiveness than permission.

Rain makes of the desert a new place, too beautiful and good for this wicked earth. The sand retained enough moisture to adhere to my fingers when I stooped to study it, and as the sun on the horizon went from cherry red to oxblood, pushing away the shadows, the great barren scape became a bright Oriental carpet: yellow primrose, scarlet Indian paintbrush, magenta fireweed, blue lupine, and the crimson pulp of saguaro blossoms, limned in white. Against the ocher and umber and pewter of the caves, canyons, and formations of granite and shale and sandstone and slate, the flaming colors of the hidden life came to glory—for me alone, it seemed, as nary a sandfly nor a lizard stirred on the rugged surface nor vulture nor eagle glided in the invisible currents of the sky, the stomach-tightening blue sky. Although before dressing for my journey I had purified my body with scalding water and borax, had fasted the day before and sterilized my system with purgatives, I felt unclean in Eden, a despicable piece of foul refuse washed up on the shore of Arcadia.

And then the sensation was gone. With the ascent of the sun, the flowers closed their petals and the features of the terrain lost their vivid and virile individuality. Everything withdrew behind a brown and swirling curtain. A breath of fetid wind blew up from the belly of old Mexico, raising billows of dust that eddied in the hollows, clumps of dead earth and decapitated cactus whirling about like exasperated rats snapping at their own tails. Diablos de polvo, these phenomena were called locally—dust devils—and truly they gamboled about like damned imps, profaning the land with their self-centered play. As I watched, several of them banded together, forming a vortex the size of a city plaza; into the spinning void vanished shards of stone shaved thin by wind and flying sand, pebbles, clumps of feathergrass, to reappear inside the brown funnel, bobbing and colliding and darkening the outer ring. The funnel grew, skipping and skidding and whipping its tail, gorging itself upon larger and larger flotsam: Rocks now, the size of fists, bunches of mescal torn from their roots. Larger still, then narrowing at the base as it expanded in height, a plume the color of sand, transparent no longer, snarling like a panther in fierce combat, gouging a path in the surface of the desert; a cyclone now, twenty feet high and growing, now charging forward in a straight line like a locomotive, now turning back along its own trail, now knifing off ninety degrees, quick as thought. Its slipstream blew stinging bits of sand in my face and lifted the brim of my straw hat, pasting it back against the crown. I held onto it with both hands and sank into a crouch in a shallow wash, frightened out of my native fatalism by a force containing more energy than my entire male line combined. Channel it, and in less than a heartbeat the Great Secret would be known. But to channel it required a force greater yet.

Thirty feet, now forty. A titan rising straight out of the desert, swallowing everything in its path and turning it into raw destructive power. I had seen its kind before, but always at a distance, a thing remote. Set loose amid a great population like that of Mexico City, any one of them would have accounted for hundreds, thousands dead, and damages to empty the treasury of the Republic. Here they were a daily occurrence and whirled out their brief voracious lives unnoticed.

I saw a thing dart from behind a rock, and thought at first it was a mesquite bush torn loose by the great cushion of air at the base of the cyclone. Then it changed directions and I saw it in silhouette, recognized the rounded tubular body with its quill-like coat, balanced upon four thin legs, the head as big around at the base as the rest of the body, tapering to a flat snout with tusks clamping tight its upper jaw like thick white sutures: a peccary and a large one, at least sixty pounds, running fast. It seemed at first to sense the cyclone's shifts and take evasive action a split second ahead of them.

Then it misjudged, wheeling left when it should have wheeled right. The tail of the twister snapped, caught the peccary, and sucked it inside before it could even squeal its distress.

I thought the pathetic creature lost. Presently, however, the funnel struck the edge of a pile of broken shale, ricocheted, and skipped to the top of a narrow butte, jettisoning debris when it landed. It continued to the edge of the butte, then leapt to the desert floor. Now my attention was diverted from it for the first time; for something moved among the pile of debris it had left behind. It was the peccary, which rose upon unsteady legs and shook its great thick-based head, appearing none the worse for its experience. This I judged a miracle. Then, perhaps in a fit of delayed panic, the creature broke into a run. I expected it to stop before it reached the edge of the butte, but it did not even slow down. It may have been blinded while inside the vortex. It ran straight off the edge and plunged, shrieking pitiably, twenty feet to the hard surface of the desert.

It took me several minutes to make my way to the spot where the peccary had landed. The cyclone had by this time vanished over a ridge. The beast lay on its side, with its head doubled under its right foreleg at an unnatural angle. Plainly its neck was broken, but it was breathing; I saw the rise and fall of its chest beneath its coarse coat. Tentatively—for the peccary is a wily, vengeful animal, capable of feigning injury to finesse its enemies within range, then lunging to rip and grind with its terrible jaws—I put out a hand and laid it upon the creature's side. I felt the double-thump of its beating heart through thick hide and wiry hair, the heat of its blood coursing through its veins. I felt the heart slowing, I felt it stop. I heard the beast's last breath rattling as it left its lungs. I knew silence.

For a long time after the peccary died I remained in a crouch with my hand on its ribcage. The cyclone was gone—left or blown out—but the beauty and tranquility that had preceded it did not return. I sensed the festering wrath of the pagan gods of the world, the beast-headed, two-faced, jealous and duplicitous immortals driven from both hemispheres by the spread of Christianity to their last refuge in the desert, where mercy and good were punished as severely as pride and evil. Here they still reigned, weakened for want of believers but powerful in their exiled union, and woe to the wanderer who depended upon his piety to see him through.

An omen, this; but I knew not its meaning. Salvation, then destruction. Why?

I did not find the Black Maria, although I carried a detailed sketch drawn by my great-grandfather in colored inks that would not allow me to mistake it. My concentration was shattered by the vision I had seen. I cut off the peccary's ropelike tail, and as I record these observations I can see it suspended over my bench from a nail in the shelf above the athanor, but I am no closer to the meaning it represents than I was upon the day I acquired it.

Salvation, then destruction.

It vexes. It maddens.

CHAPTER 12

Water and Whiskey

The senior partner in the Pecos Valley Irrigation and Investment Company stretched his long body in his stirrups and watched a twenty-mule team gouge the earth outside Roswell. Dragging a ditcher shaped like a giant spade weighted with lead, the teams followed a path outlined by a plow, to in turn be followed by a six-hitch rig pulling a scraper to smooth the ragged edges. In time, when the company finished diverting the Pecos River to fill the ditch, it would live up to the grandiose name the partners had given it: The Great Northern Canal. Just now it was an unsightly raw gash, and the stench of freshly turned earth reminded Pat Garrett of his father's plantation, with all its bad associations.

A horse drew alongside his, and Pat looked into the face of his partner. Charles B. Eddy, thick-built and sandpapery, with a short-stemmed briar pipe screwed perpetually between his molars, wrapped his reins around the horn of his saddle and glowered at the open wound. "Pure-dee ugly, ain't it?" he said. "As a cattleman I always set myself up above the damn sodbusters, but I don't see much difference now."

"You'll change your mind once it's flooded."

"Though when that'll be I don't know. I got a last notice from Chicago. They're threatening to seize the equipment."

"How much do they say we owe?"

"Twice what we got."

"What about Charlie Greene?" Pat's former publisher had joined the venture.

"Bottomed out, same as us. I'm going to Colorado Springs tomorrow. I've got an appointment with Tansill."

"The cigar man?"

Eddy nodded. "He has money to invest and he's warm on the idea. If he likes our plans, he might bring in J. J. Hagerman. Railroad man, money to burn."

"I don't like it. You can only slice up a pie so many ways."

"There's no help for it, Pat. We're in over our heads."

"Just so I don't wind up the one holding the empty pan." Pat turned his horse around and headed back toward town.

Eddy cleaned out the account and chartered a private train to bring Robert Weems Tansill, the manufacturer of Punch Cigars, and James John Hagerman, retired, to Toyah, Texas, a three-day buggy ride from Roswell and the site of the nearest station. Pat put on his good suit and a new Stetson and extended his hand when Hagerman stepped onto the platform. The railroad man, stout and rumpled from the ride, with gray in his noose-shaped beard, ignored the hand, brushing cinders from his coat. He squinted toward the sun-baked plain west of town. "This country doesn't spell water to me."

"That there's the idea," said Pat.

"Is there a hotel here without scorpions?" Hagerman looked at Eddy.

Pat said, "I lined you up with the presidential suite. Harrison stayed there last year."

The railroad man met his gaze for the first time. "I supported Cleveland."

Hagerman never addressed Pat after that. Eddy conducted the prospective stockholders on a tour of the forty-

mile canal and the pipelines in varying stages of completion
that would eventually connect it to the Pecos River. Back
in his hotel suite, Hagerman and Tansill conferred, then
sent out for champagne and cigars—General Gordons, not
Tansill's five-cent Punches—to celebrate the new partnership. Hagerman produced a checkbook bound in calfskin,
dipped a pen with a flourish, and made out a check to the
Pecos Valley Irrigation and Improvement Company for
forty thousand dollars.

Pat, watching, said, "That's Irrigation and *Investment*.
You need to draw up another check."

Hagerman blotted it. "That's just the first change."

Pat now had eighteen hundred acres three miles east of
Roswell, with a two-story adobe house standing calm as a
monastery in a shady grove of oak and pecan trees. Apolinaria had planted roses near the porch, and Pat himself
had dug up a quarter-acre of bluegrass sod and laid it in
front, making a lawn as tidy as any in town. He fed his
cattle from alfalfa he grew himself, selling the rest to
neighboring ranches, and had spent much of his first year's
profits planting and pruning the eight hundred apple and
peach trees in his orchard. Returning from Toyah, he fed and
watered his big sorrel, rubbed it down with burlap, and went
into the house, exhausted to the soles of his feet.

Apolinaria met him at the door. She was carrying Annie, their youngest. Dudley Poe, four, peeped out from
behind his mother's skirts until he recognized his father,
then came around to greet him solemnly; the boy, who
knew Pat's rages, was slightly afraid of him, although the
long man had never raised a hand to any of his children.
Pat had spotted the oldest, Ida, beating a rug in the backyard. Five-year-old Elizabeth sat on the sofa, embroidering in a hoop and pausing from time to time to run her

hand over the stitches, her blue eyes vacant. A bout with scarlet fever when she was three had left her totally blind.

"The man from the bank was here," Apolinaria said by way of greeting. "He can't give us any more extensions. He said he was sorry, but it isn't his decision."

Pat said, "I'm out."

"Out?"

"Hagerman bought up all the shares with one check. He liked my idea so much he stole it."

"Are you going to sue him?"

He laughed. Dudley Poe scampered back behind his mother's skirts. "I sold him my shares."

"Where is the money?"

"At the bottom of a ditch in the Pecos Valley. The shares were worth less than I owed."

She looked away, bouncing the baby in her arms. Her face was as pretty as when they were married, but folds of flesh had begun to appear at the corners of her mouth. Her waist had thickened and there were filaments of silver in her thick black hair. Pat had gone all silver at the temples, the tips of his moustaches were darker than the roots. He had found himself shaving his father's face.

He went into the bedroom. The bed and the chest of drawers had followed him from house to house: wedding gifts from his father-in-law, so that the house he had also given them would not be empty. His wedding picture, Pat seated with Apolinaria standing beside his chair, her hand resting on the back, shared the top of the chest with his wife's silver brush and mirror, a bottle of whiskey and a glass, and a cabinet photograph Pat had had taken with his earnings from shooting buffalo. He looked young and fierce in a new suit with his hat resting on his forearm. It had been a life without debts, a life of nights slept through without a single bad dream.

He filled the glass from the bottle and drank it down. Filled it again and opened the top drawer, groping under the stacks of shirts Apolinaria had washed and ironed and folded, until he found the long-barreled Colt he had used to kill Billy Bonney. To protect the children he kept the shells on the top shelf of the walnut wardrobe. He unlocked the wardrobe with the key on his watch chain, took down the box, and thumbed a cartridge into each of the Colt six chambers. John Poe and some others he had known made it a practice to keep an empty chamber under the hammer, but Pat didn't hold with that, more lawmen having died for want of a bullet than from shooting themselves by accident. Someone knocked on the front door, but it might have been someone else's house for all he paid heed to it. He heard Apolinaria's voice and a deep rumbling response. He was plugging the last chamber when Ash Upson walked into the bedroom without knocking.

Pat glared at the old journalist's reflection in the mirror in front of him. He had on a soiled collar and the same old suit, looking as if it would fall apart if it ever came into contact with a brush or an iron. His goatee was pure white now except for the yellow stain around his mouth, and his hair stood up on one side. His pouchy face was yellow beneath its customary gray pallor. With scarcely a glance toward Pat, he headed straight for the glass of whiskey.

He drank, then tipped his head in the direction of the big revolver. "Who's that for? Not yourself. You aren't marksman enough to hit a target as small as your brain."

"Even if I was to try it, your liver'd go first." Pat spun the cylinder.

"Your brain and my liver. I'd sooner vote for U. S. Grant." He took another drink, then picked up the bottle. "You going to shoot the son of a bitch, or just buffalo him like that lawyer Roberts?"

"Who, Grant?"

He refilled the glass and drank, swallowing hard. "Hagerman, squirrelhead. Apolinaria told me he skinned you pretty."

"You fixing to stop me?"

"No. Hell, no. The only thing worse than making your own mistakes is trying to stop another man from making his. In any case there hasn't been a good shooting in this territory since you put down the Kid. Also when they hang you it might just liven up the market for that piece of shit of a book you and I perpetrated."

"I never should of shot Billy."

Upson paused with the glass halfway to his lips. "Well, now's the time to think of *that*."

"I'm serious, Ash. Carpetbaggers like Hagerman stayed clear of this country while Bonney was about."

"Professional courtesy, I suspect. The territorial imperative." He drank.

But Pat wasn't listening. He was looking at the picture of the young buffalo hunter. "Tote up all the cattle and horses Billy stole, put it in dollars and cents, it don't come up to the interest on what Hagerman stole with just a scratch pen and a checkbook."

"The twenty-one men the Kid killed might make up part of the balance."

"That was your figure. I put it nearer four. But you see what I'm saying."

"It's a wicked old world, my friend. Why do you suppose it is I drink?"

"It wouldn't be because you got no other choice."

"Choices are for children. Bonney didn't have one. He was what he was. So are you. The difference is he knew it." Filling the glass once again, he waggled his elbow at the Colt. "Put that back or use it the way God and Governor Wallace taught you."

Pat hefted it. His expression in the mirror was sheepish. Then he bared his teeth. "You'll always be there to pull me back, won't you, Ash?"

"Don't bet the ranch on it." Upson drank.

In 1890, the eastern half of Lincoln County, containing the town of Roswell and a substantial portion of the Pecos River, broke off and renamed itself Chaves. The majority of its residents, mountain-dwelling Mexican sheepherders, had voted to honor Colonel J. Francisco Chávez, a frequent president of the New Mexico Territorial Council and the latest in a long and distinguished line to bear the name of a pioneering Spanish family with ties to Coronado, but the Anglo lowlanders who farmed and grazed their cattle in the valley persuaded the council to scrap the Hispanic z in favor of a Gallic s. The new district, in itself larger than some eastern seaboard states, needed a sheriff.

"You will hunt bad men?" Apolinaria, rocking in the parlor and nursing Annie, looked tired.

"That part of the job's changed," Pat said. "I'll probably get fat by the office stove while the deputies do the hunting, like John Poe."

"You will never grow fat."

Pat kissed her, smoothed the wiry black hair on Annie's head, and went to the barn for his bedroll. Much of Chaves was rugged country, with long empty stretches between houses, and those mostly mud shacks; hunting for votes there would be as rigorous as the search for Billy Bonney.

His first stop was the Poe ranch, where his successor in the Lincoln County sheriff's office had retired. He found a green spread with freshly strung barbed wire, a rambling house with a red tile roof and new paint on the siding. Pat's former deputy had invested his profits from the Cree sale, arranged by Pat, in a bigger and better operation than the one he had let go.

"Sheriffing isn't the same as when you left it, Pat." Poe sat on a split-bottomed chair on his front porch, scratching the head of a big woolly dog with its chin resting on his knee. He wore white Mexican pajamas and straw slippers in the middle of the afternoon and looked like Buddha.

"That's what I told Apolinaria." Pat perched on the edge of a glider with his knees on a level with his chest and circled the brim of his hat through his fingers. In the yard a Negro stable-hand washed down the spokes of Poe's buggy with a sponge and a bucket of oil soap, whistling softly. Sophie Poe was clattering china inside the house. Pat had engineered the couple's introduction, had practically pushed his old friend into the union to cinch his election in Lincoln. They had been together eight years.

"It's an administrative post. You run the county, collect taxes. There is bookkeeping involved. The irrigation project promises to bring in a lot of business from the East in the coming years. It's a big job. Complicated."

"Get to the getting, John."

Poe exhaled. "I'm supporting young Campbell. He's a successful rancher, has a good head on his shoulders, and doesn't lose it. He was just a boy when the war broke out in Lincoln. He's the first candidate we've had in years who isn't still fighting it."

Pat stood and put on his hat. Poe's eyes followed him. "It isn't personal, Pat."

"Nothing ever is with you."

"You have your ranch and your investments and your reputation. You shouldn't jeopardize them by playing around with politics."

"I should sit around in long-handles getting all suet-gutted."

Poe said nothing.

Pat turned to leave. At the top of the steps he looked back. "I'm running as a maverick. See if your boy Campbell can keep up with me."

"That would be a mistake."

"We all of us make them, John. Like when you and Tip McKinney sat playing with your peckers on Pete Maxwell's front porch while Bonney walked right past you."

The long man campaigned as an independent write-in candidate opposite the Democratic favorite. The Mexican-American majority, who harbored fond memories of Billy the Kid, including those who had never seen him, elected the young ranchman over Bonney's slayer. In April 1891, Pat disposed of his holdings in New Mexico, packed his family into a buckboard and spring wagon, and quit the territory for Texas.

CHAPTER 13

The White Sands Murders

They'd gone and brushed and pressed Ash Upson's suit, trimmed and combed his whiskers and run a brush through his hair. Pat didn't know him at first. His skin looked healthy and they'd stuffed his cheeks with something that filled out the hollows. His nails were rounded and pink and he had a rosary wound around both hands.

"I'm not certain he was Roman Catholic," said the mortuary director, a small, china-faced man with elaborate waves of creamy hair, so florid in the face that Pat suspected him of dipping into the rouge reserved for customers. "The rosary helped explain the bend in his fingers, which could not be corrected without extreme measures."

"He usually had them around a glass," Pat said. "How much for the box and burial and what you done so far?"

"Twenty-five dollars is the basic rate. For thirty I can offer six pallbearers, and two mourners for another dollar."

Pat counted two tens, a five, and five silver dollars into the director's palm. "I'll take the pallbearers. Ash didn't have that many friends to hold him up when he was alive. You can keep the mourners."

"I'll just write up a receipt."

Alone with the remains, Pat looked into the painted

face. "Well, Ash," he said, "who's going to throw me down and hogtie me next time?"

The director returned, blowing on a slip of paper to dry the ink. Pat touched one of the corpse's hands and turned to take the receipt. "Shut the box and nail it."

"Before the vigil?"

"The time to watch over him's past."

Ash Upson was buried in Uvalde, Texas. He had come there to bet on Pat's mare, which Pat had entered in the mile race at the fairgrounds outside town. After the horse had won, the old journalist had stood everyone to a drink in a local saloon, and continued drinking there after everyone else had left. Early the next morning, summoned by the agitated bartender, Pat had carried the unconscious Upson out to his buckboard and taken him to a doctor, who listened to the man's heart, pried open each of his eyelids, and told Pat he had better make arrangements.

"Well, Ash," Pat had said, smoothing back his comatose friend's unruly hair, "you quit winners."

After the graveside service—attended by Pat, Apolinaria, their four children, the professional pallbearers, and a local minister, who referred to Upson by his formal Christian name "Marshall"—Pat went to El Paso to take in the heavyweight championship fight between Bob Fitzsimmons and Peter Maher. He was getting set to leave his hotel room for the arena when a bellhop informed him that the governor of Texas had dispatched eleven Rangers to stop the fight.

"I heard they'll fight in Juarez if not in Texas," Pat said.

"So did the president of Mexico, sir. He's sending troops to stop it there."

"Where's that leave?"

"Well, Judge Bean has issued them an invitation to fight in Langtry. There's an island in the Rio Grande close by that can't rightly be claimed by the U.S. or Mexico. But there'll be a delay."

"If Wallace had sent half that many men to stop the war in Lincoln, there wouldn't of been a war."

"Where's that, Cuba?"

Pat tipped the boy a dollar for the information. "Who's in the bar?"

"A man named Raymond was there a little while ago, asking for you. He's from New Mexico."

"I don't know any Raymond. What's he look like?"

"He's a curly-headed greaser with a pointy beard. He looks clean and he talks good American, so the bartender didn't boot him out."

"He's lucky he didn't try. Numa Reymond's running for sheriff in Doña Ana County. Not Raymond." Pat gave him another dollar and went down to the bar. Reymond spotted him and waved him over to his table. The sheriff's candidate was a sleepy-eyed Mexican-American with pomade glittering in his tight curls and an obsession for clean collars. Pat had heard he changed them five times a day.

"How's the race?" Pat asked when they were seated with a fresh bottle on the table between them.

"Crooked as a dog's hind leg. There's a little matter of eighty-eight forged ballots standing between me and the sheriff's office. I'm suing to have them set aside."

"I can't help with that."

"That's not why I wanted to talk to you, Pat. The governor's here."

"Culberson?"

"No, Thornton from New Mexico. He's staying in the hotel. He wants to see you."

"What's Poker Bill want with me?"

"It's the Fountain murders."

"Ah."

Reymond drank whiskey and ran a finger along his

moustaches, flicking away the drops. "Don't act ignorant with me, Pat. You know what's being said about you in the papers."

"I heard a thing or two."

"The disappearance of Colonel Fountain and his son is all caught up in territorial politics, but at bottom it's just another range feud. Everyone thinks you're the one to get to the heart of it."

"Everyone except Oliver Lee."

"Lee as much as anyone; that's why he fixed the election to put his man Guadalupe Ascarate in charge of the investigation. Ascarate's sheriff pending the outcome of my suit; his is the name on those eighty-eight ballots. *I* know Oliver Lee had the Fountains killed on the Mesilla Road to keep the colonel from indicting him for stock theft; *you* know it, and so does the governor. But everyone in Doña Ana's either beholden to Lee or too much his enemy to make a real investigation of it. You've been away from New Mexico five years now."

"Nearer six."

"So much the better. No one's got any hobbles on you. Also you're the man who killed Billy the Kid. That counts for plenty."

"Not in Chaves it didn't."

"That was a long time ago. They've had time to think things over, and six years of pettifogging politicians strutting around pinned to badges. Gun law doesn't look so terrible next to that."

"If they think that, they must all of them have been born since Lincoln County," Pat said.

"Hear me out. Thornton's going to press Ascarate to appoint you chief deputy and place you in charge of the Fountain case. I'm prepared to drop my suit if Ascarate complies."

"Why should you do that?"

"Ascarate can't last, especially if the trail leads back to his boss. You'll succeed him as sheriff. Then you can appoint me chief deputy."

"What if Ascarate won't bite?"

"Then I'll press my suit. I'm bound to lose at the local level, but I'll appeal it right up to the territorial council. Poker Bill holds the majority there. I'll win, and when I'm sheriff I'll make you chief deputy. All I need is one term to put me in the running for the council. Then I'll resign in your favor."

"It's got more thorns on it than a prickly pear."

"I've never known you to steer clear of thorns," Reymond said. "What's your answer?"

"Let's go talk to Poker Bill."

In the presidential suite they found Governor Thornton, mournful-looking as an undertaker with his white handlebars and deepset eyes, dressed all in black to his collar, in heated conference with two men, one of whom was known to Pat. In fact, Thornton was a jovial man of healthy appetites, the joy of his family and close friends, who had nicknamed him Poker Bill for his ability to dissemble his true nature among company and settings crucial to the conduct of his territory. Even so, when he was exhausted or distracted, his wit would sometimes expose itself, to be gathered in quickly like a loose shirttail before it was noticed or remarked upon.

Pat shook John Nance Garner's hand before the governor could complete their introduction. The dapper young Texan, who held Washington aspirations, had been after Pat for so long to sell him his property in Uvalde, and so charmingly, that Pat had named his favorite mare after him. Nancy's winning performance at the fairgrounds had only added to the long man's affection.

He looked at the other man, square-built and bitter-featured, with no expression when Thornton identified him as Guadalupe Ascarate, sheriff-elect in Doña Ana County. Ascarate, in his turn, flicked ashes from the end of his cigar to the carpet and made no move to rise from the leather armchair in which he sat. His boots were exquisitely tooled and blacked to a high shine. Pat had never known a certain kind of Mexican to make a loan to a family member in need if the money could just as well be spent on a new pair of boots.

"I assume you're familiar with this Fountain business," said the governor when they had all found places. Pat, sitting legs crossed on the end of a horsehair sofa, had accepted a cigar when Poker Bill offered it from a cedar box, but declined the favor of a light. The air was blue with smoke as it was.

"Just what's been in the papers," Pat said.

"Oliver Lee's been mixed up in one way or another with every skirmish that's taken place in the Tularosa Valley since the winter of '87. In '93 he stood trial for murdering two rustlers and was acquitted on a plea of self-defense. The following year he was implicated in the ambush murder of a rancher named Frenchy Rochas, who controlled the clear-water rights in Dog Canyon. No charges were brought against Lee, but the fact is he's been piping water down to the valley from the canyon ever since. About that same time, Albert Fountain was named the lawyer for the Southeastern New Mexico Livestock Association, and announced his plans to prosecute Lee for rustling and murder.

"Last month, a range detective in Fountain's employ bought a steer from Lee's top hand, Bill McNew. When it was killed and skinned and the underside of the hide examined, the fact that the brand had been changed was indisputable. Fountain took the hide to the courthouse in Lincoln. I believe you know the place."

"I know it." Pat chewed on the end of his unlit cigar. The

graves of deputies Olinger and Bell were still visible from the building.

"When the hide was added to the rest of the evidence in its possession, the grand jury in Lincoln handed down thirty-two indictments against Lee and McNew. Colonel Fountain was handed something else, no one knows by whom: a note informing him that if he didn't withdraw the charges, he wouldn't reach home alive."

"Lee says he never wrote it," Ascarate put in. "Nobody knows who did."

Numa Reymond said, "Nobody knows what happened to Fountain, either. He and his son went missing somewhere in the White Sands on their way back to Mesilla."

Poker Bill laid his cigar stub atop the pile in a crystal ashtray, where it was allowed to smolder out. "The colonel knew his chances. Little Henry's another matter. The people of the Territory of New Mexico don't lose much sleep over what befalls a middle-aged lawyer, but when a nine-year-old boy's blood is spilled, they will have justice."

"That's guesswork." Ascarate relit his cigar. "Mariana Fountain's a jealous woman, everyone knows that. Maybe the colonel got fed up and jumped the fence."

"Along with his son." Reymond's tone was dry.

Ascarate shrugged.

"The posse found a deal of old blood on the ground where a buggy had swerved off the road near Chalk Hill," continued the governor. "Twelve miles farther on they found the buggy, abandoned, with the horses gone. Henry's hat was there, also the threatening note and Fountain's cartridge belt, with twelve shells missing. His wooden dispatch case with all his court documents was nowhere to be found."

Ascarate said, "If I was Fountain and wanted to kick over the traces and didn't want anyone coming after to drag me back, I'd write just such a note. I'd unhitch the horses, put Henry on one and climb on the other, and take off for old Mexico."

"What about the blood?" Garner looked amused. His delight in the human carnival had cut him out for a career in politics.

"It was old. It could have been cow blood. Could have been paint."

Garner smiled. "What do *you* say, Pat?"

"I didn't see it."

"Quite apart from the tragedy involved, this incident couldn't have taken place at a worse time for the territory. We're petitioning for statehood. So fresh an unsolved crime can only weaken our case in Washington." Thornton looked at Reymond. "This contretemps over the sheriff's election in Doña Ana County serves notice to the nation that we are incapable of sorting out our affairs at the local level. Will you withdraw your suit until such time as we have a suspect in custody?"

"I can't promise that, Your Honor, for the very reason that without pressure from outside the sheriff's office, Mr. Ascarate will never lift a finger to deliver a suspect to justice."

"That's a damn lie," Ascarate said calmly.

Poker Bill turned his attention his way. "May I ask what action the sheriff's office *has* taken?"

"I've had men all over that ground. That white sand won't hold a track. The county commissioners have added five hundred dollars to Santa Fe's offer of two thousand and amnesty to the man who turns state's evidence. The Masons have pledged another ten thousand. If there's anything to the talk of murder, that should shake something loose. When that happens, my deputies and I will be on hand to catch it."

"I was wrong," Reymond said. "You have lifted a finger."

"You're a damn liar."

Reymond stabbed a finger at Ascarate. "Ask *him* how those eighty-eight forged ballots got counted. Ask him who waltzed into the commissioners' court with a six-shooter on his hip and a deputy U.S. marshal's badge tacked to his shirt. It was his boss, Oliver Lee."

Ascarate started up out of his chair. The flare of Poker Bill's match distracted him. "Sit down, Lupe," said the governor out the side of his mouth, puffing life into a fresh cigar. "You back off too, Numa. Just because Fitzsimmons and Maher can't fight doesn't mean you two have to fill in. That's better." He shook out the match and tossed it onto the heap in the ashtray. "I invited Mr. Garrett so he could be present when I asked you, Sheriff Ascarate, if you would consent to assign him to a post as chief deputy with jurisdiction in the Fountain case. I suggest you pay him five hundred dollars per month, with half that sum to be provided from the territorial treasury."

"Keep your money, Governor. I run the sheriff's office. I pick my own deputies."

Reymond said, "Everyone knows who runs the sheriff's office." He looked at Thornton. "I'll drop my suit here and now if Ascarate agrees to resign. Then you can appoint Mr. Garrett sheriff."

Ascarate smiled at his cigar. "Reymond keeps forgetting he lost the election."

John Nance Garner scratched an ear. "This meeting stinks clear to Canada. I don't think it has anything more to do with who killed Albert Fountain than the moon."

Thornton sat back. He looked like an old widower. "Gentlemen, if you will all step out and let Mr. Garrett and me speak in private, I believe we can bring an end to all this wrangling without bloodshed."

Ascarate stopped smiling. "I won't be back-doored out of the office I won fair and square."

Reymond laughed. Ascarate shot to his feet, his fists balled at his sides. Reymond rose to face him. Pat stood, towering over both of them. All eyes went to him.

"I'm going down to the bar."

Garner got his hat off the peg and followed him.

Ten minutes later, Poker Bill Thornton joined them in the card room. No greetings were exchanged and he took a seat while Pat and Garner played out their hand. Pat won. Garner left to drink at the bar.

Pat shuffled. "Take a hand, Governor?"

"Draw's my game. I never saw the percentage in turning anything face up."

Pat dealt. Thornton studied his cards without rearranging them, discarded two. "What do you want, Pat?"

Pat skinned two his way. "Money."

"I heard you were well off."

"I'm broke as Job. Apolinaria's expecting again. I can't feed the four I have."

"Discussing your money problems isn't the best way to begin a negotiation." Thornton opened for a dollar.

Pat took one card for himself, saw Thornton's bet, and raised him a dollar. He said nothing.

The governor deliberated. "How much would it take to decide you to accept a post as independent investigator in the Fountain murders?"

"Who's offering, you or Ascarate?"

"Ascarate can't put on his pants without asking Oliver Lee which leg goes first. Lee will never agree to it." Thornton saw the raise and bumped him another dollar.

"That two-fifty a month from the territory still stand?"

"I'll make it up out of my own pocket if the council won't bite. It will, though. Statehood is everything."

"Throw in a hundred and a half for expenses and a bonus of ten thousand on conviction and you got yourself a detective."

"I can only manage five thousand. Money's tight in Santa Fe."

"Ten's the figure."

"Fifty-five hundred then."

"Ten."

"Six. I'm gambling with my political future here."

"Ten."

Poker Bill drummed his cards on the table. "Eight thousand, damn it. I'm calling your hand."

Pat spread out his cards. He had an ace high straight. Thornton had a full house, sixes over treys. As Pat scooped up the pot he said, "Stud's my game. I'm your man."

CHAPTER 14

Wildy Well

Now I know why they call this the Journey of the Dead."

Kent Kearney, slender and mild-eyed, uncorked his canteen and looked out across the dunes of naked gypsum for which the White Sands was named. The frozen waves put him in mind of a chart of the surface of the moon he had displayed on the corkboard in his old classroom.

"The Dead's on the other side of the San Andres," said Pat. "I prefer it to this."

Privately, the long man, who loved New Mexico in all its many moods, loathed this stretch, eighteen miles long and three miles wide, between the foothills of the San Andres and the Sacramento range. By day the sun hammered the white hills, bringing to a boil even the cold blood of the rattlesnakes that burrowed deep into them to escape the heat. By night grains of gypsum blew across the naked dunes in fine clouds like ground glass, changing the shape of the terrain like an ocean. He was unmoved by the crippling heat and the heart-emptying bleakness of the frozen waves of inescapable white; he simply had no use for country he couldn't track a man through.

The five men, mounted well and heavily armed, had drawn rein to drink from their canteens and look out across the bloodless plain. They included Pat, Kearney, a former schoolteacher who had joined the posse out of a commitment to his community, Jose Espalin, a Mexican who had shopped his gun on both sides of the border, and Clint Llewellyn and Ben Williams, Doña Ana deputies who had proven themselves enemies of county politics.

Kearney, who revered Pat Garrett's reputation, had expressed reservations about Espalin. The Mexican, tall and darkly handsome until his lips parted to show his missing front teeth, had blue eyes with all the depth of cheap silver plate. No one seemed to know what went on behind them: Not Pat, who appeared sometimes to place a man's abilities ahead of his motives, and not Oliver Lee, for whom Espalin had ridden in the past and was rumored to have taken part in the bushwhacking murder of Frenchy Rochas in Dog Canyon. When Kearney had asked Pat why he'd brought the Mexican along, the long man had shrugged and said, "He puts me in mind of Billy Bonney."

"But you killed Bonney."

"I never didn't like him."

From Chalk Hill the posse retraced the path Colonel Albert Fountain's buggy had taken on his way home to Mesilla, shortly before he and nine-year-old Henry had dropped off the face of the earth. It had not rained nor snowed heavily since that day, and the ruts their wheels had cut were still visible. They found the place where the buggy had swerved off the road, five miles short of San Augustine Pass. The sun had faded the discolored circle of earth and grass nearby, but the horses caught the scent of old blood and balked, tossing their heads and shaking their manes in protest.

"There's Ascarate's paint," Llewellyn said.

Pat studied the terrain, then pointed at a clump of mesquite atop a stationary dune. "That's the high point."

They rode to the spot, where Llewellyn and Williams dismounted and walked around, spreading the feathergrass with the toes of their boots. Former cowhands who had wintered as wolfers, they were expert trackers who knew the country well. Williams grunted, stooped to retrieve something from the ground, and went up to Pat, jingling a pair of spent brass cartridges in the palm of his hand.

"Winchester," said Pat after a glance.

"Here's a knee print." Llewellyn was crouching where Williams had found the shells.

Pat said, "I wonder how long he waited."

"Is this where it happened?" Kearney asked. "They were killed here?"

"Not here." Espalin, face invisible in the shade of his flat-brimmed sombrero, rolled a cigarette. "This was just to turn them off the road. The rifleman probably shot the boy so Fountain could operate the buggy. Too much chance someone coming along the road might see them."

Later, Kearney confided to Pat his suspicion that Espalin had spoken more as a participant than as a speculator. Pat made no response.

Williams pointed south. "Albert Junior's posse found the buggy twelve miles that way. The Colonel made a chase of it."

Pat kneed his sorrel back down to the road and started west. Kearney caught up. "Aren't we going to search for the bodies?"

"There's a hundred thousand square miles of New Mexico," Pat said. "I don't propose to dig up all of it looking for buzzard pickings."

"What *do* you propose to do?"

"Have a talk with Oliver Lee."

"I heard he went into hiding after you arrested Bill McNew."

"Lee's brother-in-law, Dub Cox, owns a spread on the other side of the San Augustine. He might know something about where he went."

"What makes you think he'll tell you?"

"Oh, he'd never tell me."

They made camp on the western slope of the Organs. Kearney started off to look for wood, but Pat called him back. "Cold camp," he said. "No fire."

Everyone unsaddled his mount except Espalin, who unloaded his short-barreled Colt and brace of Walker horse pistols, cleaned them, and reloaded them with fresh cartridges from his belt. His fingers moved so fast Kearney could hardly follow them.

"Leave the carbine," Pat said. "That way they might let you in close."

The Mexican unstrapped and laid the scabbard containing his Henry on the ground. He swung aboard the piebald and started down the slope at a walk.

"How long do we wait?" Llewellyn asked.

Pat cut himself a plug. "Till morning, if we don't hear gunshots first."

In the chill of dawn, Kearney, on lookout, challenged a figure picking his way up the slope leading a horse.

"Stand down," came Espalin's voice from the shadows. "Is me." He walked past the schoolteacher without stopping.

Pat was sitting up in his bedroll, scratching his head. His long-barreled Colt rested in his lap. When he recognized the Mexican in the starlight he asked him if there were any holes in him.

"Just my gut. Dub's wife cannot cook for shit." Espalin sat down on a rock and tugged off his boots. "Lee's there. He's got Jimmy Gililland with him."

"Gililland's a bad hat," Pat said. "He ain't got sense enough to want to see thirty. You're lucky he didn't shoot you in the back."

"I'd of done the same, but he didn't give me the opportunity any more than I gave it to him. Anyway they think I'm their man in your camp."

"Which you ain't." This from Clint Llewellyn. He and Ben Williams were both sitting up now.

Espalin grinned, showing the gap in his teeth. Then he shrugged. "Lee's finished. He knows there's paper out on him and he has no faith McNew won't give him up. He means to make a fight of it. I don't like his odds."

"Did he say where he's headed?" asked Pat.

"He and Gililland lit out at first light, same as me. He said he's fixing to hole up with Jim and Mary Madison at Wildy Well. They look after Lee's cattle at Dog Canyon and sell water to the El Paso and Northeastern. Their shack's just off the spur."

Kearney started breaking camp. When the others protested: "They have a head start. We should get mounted."

Pat threw aside his blanket and stood, stretched his long back. Bones crackled in rapid succession, like twigs igniting. "Why? We know where they're headed."

"Shouldn't we catch them in the open?"

"They've got fresh mounts. They'd just run away from us and then we'd have to start looking for them all over again." He strode outside the circle of light.

It was Williams' turn to grin. "Getting lazy in your old age, ain't you, Pat?"

"The only way to shoot a badger is to catch him when he comes up out of his hole." Water trickled in the darkness.

They rode thirty-eight miles across the desert, stopping every few miles to water the horses from their cupped hands and lead them. Their clothes were black with sweat. Leading his gray near the end of the line, Kearney asked

Llewellyn how old he figured Pat was. He got the words out between pants.

"I don't know. Right around forty-six or seven, I reckon."

"What do you reckon he eats?"

Llewellyn contemplated the long straight figure loping ahead at the front. "Bull's balls boiled in rattlesnake piss."

"I'd admire to know if he brought any extra."

"Llewellyn!" barked Pat.

He straightened. "Yo!"

"You've been to Wildy Well. What's there?"

"There's a house with a wagon shed attached. There's a barn and a pumphouse and a big old water tank on a platform."

"What's the house built of?"

"Adobe."

"Well, there's no shooting through adobe. We'll have to go in."

Sometime past dark they smelled woodsmoke. Llewellyn took note of the mountains and said he thought they were within a mile of Wildy Well. They tethered their animals and walked the rest of the way carrying their rifles and carbines. As the ranch buildings separated themselves from the general darkness, Jose Espalin took off his boots and led the way in his stockings. The house was a rectangular box, blue-white in the moonlight. The outbuildings Llewellyn had described threw square flat shadows on the ground. The galvanized water tank stood four feet above the ground on a wooden scaffold with loose earth piled around the base to discourage nocturnal creatures from nesting beneath it. Dark rust marbled with streaks of white lime bled down the tank's corrugated sides and clung to the bottom in calcified drips like stalactites. The windows in the house were dark.

The others hung back while Espalin crept up to the front door. There he swept off his sombrero and stood bent over for a full minute, listening. When he straightened, raising his hat, Pat drew his revolver and signaled with it to Williams and Llewellyn to station themselves at the ends of the house. He motioned to Kearney to follow him. Espalin stood aside as Pat leaned his shoulder against the front door, testing it in its frame. He handed his Winchester to the Mexican, fisted the Colt, spread his feet, and threw all his weight against the door.

It sprang open with a splintering sound, swung all the way around on its hinges, and struck the wall with a boom that shook the house and brought a shower of dirt and old clay down from the protruding roof poles onto Kearney's hat. Pat lunged across the threshold. Locating the bed under one of the end windows, he pivoted that way and thrust his Colt into the mounded blankets. "Throw up your hands!"

A pale-haired woman jackknifed into a sitting position, the counterpane slipping down and exposing a naked breast. She screamed.

Pat showed her the revolver. The screaming stopped as if a door had been shut.

The man lying next to her had roused himself more slowly. His face was stubbled and his hair was in his eyes. His face was puffy with sleep. He stared at the Colt as if he were trying to identify its purpose.

"Who are you?" Pat demanded.

"Jim and Mary Madison." Espalin, standing in the doorway, aimed his gap-toothed grin at the woman's breast. She glanced down, gasped, and drew up the counterpane.

Kearney came in from another room, wide-eyed and breathing in shallow gusts. He had the muzzle of his Springfield tilted up behind the head of a man walking in front of him with his hands in the air. The man was barefoot and wearing a nightshirt. "I found this one trying to let himself out through the wagon shed," Kearney said.

"What's your name?" Pat asked.

"Lon McVey. I don't know these people. I just stopped for a meal and a bed on my way to Roswell."

"Where are Lee and Gililland?"

McVey shook his head. Pat looked at the Madisons, who said nothing.

"I'll take the woman," Espalin said. "Women just generally open up to me."

Pat ignored him. "Get dressed, all of you. Watch them," he told the Mexican.

"What do I do?" Kearney asked.

"Watch Espalin." He went out.

Pat assigned the pumphouse to Llewellyn, the barn to Williams, and searched the wagon shed himself. Finding nothing there but a water wagon, he circled behind the house. A white ash ladder leaned against the wall. Pat walked past it without looking at it directly, spotted Williams coming out of the barn, and waved him over. As Williams drew near, Pat saw his gaze light on the ladder, then move on.

"Wait here," Pat said.

Williams nodded.

The long man returned to the house. Mary Madison, wearing a skirt and blouse with her hair tied behind her head, was scooping coffee from an Arbuckle's sack into a pot on the stove. Her husband and McVey sat on a pair of straight chairs, their hands clamped on their knees. Pat looked at Espalin, who shook his head and spat into a bucket.

"Anything outside?" Kearney asked.

"I found a ladder."

McVey glanced toward the ceiling.

CHAPTER 15

Two Minutes

Clint Llewellyn came in from outside. Pat looked from him to Madison. "You've got a root cellar?"

The ranch manager nodded. "Back of the kitchen."

"Take your wife and get in it. There may be shooting." To Llewellyn: "See they stay there."

McVey said, "What about me?"

"You come with us."

Jose Espalin twisted his hand inside McVey's shirt collar and followed Pat and Kent Kearney outside. They found Ben Williams still guarding the ladder. Pat pointed his Colt at McVey.

"If you're so concerned about your friends, why don't you climb up and tell them we're here?"

McVey shook his head.

Pat raised the revolver and brought the barrel down on the man's skull. McVey's knees buckled. Kearney caught him beneath the arms.

"Put him in the root cellar and come back," Pat said.

Kearney handed Espalin his Springfield and scuttled backwards, McVey's heels dragging ruts in the earth. When he returned, the ladder had been moved to the wagon shed, whose lean-to roof slanted down from the flat roof of the house. A two-foot wall shielded the house roof on two sides. Moonlight shone through chinks in the adobe.

"They can shoot down on us through those holes." Pat's voice was a murmur. To Williams: "Shoot anything that moves on top of the house. Use the water tank for cover."

When Williams was in position, Pat started up the ladder and signaled for Espalin and Kearney to follow.

The roof was covered with the same galvanized iron that had been used to make the water tank. Pat and Kearney pulled the ladder up behind them and leaned it against the roof of the house, bending up the sheet of iron along the bottom edge to keep the legs from slipping. Kearney got on the ladder and inched his way to the top, carrying his Springfield. Pat and Espalin stationed themselves at the corners.

Pat cupped his free hand around his mouth. "Give it up, boys! There's no place to go from up there but straight to hell!"

The muzzle of a rifle slithered over the top of the low wall. Kearney shouldered his rifle and fired. The big ball knocked a scallop out of the adobe.

Pat fired behind Kearney and ducked. The muzzle on the wall flashed. The slug split the air above Pat's head with a crack. There was another report from the roof. Kearney shouted and rolled off the ladder. He skidded to the edge of the shed roof, where he hung on for a moment to the bent metal. Then his grip lost its strength and he fell the rest of the way to the ground.

Williams opened fire from behind the water tank. Bullets from the roof whanged into the tank. Thin streams of water sprang out. Williams, stretched out on his stomach behind his Winchester, hunched his shoulders while the cold water splattered over him.

Pat crawled on his belly to the edge of the shed roof and lowered himself to the ground. Kearney lay moaning nearby. "Where you hit, Kent?"

"Jesus, Pat." His voice was a thin whine.

Groping in the darkness, Pat felt the moist pulp of the man's shoulder. "It's bad, Kent. The bone's shattered."

"It's worse than that, Pat."

"Hang on."

Espalin leapt down to the ground, cursing shrilly in Spanish when spines from a clump of mescal pierced the soles of his stockinged feet. A volley of shots clattered from the roof, pinning him against the wall.

The shooting ceased. Echoes of the reports growled away toward the mountains and died hissing. Two minutes had elapsed since the fighting began.

"Garrett, you hit?"

"That you, Lee?" Pat pried the spent shell out of his cylinder and replaced it with a cartridge from his belt. He was seated on the ground near Kearney with his back against the wall of the wagon shed.

"You are a hell of a lot of bastards to order a man to throw up his hands and shoot him at the same time."

"Kearney fired without orders. Are you ready to surrender?"

"I don't think I will. I've heard that you intend to kill me."

"That's just newspaper talk. All I'm fixing to do is take you and Gililland in for trial."

"Just like you done with the Kid?"

"I brought Bonney in alive once. He killed two of my deputies escaping and that's all I have to say about Bonney. You're safe in my hands. Now, will you surrender?"

Lee's laughter was louder than it needed to be. "Who do you think has the best of it? You've got yourself into a hell of a close place."

Kearney had begun talking to himself. The ground felt damper than it should. Pat pushed himself up into a crouch. From that position he could make out Williams stretched out on his stomach beneath the geyser that was the water tank. Llewellyn was still inside with the Madisons and he had lost track of Jose Espalin.

"I know it," he said then. "The question is, how are we going to get out of here?"

There was a pause on the rooftop. Then Lee said, "If you pull off, we won't shoot you."

"Just like you done Frenchy Rochas?"

"I wasn't in on that."

Pat wiped his hand on his shirt. The dampness definitely wasn't dew. "What about Kearney? He's bad hit."

"Jimmy and Mary Madison will see to him."

"I'm depending on you to hold your fire," Pat said.

Kearney stirred when Pat's clothing rustled. "Don't leave me, Pat!"

"You're in good hands, Kent. Lee has nothing to gain by not keeping his word."

"You're four to their two. You going to just tuck in your tail and slanch off?"

"I'll be seeing you," Pat said.

"In hell."

Kent Kearney died in Tularosa, where a railroad section crew Pat sent back from Turquoise Siding took him after Mrs. Madison had used a butcher knife to remove a second slug from his groin.

In Las Cruces, the newspapers were already trumpeting Pat Garrett's humiliation when the posse dragged into town. A journalist who reminded Pat a little of Ash Upson found him pouring himself a drink behind the sheriff's desk. The long man made no objection when the newcomer pulled up a chair and sat down.

"Oliver Lee says you and your posse ambushed him and Gililland in their sleep." He put on a pair of gold-rimmed spectacles and thumbed through the pages of a tattered and grubby notebook. A gnawed stub of yellow pencil rested between the fingers of one hand like a cigar.

"What they were doing sleeping on the roof is anyone's guess, I reckon," Pat said.

"I've slept on a roof of a hot night."

"Well, if I were Lee and had any pride in myself as a frontiersman, I'd come up with a better account of what I was doing. Men who could sleep through the ruckus we put up downstairs aren't the caliber that brought civilization to the wilderness."

"Did you intend to kill Lee and Gililland?"

"No. Had I intended that, I never would have gone to the trouble to obtain warrants for their arrest."

"Lee's attorney says Lee and Gililland are refusing to turn themselves in until some kind of ironclad arrangement is made to protect them from assassination."

"Everyone knows Albert Fall represents the El Paso and Northeastern Railroad, which depends on Lee's Dog Canyon station for water. It's all part of the railroad's scheme to lop another county out of Doña Ana so it can buy a whole new set of politicians. That would remove the White Sands from this county's jurisdiction. Gililland has been boasting about his part in the Fountain killings. Fall's afraid he'll confess when he's behind bars. If anything, Fall's statements are an endorsement of my ability to apprehend his clients."

"That's a fairly complex observation for our readers to grasp."

"They were all brought up on dime novels, where there's no room for politics. They all think it comes down to a fair fight between me and Lee. It's never that simple. I'd never have killed Billy Bonney if Lew Wallace didn't want to be president."

"Some people are saying that the Wildy Well fight has sullied your reputation as a lawman."

"I know who's saying it." Pat drained his glass.

"Others are saying it's typical of how you work, that you set out to assassinate Bonney and his closest friends and carried out your intentions in cold blood."

"Them that say that weren't freezing their asses off in the snow with me at Stinking Springs or sitting in the dark with Pete Maxwell waiting for Bonney to show himself."

The journalist transcribed Pat's response into his notebook, automatically editing out the phrase *their asses off*. He had more questions, but Pat got to his feet, explaining he had appointments to keep. The man looked a lot less like Ash Upson than he had when he'd come in.

"Well, Big Casino."

"What you doing, Billy?"

It was obvious to the long man what Bonney was doing. Riding across country to meet with John Chisum, Pat had altered his course when he saw a figure crouching along Chisum's north fence and recognized the green band on his hat. Billy, dressed in his working clothes and a pair of leather gauntlets that covered his arms to the elbows, was using wire-cutters to snip through the taut strands. Recognizing Pat with a broad grin, he had sat back on his heels, tugged off the gloves, and drawn a blue flannel sleeve across his glistening forehead.

"Just giving Old Jug Ears a hand with his problem," he said.

"What problem's that?"

"Cattle-poor. Poor old son's got more'n he can afford to feed. Me and the boys took pity on him and decided to help him out."

"How many are you fixing to help him out of?"

Billy was truly ugly except when he smiled; it went all

over his face and provided justification for his big front teeth. Pat thought it was the young man's good fortune that he found so many things to smile about. There were women throughout the territory, devout women who would swear on a Bible that Edwin Booth in his prime had never had anything on Billy Bonney, simply because they had never seen him in a somber study.

"Now, Pat, don't you stretch me no blankets about how you didn't cut out no calves for your own self when you was working somebody else's spread."

"No one told me you were getting up your own outfit, Little Casino. Where's your acres?"

"That's the hard part. Charlie Bowdre and I are looking to buy some land with what we realize from Chisum's beeves."

"You're not long on loyal. Seems to me you and Chisum was fighting on the same side not so long ago."

"I'm mighty glad you remember it. Old Jug Ears seems to have forgot. If I was to claim what he owed me for the Murphy men I seen to, he wouldn't have nothing to raise on this here range but a big old ruckus."

"I don't intend to sit here arguing with you, Billy. You're dead."

Bonney took off his sombrero and ran his fingers through his hair, already thinning, as if his superabundance of energy were aging his body ahead of its season. He tugged the hat back on. "I'm dead for a fact," he said, drawing up the string beneath his long wobbly jaw. "I keep on, though. They know about me in Germany, I reckon, and maybe even Rooshia. Right now the king of China might be soaking his yellow ass in his jade bathtub and reading about my exploits and derring-do. Meantime you're alive, getting all squeaky in the joints and watching your phizzle shrink up and just generally disappointing everybody that sees you, on account of you ain't as young and good-looking and full of piss as they been reading about. I ain't walking around with no wife and no litter of kids that I got to think about before I ride in with guns blazing. I don't need to lay down my arms and run away from no two outlaws on a shed roof. There's dead and dead."

"I didn't lay down my arms."

Billy got up and tucked his gauntlets inside his belt. Then he swung a leg over the bony buckskin he had ridden away from Lincoln and the bodies of Olinger and Bell. "I got to fly, Big Casino. I'm supposed to meet you in Fort Sumner tonight and get myself kilt. It says so in your book."

Pat drew his Colt. "Hold on there, Billy. I'm arresting you."

"Sorry, Pat. I got a rule about never surrendering to a man without his britches on."

He looked down and saw that he was naked from the waist down, his long hairy legs laughably pale against the coat of the big bay he had ridden in Lincoln County. His face grew hot. "Stay put or I'll shoot you in the back!"

Bonney appeared not to hear. He gathered his reins and turned the buckskin east.

Pat jerked his trigger finger. Nothing happened. Again he looked down. He was holding not his pistol but his own limp phallus. He sat there and watched as Billy Bonney rode away at a walk, whistling "Silver Threads Among the Gold."

The long man jerked awake, feeling a hot flush of shame throughout his body. He looked down and was comforted to note that he was fully dressed, in the worn leather-reinforced corduroys and old canvas coat he preferred for traveling.

He did not know immediately where he was, and the rumbling beneath his feet and the swaying of the coach, lighted only by the buttery glow of oil lamps suspended from the ceiling at the front and back, did not help. Then he remembered. He was on board the Santa Fe–Las Cruces train, headed home from Hilsboro and the trial of Oliver Lee and James Gililland for the Fountain murders. The pair had turned themselves in to Miguel Otero, the new governor of New Mexico Territory, upon the promise of safe conduct through the legal process. Pat groped in his breast pocket for a cigar, retrieving as he did so stray scraps of his cross-examination by Albert Fall:

"What did you say would be your course if given any warrants for the arrest of Lee? Did you not say that you would go after him by yourself?"

"Yes sir."

"Upon what were these warrants based?"

"Upon affidavits."

"What did you do when these warrants were sworn out?"

"Sent out a posse to serve them."

"Isn't it a fact that this posse was composed of militia—and that they pressed food from citizens?"

"Not to my knowledge."

"What was your object in sending this mob after Lee and Gililland?"

"It was not a mob, it was a posse."

Delicately, with soft-spoken phrases, the resplendent Fall, twirling with his fingers the platinum watch chain slung across his silk printed vest, embroidered a violent tapestry in which Pat headed up a ruthless gang of handpicked killers galloping roughshod across the territory, terrorizing settlers in their determination to execute Lee and Gililland without trial. Pat thought of Kent Kearney, the country schoolteacher, dead of his wounds; but by then the attorney was coming at him from another direction and he was forced to abandon Kearney—again—to defend himself. At no time did Fall's voice rise above the tone of polite conversation, nor did he address the famous former sheriff of Lincoln County in terms other than those of oily respect, and in this way he assassinated Pat's character for good and all. When the long man stepped down, he was conscious of the fact that he had been made to seem a monster, a hoary horned throwback to the dark time before the triumph of civilization and the closing of the frontier. It was 1899; the new century held no safe billet for the killer of Billy the Kid. After eighteen days of testimony the jury deliberated for eight minutes, then voted in favor of acquittal. Lee and Gililland swept out of the courtroom on a swell of backslapping, handshaking, and celebratory cigars.

Pat didn't light his when he found it, but chewed on the end, thinking about this latest dream. He had not before dreamt of encountering Bonney on the range, and in fact had never so encountered him in life; his memories of their times together were illuminated by smoky lamps suspended from pressed-tin ceilings and accompanied by the thud of broken piano keys outside card rooms packed with unwashed men. He did not wonder what the dream signified—the thoroughness of his disbelief in God and fate was such that he accepted all things as random and without design—but he was curious about where it had come from. Probably he was just getting old, pushing fifty with all his weight, and thinking too much about what he would do next.

In any case, there was nothing to be done about the former, and he was damned if he would even try to do anything about the other. In his valise in the brass rack over his head rode a letter signed by John Nance Garner, introducing Patrick Garrett to President William McKinley.

CHAPTER 16

The Pledge

The interior of El Paso's Acme Saloon was a long varnished wooden box that gleamed in as many ways as a room could gleam. Ceiling lights installed by one of the city's two electric plants reflected off the polished maroon top of the mahogany bar, the rows of bottles and white china beer pulls, and long mirror in its gilded frame behind the three bartenders in their white shirts and aprons, the oar-shaped, oiled-oak blades of the big fans swooping ten feet overhead, and the diamond stud in the green satin necktie of the faro dealer standing flaccid-cheeked and granite-eyed at parade rest behind his table awaiting his first customer of the morning. A large oil portrait of McKinley, the recently martyred president, hung wreathed in black velvet above the backbar. Pat, who had had an audience with the chief executive in this city shortly after the trial of Lee and Gililland, could scarcely connect the statesmanlike face in the painting with the blank broad countenance of the man who had told him blandly that he would consider seriously Pat's request for a federal appointment. No such action had resulted, and for two years Pat's political hopes had been as dead as McKinley.

At that hour, before the first drink was spilled and the first cigar fired up, the place smelled cleanly of moustache wax and pomade, vanilla oil and fresh-brewed coffee, bootblack and peppermint and the warm soapy water into which the glasses were plunged between patrons. The barmen, newly bathed and starched, with talcum on their pink palms, paused during setup to snatch glimpses of their reflections in the mirror, like infantrymen inspecting their uniforms before parade. Pat, the former bartender, loved that brief moment in the daily life of a saloon. In a little while the place would start to fill up with sweaty gamblers and shaky drunks. The first splatter of tobacco juice would defile the first polished brass cuspidor, and as if a starting gun had been fired the first loud braggart of the day would come strutting in on the arm of some hungry-eyed whore in her rustling skirts, layers of paint and powder, and cheap scent. Before Pat finished his inaugural beer the scrub-faced maiden of the morning would be well on her way to becoming the foulmouthed, spraddle-legged slut of the vomity night.

The man who drew his beer, a contemporary of Pat's with handlebars artificially blacked and hair combed carefully across his naked scalp, asked him if he was new to El Paso.

"New to no place," Pat said. "But this is my first visit this century. I generally do all my drinking at the Metropole, but it's all torn up now."

"They're wiring the place for electricity. We had us a mess here when our turn came, and I don't know that it was worth it. I miss gas. These damn bulbs light up places that don't need to be lit. We're always sweeping cobwebs out of the corners."

"One ducked the broom, looks like. Right up there."

He didn't look. "I don't miss coal oil, though. When I came here I was the tallest bartender in the place, and I got the job of climbing the ladder and scrubbing the soot off the ceiling. In those days the new man was expected to do everything, even empty and clean the spittoons. Now we get some drunk."

"You've worked here a spell."

"I'm the only man left who was here when John Wesley Hardin got shot. He was standing right about where you are, shaking dice with Harry Brown. Old John Selman stood in the door and shot him clean in the back of the head." The bartender stopped mopping the bartop to fix Pat with his eyes, big as brown marbles. "Now, nobody else saw this nor believes me when I tell it, but I'll swear to it on a stack of Bibles as high as your chin. Old Wes Hardin, he gave that dice cup two shakes *after* he was shot. Just stood there with his brains on his face, still trying to make the point. That's how keen he was on winning."

"Did he win?"

The bartender blinked. Then he dropped his head and resumed mopping. "I don't rightly remember whether he did or he didn't. I don't guess it means much either way."

"Seems to me it does. Seems to me anything a man does after he's dead signifies something."

"All the same, this city's a mighty dull place for his passing. There hasn't been a killing worth talking about in years, and I can't remember the last time one of the banks was robbed."

"What's doing in the Tenderloin?" Pat had been thinking of going around and looking up a whore whose services he'd enjoyed in the past.

"Oh, somebody bottoms up dead every week or so in the opium dens, but it's usually some greaser gone to spend the pesos they get from politicians to wade across the river and vote. You don't count Mexicans. There's just too much law here. It's bad for business."

"I reckon Hardin's brains on his face was good for a few rounds."

"For a month we couldn't keep the glasses filled. We could've used ten bartenders if they could move around back here without falling over each other. Everybody wanted to stand where old Wes stood and hear the tale."

"It don't matter how a man lived if he died right."

"That's the truth, mister. Old Wes just stood there and gave that cup two shakes. Stack of Bibles." He wrung out his rag over the slop bucket. "You hear Teddy's coming to town?"

"Roosevelt? I heard."

"That's how homey we've gotten here in El Paso. Old U.S. Grant wouldn't have come within a hundred miles when Hardin was around. The army wouldn't have let him. You know they started up the Rangers again just to get Hardin. The first time it took the whole Comanche Nation. Where you from, mister?"

"New Mexico."

"Billy the Kid country. Well, you know what I'm talking about then. They say Teddy's thinking of putting in New Mexico for statehood. That wouldn't have happened if the Kid was still around. He wouldn't have let it."

"Bonney couldn't even help himself."

"I guess you don't know his kind, his and old Wes Hardin's. You can kill them, but you can't civilize them. They won't stand still for it."

"They stood still when it counted." Pat paid for his beer and left. The saloon had begun to fill up.

He went back to his hotel and stretched out fully clothed on the bed to stare at the ceiling and wait for noon. That's when Roosevelt's train was expected.

Arriving at the platform, Pat found the press of rubber-neckers, reporters, policemen in helmets, and angry anarchists impenetrable. The locomotive, flags flying in front of the boiler, had just sneezed to a halt, steam boiled around its wheels and drifted across the cinderbed. The long man had on a new suit with the stiffness still in the seams and his Stetson had been cleaned and blocked recently; he had no desire to risk mussing himself. He cut himself a plug and, chewing, leaned inside the doorway to the telegrapher's while the city police sorted out the crowd. The train consisted of three cars festooned with red-white-and-blue bunting. The caboose and the coach just behind the tender would be for soldiers and the Secret Service, which had been recruiting furiously since the McKinley killing. An army sharpshooter in a sergeant's uniform stood atop the president's Pullman with feet spread, holding a Krag repeater and scanning the crowd from beneath the flat brim of his dimpled campaign hat for likely targets. Plainclothesmen in straw boaters and tight coats, virtually the only ones so attired in the blistering heat of west Texas in late summer, worked their way through the throngs, studying faces and bumping against people in search of hidden weapons. Pat, who had seen three presidents assassinated in his lifetime, thought it was all show; if Billy Bonney, wanted throughout the territory for the murders of Buck Morton and Frank Baker, could gun down Sheriff Brady on Lincoln's main street in broad daylight and ride away bold as brass spurs, then anyone could kill anyone else—anywhere, anytime he chose to do it. He'd heard the Germans were working on a gun, fed directly from a cartridge belt, that could fire several dozen rounds a minute, and the French were debating the possibility of dropping dynamite onto the heads of enemy troops from hot-air balloons. Such reports disturbed him in ways he couldn't define, although he thought it might have something to do with the fact that he had six children.

At length, the police succeeded in herding the crowd

beyond the sawhorses erected at opposite ends of the platform. A group of shaggy-headed socialists laid down their signs to help away one of their number, bleeding from a scalp wound inflicted by an officer with a stick. Pat waited for them to pass, then approached one of the plainclothesmen standing inside the nearest barricade. The man, lean and Yankee-looking beneath the brim of his boater, drew himself up a little. He was better than six feet tall and plainly unaccustomed to having to look up at anyone in order to address him.

"I've got an appointment," Pat said.

"You and everyone else both sides of the Potomac." The man had a New England accent, metallic and bitter. "Got a pass?"

He drew from his breast pocket a paragraph typed under the new White House letterhead; those he had received from McKinley had referred to the place as the executive mansion. The plainclothesman snatched it from him and read it without moving his eyes. Then he looked up. "You're Garrett?"

"I am."

"Wait here."

In a little while he came back from the train, carrying the folded letter before him like a saber. "Surrender your weapons."

Pat unbuttoned his coat and opened it to show he was unarmed.

"Thought you were *that* Garrett."

"I didn't figure Billy the Kid to be riding this train." He felt strange saying it. He had never referred to Bonney by that name.

The plainclothesman pulled a long face of contempt. He jerked his chin at the policeman nearest him, who stepped forward and pulled one of the sawhorses out of line so Pat could pass. Wiry fingers closed around Pat's upper arm. "Spit out that plug."

Pat missed the polished toe of the plainclothesman's right boot, but only because he jerked it back at the last instant.

On the platform of the private Pullman another Straw Hat, rounder in the face and kind in the eyes if one didn't look past the surface, found Pat's name in a leather-bound notebook and opened the door for him, using his left hand. Pat saw the bulge of the pistol rig beneath his left arm.

The interior of the car reminded Pat of the Acme Saloon, only no smell of peppermint or pomade and no sign of alcohol or any promise of it. The walls were paneled in red oak, and a deep fern-print carpet covered the floor from end to end. Curtains of burgundy velvet hung over the windows, tied back with ropes of gold, a row of Chesterfield lamps with copper shades swung from the ceiling between ranks of oils in gilt frames leaning out from the walls; Pat, who had little patience with *Harper's Weekly* but sometimes paused to study the lithographs while waiting his turn in the barber's chair, thought they were original Remingtons. There was a small portable bookcase, much scarred from travel, packed with volumes, a pair of deep armchairs upholstered in green plush, and a half-size roll-top desk against one wall with letters and rolled-up documents in every pigeonhole. A captured Spanish battle flag decorated the back wall next to the door and a grizzly rug, slightly moth-eaten and greatly at odds with the car's civilized appointments, sprawled at the foot of the larger of the two armchairs with yet another scrolled paper clamped in its jaws.

In the smaller chair, legs crossed to show an immaculate expanse of dove-gray gaiter, sat a trim man of sixty or so, with beautiful white whiskers and gold-rimmed half-glasses, scribbling on a sheet of foolscap on a lap desk. This was not the president. That individual, whose square stern face with its drop-wing moustaches and beribboned pince-nez hung in post offices, barbershops, and private parlors from Long Island to Long Beach, was seated at the rolltop desk in his vest and shirtsleeves with his cuffs rolled to his elbows. Pat assumed at first he was writing— the new president and most of the members of his cabinet were perhaps the most literary in the nation's history, and had been responsible collectively for more than thirty-five books now decomposing decorously in matched sets behind glass in doctors' waiting rooms in Maine and lawyers' offices in Dakota—but as he stepped farther into the car, removing his hat, he saw that Roosevelt was busy dismantling a coiled steel contraption with screwdriver in hand and his famous spectacles dangling from their gold clip.

When after a full minute neither man had acknowledged the newcomer's presence, Pat cleared his throat. He felt like a damned fool doing it. One of the advantages of having killed Billy the Kid was he had grown accustomed to all activity coming to a stop whenever he entered a room.

The man in the armchair went on writing. "Matters of state must take patience, Mr. Garrett. Theodore is in the midst of inventing a better mousetrap."

"*Rat* trap, Hay. You needn't bother pretending you don't know the difference. You saw your share when you took Lincoln's dictation." Roosevelt dropped his screwdriver, sprang to his feet, and closed the distance between himself and Pat in a bound, right hand outstretched. "Please accept my apologies for the behavior of my secretary of state. He's quite absorbed in yet another dreary volume about his years as Honest Abe's personal secretary."

"*Assistant* secretary." John Hay dipped his pen. "In any

case, twenty thousand readers have not found them dreary so far. How many copies did you say you sold of *The Naval War of 1812?*"

"It went into a second printing, blast you." The president's grip was firmer than it had to be, but Pat had been warned by John Nance Garner, and gave as good as he got. Roosevelt's gray eyes sparked approval. "What about you, Garrett? *The Authentic Life of Billy the Kid* got me through three weeks of white weather holed up in my ranch house in the Badlands in '84. I made Hay read it on the way here from Washington."

"Well, that's two."

Roosevelt laughed, a high honking bray, and straddled his nose with his spectacles. They were very thick and made his eyes seem to swim. "What do you know about mechanisms? I bought that blasted trap in Denver and haven't been able to figure out how it works. There's a rat abroad in the White House, big gray jasper whose snout puts me in mind of Henry Cabot Lodge. The staff has nicknamed him General Linares, after my esteemed opponent at San Juan Hill. Can't have that. I mean to have him stuffed and sent to the Smithsonian, but I must catch him first. I don't trust a weapon I can't understand."

"The only reliable way to kill a varmint is to wait for it outside its hole and shoot it when it shows."

"Delightful! Perfect! You hear that, Hay? Perhaps if I'd had Garrett with me in New York I'd have been spared Boss Platt. Sit down, sir. Take off your coat. It's much too hot in here for a man with blood in his veins." He glanced theatrically at the coated Hay. As Pat complied, hanging his coat on the back of the vacant armchair, Roosevelt tugged at a bellpull. When a black orderly in a white coat presented himself: "Bring us some lemonade, Atticus. Mr. Garrett is thirsty."

Pat, who had not been consulted, would have preferred

a tall whiskey; but he'd heard the president kept temperance and so sat down without comment while the servant went to fetch the refreshment.

When the lemonade was poured—John Hay, Pat noticed, let his glass stand untouched on a table, the ice melting, while he went on writing—Roosevelt gulped down half of his, set down the rest, and tramped up and down the length of the car, flapping his arms. On his way back he paused by an open window to breathe in the hot dry air. "I love the smell of this country," said he. "If you have any sort of imagination you can detect the stench of dry Aztec bones and conquistadors' armor baking in the sun. I cannot believe dear old Bill contented himself during his visit with a buggy tour and Methodist services. Had he known how little time was left him, I daresay he'd have dipped his beak deeper."

"At the risk of parroting our friends in the Secret Service, I might point out that if a certain chief executive insists upon standing before open windows in Wild West train stations, he hasn't much time left himself." Hay spoke without looking up from his foolscap.

"I've old hens enough fluttering about without another in the flock." But Roosevelt came away and sat down. Perched on the edge of his wooden swivel, facing Pat with his hands on his knees, he looked as if he were set to take off and fly upon no notice. "I'll get to the point, Garrett. I've chosen not to reappoint H. M. Dillon as collector of customs in El Paso. I'm considering you to replace him."

Pat, who had been lobbying for the position since his visit with Roosevelt's predecessor, expressed no surprise. He kept a tight rein on his elation. He had been around politicians long enough to sense an approaching *but*.

"There are no secrets on Capitol Hill." Turning slightly, the president riffled a sheaf of papers held down by the rat trap. "Since my preference became known, I've been awash in telegrams and letters urging me to reconsider. I won't name names. I'm sure you know who your enemies are."

"There's some around I haven't killed."

John Hay made a hoarse sound in his throat. Roosevelt looked as stern as his photographs, and Pat questioned the timing of his experiment in levity.

"Enemies are an inevitable byproduct of effective public service," Roosevelt said then. "I haven't much use for saints in my bureaucracy. In any case the naysayers have been counterbalanced by an equal number of endorsements from prominent local citizens and a former governor of New Mexico Territory."

Pat said nothing.

"A man of sterling qualities is needed to oversee the border between the United States and Mexico. Mind you, I'm a former frontiersman myself, and know how slight is the value of what we are pleased to call the higher principles in certain venues. I do require, however, an abstemious man in a rigorous office." The president reached into a pigeonhole. Pat, watching, could scarcely believe that all this talk of sterling qualities and effective public service had come down to a question of drink. He felt a nearly uncontrollable desire to laugh.

"Would you read this aloud, Garrett?"

Pat took the sheet of stiff paper and pronounced the words typewritten there:

"I, the undersigned Patrick F. Garrett, hereby give my word of honor that if I am appointed collector of customs at El Paso, Texas, I will totally abstain from the use of intoxicating liquors during my term of office."

"Well?"

The single syllable, dropped into the silence that followed the recitation, startled Pat out of his mounting mirth. He smiled slowly.

"Mr. Roosevelt, it suits me exactly." He held out a hand.

The president dipped a pen in the inkwell on the roll-top and passed it over, along with a ledger. Pat rested the book on his knee, placed the document on top of it, and signed with all the flourish he had.

Roosevelt beamed. "Bully."

CHAPTER 17

On the Border

Horseshit. He said it? Horseshit."

Pat, blowing a hole through the foam in his beer, nodded solemnly. " 'Bully.' That's what he said."

"Say it the way he said it."

"Can't. Not enough teeth."

"Shit. I thought that was just something them Eastie journalists made up." Tom Powers' broad Irish smile reached clear to his good eye. The other, a glass replica with the iris painted on, remained motionless in its socket. He topped off his glass from the bottle on the desk and offered to pour one for Pat, who shook his head and lifted his glass of beer in a sort of toast. They were seated in the back room of Powers' Coney Island Saloon in El Paso, which Pat had made his headquarters while the Metropole was being electrified. The Acme was too toney for him; he preferred the cigar burns on the Coney bar and the balding moose head mounted above the coatrack, collateral from an Idaho hunter who couldn't settle his tab. The back room had yet to be wired. Pat, feeling the first cricks and catches of a cantankerous old age, considered himself more at home in the soft orange glow of the oil lamp on the desk than in the glare of a tin-shaded bulb. He found the exposed cables that ran up the walls of downtown El Paso from grubby Bakelite turning-switches no improvement over gas pipe. Moreover he liked his host, who couldn't care less who shot Billy Bonney, or if he was shot at all. Scratch Home Rule for Ireland and Powers had no interest in anything that didn't directly affect his inventory.

"You serious about that pledge you signed?" Powers heeled the cork back into the bottle.

"I signed it."

"But beer's an intoxicating liquor."

"Not the way you serve it."

"That's a damn lie." The saloonkeeper grinned. "So you're a tax collector now?"

"Customs," Pat said. "I see the duty gets paid."

"Take a cut?"

Pat shook his head.

"That's good." Powers drank. "That's proper. Teddy's an honest one. I'd shake his hand."

"Not much chance of that, unless you want to get out of the saloon business."

Powers turned his glass eye Pat's way but said nothing.

The long man's office was reached by a flight of outside stairs, from the top of which a window looked out on the broad flat bend of the Rio Grande and the bridge connecting the U.S. and old Mexico; when the wind blew strong from the north, he could snap his cigar stub out the window and watch it land in one of the busy streets of Ciudad Juárez. When it turned up from the south, it brought with it the stench of the cattle pens in quarantine, the sharp-metal stink from the smelting stacks along the river, and the occasional bray of an automobile horn as one of the vehicles, shaped like a bathtub mounted on four wire-spoked bicycle wheels, chugged up Mesa Street, back-firing and startling horses. The window in the adjacent wall faced east toward Washington and the residential streets, where Queen Anne spires towered over territorial adobe and boys in cloth caps and corduroy knickers chased hoops with sticks, a practice whose point escaped the collector of customs.

The building was new and smelled pungently of fresh-sawn pine and lead paint. Pat had installed neither shades nor curtains, preferring to let the sun pour in; by afternoon the heat was so overpowering that no work could be done, at which point he adjourned to the Coney Island. There, at a corner table out of the direct line of sight from the bat-wing doors, meetings were conducted over an ostentatious pitcher of lemonade, or when the winter winds defeated the Gulf Stream, a steaming pot of coffee. Aside from that he drank beer exclusively, and then only in the privacy of Tom Powers' back room. Visitors who came to see him in the office were met by an astonishingly tall man with salt-and-pepper moustaches in a vested suit with an elk's tooth on a fob, who rose from behind his cluttered desk to grasp their hands in a dry firm grip and offer them, if they were male, a cigar from a wooden box on the desk, or if they were female, a paper cone filled with mossy water from an earthenware crock installed in the corner between the windows. Frontier history buffs looking to meet Billy the Kid's slayer were disappointed to learn that he did not use a big Colt's pistol for a paperweight, that no mementos of his peacekeeping past decorated the room, whose only ornaments were an American flag on a staff, the president's portrait in a walnut frame, and large-scale parchment maps of Texas and Chihuahua hanging side by side on the only wall not interrupted by a door or a window. His soft Alabama drawl confused them, and when he drew a pair of wirerimmed glasses from the tortoiseshell case in his breast pocket to read a document or a letter of introduction, some of them decided that this must be a different Pat Garrett.

If, however, that visitor were to say or do something to test the temper of the collector of customs, the point was settled with a speed uncommon to the sedentary life of the conventional bureaucrat.

In the spring of 1903, Pat's office door opened to an under-size man in an outsize collar, crosshatched with dirt, and cinders still on his suit from a long ride by rail. He had a narrow forehead, hollow in the temples, ears that stuck out worse than old John Chisum's, rimless eyeglasses, and a moustache like a caterpillar, from one end of which drooped a smoldering cigarette. He was carrying a broad-brimmed Panama hat that he could not have worn aboard the train; it was the only truly clean thing about him, white as milk against fingers stained black with nicotine. He held it nearly at arm's length to prevent the ashes of his cigarette from falling on it and placed it on the only clear corner of Pat's desk.

"Garrett? I'm Joseph Evans. I'm a special Treasury agent. Secretary Shaw sent me."

Pat stood and shook his hand. The man seemed to have no bones in his fingers. The collector indicated the straight chair facing the desk, but Evans missed the gesture. He strolled the room with his hands thrust deep in his pockets, looking at the maps, the portrait, the view from the windows. "Mr. Shaw is in receipt of a petition signed by sixty-three prominent El Paso businessmen calling for your removal. He asked me to look into it."

"I've seen the petition," Pat said. "I know who sent it. I. A. Barnes represents an American importing firm that does business here. He's after my job."

"Sixty-three men appear to think he's qualified."

"I'm not surprised, seeing as how they're most of them connected with the Corralitas Ranch down in Casas Grandes."

"Mr. Shaw is well aware of the Corralitas controversy.

The New York Board of Appraisers did not agree with your estimate of the Corralitas cattle's age. They reckoned between ten and thirty percent of them to be one year old or older. Your figure was slightly over half. The difference is between three dollars and seventy-five cents per head and two dollars. A substantial error."

"I've had to do with cattle for better than thirty years. I know a good deal more about their age than anyone in New York."

"Nevertheless, the decision went against you. It made the administration look bad in the papers."

"The papers here sided with me. The *Herald* knows Barnes's petition for a sham."

"Of course I was referring to the *eastern* newspapers. El Paso is the end of the world as far as most of the voters in this country are concerned."

"I'm sorry you wasted the fare," Pat said.

Evans stood with his back to the flag. The sunlight pouring through the east window made blank cutouts of his spectacles. "The party has a long-time loyal supporter here in George M. Gaither. I want you to consider appointing him cattle inspector. It will remove some of the pressure from you and recognize him for his efforts on our behalf."

"Gaither's a hack."

"This request comes directly from Secretary Shaw."

"Gaither's had his snout in the public trough for years. When the wind shifts he turns with it. He's absolutely unfit for any position under the government."

"I urge you to reconsider."

Pat played with a yellow pencil on the desk. It bore the impressions of his teeth, as did all the others in the mason jar. "I'll appoint him for thirty days. That should give him time enough to prove even to Washington he's a horse's ass."

"I felt certain you'd see reason." Evans turned to leave,

then went back and retrieved his hat. Pat wondered if he'd bought it brand new in El Paso.

Tom Powers accompanied Pat aboard the Santa Fe Railroad for the trip to the long man's neglected ranch in Doña Ana County. Pat had not invited him, and Powers had offered no reason for his decision to go. In truth, neither man had given the situation much thought. It had taken Pat the better part of ten years to find a companion with whom he felt as comfortable, and as little as if he were on display, as he had with Ash Upson. He had presented Powers with the long-barreled Colt with which he had killed Billy Bonney, and now it hung among the arsenal that decorated the wall behind the Coney Island bar.

The saloonkeeper, still attired in his town suit and fedora, perched himself on an intact section of weathered rail fence, sipping whiskey from a flat bottle while Pat wandered the yard in front of the house, kicking up clumps of drought-killed grass and testing the gate, which collapsed with a shove. The house's tile roof had fallen in and there were holes in the adobe through which a child could crawl. A family of armadillos had moved into the front parlor, building a nest inside the kiva fireplace. The nearsighted, armor-plated mammals had been migrating ever northward for three seasons, as if the end of the old century had been some sort of signal releasing them from their ancestral insect-hunting grounds. Pat, dressed as of old in a sweat-penetrated Stetson, canvas coat, denims faded white, and scarred boots, looked grim.

"What can I get for the place, Tom?"

"It depends. Any furniture in the house?"

"It's worth more than that. What do you know about land?"

"I know better than to ask someone like me what I can get for it."

"Maybe I shouldn't sell. This government job can't last. Roosevelt won't be president forever."

"Seems like he already has. But then I'm a Democrat."

"I thought you favored him."

"That's before I found out this teetotaling business was permanent. I thought he put it on to get votes. All this dry talk in Washington makes me nervous." He drank.

"Prohibition's in Kansas, I hear. Even Dodge City."

"Country's gone to hell since McKinley bought the farm."

"I ought to fix the place up, rent out what I can't ranch myself. Real estate's bound to jump now the frontier's closed."

"I wonder how you go about closing a frontier."

"I don't know. All I know is they closed it."

Powers changed the subject. "How's Gaither working out?"

"I let him go last week. He had his thirty days."

"That pettifogging Evans won't like it. They've got tight."

"Evans don't concern me. Leslie Shaw's another story. He's marked me to fall. He's in the pocket of Barnes and that Corralitas crowd. But if I can't run the El Paso office my way I'd just as soon pick Texas ticks off New Mexico cows."

The Irishman stuck his short legs out in front of him, balancing himself on his tailbone. He drank as heavily as Upson without ever showing any adverse results. Pat sometimes said he had a glass leg to go with his eye. "I'd still shake Teddy's hand," he said.

"The hand of a teetotaler?" Pat was amused.

"A popular one. If I had my picture taken with him I'd hang it behind the bar. Business would improve. I could afford to electrify the card room."

"Roosevelt's as down on gambling as he is on liquor. You'd sooner have the chance to get your picture taken with Pancho Villa."

"I don't know anybody who knows Pancho Villa."

A bench had been installed on the front porch of the Nation's Meat and Supply Company on San Antonio Street for passengers waiting to board the traction car that ran past it to put up their feet and cool the back of their necks in the shade. On his way to his office, Pat paused to take stock of the tableau presented by Special Agent Joseph Evans and George M. Gaither sharing the slatted seat. Evans sat with his head down, knees spread, and the Panama hat dangling from his fingers between them; the front of the brim and the pinch of the crown now bore the stains of handling. Gaither, all soft fat and black muttonchop whiskers in loose seersucker, small red bow tie, and a straw boater with a red silk band, worn as square across his forehead as if he'd put it on with a mitre, sat back with his elbows on the back of the bench and the soles of his saddle shoes showing, picking his teeth with a cedar splinter.

"Good morning to you, Collector Garrett," Gaither said.

Evans raised his head then. The eternal cigarette smoldered short, threatening to ignite his caterpillar moustache.

"I'd wish you the same," Pat said, "if I meant it."

"That's no way to carry on," said Evans.

Pat stood in front of Gaither. "You've been talking about me around town."

"I guess I can talk."

"You've been telling all your friends you'll have my job."

Gaither picked his teeth and said nothing.

"Did you tell anybody I said your position was permanent?"

Evans put his hat on. "Garrett, have you been drinking?"

"Answer the question."

Gaither removed the toothpick from his mouth and studied the frayed end. "I did not. I said you promised, with the assistance of Mr. Evans, to make it permanent if possible."

"You're a goddamn liar."

"Now, hold on." Evans gathered his feet to push himself off the bench.

"You're a goddamn liar too."

Gaither moved swiftly for a heavy man. He threw away the toothpick, sprang up, and hurled a fist that glanced off the customs collector's jaw. Pat swung one of his long arms in a loop that caught Gaither on the ear. After that, the fight lost its outward shape, the two men grabbing at each other's coats and wrestling rather than exchanging blows. Evans kept his distance—afraid, perhaps, of further soiling his panama. In a little while the street corner was a mob of interested citizens, some of them prominent, who seized the combatants and separated them. Police Chief Peyton Edwards elbowed his way through the throng and placed Pat and Gaither under arrest for disturbing the public peace.

"What'd they soak you?" Powers asked.

"Five bucks apiece." Pat puffed furiously at his cigar as if it were a cigarette. The Coney Island's back room was blue with smoke.

"Could've been worse."

"Only if they put us in the same cell. We had to stay overnight. I never was in jail before."

"There's not a whole hell of a lot of politicians can claim that."

"I had a wire from Washington sitting on my desk when I got out. That pettifogging Evans don't let the grass grow."

"What'd it say?"

"Shaw's appointing a special investigator to find out what Gaither and I already told Chief Edwards. He's appointing that petition-slinging son of a bitch I. A. Barnes."

"I don't know why you take it."

Pat puffed. "I never was in jail before."

Powers poured himself a whiskey. "He's going to be in San Antonio next year."

"Who, Barnes?"

"Who cares buffalo shit where Barnes goes? I mean Teddy. They're getting up a Rough Riders reunion. They're all coming, the Colonel included."

"He's up for reelection. I don't guess he can refuse."

"You going?"

"Next year's a ways off."

"That'd be the time to get my picture taken with Roosevelt, if ever there was one."

"Not if you're still in the saloon business."

"I don't have to be in the saloon business where Teddy's concerned. Tell him I'm a cattleman."

"What do you know about cattle?"

"I know enough to stay out of the business. That's more than Teddy knew."

"All right," Pat said.

"You mean it?"

"If I didn't I wouldn't be saying it."

"Thanks, Pat. I owe you."

"Just pour me one and we'll call it square."

"Beer?"

"Whiskey. What the hell."

· GOLD ·

CHAPTER 18

The Return of the Long Man

S alvation, then destruction.

Salvatio convenire destructio.

Salvación, despues destrucción.

I could not in any language, ancient nor modern, fathom the meaning of the vision of the cyclone and the peccary.

Years had elapsed since the day it was revealed to me in the desert. In the time between I had during the course of my experiments expended enough pewter to place a foaming stein in the hand of every customer in every Rathskeller in Munich, smelted nickel sufficient to plate the pivoting doors of New York and Chicago, sent enough bauxite up my chimney to build an aluminum road shining from Madrid to the Straits of Gibraltar. I had invented and prepared a solution consisting of three parts cinchona bark to one part cave mold dissolved in alcohol that had defeated an epidemic of malaria in the village, treated a score of cases of syphilis among transients, lain near death from scarlet fever for a fortnight, and been nursed back to health by the grandson of the boy who had first brought water to my rock, losing most of what remained of my hearing in the recovery. Yet I was no closer to the Philosopher's Stone and could not even guess at the answer to the riddle I had been asked.

The ancient gods that paced the barren reaches, despised

and forgotten by the peoples who had paid them homage through the million dark years before the Revelation, were low and devious. Arrogant at their height, cruel in their largesse, in their bleak exile they fed their resentment on needles and venom and amused themselves preying upon the minds and hearts of those scattered few who still heeded them. Their catechisms were meaningless, their visions conducted no light. They spent their scaly-headed, pendulous-breasted, Grendl-bodied immortality scheming new ways to bedevil those who were wise enough to mark that they did not vanish with the smashing of their temples, did not quit this world when the first unlettered Christian hoisted his cassock and shit on their altars and walked away to spread the tale. The lesson was not a lesson. The promised wisdom was muzzle.

And yet.

I kept no faith. Gentle Christianity was as dead to me as the remains of my great-grandfather's family, torn and twisted on the Grand Inquisitor's rack and flung into a pit reserved for the disposal of Unbelievers. Of the pagan creeds of the native tribes, none was as vivid as my father's narrative of my grandfather's last moments, hurled broken, blinded, and burned from the summit of a cliff by the Pueblos whose malaises he had treated, and for whose labors on his behalf he had paid them in gold and silk. I had read and been unmoved by the Book of Mormon. I found no succor in Mohammed or Buddha and thought Devil-worship a waste of expensive candle wax. The pursuit of pure Science had left me no time for pilgrimages or obsequies, even had I cared to partake in them.

But to lack faith is not to disbelieve. Whether the gods invented man or man invented the gods is immaterial; the sheer collective weight of the unthinking masses that turned out offering fealty to avoid or transcend destruction, whose solitary devotions kept lights burning in a billion bedchambers from Ice Age to Industrial Revolution, must perforce by weight of will heap flesh on graven idols and quicken it. They were unseen, these Once Exalted, but then so was the cyclone, and like the cyclone it was by their visible effect upon material earth that their strength and stature was measured.

I knew not the mechanics of augury, but thought it probable the portent I had witnessed had taxed the strength of deities already eroded by their diminishing congregation. They had not the stores to mount a practical joke. No, there was meaning to the peccary's rescue and immediate death; but I, who now had lived in three centuries, had not the wisdom to read it. Was I then a fool, a contemptible puffer like my great-great-grandfather, whose longevity was his sole virtue? Was *that* the jest engineered by the vengeful deposed gods of antiquity? I groaned and hung my head in my hands above the litter of filings and instruments that profaned my worn bench.

"Well, you ain't no ghost, and that's a fact. You told me once there's no end to a ghost's patience."

I started; for although I had not heard his footsteps on the polished stone floor, age and command had brought an edge to his tone that pierced the callosities on my eardrums. I turned around on the stool and looked upon the long man for the first time in a quarter-century.

Gaunt he was now rather than lean, like an ancient wolf in harsh winter when prey was scarce. The bones of his face stuck out like architecture, his eyes glittering like blue glass shards in the caves of Chihuahua. The long countenance was as brown and cracked as a dry lake bed. His hair and moustaches were white, and the years of stooping to hear and to be heard had rounded his back permanently. His suit of clothes was smarter than the one he had worn on his first visit, exquisitely cut from better material, and now that the railroads had come it had no need of brushing after the long journey. He no longer smelled like a French king, but entirely like harnesses that had been left out in the sun and rain. Where the nickel-plated star had been, there now depended a platinum chain with an ivory fob. The hat in his hand was a fedora, dove-gray, with a four-inch brim and a wide black silk band. The sorrow he wore was the same.

"The nostrum has run out," said I.

"Years and years ago. It never did stop even one dream."

"Did you follow the instructions I gave you?"

"A quarter of a jigger a night for two years. After it run out I switched to whiskey. That didn't stop them neither, though it did sunny up my disposition. We had us some fine talks, Billy and me."

"I have thought of you often."

He did not address that. "I didn't know the place at first. Last time I was here it was just adobe huts and the only bath in four hundred miles. Dogs taking a dump in the street. I didn't expect it would change. Funny. Where I come from just about everything has."

"A company from El Paso is testing for oil in the sand hills. If they are successful, refineries will follow. At night, they say, the flames from the chimneys reflect blue off the bellies of the clouds. They say it looks like an ocean."

"Looks like hell."

"I would not know."

"I would." He cast his splintery gaze about the room. "Nothing's changed here. I don't reckon you ever found that trick for making gold."

"If I had, it would make no difference to the way I live. My goal is perfection, not wealth." I moved my shoulders. "I am still searching. And you?"

"Well, I ain't perfect by a long shot."

It was taking longer this time for the long man to come to the reason for his visit. He had grown older, but with age had not come contentment. He was more guarded, less trustful. The years of meeting gunshot with gunshot were far behind him. In the arena in which he'd been competing, the opponent was more difficult to identify, and the weapons to fear were not those he could see. The fatal blow was as likely to come from the man at his side as from the one he faced. Words were nets, thoughts were tridents. To share intelligence was to stand naked before the enemy.

I sought to put him at his ease. "I am ancient. I have no ambitions and only one illusion. Here of all places you may speak your heart."

He nodded, and appeared to go on nodding after he'd forgotten the reason. Then he spoke.

After a time—so Pat Garrett told it—the half-naked Bonney of Pete Maxwell's bedroom in Fort Sumner came less often to his somnolent mind. Mostly it was Billy in his Spanish costume and green-banded sombrero, although sometimes he appeared in the same black hat caved in on one side and heavy ribbed sweater he had worn in the photograph that still circulated on cigarette cards throughout the southwestern United States and had even found its way to the papered wall of the cantina that had been built upon the site of Juan Flores' barbershop. He spoke to Pat of old times with Big Ear John Chisum and John Henry Tunstall the Englishman, whose death in the range war in Lincoln County had set in motion the events that cast in steel the remainder of Bonney's life and Pat's. He spoke of dealing monte in Beaver Smith's saloon. On occasion he brought cards, and the pair played until dawn, or until Pat awoke.

Sometimes Pat was receptive, and asked Billy what had become of Tom O'Folliard and Charlie Bowdre, and why they didn't come to visit. Bonney would explain that Tom and Charlie were still sore about getting killed, particularly during cold weather so that they could never warm up, and envied the long man his warm blood. "Them boys always did miss the whole point," Billy said. "They was in for the cash."

"What about you?" asked Pat.

"With me it's like cards. If you're just playing for money, you can't help but lose."

"But you lost."

"There's losing and losing."

"Billy never did make a lick of sense," Pat said. "Being dead hasn't changed him none."

Often the visits were quite ordinary, with nothing of note passing between them. Pat might as well have dreamt of branding calves on his ranch or stamping duty records at the border. The thing he dreaded—and because he could not predict when it would happen, even the ordinary visits were torturous—was the times when Bonney's amiable, slack-jawed expression would change abruptly in the middle of some folksy anecdote or while he was drawing from the deck; when his skin would grow ashen and a black band of shadow would fall across the top half of his visage, and he would shout:

"Quién es?"

Then there would be an explosion, very loud, well beyond the volume entrusted to a mere dream, and Pat would wake up, bathed in icy sweat, his nostrils burning with the stench of sulphur and cordite.

It required the half of a bottle of whiskey to help him back to sleep; whereupon another dream would come, or it would not. When it came there was no determining whether it would play itself out peacefully or end in the same disturbing way. Sometimes he put off returning to bed, and was useless all the next day for exhaustion. He feared nothing in life as much as he feared the phantasms of the night.

He did not always dream. When he did not, and when the dreams were uneventful, his life the next day would go one way or the other, as do all our days. In time, however, he came to see that the death-dream, in which he killed his friend, invariably preceded a black day in his passage.

He had slain Billy Bonney the night before he pistol-whipped W. M. Roberts on Lincoln's main street over the insulting letter to the *Rio Grande Republican*, and subsequently lost the New Mexico Territorial Council election. He was defeated for sheriff in Chaves County on a day following a night during which he had slain Billy Bonney. Bonney's death had awakened him in camp on the way to the disastrous gun battle at Wildy Well, and on the morning he traded blows with George M. Gaither he was tired and irritable from lack of sleep after a death-dream the previous night. He had not dreamt at all before the meeting with Theodore Roosevelt at the El Paso railroad station, where he was appointed collector of customs. During Roosevelt's second term, Pat one night relived in all their ghastly detail the circumstances of the night of July 14, 1881; the next day he orchestrated the infamous photograph of the president at the Rough Riders reunion with Tom Powers, notorious throughout Texas and northern Mexico for his Coney Island Saloon. Treasury Secretary Leslie Shaw made haste to bring the truth to the attention of Roosevelt, who chose not to renew Pat's appointment.

There were other such episodes, but the above serves to establish the pattern.

"Is it your belief that Bonney is responsible for all your misfortunes?" I asked.

"Not all. The sun don't shine on the same dog's ass all day, and no man's lucky all the time. But the oncs I brung up suit Billy's damn sense of humor down to the ground. Take that time he kilt Olinger and Bell and jumped jail in

Lincoln. He done it to vex me as much as to keep from getting hung."

"Ghosts enjoy a joke as well as the next man."

"It never did seem to matter to him that he was the only one laughing."

"Have you considered that the dreams may be intended as a warning?"

"Billy wasn't one to look out after other men's hides. It's what kept him alive long after he should've been cold and planted. Anyway, a warning's not much good if it don't tell you what to look out for."

I turned up a palm.

"What is it you ask of me?"

"I come down here thinking you'd have some nostrum that works where the other didn't. It's been better'n twenty-five years. I reckon that makes you somewhere around a hunnert and a quarter." Teeth showed behind his white moustaches.

"I cannot help you."

"I can't believe that. They can cure yellow fever and consumption. There's a doc in Europe claims he can make a crazy man sane. I rode from the station in a gas-powered buggy and I read where two brothers back East built a machine that flies, without a balloon or nothing."

"Time does not move so rapidly on this rock. There have been no developments."

Again he nodded.

"That tears it, then. I'm fixing up the ranch, bringing in some of them Scottish cattle Cree and Kirby went bust on. The range is fenced in, so I shouldn't have to worry about feeding them come a bad winter. I learnt a thing or two about irrigation when I was getting took by Eddy and Hagerman. What I don't ranch I'll hire out. It's still a risky living. I wanted to try and make sure I didn't dream about killing Billy before I got in so deep I couldn't get out."

"I am sorry."

He straightened his shoulders with a shrug and pulled on his fedora with the same gesture he had used a quarter century before. Perhaps it was this similarity that brought to his mind our words of parting on that occasion. The same gradual grin deepened the cracks in his face.

"I clean forgot to bring any of that wisdom you asked for," he said. "I told you I'm slow settling debts."

"I am confident you pay the ones that matter."

Pat Garrett turned and strode out, ducking below the lintel. I followed as far as the door and watched as he descended the ladder. The crown of his hat vanished below the edge of the rock. A moment later I heard a backfire from the desert floor, as sharp as a rifle report, and the rataplan of pistons. Gears meshed with a groan and then the noise faded away. I never saw the long man again.

CHAPTER 19

The Deacon

Jim Miller was not as tall nor as prosperous as he appeared. Standing at a little over medium height in two-inch heels, a sober black broadcloth frock coat (dubbed the "Prince Albert" by a canny eastern tailor who had never been closer to Victoria's late consort than his likeness on a can of tobacco) sheathing and concealing his short trunk, emphasizing the length of his legs in well-cut gray flannel trousers, he managed to maintain the illusion of height even when shaking hands with six-foot-five Pat Garrett before the bar in Tom Powers' Coney Island Saloon in El Paso. He wore a soft black hat with its wide flat brim straight as a ruler across his brows, barber-trimmed handlebars, and a brief Imperial beard in the hollow of his chin. His fair skin was burned red from the sun glaring off the snow north of Fort Worth, where he had received Pat's wire, and against it the startling blue of his eyes shone like ice shards under a threatening sky. He wore his Colt in a special holster inside the waistband of his trousers in deference to the city ordinance against carrying firearms, but Pat spotted the yellow-ivory handle against his vest when his coattail slipped open.

"Do I call you Mr. Miller or Deacon?" Pat asked.

"Miller will answer, or Jim if you're the friendly type. Every day but Sunday." His soft accent was Texan. He had left his native Arkansas while still in his infancy and no trace of it remained.

"Tom says we can use his card room."

"I don't play."

As many people claimed Miller was a duly appointed deacon in the Southern Baptist Church as claimed he had simply donned that title along with his black coat; but in speech and general behavior he conducted himself as if it were legitimate. On the rare occasion that he drank to excess, he acknowledged that he had broken but one commandment in his forty-three years, and that one fifty times. Those who had overheard him called him Killin' Jim Miller.

The photograph of Tom Powers standing among Theodore Roosevelt, Pat, and the Rough Riders, blown up and hung in a silver frame, had improved business at the Coney Island to the desired extent: the gaming room was now wired for electricity. Bright bulbs with hammered funnel shades swung low over the card stations and billiard table, their light reflecting green off the baize and illuminating the pictures of prize-fighters on the walls and the scaled-down replica of the bar in the main room. At that hour of the morning the room was deserted. Pat and Miller strode to the table farthest from the door and sat down without taking their hats off. Thus by tacit agreement they declared it a brief conference.

Pat noted with grim amusement the adjustments his companion made to avoid prodding himself with his concealed pistol. "I heard you favored a scattergun."

"I didn't figure I needed it to get a table in a saloon. They tell me El Paso's simmered down since Wes Hardin got it."

"You knew Hardin."

"Only after he got out of jail. I retained him to prosecute Bud Frazer for trying to kill me."

"I heard you killed Frazer."

"I found two barrels did the job where two juries wouldn't."

Pat, remembering the verdict in the Lee—Gililland trial, nodded. "Civilization's a deal slower in coming than electric light."

"I'm thinking it can take its time." Miller turned his concentration toward rolling a cigarette. His pink-nailed fingers were meticulous.

Pat got to it. "You know Brazel?"

"We've not met. I heard there's black blood between the two of you. Something about goats."

"Wayne Brazel's a sprout. It's the men behind him I can't stomach, chiefly W. W. Cox."

"Cox holds the paper on your ranch by Las Cruces."

"The son of a bitch is holding my cattle in Mexico till I pay it off. Only I can't pay it off without cattle. Now he's partnered up with Brazel to run goats on my property out by Bear Canyon. I can't abide a goat. More than that, I can't abide the way Cox and Brazel went around me through my boy Dudley Poe to lease the property. The deal was Brazel would deliver ten heifer calves to Dudley each July for five years. Only you don't get heifer calves from goats. All you get from goats is goats. They crop the grass down to bare ground and ruin it for cattle. Also they stink worse'n sheep. Beyond that I got personal reasons for hating goats."

Miller lit his cigarette and said nothing.

"I got Brazel arrested for herding livestock near a residence," Pat said, "but he's out on bail and court won't convene till spring; meanwhile them goats are eating my grass. If this thing is allowed to run its course I'll lose the ranch no matter which way the jury jumps. I want that goat man off my land."

"Permanent?"

The long man shifted his weight in his chair. "I'm not

hiring your gun, just what goes with it. I want you to sit in on a meeting between Brazel and me. I think he'll see reason with you in attendance."

"It's not my area."

"I'll make it worth your time." When Miller made no response, Pat went on. "I've had my life's portion of ranching. If you ain't cut out for it, it breaks your heart and your back and leaves you with nothing but dirt. If Brazel moves his goats I'll sell you the place for three thousand and pay off the mortgage out of that. Now, that's a bargain."

"You figure I'm cut out for it?"

"You can turn around and sell it if you like. Cox knows what it's worth. He'll make you a fair price, and that's damn more than you're paying. He's a mean old cob but he won't cross you the way he done my boy Dudley Poe. He's smarter than that."

"I'm not tempted."

"It's fifteen hundred acres. They aren't making any more of it. There's a spring, a house, and outbuildings. Then there's the stock."

"Cox has the stock."

"He'll free it up once the mortgage is paid. I'll run it up for you personal. Dollar a head." Pat kept his tone matter-of-fact. He had three hundred dollars in the bank in Las Cruces and owed almost a thousand in taxes.

"I've made as much as two thousand just for uncasing my shotgun. I didn't have to wait for no deeds to clear." The man in the black coat flicked his ashes into the glass tray recessed in the table for that purpose. "Where can I find Brazel?"

"To talk to him about setting up a meeting."

Miller smiled for the first time behind his moustaches. It did nothing to take the chill from his eyes. "Of course. I get paid in advance for the other."

"Let me know when you have an answer. I'm staying at Mrs. Brown's here in town."

"I know."

Pat lifted his brows. "I only moved in last week."

"Pat Garrett can't unbutton his fly without the whole Southwest knowing about it." Miller got up and left.

Alone in the large room, Pat went to the bar and leaned over it to retrieve the measured bottle from the shelf beneath. He blew into a glass, filled it, and was drinking with a heel hooked over the brass rail when Tom Powers came in. The saloonkeeper turned his good eye Pat's way. "I saw the Deacon going out."

Pat drank and said nothing.

"You know he's an assassin."

"If you barred your place to assassins, you'd be out of business in a month."

"If I was to take that notion, I'd start with him. They say he killed his own grandparents when he was eight."

"They said something like it about Billy. The true facts are never enough for some people."

"Miller blew Sheriff Frazer's head out from under his hat in Texas and stood trial for killing an Indian policeman named Collins in the Nations. That ought to be facts enough for anyone."

"I'm not a lawman anymore, Tom."

"Neither are Frazer and Collins."

"My business with Miller's legitimate. Anyway, it ain't your concern."

"It is if it goes on under my roof. I didn't electrify this place to have dark plots bandied about in it."

"You wouldn't have electrified it at all if it wasn't for me, Tom." Pat measured himself another glassful. "It cost me my job."

"I'm guessing they'll put that on my headstone."

"You owe me."

"If I didn't I wouldn't be here." Powers stepped behind the bar and held the bottle up to the light. "You're hitting this stuff square on the head these days, Pat."

"I reckon that makes me your second best customer."

"It don't matter that I'm a drunk. You've got a standing to maintain."

Pat looked at him for the first time. He had a headache. He could feel his pulse pounding in the veins in his eyeballs: Quién es? Quién es? "You ever try standing on shit, Tom? You just keep sinking. Pretty soon you're lower than the shit. I've never stood so tall as the night I shot Billy. Wish to hell I could say the same for him."

"That's whiskey talk."

"Whiskey don't lie. I believe if you was to put Billy Bonney up for governor of New Mexico State he'd win it running away."

"You ought to get out of El Paso. The town's unlucky for you. Just the way it was for Wes Hardin."

"Old Wes Hardin. They came from all over both sides of the border just to look on his corpse. More folks saw Hardin dead than Lincoln alive. You reckon they'd turn out like that to look on my corpse?"

Powers laughed and poured himself a drink. "I'll let you know in twenty or thirty years. You're a young man yet, Pat. I've got ten years on you."

"John Selman shot Hardin in the back of the head. He was standing at the bar, just like I am now. He couldn't have done it better if he'd had his pick."

"You told me you had a job waiting for you in Santa Fe. Governor Curry's set to appoint you superintendent of the territorial prison."

"That was three months back. I'm still awaiting a wire."

"Maybe it's waiting for you in Las Cruces."

"The only thing waiting for me in Las Cruces is a cattle ranch without cattle. A situation like that sure cuts down on the chores."

"You're forgetting your wife and parcel of kids. What you want to take up with that Brown woman for? She's a grass widow and not near as handsome as Apolinaria."

"She's my landlady."

"She's a whore."

"I didn't ask her profession."

"Boarders don't take their landladies on buggy rides all over town and along the river road. Not married boarders whose faces are known."

"The church ain't your true calling, Tom. I'd give it a pass."

Powers slammed the cork into the bottle. "That's a hell of a thing for you to say to me."

"I reckon it is." Pat was contrite. "Don't take it personal. I didn't sleep much last night. I had a dream."

"You'd sleep heaps better in your own bed with your own wife. If I had a wife like Apolinaria and a parcel of kids I'd sell the saloon and never leave home."

"You don't know what you're talking about."

"You don't know the company you're keeping. Whores and murderers."

Pat fished a silver dollar out of his pocket and bounced it on the bar. "I'm going back to bed."

"Wait for your change." Powers rummaged among the coins in the cigar box on the shelf under the bar.

"Put it toward a pulpit." Pat walked out with the exaggerated dignity of the true drunk.

Mrs. Brown was out when he got home. He let himself in with his own key and sank into the feather mattress on the old brass bed without taking off his boots. He fell asleep quickly, snoring to rattle the blinds on the windows, and dreamed of Billy. It was the death-dream.

CHAPTER 20

Mrs. Brown

It's wildly impractical," Mrs. Brown said.

Pat nodded agreement and sipped coffee from his thin china cup, thick and strong and black as molasses, the way he preferred it and the way only Mexicans knew how to brew it; his own attempts always wound up bitter beyond words. He wasn't really listening. They were sitting on the terrace of the El Capitan Restaurant overlooking the Mexican Quarter, and he was watching some kind of pageant going on a few blocks away. Practically every day of the year belonged to some saint or other, and the occasion was rare when one of them wasn't being celebrated. This one made use of a tall adolescent—chosen, no doubt, for his height—got up in a death's-head mask of papier-mâché, with a white linen sheet for a shroud, aboard a pale horse being led by a bent-over crone dressed all in black. A cassocked padre and a little girl in a Communion gown briskly smacking a tambourine headed the procession, looking like scraps of white paper skipping ahead of a groundwind, and the usual three-piece mariachi band—guitar, trumpet, and drum—brought up the rear playing something drunken and tinny. Pat wondered if all musicians in old Mexico were chosen for their inability to carry a tune in a bucket.

Whatever it was about, everyone was having a good

time. Children ran shouting after the performers and the watchers on the boardwalk beat their hands and cheered and sang along with the music: "La muerta, la muerta, viva la muerta." The more macabre the trappings, Pat reflected, the more greasers seemed to like it. It was no wonder they had so many revolutions.

"It's burgundy velvet, with a robin's-egg blue linen yoke and a full skirt that wraps around," Mrs. Brown was saying. "The hem is trimmed with chantilly." She pronounced the word with a hard *ch*. Pat had never heard it before, but assumed it was French and that she was making a mess of it. He'd been to New Orleans, and Mrs. Brown had spent her whole life in Texas, and not more than a day or two of that on the polite side of town. "I saw it in Birnbaum's window."

"How much?" Pat asked.

"Forty dollars. Mrs. Birnbaum said they're selling the same dress in St. Louiš for sixty," she added quickly.

"Tell her to sell it in St. Louis."

She looked down at her plate of ham. It had grown cold and she had not so much as dented it with her fork. "You haven't bought me anything in a long time."

"I bought the dress you've got on, and the hat." He'd thought it was a damn silly hat at the time, the black straw brim bent up on one side and pinned to the crown, dyed ostrich plumes on the other, and time hadn't increased his affection. "I'm buying that supper you didn't eat." He resolved to smoke a cigar and put it out in the center of the ham slice when he left, just to keep the management from serving it to another customer and collecting twice. He had lost a young fortune at cards and horse races in his lifetime and didn't mind wasting his money so much as paying to look the fool.

"If you loved me you wouldn't keep track."

He got out his wallet to pay the bill and leave, with or

without her. Then he took out a twenty-dollar bank note and two tens and laid them on her side of the table. "Tell Mrs. Blumberg I ain't paying no tax."

"Birnbaum." She made a purring noise and placed the notes in the bottom of her reticule. She had fine eyes, large and dark like his wife's, but heavy-lidded, as if she hadn't got enough sleep; which in his experience was a true thing. Her nose was thin and too long and she had bad skin, but she made up for these faults with an abundance of tawny hair that he didn't think was dyed. She wore it swept up; when the pins were removed, it spilled like rich grain to her shoulders. Although soft and doughy around the middle when she undid her corset, in bed she grappled ferociously, all teeth and sharp nails and sinewy coils that kept him from breathing, making the release when it came as explosive as a Howitzer. Apolinaria by contrast lay submissive and unmoving, neither resenting his needs nor enjoying them, accepting them with the passive gratitude of a penitent. He loved Apolinaria; not as passionately as he had loved her sister, dead these thirty years, but with the fullness of affection due the mother of his children and the companion of his age. He needed Mrs. Brown. Her conversation bored him, and it had occurred to him that if she were to drop out of his life—fall into the Rio Grande and drown on her way across the bridge to purchase her medicinal opium, or leave him for the Mexican policeman he knew she stayed with while in Juarez—he would miss her for a while the way he'd miss masturbating if his wrist were sprained, but that would be all. Her absence would cause him more irritation than grief.

He was still a little cloudy on how they had come to keep company. Tom Powers, whose taste in whiskey Pat also considered inferior, had been working on her romantically, and had introduced her to him along with her girlfriend, a younger and far more interesting woman with an

infectious wit, to whom Powers had presented Pat as the
famous Sheriff Garrett of Lincoln County. The long man,
pleasantly drunk and in a mood to charm, had barely noticed Mrs. Brown in favor of her friend, but as the evening
wore on and the Coney Island grew crowded and smoky
he found himself standing with his arm around her waist
while the other woman receded into the predominantly
male assemblage. One-eyed Tom, diplomatic to a fault,
withdrew as well. The next day Pat awoke in Mrs. Brown's
bed, and by the end of the week he had moved his belong-
ings from his rented rooms on Texas Avenue to her house
on Eighth Street, from the bedroom of which could be
heard the cries of merchants selling avocados and melons
in the farmers' market in Juarez. He was contented enough
with her favors, whose variety convinced him, if indeed
her general manner did not, that she had at one time or
another made ends meet with their assistance, and was seldom bothered by the empty-headed prattle that in her
passed for conversation, but in his darker moments he
could not avoid the conviction that somehow in the course
of that alcoholic evening she had bewitched him against
his will. He did not trust her.

She had a first name, something classical that he couldn't
pronounce (*Apolinaria* had thrown him for a year, and
even after all this time he could not say it the way a Mexican did), and so when he made reference to her and
thought of her it was as Mrs. Brown. He never addressed
her by name or private endearment. In truth, every conversation they had had, she had initiated. His relationship
with her was entirely responsive except in bed, and even
there she commenced matters as often as he. The first time
this happened he was surprised, and perhaps shocked; for
he was accustomed to a degree of passivity even in those
partners for whose time he paid. Certainly this was always
the case in the marital chambers. To find the positions re-

versed disconcerted and excited him in equal measures. Mrs. Brown appeared to enjoy herself whether she was giving pleasure or taking it. She had never once refused him. He made that allowance for her, and when he bothered to contemplate the affair he decided that was the one thing that sustained it. When it came to the physical act of love she was a giving creature, generous and sweet. He came as close to loving her then as he ever would.

She claimed to have lost her husband in the siege of Santiago, but the circumstances of his death as they were explained in a wire she insisted she had received from the War Department kept changing. Pat had heard from various sources that "Mr. Brown" was alive and operating a house of loose ethics in Fort Worth, that he had expired of a belly wound inflicted by a mulatto named Pullman Beal during a fight over Mrs. Brown in an Amarillo saloon, and that she was married simultaneously to a Brown in Del Rio and the Mexican policeman in Juarez. Pat believed none of the stories. He believed all of them. He didn't lose any sleep wondering whether any of them was true and would not have cared if the most sordid turned out to be fact. In his fifty-eighth year, he was a man without illusions.

He knew what was said about him when he was seen piloting a buggy through city traffic with Mrs. Brown beside him on the seat, hatted and shaded beneath a spread parasol, or strolling down San Antonio with her on his arm, pausing at every store window to admire the merchandise on the other side of the glass. They said—these cattlemen's wives in silk drawing rooms only once removed from the parlors of whorehouses where they had met their husbands, these oilmen in their silk hats and morning coats who nipped into the Mexican quarter at dusk to explore the pleasures of working women—that Pat Garrett had "gone to the bad" in the company of his hired whore, that her wicked wiles had besotted him and turned him off the true path. She was responsible for every wrong decision he had made since he came to El Paso. But for her, they said, he would have restrained himself from fighting George Gaither on a public street in broad daylight like a common tough. Her influence had caused him to throw reason to the winds and smuggle Tom Powers, that one-eyed whiskey-slinger, into a photograph next to President Roosevelt, soiling the dignity of that high office. Time and the actual order of things had no effect upon such talk. Such talk made no room for a man's ability to make his own mistakes. They had to be charged to liquor or, preferably, a woman of slim virtue. It made for more entertaining discourse.

For all their whispers they cared nothing for respectability or appearances. They were the sons and daughters of embezzlers and consumptives, driven west to escape their pasts or to prolong their lives; civilization had come with them like lint caught in the cuffs of their trousers and on the hems of their skirts. Their heirs pretended to guard that fragile culture against the actions of that same breed that had brought it. In fact they would find life intolerable without the diversion of an occasional fall from grace. Pat compared himself to the *Police Gazette* and the herky-jerky images of frantic firefighters and disrobing women projected twice a month onto the stage of the opera house for the enjoyment of patrons, and had commented to Mrs. Brown that they ought to charge admission every time they went out in public. He was the same man he had always been, he had not changed. The generation that had grown up since Billy Bonney's death expected his slayer to behave like the abstemious, poetry-spouting heroes in *Beadle's Dime Library*, and when he had not, they drowned their disappointment in lascivious gossip. He despised himself whenever he thought about how much of his life he had squandered currying the favor of such as they. Everything he had done since he left Pete Maxwell's bedroom in Fort Sumner he had done for their approval.

Not killing Billy, though; no matter what they said about that, that he had done for himself alone. He had not killed the badger to protect his mother's chickens. He had killed the badger because he had wanted to kill the badger.

"Patrick, are you listening?"

"No."

"Silly man." Mrs. Brown was pulling on her elbow-length gloves, elaborately attending to the details. She smoothed the gauntlets along her forearms and worked a fingertip between all the fingers, seating the material firmly. At her insistence, Pat had bought them for her from a shop that catered to gringos on the Mexican side of the river. He had been in a good humor at the time, and had even foreborn to point out that it seldom got cold enough on the Gulf Stream to make them anything more than a nuisance. She was forever forgetting them and sending him back for them; as if anyone would bother to steal them unless he was on his way to Montana. "I said a new dress isn't much good if I haven't a place to show it off."

"Put it on and take a walk down San Antonio. You'll see everyone you know and some you don't."

"I was thinking of the opera."

"No."

She thrust out her lower lip. It made her look like a rat terrier Pat had had when he was eight. "You haven't taken me anywhere in a long time."

He started to sweep a long arm around the El Capitan's terrace, to force her to give evidence that it didn't qualify as somewhere. His gaze fell upon Jim Miller, making his way toward Pat's table from the interior of the restaurant. He resembled a Mormon in his long black coat and flat-brimmed hat. When he spotted Pat he stopped and jerked his head. Pat placed his crumpled napkin on his plate and rose.

"You're not leaving me alone to talk to that horrible man." Mrs. Brown's face was pale, a danger sign.

"Pretend I'm in the crapper."

He joined Miller on the other side of the arched passage, where they crowded next to the wall to avoid collisions with steaming tamales and cooked pheasants. They didn't shake hands.

"You're not hard to find," Miller said in greeting.

"I wasn't hiding."

"I meant you cut a wide swath in town. Everyone seems to know what you're about."

"Tell it."

"Brazel's willing to sell out if his price is met."

"I ain't buying any goats."

"You don't have to. I can find a buyer who'll make me a better price than what Brazel's asking. He's got twelve hundred goats he'll let go for three-fifty a head, then he'll cancel his lease. He's having a contract drawn up."

"For a man who says ranching ain't his area, you're sure starting to sound like one," Pat said. "I didn't figure you for a goat man."

"I don't intend to keep them long enough to be one. Your offer still stand?"

"I don't make any I'm not prepared to back up."

"All right, then."

When Miller left, Pat returned to his table and sat down. Mrs. Brown's face was dead white. "I loathe being stared at in restaurants."

"You get used to it."

"Now you're having fun at my expense. I don't see what there is to grin about."

"Calm down, old girl," Pat said. "What opera you thinking of going to see?"

CHAPTER 21

Old Haunts

No city, as Pat saw it, managed to look more like itself than Santa Fe, while having changed so much in everything that counted.

The Palace of the Governors looked the same. Strings of dried chiles still decorated the verandah, and Indians still sold their pots and beadwork in its shade, never once looking up into the faces of customers as they haggled. But Lew Wallace no longer spread terror inside its six-foot-thick walls, calling for more and better maps of the territory like the general he was while Jorge, his old manservant, hastened back and forth emptying and replacing his brimming spittoons. In the governor's chair, clean-shaven, quiet-spoken George Curry now sat placidly signing ordinances against the operation of automobiles during peak hours and drafting addresses to the Women's Christian Temperance Union. Outside the plaza, the gubernatorial term of Miguel Otero had furred the lines between the Mexican quarter and the city proper, but to Pat's mind, emancipation had only served to make the Spanish-speaking population as edgy as the Anglos. Free now to compete commercially with their fair-skinned neighbors, the Mexicans were less cheerful, more guarded, and tended to contaminate the bills of fare in their cantinas with veal in champagne sauce, strawberry short-cake, and Kentucky rye. In the largest Hispanic enclave north of Chihuahua, it was sometimes impossible to order a decent tortilla with green chiles or a bottle of mescal that didn't taste like horse liniment.

Pat's first stop, after pausing to cut the cinders in a saloon run by a young Spaniard who entertained his clientele with Caruso playing on a Parlograph behind the bar, was at Señora Leones' whorehouse, respite in years past from Wallace's harangues, only to find that an ice cream parlor had moved in. From there he went to a three-chair barbershop and paid nearly a dollar to have his neck trimmed, his chin scraped, his nails pared, and his boots shined to a finish like black oil. He spent his last quarter on a Hidalgo Perfecto and had to burn a light off the apprentice barber, a sullen-faced half-caste in his teens with vaseline in his hair and pimples on his forehead. The train ticket had cost twice as much as anticipated. Pat was broke.

After waiting some little time in the narrow wainscoted reception area where a secretary in a shirtwaist and long skirt with her hair tied up with ribbon chattered at a big black Remington typewriter, Pat was allowed into Governor Curry's sun-splashed office. The window overlooking the plaza left so baldly open gave him pause. In the past he had been accustomed to meeting Lew Wallace there in the dim golden light of a globe on the desk, blinds drawn and shutters latched against Billy Bonney's threats to kill the governor for breaking his promise of pardon; that the chief of the territory should go about his business naked to the world struck the long man as unseemly and somehow indecent. He was scarcely mollified by the pudgy Curry's obsequious greeting and flabby handshake. Wallace, ever the general and conscious of the gulf that separated the commander from his subordinates, had never offered his hand nor risen from behind the great leather-topped desk with great brass tacks all around.

"I believe this is your first visit to the capital in some

years," said Curry when the pair were seated, Pat in a straight-backed chair of Mexican design with his fedora in his lap. "What do you think of the place?"

"It's grown a mite. More brick buildings, less adobe."

"We're encouraging that. Mud walls don't hold up to the vibration of heavy machinery. There's talk of an automobile plant and a print factory. Bit of a shock for you old-timers, I imagine."

"I was the same age as you when you ran the Brock Ranch. I reckon we're both older by the same thirty years."

"So we are. Those days seem a long time gone. Dead as old John Chisum. Now when you bring up the war, most folks think you're talking about the one with Spain. I suppose that's as it should be. Living in the past has been the ruin of Dodge City and Tombstone. Wyatt Earp's a fight referee. Bill Tilghman's gone into national politics. The new breed of marshals and sheriffs make their rounds in flivvers with court orders in their pockets. I don't believe half of them bother to carry weapons." His liquid brown gaze went toward the bulge of the bulldog revolver in Pat's side pocket.

Pat saw where this was going. He leaned forward and helped himself to a cigar from the humidor on the desk, carved from native piñon. Curry had not offered. "Once every couple of years, some young cowboy gets a pimple on his ass and takes a shot at me. They all want to be Bonney, you see. I ain't as popular as Tilghman, and Earp always was a sack of horseshit. That business in Arizona should never have happened. I got brothers too, but we don't travel in a herd. What about that appointment, George?" He bit the end off the cigar and, unable to locate a cuspidor, took the piece out of his mouth and put it in his pocket.

Curry shifted his weight in his swivel. He had taken a bad spill off a mustang during the trouble in Lincoln County, and Pat suspected his back still bothered him.

"I've decided to keep Olaf Burnsum in the prison superintendent's position for the time being. He's doing an adequate job. There hasn't been a disturbance among the convicts in years."

"That's because they go over the walls like water."

"That's not at all true. This is a difficult time to make changes, Pat. I have no guarantee that my own appointment will survive the next administration. Roosevelt has indicated he won't seek a third term. He wants to run his secretary of state. If Taft loses to the Democrats—" He spread his hands, then let them drop to the arms of his chair. "Let's just say, this isn't the time. After the elections in November, assuming we carry the day, if you care to resubmit your application—"

"Damn it, George, I was counting on this job. My ass is poking through my drawers. I got eight kids and they all have to eat till November."

"Perhaps if you stayed at home more, and worked the ranch." Curry's jowls folded over the corners of his disapproving mouth.

"My ranch is overrun with goats," said Pat darkly, "and I reckon I ought to have thanked you more for carrying the sheriff's election for me in '80 with a jug of whiskey and the wetback vote."

The governor's broad brow clouded. "That was the frontier. If you can't see the difference, maybe it's time you retired from public life." He softened his expression. "Do you need money?"

Pat clenched and unclenched both fists. He reached up and took the unlit cigar out of his mouth. "George, I'm in a hell of a tight. I've been trying to sell my ranch, but no luck until this goat thing is settled. For God's sake lend me fifty dollars to keep me till I leave for home."

Curry unlocked a desk drawer with a key attached to his watch chain, drew out a checkbook bound in yellow calfskin, shook down the ink in a gravity pen, and began writing. "When you say *home*," he said, rocking a blotter over his signature, "are you referring to Las Cruces or El Paso?"

"I haven't had a home since I left Alabama when I was three." Rising with the check in his breast pocket, he nodded at the governor. Neither man offered his hand. "Thanks, George. This is just a loan."

"You're good for it."

The tone of both men's speech bespoke the likelihood that the debt would ever be repaid.

The curved-dash Oldsmobile jittered out of a cloud of its own dust, bowed alarmingly but flexibly in the middle when one of its spindly wheels dipped into a chuckhole, and sputtered to a stop beside the boardwalk where Pat stood, far enough back to prevent the drifting grit from settling on his boots. The motor went on galloping a full minute after the ignition had been switched off, then died with a wheeze. Instantly a thick cloud of steam poured from the radiator. The driver, a stout young Hispanic in goggles, a duster, and a cap made from ticking, hopped down from behind the wheel, unhooked a goatskin bag from the spare tire on the back, and with a red bandanna wound around his right hand unscrewed the radiator cap. Pat felt the moisture on his skin from the geyser, whose force could not remove the broad white grin from the driver's dark face.

Emerson Hough, all eastern dignity even with dark stains on the crown of his dove-gray Stetson from the condensing vapor, stepped from the Oldsmobile's running board to the boardwalk with the easy assurance of an old seaman quitting his launch for the jetty. He wore an ankle-length duster over a tweed suit and garish yellow gaiters laced to his knees. He had a broad face, clean-shaven but for a military brush moustache flecked with gray, and pale eyes set in thickets of sun-creases, sparked with gentle good humor. He was, after Owen Wister and Zane Gray, the most popular writer of frontier stories in the United States.

"Pat, I see the life of the gentleman rancher has not made you fat." He did not smile with his mouth when he took the long man's hand in his firm grip, calloused at the finger ends from the keyboard of his Oliver typewriter, but the warmth in his eyes made the driver's grin look empty and false.

"You're fat enough for us both, Em."

Hough patted his stomach. "It's all this deep frying out here. Back home I'm content with tea and toast."

"What do you think of Lincoln?"

The writer looked around at the patched adobe and weathered clapboard, the loafers lounging in front of the general merchandise. A dog with running mange lifted a crooked hind leg against a wooden trough containing nothing but dust. "I think the county seat should be closer to the railroad than Carrizozo. Where is the famous courthouse?"

"We're standing in front of it." It was a two-story territorial style with two wooden staircases wobbling diagonally from the street to a balcony in front.

"Were there bars on the windows when the Kid made his break?"

"No. The town didn't have a jail then, so I placed him under guard in an upstairs room."

"It would be better with bars."

"He didn't make his play from inside. He shot J. W. Bell on the outside stairs and Bob Olinger from the side window with Olinger's own shotgun."

"I heard they taunted him."

"Bob did. He was a mean son of a bitch. J. W. wouldn't raise his voice to a dog."

"Did he draw on the Kid?"

"No. Billy shot him twice in the back while he was running from that smuggled gun."

"We might have to do something with that. Readers today want a Billy who's smarter than paint and kind to old ladies."

"He was a tricky little shit."

In the hotel room Pat had arranged for him, Hough unstrapped his suitcase, found a bottle of gin, and filled two glasses, handing one to Pat. He shed his boots and gaiters for a pair of worn leather slippers and sat in a straight chair at a drop-front secretary while the long man stretched out on the bed, his boots protruding over the footboard. "What is it you want from me, Pat?"

"I don't look at it like that. Last time I saw you in El Paso you said you wanted to poke around the Southwest for material. You need a guide for that."

"Are you volunteering?"

"I ain't volunteered for a single thing since I ran for sheriff in Doña Ana County. You read my book?"

"The last part. I thought the first part was a mess of cowflop. Upson must have been plenty drunk to have come up with it."

"Ash was plenty drunk most of the time. He said that's what sells books—the cowflop, not the drinking, though if that was true he'd have been rich as Croesus. Well, it was a poor job and I went along with it. I can't see as we'd do any worse telling the truth."

Hough refilled both glasses, then smacked the cork back into the bottle with finality; he was no Ash Upson. "Well, there's truth and truth. You have to cut the gin with something or no one will want to drink it. Are we talking about collaborating on a new life of Billy?"

"What do you think?"

"It's all right as far as it goes. It's not ambitious enough. Grosset and Dunlap want me to write a new and complete history of the war in Lincoln County. You know the kind of book: embossed covers, painted starbursts, prominent American flag. You'll find one in every parlor from Leadville to Union City."

"Where do I fit in?"

"Primary source. Of course you'll be paid a fee."

"Royalties?"

Hough shook his head. "It's the market, Pat. My hands are tied."

Pat took a drink, held it, then swallowed. The gin burned all the way down. "How much?"

The writer stood, took a yellow leather billfold out of the breast pocket of his tweed coat hanging on one of the bedposts, and thumbed out five twenty-dollar banknotes, which he laid on the maple nightstand. "Consider that an advance against expenses. New York takes too long. I'm still spending the royalties from *The Mississippi Bubble*."

"Thanks, Em. I'm short until I resolve this goat business."

"I heard you were in real estate."

"That went sour. The bookkeeper cleaned out the safe and lit a shuck for old Mexico."

"You should have stuck with keeping the peace."

"Better class of people," Pat agreed.

Hough finished his drink. "Where do we start?"

"Stinking Springs."

"Sounds pretty."

"It used to be. I can't answer for it now."

The horses they had hired—fat, town-kept, more accustomed to picnic rides on the flats outside Lincoln than hard gallops up standing country—found the going rougher than had the lean, experienced mounts the Garrett posse had ridden through the heavy December snows of twenty-eight years before. A late January thaw had turned the drifts on the ridges to greasy slush, the runoff standing in vast brown puddles that splattered Pat's slicker to the elbows and surprised uncharacteristic blasphemies from Emerson Hough when rooster tails splashed his face and neck, chilling him to the bone. The river was sluggish with mud and floes of dun-colored ice piled up like discarded mattresses in the bends. Hoofs slipped and scrabbled in the slime that coated the grades. The men stopped often to let the horses blow. Pat, helping himself to a slug of hot coffee from a vacuum bottle, confessed that if they'd made this kind of time in '80 and '81, the Kid would still be terrorizing the countryside.

"That's hard to picture," said Hough. "A fifty-year-old Bonney."

The shack took finding. The slant roof had fallen in, splaying out the walls, and the pine timbers and siding had rotted and settled into an orange mulch to match the carpet of sodden dead needles that surrounded them; from any distance it looked like one of a hundred treefalls lining the river. They picked their way down the slope where Pat, Lon Chambers, and the others had stretched out on their bellies in the predawn, dismounted and tethered their horses to the fallen ironwood roofpoles. Lengths of squashed and rusted stovepipe and a corner of iron bedstead stuck up out of the debris, looking like the calcified skeleton of an extinct beast.

"Not much left," Pat said. "Two more years and you won't be able to find the spot."

"Are you sure this is it? It doesn't look like the kind of place the Kid would choose to make a stand."

"He didn't. He thought we wouldn't follow him in no blizzard. Billy always did underestimate his friends."

"You mean his enemies."

"Everybody liked Billy."

Pat walked back and forth in front of the ruined house, measuring with his stride. He stopped. "Right here's where Charlie Bowdre was standing when he was shot. I got him first, through the lungs. He was carrying a nosebag. I thought it was Billy coming out to feed the horses."

"You and Bowdre knew each other."

"I knew all of them, him and Rudabaugh and Tom O'Folliard and Billie Wilson and little Tom Pickett. Billy was the only real card player in the bunch. Dead now, the lot, and not a one of them in bed, neither."

"Are you sorry?"

"I wouldn't trade, if that's where you're headed." He scraped a clot of mud and pine needles off his boot heel against the edge of a foundation stone. Then he looked at Hough. "You know Billy stood Charlie up, all shot to pieces as he was, and stuck a pistol in his hand and shoved him back out the door to draw our fire. They was fixing to go partners in a ranch when they'd rustled enough."

"He must have been crazy."

"Everybody said so."

He kicked at the loose weeds and other rubbish inside the foundation. "We left Billy's horse right here, where I dropped it to block the door. I reckon coyotes carried off whatever was left."

Hough's smile was tight beneath the brush moustache. "Maybe he came back for it. Maybe they're ghosts together."

"That ghost talk's horseshit." Pat jerked loose his horse's tether and mounted. His face felt tight.

The writer opened his mouth, then shut it. He followed suit, looking puzzled. They spurred the fat, complaining horses up the slope.

* * *

When they reached Fort Sumner they didn't even step down. It was dry there. A cold wind skinned crystals of white dust from the ground and knifed through their coats, Pat's a good one made of heavy bearskin, Hough's tailored in Chicago with a red silk lining that must have felt like ice when he first put it on. There was nothing there but a stone well heaped high with sand and a maze of broken adobe walls. The town had picked up and moved down the road when the wells went dry. The desert was busy reclaiming what was left. They had glimpsed its only apparent resident, a fat gila, waddling toward the cover of a granite shelf, when they'd drawn rein.

"Bonney hung out *here?*" Hough asked.

Pat leaned on his arms, folded on his pommel. "You could get anything you wanted in Fort Sumner: Girls, cards, tequila. Steaks as thick as your arm. The best fighting cocks west of St. Louis dropped their feathers behind Pete Maxwell's place, and that's the best in the world. If Billy ever thought about heaven, this here's what he had in mind."

"Hard to imagine, even for a writer."

"I can't hardly tell where Pete Maxwell's was."

"Approximately."

Pat pointed. "He was hunkered right there with some of the locals. I'm sure now it was him, though I didn't see the green hatband in the dark. He walked over there and let himself over the fence."

"That's when you went to see Maxwell."

"I was sitting with him in the dark when Bonney come in, asking Pete who those fellows were outside. I knew his voice. He'd walked right past Poe and McKinney. I shot him twice while he was still asking who it was."

"Where's the grave?"

The long man stirred himself and put his heels to his horse. He led the way to the ruins of the old fort wall, where a cluster of sorry weathered wooden markers lolloped about at crazy angles. After a few minutes spent picking their way among the sunken graves, most of which were no longer marked, and some of which had given up their charges, they reined in. Pat shook his head. "Floods and weather. There's no telling which one's his."

"Or if he's still here," Hough said.

CHAPTER 22

The March of the Toreadors

Pat was relieved to see, when he got in from the El Paso station, that Mrs. Brown was out, even though the late hour meant she was probably across the river sharing the bed of her Mexican policeman. He hadn't the energy to keep up with her chatter, which would probably have led to a fight, and he was too tired to take his boots in hand and try to sneak between the sheets without stirring her awake. Visiting the scenes of his youth only to find the features he best remembered in an advanced state of decomposition had depressed and exhausted him. It was like receiving news of the death of an old friend or elderly relative, despite whose late infirmity he could convince himself he could always go back to his earlier happiness, only to find that door slammed resoundingly and forever by fate. The thoroughness of the decay had appalled him. In his mind it was all so fresh. He felt the weight of his years.

In the dark he undressed completely, his long underwear peeling like greased paper from his armpits and crotch. He could never remember where Mrs. Brown put his nightshirt after washing it—she refused to drape it over the back of a chair beside the bed, as he was accustomed to in Las Cruces—and he didn't feel like lighting a lamp and pawing through drawers. The soles of his naked feet shrank from the surface of the wide floor planks, worn smooth

and cold as polished stone. The stove had gone out, he
lacked the will to start it up, and so he slid quickly beneath
the heavy quilt and shivered while waiting for the heat of
his body to fill the cavity where he lay. The air smelled
musty and damp. There had not been a fire in the house
for a week, which meant that Mrs. Brown had left immediately after seeing him off from El Paso.

He should have stayed in Las Cruces. There, Apolinaria
had welcomed him as warmly as if he had been away only
a few days and sat him and his guest down to a hot meal
of fresh tortillas and peppers that stung their tongues, with
gallons of strong coffee served hot enough to raise blisters. After dinner his children had scurried to find his
favorite pipe and tobacco and lined up to report on late
developments, carefully avoiding the subject of the goats
at Bear Canyon. That chore fell to Dudley Poe—already
out of his father's favor for allowing himself to be taken
in by Cox and Brazel—who came by the next morning
during breakfast. At twenty-one the young man was as
lean as Pat although not nearly as tall, with his mother's
dusky skin and a languid way about ranch work that belonged as much to his Garrett blood as his Mexican. On
several occasions, he said, he'd been forced to herd the disagreeable creatures away from the house, where they had
worried nearly all the paint off the northeastern corner
rubbing it with their horns, and once they had pulled down
a clothesline, dragging his mother's washing through the
dust of the backyard. Pat advised him to shoot them the
next time they wandered inside range.

Later, showing off for Hough while they were riding
near Bear Canyon, Pat had fired his Yellow Boy Winchester at one of the animals grazing along the lip. The
hammer snapped on a punk shell.

"The same goddamn thing happened the day I had

Oliver Lee square in my sights," he'd said, ramming the carbine back into its scabbard.

He should have stayed. Telling Apolinaria good-bye had set him low. She was too much the saint in their bedroom and could be shrill as a bitch coyote when he tracked mud into the parlor or scratched a chair rung when he forgot to take off his spurs, but she was worth more than all the Mrs. Browns in Texas. He could not abide looking out a window he had paid for and seeing goats.

"Quien es?"

He did not know he'd slept. He was lying there in the bed Mrs. Brown had brought with her from Fort Worth. He could see her dress form standing in the moonlight skating through the window, reminding him of the torso of a Chinese prostitute, armless, legless, headless, found behind a crib in Lincoln County when he was sheriff, a case he hadn't solved. When he'd asked Mrs. Brown to put it in some other room, she'd laughed at him and ignored the request. It was demonstrably her room. But there coming through the door from the hall was that half-naked figure he'd seen in Pete Maxwell's bedroom, and indeed every bedroom he'd slept in since that night. The knife was in the man's hand, his stockinged footfalls were silent. He smelled pungently of greasewood fires and semen, sweat and sulphur, horse and rawhide and tequila and other men's butchered cattle. Pat knew Billy Bonney's special scent as well as any stray yellow dog he fed scraps to in Fort Sumner.

"Quien es?"

He drew his big Colt's and fired; fired again, screaming over the second report. Screaming because, in the flare from the first, he saw the young man's face clearly, though not in time to stop his finger from squeezing the trigger again. It was his own face, not Billy's; his own face, yet not his own, younger than he had been in 1881, gentler, with

Apolinaria's great dark eyes. The face was Dudley Poe's. He had slain his son.

He was awake a long time, and had lit a lamp and explored every room of the house, before he satisfied himself that he had only dreamt, that the dream had merely found a new path toward torment.

The next morning he went to see Deacon Jim Miller, but the woman who kept his boardinghouse, a fat Mexican and former madam who had turned out her girls and hung out a new shingle in response to a city ordinance zoning low commerce out of her neighborhood, told him he was out. The building had been a bishop's house during Spanish colonization; a separate carriage house stood in back. Pat found Miller currying his horse inside. It was a short-coupled strawberry roan, sixteen hands high. Its hooves had been waxed recently, and although its coat shone, Miller continued to work at it with his hands inside the straps of the best-looking set of matched combs Pat had seen in a long time. The Deacon was in white lawn shirtsleeves with the cuffs turned back to his elbows. His forearms were hairless and corded with muscle. Without the coat, in his squared-off hat and black vest he looked less like an undertaker and more like a preacher at a tent revival. He breathed heavily as he worked and a glassy sheen of sweat coated his face.

"You'll rub the hide right off that pretty horse if you ain't careful," Pat said.

Miller, whose back was turned to the entrance, went on combing as if he'd been aware of the other man's presence right along. "There is an order out here," he said. "Horses first, guns next. There are nesters dead in the Panhandle who forgot that."

"What's Brazel about?" He didn't want to know any

more about the nesters in the Panhandle. The rumors he'd
heard had involved shotguns.

"I talked to him Saturday. It seems he miscounted."

"Money or goats?"

"The price is still three-fifty a head. Only instead of
twelve hundred head it's eighteen hundred."

"Who does his counting?"

"That's neither here nor there. It's an additional two
thousand dollars. I haven't that much to spend."

"The deal's off, then."

"It doesn't have to be."

Pat said nothing. The scrubbing of Miller's brushes was
the only sound in the stable.

"Brazel is on his way back to Las Cruces," Miller said
then. "He's taking a buckboard over the Mail-Scott Road. A
man on a good horse taking the Freighter's Road could overtake him easily."

"Why would he want to do that?" Pat asked.

The currying stopped. Miller clapped the combs together, placed them in a worn leather satchel on a shelf
containing an old lantern and a bucket of coal oil, and used
a chamois cloth to wipe his hands, paying particular attention to the nails. "I'm as good with a rifle as with a shotgun,"
he said. "I favor a forty-four-forty Winchester. You can't
tell from the slug whether it came from a long gun or a
pistol."

Pat produced a plug of Levi Garrett's and his pocketknife. He sliced off a chew the thickness of a dollar and
popped it into his mouth. When the saliva came he spat a
jet at the stone foundation. "I do my own shooting. When
I do it."

"A man's eye at sixty isn't what it was at thirty. It won't
cost you," Miller added. "I have a brother-in-law, Carl
Adamson. We'll buy your ranch for three thousand, just
like you and I agreed, and pay you a dollar a head to drive

those cattle up from Mexico. That makes the goat problem ours. It won't concern you how we handle it."

"It ain't the way I care to profit."

"Look on it as a courtesy. Cox holds the mortgage on your spread, and he's in with Brazel. I can go to him with the same deal."

"Go to hell."

Miller took his black coat off a nail, brushed it with the edge of his hand, and put it on. Pat noticed the special harness for his shotgun stitched to the lining. "That's a mistake," said the deacon.

"More than likely. At sixty, one more don't matter all that much." Pat left.

Tom Powers, taking the sun in a captain's chair in front of the Coney Island, listened without expression to Pat's account of his conversation with Jim Miller. He had a bottle of tequila on the window ledge beside him.

"Miller's a bad hat," he said when Pat finished. "Don't let him see your back."

"I don't believe that story about his killing no fifty men. My pa was a colonel in the Confederate Army and he didn't see that many kilt the whole time he was in. Ash Upson said Billy Bonney killed a man for every year he lived. I wouldn't go above six."

"Six or sixty, what's it matter? One's plenty if it's you. Stay away from Miller."

"I am done with him. I'm done with ranching, too, just as soon as I get rid of them damn goats."

"Go back to Las Cruces. El Paso is no place for you."

"That's just what I'm fixing to do, Tom. I come to say good-bye."

Powers got up and stuck out his hand. "You watch all

around and up and down. You've got more enemies than any man I know, and I'm in the saloon business."

"You don't need a lot of enemies to have to watch yourself," Pat said.

He went to the El Capitan for the kind of breakfast he preferred when traveling, rare steak and runny eggs and fried potatoes swimming in grease, washed down with three cups of thick black coffee. Across the river a fresh group of Mexicans, or perhaps they were the same, were having a celebration, this one somewhat less morbid than the one he had witnessed the last time: A pair of boys capered down the street sharing a black crepe cover, one in front wearing a papier-mâché bull's head complete with scarlet-stained horns and a painted snarl, his partner behind, flipping a tail made from a frayed length of rope. Bawling convincingly, they undulated along, sometimes charging into the crowds that lined the street, forcing them to scatter in mock fright, while the ubiquitous band followed, playing "The March of the Toreadors." Performers dressed up as picadors darted in and out and pretended to puncture the beast's back with banderillas. At length the matador appeared, borne upon the shoulders of half a dozen brightly dressed newcomers, who set him on his feet before the bull. The boys in the black costume pawed the ground, lowered the head, and charged, enabling the bogus matador to wheel his red cloak in a passable veronica, then twirl on his heels and apply the death-stroke. As the collapsible sword seemed to sink between the shoulder blades, a girl in a frilly black dress and a mantilla came forward carrying a pot with a ladle and basted the crepe with red liquid to represent blood. The ersatz bull reeled, tossed its head, wobbled, and fell with a resounding groan, the boys inside rolling over onto their backs and kicking their feet. The matador bent over the "carcass" for a moment, then straightened with a leap, displaying a severed black papier-mâché ear in each outstretched hand. The crowd shouted "olé!"

Pat reflected that the bullfight season was starting early this year. He had been to only one fight and hadn't enjoyed it. Some people felt bad for the horses that were gored when the picadors rode too near the bull, but these were bony, spavined nags destined for the gluepot anyway. Some feared for the men, but to Pat's thinking if some damn fool was determined to get himself gutted he oughtn't to expect tears when it happened. It was the bull Pat felt bad about. The dumb brute never had the luxury of choice, and even when it managed to kill the one who was out to kill it, the picadors stepped in and slaughtered it. It was a harsh world for bulls.

Mrs. Brown was still out when he got back. He pulled his valise out of the closet and packed carelessly, not bothering to fold anything since she never bothered to iron anything anyway, though he bet she put a nice crease in her Mexican's uniform pants. When he took his shirts from the bureau he found a letter he had received recently from Emerson Hough and reread it. The Lincoln County War project had foundered in New York, but Hough's new publishers had commissioned him to write a serial entitled *The Story of the Outlaw*. They had further agreed to pay Pat two hundred dollars for his cooperation, that amount to be returned if the completed book failed to make expenses. "While its changed arrangement makes it general in application and not applicable to any one locality," Hough wrote, "it may surprise me by making money, in which case I think you can depend that I will do the right thing by you."

He crumpled the letter and tossed it into a corner. Then he strapped up his valise, flipped his key onto the bed, and went out to catch the noon train.

CHAPTER 23

Leap Year Day

At half-past 4 A.M. Saturday, February 29, 1908, Patrick Floyd Garrett made love to his wife.

They had been awakened an hour earlier by a ranch hand, who reported he'd glimpsed someone prowling around behind the corral. Pat tucked his nightshirt into the corduroy trousers he'd worn the previous day, pulled on a pair of boots and his bearskin, snatched up his folding Burgess shotgun from the corner near the bed, and went out with the hand to investigate.

"What did you see?" Pat asked.

"Just something moving. I'm sure it was a man. He was all dark. I think he might have had on a black coat."

The night air had a snap to it, but the ground was still soft from the last thaw. Pat struck a match and put it to a lantern. Fresh bootprints crossed a bare patch of earth and vanished into the grass beyond.

"Vagrants come to the door sometimes," reported the hand. "There's a deal of cowpunchers afoot these days since they fenced the range."

"Well, stay awake."

Pat climbed back into bed, but he was too alert now to sleep. He found the hem of Apolinaria's shift and pushed it up to her hips.

She started. "Your hands are like ice."

He withdrew them from her bare skin. "I reckon I can do this without hands," he said.

She felt hot when he entered her. Mrs. Brown was always chilled—he was forever getting up to feed the stove, even on nights when he would have been comfortable with the window open—and he had almost forgotten how much he missed Apolinaria's warm Spanish blood. Within minutes he was sweating. His release came soon after, an explosive shudder.

He was wide-awake now. He had an appointment with Wayne Brazel and Carl Adamson, Jim Miller's brother-in-law, in Las Cruces that morning, to settle the business of how many goats Brazel had to sell. Sometimes a careless shaver, he now handled the ivory-handled razor with precision, pinching his nose to get at the short coarse hairs that grew in the creases of his nostrils and trimming his moustaches with the long-bladed steel shears from his toilet kit. He dressed just as carefully in his best linen shirt, boiled blue-white and ironed by Apolinaria, the good black broadcloth suit he had worn for his first meeting with Roosevelt, stovepipe boots he'd blacked himself—a chore he trusted to no other—and a string tie, which he did over when he could not get the ends even the first time. He didn't want anyone taking the impression he wasn't familiar with the niceties of civilization.

Breakfast consisted of Apolinaria's corn bread, hot and crumbling in pools of melted butter, rashers of crisp bacon, fried eggs slightly overdone—her only failing in the kitchen—corn fritters drowned in honey, and of course coffee strong enough to float a boot, his wife being the only woman in the world who had the sand to throw in that extra handful of ground beans. Almost the entire family was gathered in one room: Dudley Poe's grave-eyed older sister Ida, married now but living on the ranch while her husband looked for work in Texas; eighteen-year-old Elizabeth, sightless since childhood, home on a visit from the Texas School for the Blind in Austin; twelve-year-old Patrick Floyd, Jr.; nine-year-old Annie; little Pauline, Pat's favorite at age eight; four-year-old Oscar; and Jarvis, the baby, at two and a half already displaying signs of growing up to look the most like his father. Dudley Poe had spent the night in town and would join Pat and the others at the meeting. The children's mother sat at the opposite end of the trestle table from Pat, watching closely for crimes of etiquette and the occasional smuggling expedition from the table to the dog. In the presence of such substantial proof of his claim upon the twentieth century, Pat felt invincible, and in uncharacteristic good humor. When Annie helped herself to a third portion of corn bread he chided her for her plumpness, then winked to remove the sting when her lower lip began to quiver. Apolinaria reminded him to go easy on Dudley Poe for his part in the Brazel mess. He told her not to worry. "Brazel promised calves. He knew goats don't throw calves. If I didn't know him for Cox's bootlick I might have went for it my own self." Relieved, she smiled brilliantly.

Apolinaria and the girls were clearing the table when the hand who had awakened Pat early that morning came to the door to announce that a two-horse buggy was coming down the ranch road. A few minutes later Carl Adamson drew the buggy up before the porch and got out. He was a good foot shorter than Pat but outweighed him by twenty pounds. The stout newcomer wore a brown bowler and a tan coat whose hem swept the tops of his Wellington boots, the coat unbuttoned to expose a vest strung with fraternal medals; he jingled when he stepped up onto the porch to shake Pat's hand. He had a pink, youthful, clean-shaven face and glass-blue eyes that reminded the long man of the insulators on telegraph poles.

"The sky looks mighty like snow," Adamson said by

way of greeting. "There is no good purpose your catching your death on horseback."

Pat said, "I reckon I rode through heaps worse before you were born." But he went back to the door to tell his wife good-bye.

"I don't like him," Apolinaria whispered. "He smiles too much."

Pat showed his teeth. "You're always telling me I don't smile enough. You're powerful hard to please, old girl."

"I don't like him," she said again.

"If I only did business with men I got on with, we'd be in even worse shape than we are. I've got a good feeling about this. Our money problems are about over."

The road, narrow and rutted, wandered past the former boomtown of Gold Camp, inhabited now by prospectors motivated more by habit than hope, prostitutes too old and fat to move on, and the odd armadillo, across San Augustine Pass between the peaks of the Organ Range, through Organ, and down to Las Cruces. The sky was low enough to touch and the landscape was all the same dour shade of gray.

"Desolate country," Adamson said.

"There ain't a square inch of it not crawling with some kind of life." Pat elaborated to keep his mind off the damp chill; he had driven off without his topcoat. "When Geronimo was about you took your hair in your hands every time you went out."

"They sent that old bastard to Florida. They should have hung him in Arizona."

"He'd agree, I reckon."

A mile farther on, Adamson leaned over and craned his neck to peer back up the road. "Now who's this? Not some Apache who hasn't got the news, I hope."

Pat looked. "It's just my daughter on her mare. Let her catch up."

They stopped. Pauline, tall for her years and slender, an

accomplished horsewoman at eight, slowed from a gallop to a trot, then drew rein alongside the buggy. She had her father's bearskin folded across the pommel of her saddle. "Mommy says you'll catch your death." She was panting.

Pat climbed down and lifted her off the saddle. He kissed her on the cheek, tickling her with his moustaches so that she screwed up her face and turned it away. "Gracias, azúcar. Take good care of Mommy, and I'll bring you back a pretty." He took down his coat and helped her back astraddle. She was still watching when the buggy rattled over the next hill, putting the country between them.

"I never dreamed you had so many children," Adamson said.

"Me neither. Every time I look up it seems there's another." Pat felt uncommonly good.

From the pass they could look across La Jornada del Muerto, the long man's favorite route to the border. A split in the clouds spilled red morning sunlight onto the sand, reminding him that it was soaked two feet deep with the blood of Spaniards, Indians, mountain men, prospectors, and settlers, not to mention Albert Fountain and his young son, forever to be unavenged. Pat had chased buffalo across it, Billy Bonney, too, and been chased across it by Apaches. He had thought to irrigate it and make it green, but he was glad now he had lost the chance. To do so would have been like chaining a lion. He never felt so alive as when he was crossing its hammered arid surface. For this reason he could never bring himself to refer to it by its name in English. He did not even think of it in private as the Journey of the Dead.

The jangling of Adamson's medals brought Pat out of his reverie. The stout man had taken out his watch and snapped open its face. "We're making excellent time," he said. "There's a chance we'll overtake Brazel on his way in."

"I'm for getting this business over as soon as possible."

"All the more reason to make haste. We'll celebrate with drinks in Las Cruces." Adamson returned his watch to his vest pocket, shifted the reins to that hand, and gave them a flip. The matched grays broke into a canter.

Organ was a scattering of adobe huts that looked as they might have when Coronado came through, log buildings constructed of mountain pine that were nearly as old, and a clapboard general store that had thrived on the first push of miners and now hung on with help from the hollow-eyed men who continued to sift through the sand for the glitter of their lost youth. They would always need coffee and tobacco, the open front door seemed to say; there may yet be a strike. Bow-legged overalls and stiff suits of long johns swung like board signs from the clotheslines strung behind the buildings, reminding Pat grimly of the washing the goats had spoiled. He felt his good mood slipping away through the loose grains of sand churned up by the buggy's wheels.

Everything looks so old, he thought. *It was all so new and stinking of green wood and sawdust.* He spotted an old man sitting on a chair splattered with whitewash on the front porch of the assay office, his white beard stained yellow all around the mouth, and he thought, *I'm old, too, by God; older than all the sorry-looking horses in this town strung end to end.*

"What an ugly place," Adamson said then. "A flood here would bring nothing but improvement."

"The prettiest whores in the territory used to hang around in front of that store. Cowboys without a nickel to their names used to ride in for sixty miles just to get a look at them."

"That must be why they moved on. They couldn't have made any living off the locals either."

Pat lapsed back into silence.

South of Organ the road forked. The Mail-Scott Road,

a relatively smooth route, meandered among the foothills, while the Freighter's Road bucked and jounced the short way into Las Cruces. They came together two miles north of the town, but travelers generally chose the longer Mail-Scott in deference to their fillings. Just ahead of the fork, Pat directed Adamson to haul up in front of Russel Walter's livery stable. He recognized Russel's son Willis standing in the bed of a wagon, scooping alfalfa through the open door of the stable's second-story loft.

"Have you seen Wayne Brazel?" Pat asked.

Willis pointed his tines down the Mail-Scott Road. "He just left."

As they turned down the fork, Pat saw two riders stopped with their horses nose to nose a half-mile down. At the buggy's approach one of the riders backed off, wheeled his mount, and dug in his spurs, kicking up a thick cloud of dust as he galloped down the road. The long man's eyes weren't as good at a distance as they used to be. The horse was either a sorrel or a strawberry roan.

Brazel, sitting a blaze-faced black with his blanket roll across his cantle, was a tall, loose-jointed thirty, slender rather than lean, with no hair on his face and thickish lips twisted into the kind of permanent smile that Pat in his youth had enjoyed knocking off the face of many a fellow cowhand and hider. He had on a town suit and a new gray Stetson that he nudged back with a knuckle to avoid staining the brim with sweat from his fingertips.

"You're off to a quick start," he told Adamson.

"I wanted to get to the livery before all the best vehicles were spoken for." The stout man tried out a smile, which faded in the awkward pause that followed.

Pat ended it. "Who's that you were talking to?"

"Some drifter." Brazel took up his reins and coaxed his black into the road.

"Not a lot of those around these days."

"Folks stay put now," Adamson agreed. He started the horses moving. Brazel rode alongside. Plainly Adamson was a man who disliked silence. "Yes, there is not much now of this blowing with the wind. When folks get the urge to move they motor out into the countryside for a picnic or what-have-you. I don't care for it myself."

"What, picnics?" The rider looked puckish. It was those thick lips, in a mouth too narrow for his face.

"Motoring. Automobiles in general. You can't hear the birds singing for the noise. And then there are the punctures. No, sir, I don't care for it at all."

"I don't know. I'd sooner ride on springs than bones and hay."

Pat made a noise of impatience. At that point the road narrowed. Brazel struck out ahead, and for a time there was no need for conversation. Then it widened again and the rider fell back beside the buggy. In his desperation to avoid embarrassment, Adamson chose a poor subject for jest. "Are your goats kidding yet?" He chortled.

"They must be," Pat said. "I can't feature how twelve hundred got to be eighteen hundred otherwise."

Brazel's smile changed. "I missed counting a bunch in Bear Canyon."

"I reckon you're as bad at numbers as my boy is at judging character."

Adamson jumped in. "See here. There's bad feeling between you two and Cox, and to put it right Miller and I are willing to buy the original twelve hundred goats. We don't want even that many, but it's part of the price Mr. Garrett is asking for his ranch."

"If I don't sell the whole bunch, I won't sell none."

Alameda Arroyo was coming up, a jagged-edged pool of shadow under the overcast. Adamson pulled back on the horses and handed the lines to Pat.

"Puncture?" The friction with Brazel was restoring the

long man's humor. Nothing brought him down lower than a false civility. He liked things out in the open. He seemed to be one of the few left who did.

"I have a weak bladder." Adamson climbed down and hurried behind a clump of mescal, unbuttoning his fly.

Alone with Pat, Brazel smiled down at his nails. "Maybe I'll just hang on to that lease."

"It don't make any difference what you do. I'll get you off the land somehow."

"Cox is right about you, Garrett. You're a muleheaded old son of a bitch."

"Goddamn right."

When Adamson returned, Pat gave him back the reins and stepped down to the ground, taking his folding shotgun. "I believe I'll bleed the goose myself."

"Do you always bring along a weapon?" The stout man laughed nervously.

"Ever since Lincoln County."

Disdaining the cover of brush—his dingus was in proportion with the rest of him and he wasn't ashamed to haul it out into the air—Pat turned his back to the buggy and pissed into the dust, balancing the shotgun along his left forearm. The air was getting colder; his urine steamed. He smelled iron. His joints ached. That meant snow, and plenty of it. It was going to be a regular Stinking Springs winter, perhaps even as bad as '86. Maybe the damn goats would all freeze to death. Maybe God, if He did exist, would take pity on the frontier and blast down every stick of civilization, every last brick shithouse and oil derrick and cattlemen's trust, put the territory back where it was when he came to it in '77. Pretty señoritas and bandidos with gold teeth, asshole-ugly longhorn steers and Apaches as mean as bloody turds and tortillas deep-fried in buffalo lard.

He'd had to pee worse than he'd thought; he had a partial erection. It had been good that morning with Apolinaria, he remembered. Damn good, for a man bearing down on fifty-eight. He wondered if there were any cute whores left in Las Cruces. Some of them might be granddaughters of the ones he'd known, in which case he might be committing incest. Old man dreams. What was that tune the tricky little shit loved to whistle? "Darling, we are growing older."

He finished. He shook the dew off the lily and buttoned up. He was passing the last one through the eyelet when he heard a noise behind him. He started to turn his head. *Billy?*

CHAPTER 24

The Rock and the Desert

The cruellest jest the old gods ever played is to withhold truth until the very moment it no longer matters. The change is coming. I feel it in the weakness of the hand that must pause, even in the midst of a word, as I write upon these sheets; in the coldness of my lower limbs despite the suffocating quilts and native blankets with which my poor pallet is heaped; moreover I feel it in my thoughts, which will not stay to their purpose as of old, but fly in all directions like startled birds and are compelled to resume their perch only through great effort on my part, which drains the little strength I still possess. The store is depleting, it shall not be restocked in this pale. I must write until I can no longer will the pen to move.

There is no formula for the transmutation of base metal, this I now know. Gold is gold, lead is lead. A hedgehog cannot soar, nor an eagle suckle its young. The Black Maria, if it ever existed, is but a fungoid growth, good only for adding flavor to one's repast, if indeed it is not deadly poison. My great-grandfather, whose memory I have placed above all others, was a puffer and a charlatan, more culpable than his father who gulled a king, for he has made the descendants of his own blood the victims of his lies. He did not create silver from quicksilver, as he recorded in his notes. He merely sought by them to live beyond his span, and in his blind arrogance had not the wits of a low-born fool, who knows that in the infinity of time all must be revealed and every ruse made transparent. In this, he had at the last fallen prey to his own deception. The pages he had written comprised the last fuel I fed to the athanor. The brittle parchment offered itself to the flame like a disenchanted maiden stretched upon the conjugal bed and was gone up the chimney in the drawing of a breath.

There is no Philosopher's Stone. My life, long though it has been, is but an empty vessel, open at both ends, so all that was poured into it passed through the bottom and vanished into the sand, wasted. My line, more ancient than all of Europe's great dynasties, has been an extended irrelevance, a row of antique snuffboxes twinkling facetiously upon the shelf of a collector of amusing obsolescences. In our time, we had represented knowledge, and all that was awesome and holy there attendant. Kings envied us our independence. Popes feared our freedom from superstition. We knew all that was known, had read every tract, dismantled and examined every discovery from the charts of Copernicus to Galvani's coils, and declared it insufficient. We had dared to strike out into the dark part of the universe in search of yet more illumination. We were Oedipus and also the Sphinx, Columbus and Mohammed, Tamerlane and Tesla, Odin casting his eye into the Well of Wisdom and Paul addressing the Corinthians. We were the conductor and the light. Albertus the Great, demonstrating his ability to coax St. Elmo's Fire from the vane atop the cupola of his house to an iron staff in his hand, and from the staff to a silver goblet held by his son, without harm either to man or boy, kept in thrall for an afternoon an audience that outnumbered all of Caesar's legions, and dispersed them with no weapon other than that same slender staff and his own formidable will when they cried sorcery and surged forward to seize and crucify him. In those days education was looked upon as a treasure bestowed upon the chosen by divinity, like dominion. But Magnus was as deluded as the rest of us. The truth had passed us by, or we had passed it heedless, beguiled like an infant by a glimmer in a false mirror. We had sought to write the book, and been consigned to a nota bene entangled in the close print of the index.

The athanor has grown cold. No coals glow there for the first time since 1680. The remaining villagers must wonder that there is no curl of smoke from the chimney. I do not miss its light, although I lament the loss of heat. The great-grandson of the boy who first brought water to my rock now brings hot broth to warm my stomach and slow the creeping weakness, but he is eager to look for work in Mexico City, and though he is too much his father's son to express it, he is impatient for my death and his liberty.

I do not begrudge him his restlessness. Had I a son I would not have called upon him to serve an indenture that has already consumed too many lives to no purpose. Moreover, the village is dying, as I am dying. I witnessed its conception, when I was a young man of seventy and my simple hut was the only structure made by man for a hundred square miles. I had measured its slow growth in the beginning, and when the norteamericano petroleum interests came to test-drill for oil I had heard, as on a sudden, the drawing of saws and percussion of hammers, the braying Klaxons, chortling motors, whizzing cable, hydraulic sighs, and all the rest of the din of solvency in the new century. When the wells produced nothing but dust, I had seen the flatbed wagons and great rubber-tired trucks roll northward, carrying the heavy equipment home. The merchants had followed, leaving their buildings to peel and pucker and fill with jackrabbits and tumbleweed. Now when the wind blows, doors open to admit no one and shutters slam to repel nonexistent invaders. Mute signs, their painted

legends worn away, creak when they swing and occasionally fall, with no more noise than is made by a leper's
fingers dropping away. The wooden oil derricks are gone.
The last of them collapsed from dry rot after the others
were eaten by fires no one bothered to extinguish. In another year all the roofs will have fallen in; in five, even
the foundations will be covered by the jealous desert, and
from the vantage of my rock, all will be as it was when
the Aztecs abandoned Popocatépetl for the caves of
Chihuahua.

But I will not see it.

I have given the boy detailed instructions for the disposition of my remains. This I have done in person, for like
all the others who are left in the village he has no knowledge of letters, the last of the padres having been recalled
from this parish two years ago. I wish to be laid out upon
my bench in my father's velvet robes, my hands folded
upon my breast with the pages containing my notes, the
complete record of my empty existence, these sheets
included, between. I further direct that the hut be set ablaze,
and that the flames be allowed to burn themselves out,
down to the naked stone, so that nothing survives, least of
all the herbs I have cultivated these hundred years. Those
that remain must be left to whiten and shrivel in the pounding heat and fall to dust, which the wind will then seize
and scatter along with my ashes. The rock alone will stand,
the rock and the desert and those things that belong to it.
It will be unchanged from the place my father saw when
he came south to escape my grandfather's fate. In this at
least my vision will succeed where Pat Garrett's failed.

Of the long man's fate I remained ignorant for many
months. In the spring of 1909, a professor of zoology at
the University of Texas paid me a visit in the course of his
Mexican sabbatical, examined the stuffed armadillo hanging from my ceiling, and declared that it represented the

only known specimen of its particular subspecies extant. I declined to sell it, but I gave him permission to measure it and make detailed sketches, in return for intelligence from the north. At present, he reported as he laid out his instruments and colored chalks, all of New Mexico and Southwest Texas was buzzing over the recent verdict in the Pat Garrett murder trial.

So far as was known, Pat died instantly when a bullet smashed into the back of his head, fired from either a revolver of standard manufacture or a breech-loading rifle in the identical caliber. The position of the body, lying on its back with one glove removed and its trousers partially unbuttoned, suggested clearly that the long man had been ambushed from behind while relieving his bladder alongside the Mail-Scott Road, and yet Wayne Brazel, who stood trial for the killing, claimed to have struck in defense of his own life. His testimony, supported by Carl Adamson, that the dead man had threatened to get Brazel off his land one way or another, and the fact that Pat's Burgess shotgun was found next to his body, were entered into evidence and let stand by an indifferent prosecutor, who failed to summon key witnesses in support of the territory's case or produce subpoenaed documents suggesting a conspiracy involving Brazel, Adamson, Deacon Jim Miller, and W. W. Cox before and after the killing. An apathetic jury deliberated for fifteen minutes, then delivered a bill of acquittal. Two hours later the ex-defendant attended a barbecue in his honor at Cox's ranch.

The men who gathered in Tom Powers' Coney Island Saloon to drink, play cards, and discuss politics and local events were of the general opinion that Brazel was a stalking-horse, put up to draw fire for a deed for which he was not responsible. Some fixed the crime on Adamson, who had not the luxury of a plea of self-defense, while others named each of the legion of enemies Pat had made in Texas and New Mexico, including one or two of Billy Bonney's compatriots whose deaths went unrecorded and so were believed to have wandered the West for nearly thirty years, awaiting their opportunity to avenge him. One provocative theory, that Bonney was not dead at all but had come out of hiding in old Mexico to slay the man credited with slaying him, enjoyed a certain popularity until someone thought to ask what motive he might have had to take the life of one who had not, after all, taken his. Still others preferred Jim Miller. These identified Killin' Jim as the mysterious horseman with whom Brazel had been conversing on the Mail-Scott Road when the buggy carrying Adamson and Pat arrived to separate them. There were a thousand lofty places in the vicinity of Alameda Arroyo where a man armed with a Winchester could station himself and shoot the proprietor of Bear Canyon Ranch at long range.

Partly because Miller was widely hated and feared, and partly because his murderous celebrity suited the murder of so celebrated a victim, the Miller Solution, as it came to be known, spread rapidly. By now it has entered the legendary annals alongside Ash Upson's claim—based on nothing but his own imagination, colored with printer's ink and cured with alcohol—that at the time of his death at age twenty-one, Billy the Kid had slain a man for every year of his life; and there it will remain, as permanently as James Butler Hickok's last hand of cards and the old woman in Missouri whose mortgage Jesse James took it upon himself to pay off with money stolen from the same bank that issued it. But by the time the men of the Coney Island arrived at this conclusion, the point was moot. On April 19, 1909, the same day the jury in Las Cruces declared Wayne Brazel innocent of the crime with which he was charged, a masked mob pulled Jim Miller from a jail in Texas where he was awaiting trial for the brutal murder of a local man and hanged him from the rafters of a livery barn nearby. As if to ordain the event, one of the vigilantes draped Miller's sober black coat over his body where it lay among the loose hay and horseshit after it was cut down.

Whether because of outrage over the affront to justice or because of an Old Testament faith in blood cleansing blood, the manner in which Pat Garrett was beheld underwent a dramatic change in the months following his death. Old enemies waxed sentimental upon his subject, and friends vexed by his complicated personality forgot his inconsistencies and dwelt upon his more sterling characteristics. The public in general, which in response to the inundation of paperbound novels deifying Billy the Kid had been wont to consider his killer in a category with Bob Ford and Jack McCall, assassins of Jesse James and Wild Bill Hickok, respectively, now took into account his official status as a peace officer and the long months spent combing the backcountry for Bonney's trail, and awarded him a place among the great lawmen of his day. Copies of the disastrous *Authentic Life of Billy the Kid* surfaced from mercantile storage rooms where they had lain neglected for three decades, and inquiries were made to Apolinaria Garrett by a major publishing company in New York in regard to a new edition, to be edited and annotated by an established authority on the history of the Lincoln County War. A maker of moving pictures, having relocated in California to escape an injunction brought by the Edison Company to protect its patent on the filmmaking process, had announced plans to produce a two-reel feature dramatizing the young bandit's career, with equal attention paid to Bonney and Garrett. The resurrection was in full cry.

My relationship with the long man is more difficult to interpret. Although I did not hear of him for years at a time, when news did come I experienced, as in a sudden burst of illumination in a dark room, the whole of his thoughts and emotions as they occurred throughout the long silences, as if they were my own, delayed by deep preoccupation. I am a man of science; prescience lies outside my field of study. It may be that because we were both seekers by nature as well as by profession, more compelled by the search itself than by the bitter disappointment of the result, we shared a consciousness. Or it may be that I am a vassal of my imagination. Certainly the evidence of my life and my line is sufficient to prove my capacity for selfdelusion. What does it matter, since this record must die with its author?

One success at least I may claim, and that is the answer to the riddle of the cyclone and the peccary. The old gods, accustomed as they are to chaos and conflict, are bored unto death by their inaction in this desert exile, and must amuse themselves with challenges, counting games and the like, to forestall decay. The great Leonardo, whose mind and energies were too adept even for the diversions of the Renaissance, recorded his observations and conclusions backwards, inscribing in his fine hand from right to left, so that he who would benefit by them must turn the pages to a mirror. So too did the pagan immortals write the object of the lesson of the natural force and the dumb beast. Thus, destruction does not follow salvation. The truth is in the reverse.

All things that come from clay go back to it in the end. Save gold.

> Francisco de la Zaragoza, Viceroy in Absentia,
> Durango, Mexico,
> 1782–1911

CHAPTER 25

Transmutation

Well, Big Casino."

"Well, Little Casino."

"Come far, looks like."

"Just down the Jornada. It ain't so far when you know the way."

"I think you know all these boys: Tom O'Folliard, and little Tom Pickett, and Billie Wilson, and old Charlie Bowdre, and there's Rudabaugh."

"How do, boys."

"I sure hope you brung money, Big Casino. We been pushing around what was in our pockets when we got here for ever so long. We wore the injun's head clean off all the pennies."

"I'm fixed okay, I reckon. Only it don't look like Charlie's so glad to see me."

"You know Charlie. It took him the best part of forever to put aside my pushing him out the door at Stinking Springs. He'll come around. Look at Tom. You shot him all to pieces at Roswell and he don't bear no grudge no more."

"Tom always was a Christian."

"Take my seat, Big Casino. Could be it'll bring you more luck than it brung me."

"What's the game?"

"Five card, nothing wild. Excepting me, of course."

"Whose deal?"

"Yours. With these boys I got so I don't know what it's like to get one off the top."

"Stop that whistling."

"Sure thing, Pat. You're dealing."

The
Undertaker's
Wife

To the memory of Richard C. House:
conqueror of space and time

Let us be honest—we don't believe in an afterlife. (If you do, it makes no sense for you to ever visit a grave.) So we go to the body. It is the best we can do.

—DAVID CARKEET, *I Been There Before*

FUNERAL, *n.* A pageant whereby we attest our respect for the dead by enriching the undertaker, and strengthen our grief by an expenditure that deepens our groans and doubles our tears.

—AMBROSE BIERCE, *The Devil's Dictionary*

The savage dies—they sacrifice a horse
To bear to happy hunting-grounds the corse.
Our friends expire—we make the money fly
In hope their souls will chase it to the sky.

—JEX WOPLEY*

*Ambrose Bierce, *ibid.*

I

The Undertaker's Art

If the Dismal Traders (as an eighteenth-century English writer calls them) have traditionally been cast in a comic role in literature, a universally recognized symbol of humor from Shakespeare to Evelyn Waugh, they have successfully turned the tables in recent years to perpetuate a huge, macabre and expensive practical joke on the American public.

—Jessica Mitford
The American Way of Death

CHAPTER 1

Elihu Warrick entered his first-class stateroom aboard the Michigan Central, laid out his cigars and placed his portable bar in its morocco-leather case on one of the seats, removed his shimmering silk hat and gray Chesterfield, and gave them to the porter for brushing. When the porter returned forty-five minutes later, carrying the items in a new pair of white gloves, he found Mr. Warrick slumped on the seat opposite the bar and cigars, indisputably dead.

Certainly the porter, who had performed as an orderly in a Negro troop hospital during the war with Spain, was disinclined to dispute the fact. There was the matter of the pallor of the overfed face, like tallow in contrast to the weighty black moustache, too obviously a beneficiary of Dr. Rose's Old Reliable Hair and Whisker Dye, and then there was the confirmation of the round blue hole in the right temple, burned and puckered at the edges, and Mr. Warrick's thumb inside the trigger guard of the Forehand Perfection Automatic Five-Shot Revolver in his lap.

The porter laid the folded coat on the seat next to the bar and cigars, stood the silk hat atop the coat bottom side up to protect the brim, leaned across the body, and opened the window to let out the sulfurous stink—of the exploded cartridge combined with the passenger's voided bowels, not of the cigar, which continued to emit a pleasingly expensive masculine perfume from the smoking stand where its owner had placed it half-smoked. The young Negro was mildly upset. Mr. Warrick was reputed to be a generous tipper, and he'd neglected to lay out a gratuity.

To help himself to a cigar from the open silver case violated railroad regulations as well as the porter's own standard of conduct. Instead he poured an inch of brandy into a small silver-plated cup from the crystal decanter strapped inside the portable bar, flipped the brown liquid down his throat, polished the cup thoroughly inside and out with his handkerchief, and returned the cup to its loop inside the lid. With the spirit's heat spreading up from the floor of his stomach, he went to find the conductor.

Hairline cracks radiating from the death by his own hand at age fifty-four of the well-known Chicago speculator, railroad investor, and meatpacking magnate reached as far north as Ontario, where he'd maintained mining interests, and as far south as Venezuela, where his gifts to several key cabinet members had secured extensive investments in the trade in rubber and balata, a principal ingredient in the manufacture of gutta-percha and chewing gum. The Texas cattle industry was concerned, as were his associates in New York City, who through their attorneys moved swiftly to demand an audit of all his books; for in the world inhabited by Warrick and his class, suicide had but two motives, money and women, and as the second was invariably tangled with the first, it little mattered which was the specific cause. This latest disaster, occurring when the bloody gash of the 1893 Panic had not yet healed completely, further eroded stomach linings already worn as thin as vellum.

As it happened, the news reached John C. Broughty at Windvale, his twelve-acre estate on Long Island, just as he was showing an early holograph manuscript of John Donne's 1624 poem "No Man Is an Island" to a baron from the court of Kaiser Wilhelm II. The baron was considering trading some documents signed by Frederick the Great for it, along with mineral rights in the Ruhr Valley. Broughty, seventy-three and determined to extend his mastery of the nineteenth century into the twentieth, listened to his butler's announcement that a gentleman awaited him on the telephone, invited the Herr Baron to examine the parchment at his leisure, and excused himself to squeeze into the cork-lined closet he'd installed in his front hallway to accommodate the instrument. The caller was a railroad dispatcher in his employ, relating the circumstances as they'd been wired to him by the conductor on the train from Chicago to New York City. Broughty cross-questioned the man, who assured him that no one knew the details apart from himself, the conductor, and the porter, both of whom the dispatcher had admonished by return wire to say nothing to anyone.

"And the telegraphers, of course," he added. "But they're bound by the seal of the profession."

"Bind them by mine as well. I own sixty thousand shares in Western Union. What about the police?"

The dispatcher replied that he'd arranged for the man in charge of the Michigan City branch of the Pinkerton National Detective Agency to secure the stateroom when the train stopped there and to exercise his discretion with the local authorities. Broughty knew the detective's name, and approved of this decision. He shouted instructions to remain by the telephone, got the operator on the line, and placed a call to his attorney.

He smoked the better part of a cigar while waiting for

the connection, with the door open to let smoke out of the closet. Pulling it shut and extinguishing the stump, he made arrangements for an immediate audit.

"My firm represents Warrick," the attorney shouted back. "Shall I inform the widow?"

"Ask her to make no funerary decisions until I've spoken with her."

"She'll want to know why."

"She and Warrick have benefited from my counsel for twenty years. Send your best man to remind her of that. Your most diplomatic man. Go yourself."

His next call was to Gordon Lindsey, his personal secretary, whom he instructed to call and wire his associates with the news of Warrick's sudden death, sans details, and a request to come to Windvale at their earliest convenience that evening. Then he pegged the receiver and returned to his guest.

By eleven o'clock, five men who had twice rescued the United States Treasury from bankruptcy were gathered in Broughty's neoclassical library, which was fresh out of barons but well supplied as to illuminated manuscripts, European incunabula of the fifteenth and sixteenth centuries, and other literary spoils plundered from the capitals of the Old World. Between the glazed book presses and above the Levantine marble fireplace hung a new portrait of the owner, while below and in front of it, its subject struck the same unconscious pose, one thumb hooked inside the watch pocket of his vest and his good ear turned to the world. He was famously deaf in the other, the result of a childhood encounter with an exasperated streetcar operator whose one brush with history was to box the ear of the future most powerful man in America.

In the painting and in person, Broughty's face frequently surprised people who knew him only by reputation. White-haired, pink-skinned, and clean-shaven, with the suggestion of a chronic smile about the mouth, he resembled one of those kindly corner druggists who were routinely taken advantage of by wholesalers and their own delivery boys. Governor Roosevelt, less easily impressed, had denounced him as "the greatest threat to free competition since the Golden Horde."

The four influential guests listened to the news about Warrick without interrupting, while Broughty's secretary, pockmarked and side-whiskered, sat with his hands folded in his lap, his writing block out of sight for the first time in memory. Cicero Lewiston—banks, shipping, and chocolate—was the first to break the silence. He was the fattest man in a company of notorious trenchermen.

"Did he leave a note?"

"None was mentioned. If he did, we'll get it from Pinkerton's."

"We can either start unloading stock first thing in the morning before the price drops, or buy more at noon when it's down and counter the run." This was James Oliphant, railroads and mining, bald as a china plate beneath his gray bowler. "I don't see any third alternative."

Broughty said, "There will be no run."

Lewiston said, "The man killed himself. Stockholders are sheep. They'll stampede."

"Sheep follow," Broughty corrected. "Cattle stampede. Never without reason. Outside of this room, only five men are aware Warrick's death was suicide. You all know young Lindsey." The secretary was fifty. "It shouldn't be necessary to swear us five to secrecy as well. Warrick's wife doesn't know. I didn't even tell my attorney."

"Still, it's five too many." Ignatius Frank, refrigeration. Thirty years after Louis Napoleon named him an honorary chevalier of France, he still waxed his whiskers after the fashion of the defunct imperial court. "It's bound to come out."

"Rumors."

The host snarled the word the same way he said, "The press," at whom he'd been known to raise his stick.

"Rumors are as bad as the truth. Worse." R.W. Gilbert, who held the patent on the Gilbert Hydraulic Perpendicular Railway—elevators—was a sallow-faced old widower who managed to depress people when he wished them a happy Christmas.

"I'm not saying the market won't react," Broughty said. "It would do that if he'd died of apoplexy. It will adjust itself once the rumors are refuted by fact."

Lewiston was a man for the basics. "What fact? The man killed himself."

"The fact of his corpse."

"Naturally, the coffin will be closed." Gloomy old Gilbert was an authority on funerary practice. Since burying his wife, he'd attended thirty such services, many of them for complete strangers. The society correspondent for *Harper's Weekly* reported that he traveled with his own casket (as the genteel class were calling it now), in case he expired during a business excursion far from his Fifth Avenue brownstone.

"Naturally, a closed coffin would only fuel further rumors. He will lie in state, and the viewing will be open to the public."

Even the redoubtable Gordon Lindsey was agitated by Broughty's declaration. He unfolded his hands and refolded them the other way. The others yawped like terriers; all except Gilbert, who stared at the Turkestan and howled like a basset. Broughty lit a cigar, breathed the smoke in through his nostrils, and waited until the protests had crested. Then he said, "Connable."

This had the effect of dropping a lid on the noise. This time, bald Oliphant was the first to speak. Of all those present, he was the only one who had fought in a war, as a volunteer with the First Division in Mexico in 1846. "Have you ever seen a corpse with a bullet in its brain? You don't just cork the hole and plaster it over."

"I would imagine that's just what you do," said Broughty. "I'm sure there's quite a bit more to it, but it would seem to be some variation on that principle." Broughty waved his cigar. "Gentlemen, I don't know for a certainty that the thing is possible. If it is, Dick Connable's our man."

At the time this conversation was taking place, Richard Connable was four hundred miles away, playing canasta with his wife and another couple from their neighborhood in the two-story brick house he owned on Delaware Avenue in Buffalo. He was a large man in his late fifties, thick-shouldered and burly, and clean-shaven like John C. Broughty, but less benevolent in appearance. This lack of warmth was a practice of long standing, assisted by the blue-tinted lenses of his wire-rimmed spectacles, which protected his weak eyes from glare and masked the only truly expressive feature of his face. Although he still went about in stiff collars and neckties, the striped and colored shirts he wore in place of the conservative white of old, combined with the dark glasses—*cheaters*—put observers in mind of a professional gambler; but not if they'd ever played cards with him. He was constitutionally incapable of reading his partner's signals and always had to be reminded when it was his turn.

In truth, he loathed parlor games. He found them as tiresome and time-wasting as the couple he and Lucy were playing against that evening. Sitting there holding his cards, listening to the clock knocking out the seconds of his life and watching the faces distorted in concentration, hands restlessly shifting the pasteboards from one arbitrary position to another, he realized most vividly that to retire was to sit back and wait for death. He only played because his wife seemed to enjoy it; and Lucy enjoying *anything* was worth the trade of several hours' morbid contemplation of the Inevitable.

The neighbors weren't bad company—not bad in the sense of a prospector who hadn't bathed in eight months, or a settler turned cannibal, gloweringly watching him inject arsenious acid and potash into the veins of a cadaver, banishing it from the bill of fare—just dismally predictable. He was a former engineer in charge of widening and dredging the Erie Canal, she a former New York City debutante, and most of their conversation had been stuck in a tunnel since 1862. Had Connable brought their attention to the fact that the century was only three months from turning, he would half expect them to blink and fall to dust. Theirs was an earlier generation, one he had spent much of his career preparing for burial, and yet retirement had flung them all into one camp.

The Engineer and the Debutante won the rubber, as usual, and square on the chime of midnight the Engineer hauled out his heavy gold watch, popped the face, and said, "Well—"; and Connable knew they were only twenty minutes from leaving.

When they'd gone, he locked the door behind them, lit a lamp, and turned out all the gas fixtures on the ground floor, then climbed the stairs by handheld lamplight to the bedroom. He savored that solitary time in the soft glow and would miss it when the house was electrified. Half the city was engulfed in white incandescence, with the other half expected to follow next year. Lucy wanted it, and that was the end of that.

He turned out the lamp before entering the bedroom, undressed in the dark, and dropped his nightshirt over his head. Lucy was already under the covers, breathing evenly. He climbed in beside her, without hope that his insomnia would spare him this night or any other. He was awake four hours later when someone pulled at the bell downstairs.

Lucy Connable awoke slowly, and was only aware that Richard was shaking her by the shoulder when she opened her eyes and saw his face, inches from hers with his tinted glasses pushed down so he could see her over the tops. The lamp he always carried from downstairs glowed on the nightstand on his side of the bed. He was fully dressed, in the suit he'd worn earlier that evening and one of the white shirts she hadn't seen in months. He was speaking her name gently.

"Is it Victoria?" She pulled herself upright.

Instantly she realized her mistake, saw the pain on his face.

"A man named Lindsey is downstairs," he said. "He came here straight from New York. He works for John C. Broughty."

"Broughty?" She saw columns in the *Ledger,* a headline. The name meant nothing beyond that. She smelled gin on Richard's breath.

"The Manhattan millionaire. He's offering me a client, a man named Warrick. He's in a parlor in Cleveland. They took him directly from the train station and knocked up the owner. Five thousand dollars for one day's work."

"Cleveland?" She couldn't seem to stop repeating names. The fog began to clear. "Richard, you're retired."

"Five thousand dollars, Lucy. We can sell this house and build a better one out West."

She didn't say, "West?" She asked him the time.

"It's nearly dawn. Lindsey hired a carriage. We can make the six-fifteen if we leave soon. I'll be back by dark."

"It's too much money. It must be criminal."

"This is John Broughty, not the Shrunk brothers. He wants to exhibit the client. He doesn't want to stuff him in a sack and dump him in Blackwell's Bog. If that were the case, he wouldn't need me." He straightened. "This is your chance to clean my study. You complain I never leave it."

Then he was gone.

She waited until she heard hoofbeats echoing down the empty block, then rose, stuck her long narrow feet into an old pair of Richard's slippers and, hugging her arms in her nightdress, went downstairs, carrying the lamp Richard had left for her. In the kitchen she found the quart of gin where he was hiding it now, behind a can of Royal Baking Powder in the cabinet above the sink, and drank from it.

She was fifty-five, and under no illusion that she didn't look her age. Always slender, she'd begun to lose weight lately, although she ate as much as ever and took little exercise. The skin of her face had grown shiny where it stretched over bone. She no longer saw out her right eye, a recent and sudden development she took pains to conceal from her husband.

She wore her rusted-iron hair long, braided for sleep and pinned up during the day, caught with ivory combs on the rare occasions they went out together. In younger years, she'd been what in fashionable quarters was called a Handsome Woman, never a beauty; she considered herself plain and always had. The closest her parents had ever come to confirming that description was when they'd referred to young Connable at the time of her wedding as a Good Catch. Her cousins had all married doctors. She'd known where she stood in comparison.

She took another drink and stood on tiptoe to slide the bottle back into its nook. She didn't want to take so much she'd have to replace it with water from the tap. This morning was the first in many years she'd known Richard to take a drink any day other than January fifteenth. She couldn't take the chance of his noticing the substitution.

She drew aside the curtains over the kitchen window and watched the first zinc-colored light spreading behind the Muellers' house on the other side of their lot. It chilled her, despite the flush of the gin. She wished she'd thought to put on her robe. Reaching up to recover and replace the bottle had claimed the strength she needed to climb the stairs.

A house out West. Richard hadn't mentioned it for as long as they'd lived in Buffalo. Which was as long as it had been since either of them had spoken Victoria's name aloud.

CHAPTER 2

The Pinkerton detective's name was Stockfinger. The call from the railroad dispatcher had reached him at his office on the second floor of a former cement factory in Michigan City, where he'd been spending most of his time since his wife had left him at Christmas.

He'd been with the Agency twenty-two years, having joined shortly after the successful prosecution of the Mollie Maguires in Pennsylvania based on undercover evidence presented by the legendary James McParland; but Stockfinger was an unconvincing liar, and so had subordinated his dreams of intrigue and disguise to his superior skills of investigation and administration. When it came to retrieving microscopic traces and classifying them in columns one hundred feet long, no one at The Eye was better.

In appearance he was small and tidy, wore his suits tight, and combed his fair moustache straight out from the center in a stiff-whisker effect some found unfortunate: *Rat-faced* was the word his wife had used in her valedictory. He detested hats, which he considered the leading cause of premature baldness in men, and had used the occasion of Allan Pinkerton's death to flout the Agency's uniform code and step out uncovered in all weather. In stores where his was usually the only bare head on the customer's side of the counter, he was often mistaken for a clerk.

Listening to the dispatcher, he committed the train and track number to memory—his lingering infatuation with the clandestine prevented him from writing down information that might be seen by unauthorized eyes—and inquired about expenses, implying that certain arrangements might be necessary that could not be recorded. He was assured that Mr. Broughty would be reasonable in this regard. Stockfinger rang off, withdrew one hundred dollars in banknotes and twenty dollars in gold from the safe in his office, and entered the amount in the ledger under Discretionary Expenditures. He then transferred a number of items from a locked drawer in his desk to a leather bank satchel and went out.

At the Michigan Central station, the conductor, a Low Country German named Schilling, read his card and escorted him to a Pullman car, aboard which a colored porter unlocked the door to Elihu Warrick's stateroom. Upon closing the door behind him, the Pinkerton's first act was to stuff a corner of his handkerchief into the keyhole. The porter or someone had drawn the blind over the window.

The portly man slumped on the seat was obviously dead, but Stockfinger pressed his fingers into the folds of fat on the neck to confirm the absence of a pulse. The skin was cool to the touch. He made a mental calculation and entered an approximate time of death on his own shirt cuff with an ink pencil. The man's pockets contributed a number of items to the seat opposite: a ring of keys, a platinum watch, a small memorandum book with a gold pencil attached to it by a tiny chain, and a calfskin wallet containing seven hundred dollars in banknotes, two double eagles, and his train ticket. These things Stockfinger handled with his spare handkerchief and laid out in the order in which they'd be returned. The latest entry in the memorandum book was a barber's appointment, dated yesterday. There was no note.

Working by lamplight and using the instruments he'd brought, the detective applied the Galton System to the fingerprints on Warrick's watch, wallet, portable bar, cigar case, and the revolver he'd removed from his lap, took an impression from the dead man's fingers, and quickly established that someone other than Warrick had handled the crystal decanter labeled BRANDY. This fact he committed to memory in case it became convenient. Instinct told him the man had not been murdered for his spirits.

Further tests told him the man had probably not been murdered at all. His right hand smelled sharply of spent powder, and a tape measure applied to his right arm confirmed he'd been capable of placing the muzzle to the spot where the wound had been inflicted. The writing in his memorandum book bore a right-hand slant. The wound matched the caliber of the revolver and there was an empty cartridge under the hammer. A bullet had passed through the barrel recently. The powder flash had made crackling of the surrounding skin upon contact.

The detective returned the personal items to their original pockets, placed his instruments back in the satchel, and snapped open the door to the corridor. The porter shot upright from his slouch against the door of the stateroom opposite. If he'd tried listening at Warrick's door, he'd given it up as a bad job.

"Where is his luggage?" Stockfinger asked.

"He had none, sir."

"He booked a compartment to New York City without bringing any bags?"

"No, sir. I mean, yes, sir. Just the spirit case."

"Get the conductor."

Schilling's face throughout the Pinkerton's instructions

wore an expression of Teutonic gloom. When he interrupted to recite a passage from the railroad manual regarding the containment and transportation of the remains of deceased persons, Stockfinger explained that his directions came from the man who wrote the manual, and offered him a hand in the palm of which was folded a banknote. The conductor took it. The detective handed the porter a ten-dollar gold piece and watched as it disappeared inside his white glove.

The porter relocked the door and Stockfinger returned to the office to write his report. Headquarters in Chicago had approved the purchase of Remington type-writing machines for all the branches, but he preferred script, using telegraphers' shorthand. The girl he'd employed through an agency would transcribe the material tomorrow, with carbon copies for Chicago and the client in New York. Before his final paragraph, he paused to roll and smoke a cigarette, then dipped his pen and wrote:

> Finally, fact that Subject, a man of clean habits and accustomed comforts, bought a ticket for an overnight train to New York City without bringing a change of linen strongly suggests he did not intend to complete the journey, corroborating evidence above and leading this investigator to conclude that Subject took his own life for reasons unknown at this time.

He read what he'd written, made corrections, placed the pages in a leather folder, and locked it in the safe. He had not mentioned that the assignment had cost the client only sixty dollars thus far, apart from fees, nor did he adjust the amount he'd recorded in the ledger. Stockfinger intended to retire in three years, and William Pinkerton held a Scot's own view of pensions. John C. Broughty would certainly never miss the difference.

The mortal shell of Elihu Henry Clay Warrick, a director
of the Chicago, Rock Island, and Pacific Railroad, heir to
Warrick & Company Meats and Dairies, principal shareholder in Columbian Shipbuilders and Hiawatha Iron,
owner of the Wing's Metallic Mill Bush patent, and a
thirty-third-degree Mason, was conveyed from the Michigan Central tracks in Cleveland in a grocer's delivery
wagon to Millard & Sons' Mortuary on Detroit Street, a
short walk from Lake Erie and seven blocks from the rail
yard. When the wind blew from the direction of the docks—
and it never blew *toward* them—it brought with it a solid
stink of fish and rotting timbers. At one time the brick
house had belonged to one of the city's wealthy early merchants; more lately it had operated as a brothel, and the
infusion of several years' worth of formaldehyde and flo-
ral displays had not eradicated the miasma of disinfectant
soap and perfume-by-the-jug that hung over it like yellow
fever. The location had been selected for its convenience
to the railroad terminal, to minimize the chances of discovery en route.

Upon entering, Richard Connable ignored the hand
extended by the owner, a dried old stalk in a cutaway, waistcoat, and striped trousers that looked as if they were all
one piece and hooked up the back, like a burial suit. Presumably this was Millard *père*. Accompanied by Broughty's
man Gordon Lindsey, and with the ancient mortician
limping behind, the visitor strode down a gaslit corridor
flanked by curtained archways and crossed through a coffin display room reeking with cheap furniture oil to the
room in back where the cadavers were prepared.

This room was electrified, but no less dim than the corridor; the naked bulb hanging by a twist of cord from the
ceiling wore a fine coat of soot, as did most of the objects
in the room. The air was heavy with ammonia and the
smell of mold from an icebox that hadn't been scrubbed

in weeks. Connable walked around the corpulent figure stretched out on a bench in the center, stopped before a set of homemade shelves, and lifted a sooty brown bottle to the light. The contents were caked hard at the bottom.

"Is this as much cinnabar as you have?" he asked Millard.

"We never restocked." The old man's voice was thick with catarrh. "Most of our customers can't afford that method. We went back to camphor."

"One to six?"

"Four."

A pair of dark and surprisingly lively eyes regarded him over the tops of the tinted spectacles. "An ounce of camphor to four of spirits of wine? What do you do, drink the rest and charge it to the client's account?"

"Certainly not. I'm a man of temperance. We use water."

"From the lake, no doubt; and tack on a city fee for good measure."

Millard's mouth opened and closed twice. Nothing came out.

Connable replaced the bottle in its clean circle in the dust and soot on the shelf. He browsed among the jars and cans and bricks of some material that looked like chocolate. "What about potash? Glycerine? Acetate of alumina? At this point I'd settle for turpentine. Good God!" He hoisted an evil-looking gallon can by its bail and brought his nose close to the black glutinous stuff that had spilled over the edge and congealed down the outside. "Tar. Did you run out of quicklime?"

"It's a reliable preservative."

"So is brine, and you can make pickles while you're about it. Who taught you the trade, the butchers at Tyburn?" Connable let the can drop with a crash.

"Gentlemen—" Lindsey began.

"Our customers are working men and women. Dock laborers, teamsters, laundresses. They can barely scrape enough together to keep their loved ones out of potter's field. We don't have your fine practice, Mr. Connable. You'll have to go to Krauss's on Broadway to find anything like it." Millard gurgled and spat into a brittle handkerchief.

"Krauss's it is. And have them send a proper hearse. This is a fellow human creature, not salted pork." He tipped a hand toward the body on the bench, acknowledging its presence for the first time.

"You can make those arrangements yourself. I got up out of a warm bed at your people's request. I didn't ask for the work."

"The fact you can sleep at all confirms my impression of your establishment." Connable strode from the room.

Lindsey gave the old man a banknote for his trouble, recorded the figure in the account book he carried whenever he went abroad on an errand, and hurried out behind his companion.

He found him standing on the columned front porch, wiping his spectacles with the tail of his coat. Lindsey produced a folded square of white broadcloth. Connable accepted it. The secretary stepped off the porch, whispered a few words to the driver of the carriage they'd hired at the station, scribbled on the back of a card, and sent him off with it and a dollar. When Lindsey returned to the porch, Connable gave him back the handkerchief.

"Thank you. It's a wonder I didn't come away without my trousers."

"I imagine the close work is hard on the eyes." The secretary had noticed him squinting in the medium-gray sunlight.

"No, it's the corrosive chemicals. My tear ducts crumbled away years ago."

"Is that why you retired?"

"No."

Lindsey looked out at the street, which wasn't much less

depressing than the back room of the funeral parlor. Last night's slops made puddles in the jagged holes in the macadam. A native New Yorker, he hadn't suspected life on a lake would so closely resemble the First Street wharf.

"You should know I approved of the location, and the delivery wagon. It was a matter of expedience. I didn't think it would be this bad."

"You have no idea how bad it can be. Although I wouldn't put it past that old fraud to spread one coffin over five plots. I can't do the work your employer wants with the materials in there. And I need better light."

"I hope Krauss's will serve."

"I'm sure it will. You can trust a charlatan like Millard to know who's best. I hope you paid him enough. Otherwise he'll come back for more. He may regardless."

"Mr. Broughty understands he has to pay more for certain services than most people. He doesn't begrudge some profiteering. He draws the line at extortion. Far more important men have been ruined for less."

"I heard Jim Hickok make pretty much the same speech in Hays City. He said 'killed,' but I suppose it comes to the same thing."

"You knew Wild Bill Hickok?"

"Not well enough to call him Wild Bill."

Lindsey waited, but nothing more was forthcoming. His employer had made a discreet choice.

"I'm sorry it couldn't be done at your establishment in Buffalo," he said. "If Warrick isn't lying in state in three days it won't look well."

"I can send out for anything they don't have. Now that I'm out of the trade, Krauss can have all my secrets and be damned. If there *is* a Krauss. A fictitious German name never turned away business. Broughty will stand the cost?"

"I'm authorized to pay any and all expenses up to a thousand dollars."

"It won't come to a tenth of that. Warrick isn't Pharaoh."

"I noticed you never looked at him."

"The rupture is less than two centimeters. I can fill it with paraffin and cover it with cosmetic. The coloring may prove a challenge. Without having met the man, I assume he suffered from accelerated circulation and probably a bad liver. I'll need plenty of rouge, and white aluminum to dilute."

"I guess you did look at him."

"There wasn't any point in trying to examine him closer in that light. But I've worked by tallow. If you train what God left you, you see things that stronger eyes miss."

Lindsey was surprised. "I didn't think morticians believed in a higher power."

"They don't. That crook inside is a mortician. I'm an undertaker."

"I wasn't aware there's a difference."

"You'll learn soon enough, if you have the stomach for it."

CHAPTER 3

Uter Krauss was an Austrian of German descent who'd fled Europe in 1870 to prevent his son from being pressed into military service. His wife died during the rigorous ocean crossing, and Krauss now wore a black band of mourning for his grandson, who'd joined the U.S. Army during the Spanish War and died of fever aboard a troop ship anchored in Havana Harbor. These events had contributed to his lifelong tendency toward fatalism.

He himself had learned the rudiments of his trade in a martial setting, preserving the corpses of officers for transportation home at the time of Austria's invasion of Italy in 1866. He'd interned in a hospital before the war and had served briefly as a medical orderly, but mortuary science had interested him more than medicine. Krauss's was the oldest established funeral parlor in Cleveland, serving mostly upscale residents of the city and nearby Lakewood. The mansarded building, home to a gentlemen's club until it lost its lease following a fatal pistol duel in the dining room, occupied a corner lot on Broadway, with a carriage house behind it for the hearse and double doors installed in back for the passage of caskets. Well-mannered flowers grew in cedar boxes under the windows and bordered the limestone front path.

The proprietor was tall and fine-boned, parted his

thinning white hair in the center, and at age sixty stood erect in black mohair suits he had made to his order. Envious competitors referred to him behind his back as "Herr General," unsuspecting that he was a habitual contributor to pacifist causes.

"Mr. Connable. A great pleasure." He snapped a bow over their clasped hands in the quietly decorated foyer. Both hands were maintained carefully, with nails round and white, but contact with various acids had mottled the skin permanently. Neither man wore the gray felt gloves uniform to the trade, a professional courtesy. Connable's grip was firm, unaffected. He was younger than anticipated. "My associate is in back, preparing the client." He preferred this verb to "undressing and washing." "I trust you're satisfied thus far?"

"I've never seen a finer pair. You have new tires."

"We replace them each spring. They crack in this lake climate every winter."

"I imagine you've an eager buyer in Millard."

Krauss's tight-lipped smile was noncommittal. He never criticized his colleagues.

"Mr. Krauss, Mr. Lindsey. Lindsey represents our friend in New York."

He shook Lindsey's hand. In his side-whiskers, with powder caked in his pox scars, the secretary looked like a would-be robber baron who had abandoned his dreams in order to serve one. "Shall we discuss arrangements?" Krauss asked.

"That isn't necessary," Lindsey said. "Our friend in New York will meet all your requirements. I assume your associate is aware of the terms?"

"He is my apprentice. You may assure your friend that he represents this firm as much as I." No names other than Connable's and the secretary's had accompanied the earlier message; but Krauss had served the city's politicians and their financiers for years and knew whom Gordon Lindsey represented. He turned toward Connable. "We employ the Frankfurt Method, as practiced by Herr Wiesel. It's similar to the Florentine Process, but less time-consuming, and the results have proven most satisfactory, even when the client is disinterred after several years. It involves glycerine and methylic alcohol."

"We aren't concerned with disinterment," said Lindsey. "It only has to pass muster until the coffin is closed."

"I prefer formaldehyde to methylal," Connable said. "It travels better. The client has a long journey ahead of him."

"Eight hours by rail is hardly an Odyssey. Our clients prefer methylal for its pleasant odor."

"That's what flowers are for."

"At Krauss's, we enhance. We don't conceal."

Connable smiled faintly. "At least we agree on the glycerine."

"Well," said Krauss, and tipped a hand toward the foyer's back entrance.

Lindsey stepped that way. Krauss turned his palm slightly. "I discourage observers," he said.

"I'm sorry. That's one of the terms."

Krauss glanced at Connable, whose expression was unreadable behind his colored lenses. "How is your constitution, Mr. Lindsey?"

The secretary hesitated. "I was fourteen when the draft riots broke out. I've seen men blown open in a public street."

"It's not the same," Connable said. "In that back room, we're going to pull a man apart and put him back together, and do it in such a way that it looks as if we did nothing at all. Ours is an invisible art. That's why I agreed to your terms. I want your employer to know what he's paying for."

* * *

Uter Krauss's back room—unsentimentally referred to, by both him and Connable, as the morgue—did not belong to the same world as Millard & Sons'. Electric bulbs set in a row of ceramic fixtures in the ceiling shed even light on the furnishings and floor, which was made of slate and declined slightly toward a sump at the back, as in a butchery. The slate shone from recent scrubbing, as did the white porcelain sink and zinc countertops, rows of cabinets faced in white enamel, and a sort of trough raised on four stout legs in the center of the room, porcelain also, with faucets built into one end and a drain in the other. At seven feet long and three feet wide it was more than large enough to accommodate the naked man who lay in its recess, at a thirty-degree angle with the head elevated above the feet at the drain end. His skin wore a bluish pallor, like skim milk, and the angry puckered hole in his right temple was of a shade slightly darker than billiard-cue chalk. His genitals, plum-colored, looked comically small at the base of the huge, swollen paunch. Gordon Lindsey was aware of a smell of carbolic and stale meat.

The apprentice's name was Nuttle, and he looked more like one of Millard's dockworker customers than what Lindsey had expected to find employed in a charnel house; popular fiction had led him to believe that all the men who worked closely with the dead were gaunt caricatures of animated corpses, like vampires in woodcuts found in penny dreadfuls. Thick and slope-shouldered, with features bunched like fishermen's floats, he wore a leather apron over a coarse gray work shirt with the sleeves rolled up above his biceps. In fact, excepting the desiccated Millard, everyone the secretary had met so far in the dismal trade appeared to be well fed, with a high color. Nuttle's huge hands reminded him of a dishwasher's: red, chapped, and unnaturally clean, as if they spent most of their day immersed in scalding water and a solution of harsh soap. He was washing them at the sink when they came in. Elihu Warrick's fine clothes lay in a heap in a corner and his implausible black hair was slicked back and glistening. He'd just been bathed.

The young man had been busy with other things as well. A tray of stainless-steel clamps, scissors, scalpels, augers, and forceps glittered on one of the zinc countertops, next to another tray on which had been placed a half-dozen syringes, laid out in order of size, with the smallest about five inches long and no bigger around than a pencil and the largest as big as a grease gun; this last would require two hands to operate. Adjoining that counter at a right angle was another that ran the length of the back wall and supported an assortment of steel and enamel bowls and basins, pumping mechanisms of black rubber and painted metal, coils of rubber tubing, and a graduated set of what looked like furniture clamps made of varnished wood with iron screws. Disregarding the presence of a corpse, the room seemed to be a combination operating room and bicycle repair shop.

Connable's examination of the deceased began with the hands, with particular attention paid to the nails. He inspected the toenails as well, then directed his attention to the head and neck. He rolled back the eyelids and turned the head right and left in the light, an action accompanied by an involuntary lifting of each shoulder in turn, rigor mortis having set in. The body moved all in one piece, as if petrified. He pressed a hand to the neck on either side of the jaw. It put Lindsey in mind of a physician examining a live patient, and he was disappointed when he didn't pry open the mouth and press down the tongue with a flat stick.

"No jaundice evident," Connable said.

"Good. We're low on Number Ten paste. We had an

epidemic of scarlet fever in April." Krauss tested the plunger of a syringe in the middle range. It made a wheezing noise.

Connable looked up at Lindsey. "In cases of jaundice, the embalming agent turns the body green. It takes a lot of masking paste to reverse the effect."

"Oh."

The two men had traded their coats for leather aprons and turned back their cuffs, revealing powerful forearms as hairless as a woman's, spotted like their hands. Hovering over the cadaver in their cravats and homely bibs, they resembled figures in a painting on John C. Broughty's gallery wall of a dissection in the theater of the Royal College of Surgeons in London. Despite the sterile modern surroundings, the whole thing was redolent of the eighteenth century: latter-day wizards performing alchemy on the newly dead.

His examination finished, Connable selected a scalpel from the tray of surgical instruments. "Preference, Herr Krauss?"

"Doctor, actually," he said. "I don't insist upon it. The choice is yours, Mr. Connable. I'm only assisting."

"I favor the subclavian."

"Jugular for me. I had an unfortunate experience."

Connable smiled. "Anatomy class?"

"The Custozza battlefield. *Very* shortly after somatic. I wasn't informed."

"Gushing," Connable told Lindsey. "A practical joke as old as Giza."

"Oh," again. They were having sport with him.

"Not a problem here." Connable frowned. "Both, I think. There's a time factor."

"That being the case, I'll take the subclavian. One must get back on the horse." Krauss bent over the tray. To Lind-

sey's surprise, the instrument he picked up was not a scalpel but a wicked-looking knife with a straight, nine-inch
blade like a bayonet's and a wooden handle. Connable
stood back while the owner of the parlor inserted the point
just above the great belly and jerked it toward his body,
slicing at an upward angle and stopping at the breasts, flippers
of inert gray flab like an old woman's. Lindsey flinched,
but very little blood oozed out. Krauss made two more quick
incisions, straight across, and peeled back a flap. The secretary saw the inside of a man's rib cage for the first time.

He was more fascinated than revulsed. What he'd seen
in 1863 had been so fleeting, and there was so much blood
and spilled entrail, that he'd come away with little but a
horror to haunt his nightmares. He found himself leaning
forward for a closer look as Krauss dropped the knife rattling into an empty basin, chose a scalpel, and reached inside
the cavity to nick a vein near the sternum. Blood trickled,
more swiftly than from the first incision, but still not the
gusher Connable had described. Connable meanwhile leaned
across Warrick's neck and cut a slit under the right corner
of his jaw. This brought forth another scarlet trickle. Together, and with the assistance of the bull-shouldered Nuttle, the two men lifted the body with a chorus of grunts and
heaved it onto its side, then over onto its face. Lindsey stared
at the pale, purple-streaked buttocks and heard liquid gur-
gling down the drain at the foot of the trough.

"Scheisser!" Krauss, older than Connable and less
stout, leaned panting on the counter covered with pumps
and tubing. "Like landing a whale."

"One of the disadvantages of serving the gentry." Connable unhooked his spectacles and dragged a sleeve across
his streaming forehead. "The famished poor are invariably
easier to manipulate, but can't pay."

Nuttle watched them with an expression of bemused

contempt. The young man's breathing was normal, his face barely rosy. The secretary understood then why the emaciated Charons of fiction existed only there in any quantity.

Someone groaned, long and plaintively. The sound was coming from the corpse. Lindsey felt his own blood draining from his face.

"Mr. Warrick's last testimonial," Connable said. "We just released a pocket of trapped gas. If you like, you can interpret it as the soul leaving the body."

Lindsey, who had been raised in the Episcopalian faith, had converted to Presbyterian when he came to work for Broughty. He resisted the urge to cross himself. "Are you absolutely certain he's dead?"

Connable thumped Warrick's shoulder sharply with a finger. It sounded like tapping an oaken plank. "Not an isolated concern. One of the side benefits of the embalming process is to prevent premature burial. My theory is that was its original purpose."

"Poppycock," Krauss said. "Why not just hit him with a mallet?"

"I don't debate the point. The man who taught me the trade always stuck them with a pin, just to be sure."

Lindsey watched, repelled and fascinated, as Warrick's blood swirled down the drain. "How long does it take?"

"To complete evacuation?" Connable looked at Krauss. "Twelve to twenty minutes?"

"Longer in this case, I think. None of us has more than eight quarts of blood nor less than six, but this long past death the coalescence is advanced. Think of it as the dregs of an old bottle of wine that has been stored improperly."

Lindsey didn't appreciate the comparison. He'd been looking forward to a glass of Madeira when the assignment was finished.

"At least no one is chasing us with stones," said Connable.

"Stones?"

"Yes." Krauss lifted his brows at Nuttle, who rubbed his chapped hands together with a noise like turning over dry pages. He spoke haltingly. "The first Egyptians understood the importance of letting blood, but it shamed them before the gods. The person who made the first cut was forced to run to avoid being stoned to death by his companions."

"Pagans."

Krauss nodded. "A great deal has changed in three thousand years."

"Yes, they no longer use stones." Connable excavated his watch from under his apron and observed the sweep of the second hand. He appeared to be timing the bleeding.

"Is everyone in the mortuary profession an authority on its history?"

"I'd bet a dollar to a drag hook that old quack on Detroit Street doesn't know Babylonian from Aztec," Connable said. "But sooner or later it all comes back to the Egyptians."

Nuttle, his eager expression faded, opened a cabinet and began removing bottles from shelves and lining them up on a clear space of counter. Lindsey could read some of the labels: GLYCERINE, BORAX, PHENOL, METHYL ALCOHOL.

Krauss shook his head. "No, formaldehyde."

"I'm not sure we have any."

"Try the pantry."

The hulking apprentice opened a narrow door in the end wall, which Lindsey had assumed belonged to a broom closet. The recess behind it contained shelves like those in a cook's pantry, stacked three deep with jars, bottles, square tins, squat canisters, and sacks of what looked like flour, stored in rows on the floor with their contents stenciled on the fronts. He wondered what use an undertaker had for mortar. Nuttle retrieved an amber bottle the size of an earthenware jug with a thumb handle near the mouth, shook it, and stood it on the counter. It sounded to be half full of liquid. He shut the pantry door and returned the alcohol to the cabinet.

Krauss tested a pump while Connable lifted the largest and most sinister-looking of the syringes and drew out the plunger, suctioning air through the hollow needle at the end. The noise was not unlike the sound that had issued from the dead man's insides when he was turned over. Lindsey shuddered at this fresh reminder. When Nuttle began pouring formaldehyde into a large enamel bowl, Connable put down the syringe and moved to his side, touching his elbow when he tilted the jug back upright.

"More."

Nuttle looked at Krauss, who shrugged. The apprentice resumed pouring. A strong, gaseous stench stung Lindsey's nostrils at a distance of ten paces. Krauss reached under one of the suspended cabinets and snapped a switch. Fan blades clattered, settled into a hum, and the fumes began crawling toward a tin plenum mounted beneath the cabinet. The air cleared.

"Enough," Connable said, and reached for the bottle marked GLYCERINE.

Lindsey found himself losing interest. Contact with the fumes, and twenty-four hours without sleep, caused his mind to drift from what had become a mundane operation after all. Even the corpse had become nothing more than another property in a room that had lost much of its mystery. He'd found more to divert him watching a photographer blending his chemicals under a red lamp, the images etching themselves on the glass plates as if by an unseen hand.

Connable clapped his palms together sharply, starting him out of a standing doze.

"Porter's duty again, gentlemen," he said. "Mr. Warrick is done on this side. A hand, please, Mr. Lindsey. Young Nuttle's the only one here who's stronger for the time elapsed."

CHAPTER 4

She couldn't see the lake through any of the windows in the house in Buffalo, but she felt its damp bite.

Richard, who on impulse would buy a gold-headed stick for himself or an imported lace shawl for her, was economical about coal and electricity, and no matter what caprice might bring the chill of Canada across the lake in midsummer, the furnace remained cold from the first of May to the first of October. Today the plaster was damp, and Lucy thought it odd that Richard might be feeling the effects of the same lake at this moment, in a place that was as foreign to her as the rice paddies in China. If she'd ever been to Cleveland, it was aboard the train while she slept. She couldn't picture it.

When she'd rested enough to climb the stairs, she put on the dress she wore most often these days when she went out, pale blue with a white ruffled collar. She owned two skirts and shirtwaists, which she'd bought on impulse the first time she saw them in a shop after reading about them in *Harper's,* but after wearing each once in public, she'd lain them to rest in the bottom drawer of the bureau where she kept her wedding dress. She had her mother's long waist and had constantly had to visit a water closet to tuck in the flapping ends. She'd had to face the fact she wasn't a twentieth-century girl. Which was just as well.

Buttoning the collar, she was horrified to learn that it left a gap of an inch between it and her neck. The effect in the mirror was of an old woman shriveling away inside her clothes. It had been just ten days since she'd worn the dress last; she hadn't realized she'd lost that much ground. She hadn't the energy to take off the dress, find her sewing basket, and move the buttons—not enough to do all that and then put the dress back on and still go out. Her most recent maid had given her notice three weeks ago, with no replacement in sight. Servants in Buffalo were by and large Irish, a superstitious race who'd sooner serve a Jew than go to work for an undertaker's wife. The colored were even more inclined in that direction, commonly crossing to the other side of the street while on their errands to avoid passing in front of the house. Richard had been forced to padlock the doors to the coal bin to discourage their bolder children from sneaking into the basement on All Hallows' Eve, looking for skeletons.

She rummaged through her jewelry case, found a pin attached to a tiny garnet, like a drop of pigeon's blood, and transfixed a fold in the collar, snugging it to her throat. Her hands shook, and she lowered herself to the chair in front of the dressing table to conserve strength. The mirror, an oval of beveled glass in a tiger-maple frame, showed a face that looked as if it had been drained of color by the red stone beneath the chin. She busied herself among the pots, jars, and atomizers on the table, painting life on her features the way she'd done so many times for the women and young girls who had passed through Richard's back room.

Suddenly she was weeping, her shoulders shaking, tears cutting channels through the powder and streaking her collar pink. She had to erase the face she'd painted, start all over again, and sponge at the stains with a handkerchief dipped in toilet water. She did all this with her head cocked to the right to the advantage of her good eye.

The result, when she'd dressed her hair, was matronly, but no longer ghastly, and after sitting five minutes with her eyes closed, she rose, pinned on the hat that went with the dress, and went out with her reticule wound around her wrist by its strap; a trick she'd learned in San Francisco to foil snatchers.

On the sidewalk she wobbled, and would have gone back for her parasol for its support had she not known that the effort would exhaust her reserves. Soon she would need a cane, and then there would be nothing for it but to tell Richard what was happening. For a man with his attention to detail, he was elephantiacally nonobservant, always seeing what he expected to see, nothing more or less. As much as she ached for his return, she feared it, for the clearer vision that came after even a brief absence. He would see, and be concerned, and ask questions, which to answer would be to make the thing real. The thought was a blow. She had to stop walking in order to concentrate on not collapsing. That emergency passed, she would have turned around and gone back into the house if the street-car hadn't come along at just that moment.

The tracks went right past the house, which was one of the things that had decided Richard and Lucy in favor of the site; after so many years in temporary towns built of unpainted clapboard on old Indian trails, they had selected Buffalo for its civilized comforts. The pace there was less frantic than in New York City—a place whose society Lucy hated—but lively enough to forestall the crippling ennui of prairie life, with the tantalizing promise of ice cream shops, separate clothing stores for men and women, restaurants, and theaters, all within five cents' journey from their doorstep. They'd had their sorrow even then, but also their health.

The driver, a middle-aged man with the battered face of a prizefighter under his patent-leather visor, pulled in the mule and didn't get up from his seat to help her aboard. He wasn't the regular man. When she'd pulled herself up the steps and dropped a nickel through the slot, she asked him what had happened to Jimmy.

"Gone to Alaska, just like everybody else. Come back with a tubful of gold and an Eskimo wife. There's room in back." He gave the reins a flip. She clutched at the seats as she made her way to the rear. None of the men aboard offered her his seat. That was one thing she missed about the old life, the courtesy shown by the lowest desert rat.

She almost missed her stop. She jumped awake, pulled at the bell, and was forced to endure the driver's drawn brows in the mirror mounted under the roof as she shambled toward the front of the car.

She walked the half-block to the one-story stucco building that sheltered Connable & Haight. There was a sign out front now, lettered tastefully in silver on black. At the beginning of the partnership, Richard had insisted that the building remain anonymous; rancor remained from having to hang a shingle beneath those of a succession of barbers and dentists, and in those days Buffalo was small enough, and Richard's reputation well enough known, to draw trade from the local wealthy and prominent from no advertising other than a single line in the city directory. To his credit, C.F. Haight had waited a discreet eighteen months after Richard's retirement before posting the sign. By then, a half-dozen similar establishments had appeared to serve those who hired broughams to follow hearses to cemeteries featuring sealed underground vaults and something called Perpetual Care, which usually meant a gardener to weed the plantings and chase away stray dogs and unsupervised children. Family visitations to tend the graves and eat picnic lunches ceased to exist almost overnight.

She used a wrought-iron railing to scale the three marble steps to the door, which jarred an overhead bell when she opened and closed it, and waited for someone to join her in the foyer, redecorated in velvet and brocade. A Certificate of Public Recognition, calligraphed in gold leaf and signed by a former mayor and a pastor of the Lutheran Church, hung in a polished walnut frame above the coatrack. She remembered the typhus nightmare, and Richard's charitable service to the relatives of the victims, that had inspired it. For four days he'd never left the building, working twenty hours at a stretch and sleeping on a cot in the morgue, and afterward had nearly died from bronchitis brought on by exhaustion. No one had offered Lucy a certificate for the week she'd gone without sleep, nursing him to avoid pneumonia. A faint squeeze of her hand from Richard when the fever broke had meant more to her, but they might have had the ceremony somewhere else than a gentlemen's club, where women were barred.

She felt faint, and her forehead was clammy, but she remained standing, supporting herself with one hand on the registration stand where books were spread open for the mourners to sign. She was afraid if she sat on the hickory bench she wouldn't be able to get up.

"May I help you?"

At first she failed to recognize the young man who'd come in through the curtained arch at the back. He was tall and deeply sunburned, with the suggestion of a moustache, and wore his dark gray cheviot suit buttoned snugly all the way to the cravat, military fashion. Then she smiled. "Charlie, is it you?"

"Charles Haight, Junior," he said; and then stiffness gave way to astonishment. "Mrs. Connable?"

"You have on long pants!" Her hand sped to her mouth. She hadn't laughed in so long the sound embarrassed her, as if she'd belched. "I read in the *Ledger* you were in the Philippines. I thought at the time, *He must have recovered from that skinned elbow.*"

He colored under his sunburn. "I've been back three weeks. Is Mr. Connable with you?"

"He's away. Working, actually. Not in competition with your father," she added quickly; wondering if she'd said too much already. She found she didn't care. Men and their sacred societies, their unspoken confidences and secret handshakes, had no hold on her. "Is he in?"

"He left for Albany yesterday. Clifford Johansen suffered an apoplectic seizure at the party convention. His widow engaged the firm to bring home his remains."

She had no idea who Clifford Johansen was, or what party he might attend. Politics were nothing more than the biggest fraternal order in the world, with tall hats instead of turbans, and exclusive only of women. She hadn't read a front page since Mr. Garfield's death. Richard's chief concern at that time had been whether to submit a bid for the arrangements.

"Oh, dear," she heard herself say, and stumbled against the registration stand. She had never said, "Oh, dear," before in her life.

Charlie strode forward and cupped her elbow. "Are you ill?"

"I just need to sit."

"The air in here is close." As indeed it was; that familiar oppressive concoction of wood oil, cut flowers, and dust overlooked in the swags. "Can you make it to the office? It's in the same room as always." He had an arm around her now, supporting her.

She nodded, and leaned on him as he swept the curtain aside with his free hand and walked with her down the short hallway to the mahogany door that still bore Richard's name lettered in gold. Dear, good Charles had not scratched it out nor covered it with a plaque bearing his own. She'd said nothing, but had not taken Richard's side in the estrangement that had changed them from friends to polite acquaintances, coolly touching their hats when they met on the street.

On the way, she and Charlie passed another arch belonging to a second viewing room separate from the original parlor off the foyer. It was where they'd kept the folding chairs before. Business was good. But then, how could it fall off?

"May I bring you a glass of water?"

She was seated now, in a tufted leather chair facing a desk bare but for an immaculate green blotter and C.F. HAIGHT engraved on a marble trivet. The walls were paneled in cherrywood and hung with pastels, of meadows and ponds and Alpine landscapes, soothing to the eye and healing to the heart, however temporarily. In Richard's time there had been shelves of Browning and Tennyson with gilded spines, selected for the same purpose. It was as difficult as ever to distinguish at what point professional compassion became set dressing.

She was aware of young Charlie bent over her, holding her wrist with a thumb on her pulse, concentration on his face. Had he done this same thing in some ruined canebrake, waiting with a wounded brother soldier for an orderly to come in answer to his cry? Was this the same face, pale and half-hidden behind his mother's skirts (poor, dead Madeleine, eight years since she lay in the front parlor) the day a precedent broke and the partners' families mingled for the first time? Lucy hadn't realized they had a past here.

"Mrs. Connable?"

He'd asked if she wanted water.

"Have you tea?" Immediately she regretted asking. She wasn't in a restaurant.

"I have some brewing, as a matter of fact. I'm expecting a client this afternoon."

Smiling, he patted her hand and went out. Evidently the function of her heart had reassured him. Its sudden stop was what he'd feared. Where he'd been, there were no long tedious downward vortexes. He'd been to war and thought he knew death.

She closed her eyes. When she opened them he was coming through the door, balancing a steaming cup on its saucer. Connable & Haight was still using the pattern she'd chosen, a gold stripe on translucent white porcelain. It bore no resemblance to the cold shining fixtures in the back room. The sight revived her to some extent.

The lemon was too strong, but the aroma of the brew was bracing. How hard it had been to come by in so many places, and how wonderful the taste when she'd managed to find it, whether drunk from English bone china (Tucson, of all places) or battered tin (Creede, Billings, stagecoach stops without number). She warmed her hands around the cup and smiled up at the mask of concern that was Charles Junior's face.

"Thank you. I haven't been well."

It amazed her to discover how easy it was to make this confession to this young man she'd known better as a child, but could not be said to have known at all. They hadn't been together in the same room since his mother's services.

"Do you need a doctor?"

"Certainly not. The air was chilly earlier, and I over-dressed for the season. Old women will, from time to time." And so she'd turned it into a lie at the finish.

Charlie's smile was relieved. "You're not old. You're one of Buffalo's great beauties."

"Have you seen the competition?"

He laughed, surprised, and looked embarrassed after-ward. There were no signs about the place reading UNSEEMLY AMUSEMENT IS PROHIBITED, but there might as well have been. None of Shakespeare's rakish grave dig-gers need apply for a position with Connable & Haight. He circled behind the desk and sat down. His eyebrows arched in polite invitation.

She sipped her tea. It was the right amount of lemon after all. Lately, everything seemed to be amplified to an unpleasant level. The first touch of her softest flannel nightdress made her skin recoil, and she could no longer bear the music coming from her own gramophone. Fresh asparagus, a smell she'd adored and had missed in the desert, nauseated her. Life seemed to be withdrawing from her instead of the other way around.

She set the cup in its saucer with a click. "So. You've come home to work with your father?"

"For the practical experience. After graduation, I'm moving to California and opening a parlor in Los Angeles. It's become an important citrus-growing center since they completed the railroad to San Francisco. The population has more than doubled in ten years."

"You're going to college?"

"I've enrolled in a course in mortuary science at New York University. The term begins in September."

"What can they teach you there that your father can't?"

"Modern techniques. I'm counting on the diploma to attract the right trade. One doesn't start out with a certificate of public recognition."

"I suppose you'll call yourself a mortician."

"*Funeral director* is the preferred title now. We're trying to get death out of the commercial end."

"And how do you propose to do that?"

He shifted his weight in his seat; his father's seat, which appeared to fit him poorly. "Not all of the details belong in polite conversation."

Charlie had become a prig. Well, he'd come into it honestly, although Charles Senior had been aware of the tendency in himself and had fought against it. Perhaps the war had brought it out. She'd never known killing to build character, no matter what that old fraud Buffalo Bill had said in Denver.

"I'm not a civilian you need to cosset," she said. "I've washed and painted corpses—*clients,* Richard called them; never the survivors. Maybe that was the start of all this pussyfooting new language, but he's always been proud to call himself an undertaker. So was your father, at least at the start. There's death in the thing from one end to the other. You can't hang paintings and drapery and pretend you're selling real property. No one ever built a house on six feet of dirt."

"I didn't intend to upset you."

He looked alarmed. She supposed she presented a horror when she was angry. The skull would show. She sat back then, more drained than the trip had left her. She wished she'd thought to send round a message to find out if Charles was there. But he wasn't, and Richard would be home in a few hours. She didn't know when he'd be out of the house again, or if she'd have the strength to repeat the journey. She drank some more tea, but it was growing cold. She leaned forward and set the cup and saucer on the edge of the desk. "I've come to make arrangements."

Concern came back, chasing away his fright. She couldn't tell if it was sincere or automatic. "Is it Mr. Connable?"

"No, Charlie, it isn't. I want to see the book. I assume funeral directors have a book the same as undertakers and morticians. Or must I order my coffin from Sears and Roebuck?"

atgut," Connable suggested.

Uter Krauss opened a shallow drawer in a yellow oak cabinet built beneath a counter, drew out a wooden spool wound around with shiny, transparent membrane that looked like fishing line, and held it up.

"Heavier. The stitches must hold. The yard engines in Chicago don't care what they bang about when they switch tracks."

Krauss traded the spool for another. "I generally reserve this for closing the cavity. It's too coarse for finish work."

"The moustache will conceal it."

The owner of the parlor beckoned to young Nuttle, who took the spool, along with a crescent-shaped needle, longer and thinner than any Gordon Lindsey had ever seen. With surprising deftness, the apprentice's meaty fingers threaded the needle, made a loop, cut it free with a pair of short-bladed scissors he took from a pocket in his apron, and knotted the ends. Connable accepted needle and thread and bent over Elihu Warrick. Lindsey watched closely as he stitched shut the dead man's mouth, directing the needle through the gums, beneath the upper lip, and out the left nostril. He tied off the end of the thread, cut it with surgical scissors, and returned the needle and spool to Nuttle, who put them back in the drawer.

Embalming came next, a purely mechanical process involving one of the pumps from the counter. Nuttle blew through a coil of rubber tubing, fitted one end to a nipple at the base of the pump, which he had set on the floor, and submerged the other end in the bowl he'd filled with glycerine, formaldehyde, and a tiny amount—the secretary would have described it as a jiggerful—of borax. The recipe appeared to be Connable's own, and had astonished Krauss, who confessed to a preference for more borax and less glycerine; the latter, it seemed, was more expensive.

"To whom?" the visitor had replied. "He'll have trouble enough getting that belly through the eye of the needle, biblically speaking."

"As you say. I myself am not a Socialist."

"Mr. Warrick is no longer a capitalist. He's joined the masses."

Krauss glanced at Lindsey, then leaned close and whispered in Connable's ear.

The latter shook his head. "We're not profiteering. Glycerine restores flexibility to the skin. Formaldehyde is the more reliable preservative. Borax is a binding agent, nothing more. Mr. Lindsey, I'll put that in writing for our friend in New York, in case you don't remember it."

"I'm satisfied," Lindsey said.

Connable made an incision in the left side of Warrick's neck.

"The heart feeds blood through the arteries to the other organs, which then expel it through the veins." He was addressing Lindsey as if he were a medical student in an operating theater. "All the impurities are filtered through the liver. You might want to remember that the next time a waiter in Delmonico's serves you pâté."

"Or perhaps not." Krauss was amused.

"Therefore, we drain blood from the veins and introduce the embalming agent through the arteries." Connable inserted a thin nozzle at the end of a tube attached to the top of the pump. "Any officer who directs traffic in Manhattan could explain why."

He stood back while Nuttle seized the pump's handle and slid it up and down rhythmically, slurping fluid from the bowl when he drew up and exhaling it into the artery when he pushed down, Connable holding the nozzle in place. The tubes flexed like snakes as the stuff coursed through them. Connable watched Warrick's face closely throughout the procedure. Lindsey looked—and thought he saw the beginnings of a glow of health. Connable held up a hand. Nuttle stopped pumping.

Krauss, assisting, pressed a thumb to the spot where the nozzle was extracted while Nuttle opened a flat can labeled BRIGHT'S PARAFFIN WAX and Connable scraped up a tiny portion of its contents with a fingernail. He rolled the portion between thumb and forefinger. Krauss withdrew his thumb and Connable smeared the spot. He inspected the bullet hole in the temple, then applied paraffin there as well. Lindsey thought of a bicycle tire being patched.

Connable retrieved his scalpel and bent over Warrick's groin. He flicked the fingers of his free hand against the inside of a fat column of thigh, like a carpenter looking for a stud, then cut a slit with the scalpel and inserted the nozzle. Nuttle resumed pumping. This part of the procedure took longer—twenty minutes, by the secretary's watch—at the end of which the bowl was nearly empty. The nozzle was withdrawn, paraffin applied, and Nuttle dismantled the tubes and returned them and the pump to the counter.

The apprentice had washed the wicked-looking knife in the sink, rinsed it, handle and all, with alcohol, and wiped it dry with a cotton cloth. Without waiting for instructions, he gave the knife to Connable, who used it to extend Krauss's original incision to a point three inches below Warrick's navel.

"Trocar, please, Doctor." He slid the knife into its basin.

Krauss handed him the Brobdingnagian syringe and switched on the ventilator fan; not in time to prevent an odor of foul ferment from reaching Lindsey's nostrils. The secretary took a step back and pressed his handkerchief to his nose and mouth while Connable probed the cavity at various angles with the syringe, drawing the plunger out and filling the metal tube with the contents of Warrick's stomach and entrails and depositing them in a fresh bowl, which Nuttle had positioned under the fan.

"Excuse me—" Lindsey's mouth filled with bile, interrupting the urgent request.

"Through there." Krauss, who had been watching him, indicated a door in the wall adjoining the pantry. Lindsey found the water closet there, just in time.

After pulling the chain, he ran water into the tiny sink and bent to splash it onto his face. He dried off with a thin towel and looked at his reflection, pale as Warrick's face, in the mirror above the basin. "Sons of bitches." He wet his comb and tended to his hair and side-whiskers.

Hearing the toilet flush, Nuttle chuckled over the mortar he was mixing with a wooden spatula. He used the same bowl that had contained the embalming fluid. Krauss told him to be quiet.

"Harsh medicine, Mr. Connable. Was it necessary?"

"It was his choice. Or rather his employer's." He smeared Warrick's face with petroleum jelly; chemical leakage raised blisters on untreated dead skin, requiring trimming, additional cosmetics, and delay.

"You might have prepared him."

"Millionaires always think you're cheating them. The self-made ones all fancy they could do the job themselves if they had time. I'm counting on Lindsey to provide a detailed report."

When the secretary came out, gray-faced but steady on his feet, Nuttle was holding the bowl while Connable ladled mortar into the empty cavity with a wooden scoop. He asked Lindsey how he was feeling.

"Well enough, thank you." His voice was tense. "Won't that make him too heavy to carry?"

"Some years ago I invented a new composition, involving cellulose and nitrate, which is much lighter; but I was jealous and kept it from the rest of the trade, so Krauss hasn't the ingredients. This mixture is too soupy ever to set. The consistency is close to the natural. It's heavy enough to remind the pallbearers they're carrying a substantial citizen. Not so heavy they'll drop him on the church steps."

"Still, there is no predicting an amateur's lack of grace," Krauss said. "We had a scandal when a pallbearer did just that. The casket split and the cadaver spilled out, along with several back numbers of the *Plain Dealer*. It was made of newspapers and paste and heavily varnished. Not one of ours," he added quickly.

"I'd venture to guess whose. We'll need another batch," Connable told Nuttle. "I doubt Mr. Warrick missed a course in his adult life."

Lindsey said, "The last time he dined with our friend in New York, he started off with a whole shepherd's pie. I understand the servants are still talking about it."

Connable grunted. "He was the vintner's friend as well. I examined his liver while you were out of the room. It's as shriveled as an orange. That bullet cheated him out of six months at the outside. Have a look."

"I thought cirrhosis enlarged the liver." Lindsey kept his distance from the basin.

"Not in the late stage. The spleen was enlarged, and the legs retained water. I saw quite a bit of that in Barbary;

Nob Hill is only a generation removed from the bagnios on Pacific Street. The swelling is why I inspected him for jaundice. It doesn't always occur. It didn't in this case."

"Was he in pain?"

"Not my area. Doctor?" Connable returned the scoop to the empty mortar bowl. Nuttle took it away to mix more.

"His discomfort would have been considerable," Krauss said. "Gastric pain, severe indigestion, vomiting."

"Loss of appetite?" Lindsey was staring at Warrick's belly.

"The distention is dropsical, not a matter of overfeeding. The contents of the stomach were bilious. He hadn't eaten solid food in at least twenty-four hours. Pain? Yes, definitely. No more shepherd's pies."

"Did he know he was dying?"

"How could he not?"

"I'll ask his physician. Our friend would be relieved if Warrick's suicide had nothing to do with money or women. It would make this whole episode unnecessary."

Connable wiped his hands on his apron. "That's why I brought it up. Please tell our friend if he'll compensate me for my time and Dr. Krauss for his and the use of his parlor, our work is finished. No bonus required."

"You can't just leave him like that."

"Certainly not," Krauss said. "I'm not running an emporium. I cannot have inventory piling up in the back room. You must make arrangements."

Lindsey looked at his watch. He snapped shut the face.

"Proceed, please, gentlemen. The market's a woman. You can't shake it loose from its first impression with logic. If Warrick's doctor confirms he was dying from cirrhosis, it shouldn't be difficult to persuade him to sign a death certificate to that effect."

"That's your decision," Connable said. "In any case, I didn't hear it. I was concentrating on my work."

Krauss said, "I, too, was distracted."

Nuttle, mixing mortar, said nothing.

"No one will ask." Lindsey pocketed his watch. "This makes it absolutely crucial his body appear unblemished."

"It will be," Connable said. "There is no appearing about it."

Nuttle used the toilet in the water closet to dispose of the offal from Warrick's insides. Lindsey was grateful he hadn't known of this use for the receptacle when he was kneeling in front of it. When the apprentice finished cleaning up, Krauss sent him to a laundry to have Elihu Warrick's suit pressed and his shirt and stockings laundered. His underwear, soiled beyond reclamation, had gone into the trash barrel behind the building.

"Tell them one hour," Krauss said. "Accept no excuses."

When Nuttle left, carrying his bundle, Lindsey observed that the parlor must be one of the laundry's biggest customers.

"I'm a distant fourth, behind three of the most popular restaurants in town. However, I am a Freemason, as was Mr. Warrick—the monogram on his waistcoat is unmistakable—and so are the owners of two of the restaurants. The third is a Jew. The laundry will cooperate."

As he spoke, Krauss threaded a needle, straight and stouter than the curved one used earlier, and handed it to Connable, who proceeded to stitch shut the body cavity.

Lindsey said, "When you told me you were going to pull him apart and put him back together, I thought you were speaking figuratively."

"The man I apprenticed to would think it vastly incomplete." Connable's fingers flew; the secretary thought he would have made an admirable tailor. "No trepanning, no evisceration. In another twenty years, I suppose, we won't cut into them at all, just run some sort of hose up the ass and pump them full of Cream of Wheat. If I'm any judge, Old Man Millard guts them like a fish, paints the insides with tar, and dumps the scraps in the lake along with the remains of his supper. Then he charges the survivors for all that gear on his shelves he hasn't used in years. It's a short enough hop from there to wrapping them in newspapers. Am I right, Doctor?"

"I'd rather not say."

"Quite right. If the Knights of Columbus take back Cleveland Heights, you might wind up on Millard's bench someday. Any of us might. If it gets back to him or his sons you've been gossiping about him, he'll slip an empty box into your grave and sell you to a medical school."

"If what you predicted comes to pass, I might end up in a museum instead, in a glass case next to a stuffed fox. We buried my grandfather in Baden, in a cedar box, at his request. No embalming was done. He said he wanted to return to the soil as soon as possible. Which is the more honorable fate?"

"An odd philosophy, coming from an undertaker." Connable finished stitching. He tied off the thread and snipped the rest free.

"What about you, Mr. Connable?" Krauss asked. "What plans have you made for your immortal rest?"

"To be honest with you, I've never given it a thought."

Lindsey watched as the two men spread a sheet over Warrick's body from head to toe. "What are you doing?"

"A gesture of respect," said Krauss. "I didn't know the gentleman, but I assume he wasn't in the habit of spending his idle hours lying about naked. He wasn't an anarchist."

"But you haven't made him presentable."

Connable wiped his hands on his apron. "The tissues need time to absorb the fluids. Otherwise it's like painting a wet canvas. When it dries, the pigment cracks."

"How much time does it take?"

Krauss said, "Eight hours."

Something struck Lindsey's tender stomach from inside. "The last train to Chicago leaves in five!"

"Two hours," Connable said. "We need that much time to dress him, anyway. We don't want to smear him manhandling him into his coat."

Krauss shook his head like a Prussian bull. "Six is a gamble. If you rush it beyond that, I won't be responsible."

"I will be. That's another reason I favor formaldehyde over methylal. It works faster."

"This is a craft, not an industry. We're not manufacturing ladies' hats for Montgomery Ward."

"Two hours. He may need touching up before he meets his public. I recommend Frank Small, at Craidlaw's in Chicago. I trained him."

Lindsey said, "Our friend would feel more at ease if you made the trip with Warrick and touched him up yourself."

"No."

"Naturally, your fee will be adjusted."

"No, Mr. Lindsey."

Nuttle returned, reporting that the laundry had promised results within the hour. Connable and Krauss spent much of that time in front of an open cabinet, taking chemicals off shelves and arguing about their various properties. Lindsey sat on a stool, and was addressed only when he put a cigar between his lips and struck a match. All three men shouted at him to put it out. It seemed most of the agents involved in preserving dead tissues were highly volatile. He extinguished the flame and chewed the end of the cigar for the nicotine.

Warrick's black suit and white dress shirt were delivered on hangers—to the foyer, evidently by a messenger who would come no nearer than that to the rear of the establishment. Nuttle brought them back, and Lindsey watched as the three men made ready to dress Warrick in the splendor in which he'd expired. Connable turned to the secretary with the freshly pressed trousers in hand. "You may want to take some air."

"Why?"

Krauss said, "Rigor is still present. In order to put him into position, it will be necessary to break his arms." He took a crowbar from a drawer and handed it to Nuttle.

Lindsey accepted the invitation. His cigar came from John C. Broughty's private stock, and took an hour to smoke. By that time he'd become familiar with the comings and goings in the busy neighborhood at that hour. There was a saloon on one corner, with a side entrance for ladies, and two doors down from it an ice-cream parlor, as white and shining as Krauss's back room. The houses were gimcracked and painted recently, one out of three equipped with its own carriage house. The neighborhood did not seem to belong to the same city where Millard & Sons practiced; but then Uter Krauss did not seem to belong to the same profession, and Richard Connable was as a visitor from the Holy See. He was sorry the man wasn't more likeable.

He paused once on the sidewalk to listen to the chugging of a train. Krauss's was a mile from the nearest track. After a long interval, a bonneted vehicle turned the corner and the operator, dustered to the ankles and gauntleted to the elbows, guided the shuddering piece of machinery up the street. He touched his visor as he passed the pedestrian. Cleveland was not so far behind New York City.

He returned to the parlor and found Connable, Krauss, and Nuttle hard at valet duty. A pine plank lay the length of the trough with Warrick stretched fully dressed upon it, wooden clamps holding his feet and head in place. Nuttle coaxed a liquid shine from the millionaire's patent leathers with a horsehair brush while Krauss shaped the nails of his folded hands, plump and pink, with a file and Connable brushed his hair and pointed the tips of his moustache with paraffin. Warrick's face appeared flushed, as it had in life, and the portion of lower lip that showed where the moustache was parted glistened with moisture. The whites of his eyes glistened also beneath his lowered lashes. He truly appeared to be in the midst of awakening from sleep.

Lindsey walked around to the other side. He thought he'd become confused about the location of the bullet hole.

"The right." Connable tweezed a stray eyebrow hair and cast it to the floor.

Lindsey returned to that side and bent close. He saw only uninterrupted skin.

"Common cheesecloth," Connable said. "It reproduces pores more faithfully than anything in the catalogue."

"It's remarkable."

"Rubbish. I've always found my wife's work more satisfactory. There's something wrong with the lip."

"It's sorcery."

Krauss, straightening, stepped back to inspect the corpse from head to foot. Then he stepped forward and shook Richard Connable's hand. Lindsey was astonished. There were tears in the Austrian's eyes.

II

The Undertaker's Son

And Joseph commanded his servants
the physicians to embalm his father;
and the physicians embalmed
Israel.

—Genesis 50:2

CHAPTER 6

She would always consider herself a twin, with one tender side, as if a wall had collapsed suddenly, exposing it to the elements. And with that tenderness came a sense of shame, because she had been born eight minutes ahead of Luke and had failed to protect him as an older sister should.

Apart from sharing the same birthday, they were as different as different came. Their mother was descended from the French who founded Monroe, Michigan, their father English; and while Lucy banked her emotions in true Anglo-Saxon fashion, her brother was quick to feel a slight, and as quick to protest it, exploding in volcanic rage, his color high and his dark brown eyes on fire. When in third grade he'd leapt on the back of a classmate twice his size over some disagreement, it was Lucy who'd come to his rescue, swinging her schoolbooks by their strap and dazing the larger boy long enough for Luke to take to his heels and flee retaliation. Later she received without expression his shrill complaint that she'd humiliated him before the male half of the school. Alone in her bed, she'd cried all night.

But she hadn't been present to prevent Luke from lying about his age and joining the First Michigan Infantry just weeks after the Confederacy fired on Fort Sumter, or to warn him away from the ammunition shack the first day of training at Fort Wayne in Detroit, when a stray spark from a chimney set off the powder inside, obliterating the shack and driving a splinter of door the length and shape of a bayonet through his skull as he was walking past. No medals of valor accompanied the plain box in which his remains were sent home, and the letter of condolence from the War Department was reserved; it was no hero's end to blunt the pain.

Lucy's mother, never a well woman, took to her bed. Her father, a pharmacist, treated her mother with alkali and tonics and refused to go to the train station to accept the body. He'd maintained neutrality in the war, which he considered a scheme by the government in Washington to seize control of the cotton trade in the South, and blamed Luke's betrayal for his mother's misery. Concern for his wife's condition had for years taken precedence over his patriarchal responsibilities. The errand fell to seventeen-year-old Lucy.

A porter directed her to the baggage room, where a clerk read the tag attached to a box made of reinforced pine, scarcely distinguishable from a number of crates stenciled with the names of farm-equipment manufacturers, and took her into a tiny office to sign the certificate of receipt.

"Where you want him took, miss?" He rocked a blotter over her signature and filed the paper in a box on the desk.

"I don't—home," she said. It was some disjointed dream. Luke had turned into a box and she was telling the man where to deliver it.

The clerk looked embarrassed. He was a bald New Englander with a mariner's beard that encircled his otherwise clean-shaven face and shallow dents all over his shiny scalp, as if it were made of hammered tin.

"They don't—I mean to say, miss, there's no *restora-*

tion. You need an undertaker before you open him to view, and that's no proper coffin he's in."

"I don't know any undertakers."

He rummaged among a pile of papers and telegraph flimsies, uncovered another file box, and thumbed through the cards and receipts inside. He handed her a white pasteboard.

"This here's the fellow comes through the most. Lots of folks in Detroit use him instead of the locals. He's a fine man, miss. Very clean." His own broken nails were stained black and one side of his face was smeared with dust.

The card was engraved on heavy stock, bordered in black:

JANUS R. CONNABLE
Obsequies
79 Monroe St.   Monroe, Mich.

She slid her thumb over *Obsequies,* hand-lettered in copperplate and raised slightly above the surface. She recognized the name from the sign in front of a brick house on the route to church.

"Thank you." She put the card in her reticule, drew it shut, then reopened it hastily and retrieved a twenty-five-cent piece from the interior.

He stopped her with a palm. "That's unnecessary, miss. Do you need a cab?"

She preferred to walk. He gave her a claim ticket—it was marked BAGGAGE—and she went out without looking again at the box.

Restoration. Yes, she supposed restoration was what was required. Her mother had sent out a sideboard to be restored, a family heirloom built by hand by a craftsman in Marseilles. It had come back with no chips in the marble serving surface and its shattered leg replaced with one that was a shade lighter than the others. She would have her brother restored.

The house was square and solid, and despite some modernization—particularly the enlargement of windows originally designed to shutter easily during Indian attacks—still bore signs of having been built to sustain a siege. The slate roof would repel burning pitch hurled to drive the occupants into the open, and there were no old-growth trees from which an invader might gain access to the second story. But the iron fence that encircled the lot was strictly ornamental, the scrollwork gate oiled recently so that the hinges turned on their pins without a whisper. A small sign mounted on the wall next to the door advised visitors to KNOCK THEN ENTER. She raised and lowered the small bronze knocker twice, then turned the knob.

The foyer was large and open, not at all oppressive, with a varnished oak staircase leading to the upper floor. Sunlight flooded in cheerily through unshaded windows. It was her first visit to a funeral parlor, and it answered to none of her preconceived notions about what a house of death would look like. She wondered if she'd entered someone's house by mistake.

She'd been standing there less than a minute when a man approached her, following a runner extending to the back of the house. He was forty, erect, slim-waisted, and dressed somewhat behind the fashion in a black coat with velvet facings and a swallowtail over close-fitting trousers, almost like breeches in their effect. He wore a high collar and a black silk stock, and Lucy thought she had never seen a man with a face so gentle. His eyes were pale beneath brows that slanted up from his temples and he wore no whiskers of any kind. He was, as the baggage clerk had said, very clean.

"Good afternoon, miss. Are you with the family?"

She almost said, "Yes." The man's voice, in the middle register, was so reassuring, and his tone so understanding, that for a moment she thought he must know what family she was with.

"I'm—my brother's at the train station," she said. "The man gave me your card." She fumbled it out and proffered it as if it were a ticket she needed to enter.

He accepted it, read it as if it were someone else's card, handed it back. He lowered his head. "My name is Janus Connable. This is my establishment. Miss—?"

"Brookside. My brother's name is Luke. They have him in baggage."

His expression changed. She saw her own pain reflected in his face. "Please come in and sit down." He tilted a hand in the direction from which he'd come.

"We're hosting a visitation this evening." He escorted her past a pair of pocket doors that seemed to belong to a drawing room. "The family has asked that no one be admitted until they arrive. Please forgive me if I seemed rude."

"Of course. I mean, you weren't."

"I'm very sorry about your brother. He must have been young."

"We're twins."

His silence said much.

The room, at the back of the house, was very much like a parlor in someone's home; she had the impression it was not the room to which mourners were generally admitted. Some time would pass before she learned this was the intended effect. There was a rug, a piano, and lithographed prints leaning out from papered walls, uniformly faded in the strong sunlight streaming through the west windows. He drew a shade without appreciably darkening the room and asked if she would like water or tea. She declined. They sat facing each other in tapestry chairs worn threadbare on the arms.

"Was your brother in the army?"

"Yes."

"He's our first," he said. "We expect more soon. The news from Virginia is bad."

"He never got to Virginia." She told him what had happened. At the end he rose and offered her his handkerchief. She accepted it with a nod. She couldn't speak.

He stood near the window and waited until she was quiet. "I must ask you your preference in the matter of lying in state. I'm afraid it's a question of whether you wish family and friends to remember him as he was in life."

"I don't care about the others. I want to say good-bye to my brother. I won't do it through a box."

"There is expense involved. Would you rather I spoke with your father?"

She unclasped the brooch she wore atop her collar. It was fashioned of ivory and set in silver. "This cameo was a present from my grandmother. I was told it belonged to a countess in the court of Louis the Sixteenth of France. Will it be enough?"

He took his hands from behind his back and let her lay it in his palm. "I'll give you a receipt before you leave. We can discuss details now, if you like."

"Please send someone to the station. I can't stand thinking of him in baggage."

"Please excuse me." He left the room. She heard stairs creaking overhead, and heard them again moments later, this time under the combined tread of two pairs of feet.

"Miss Brookside, my son, Richard. Richard Connable— I'm sorry, I haven't your Christian name."

"Lucy."

"Miss Brookside."

She'd wiped her eyes and blown her nose, drawn a shuddering breath to collect herself. She gave her hand to the young man, who touched his fingertips to hers and bowed from the waist. He was shorter than his father by an inch and built more solidly, almost along the lines of the house. His trousers were cut loosely in the modern fashion and he wore a frock coat, but as to neckware he followed his father's quaint example, with a silk scarf—what used to be called a stock—wound around a high collar. He had dark curly hair, burnsides trimmed square at the corners of his jaw, and fine gray eyes. She thought him handsome, but his manner less warm than Janus Connable's. He seemed to be searching her face for flaws. That made her lower her eyes and turn her head away, for she had many.

"I'm sending Richard to the station. He's made great progress in the area of facial reconstruction, and will tell us if it's recommended. Did they give you a ticket?"

She handed it to the young man, who bowed again and left. His father glanced at a nickel-plated watch and returned it to his coat. She'd noticed there were no clocks. "The examination will take time, and I'm afraid we have that visitation. Can you return tomorrow morning, and will you bring your father?"

"My father is with my mother, who's ill. But I will be here." She stood.

"Thank you for selecting us, Miss Brookside. We'll do our very best."

Late that evening, the bell rang at the front door. Lucy, in her nightdress, was in Luke's room, sewing a button onto the suit he'd worn to church; she didn't know what condition his uniform was in, or if burying him in it would upset her father further. The light under her parents' door had been out for hours. She pulled on a shawl and carried a candle downstairs. Pulling the curtain aside from the front window, she saw Richard Connable standing on the porch. He had on the suit he'd worn earlier, with an absurd tall hat tucked under his right arm. She opened the door six inches.

"I'm sorry to call so late," he said. "I found your address in the directory."

"Your father asked me to come in tomorrow morning."

"I realize that. I'd like to get started tonight."

"What's preventing you?"

He looked embarrassed for the first time. It softened her opinion of him a little. There was a stiff arrogance about this young man—hardly a man; she judged him to be only a year or two older than she—that reminded her of Luke's less personable side.

"I'd hoped you might have a likeness of your brother. A daguerreotype or a photograph. It would help to have a model from life."

His expression was doubtful. Families that could afford photographic portraits lived in houses less modest. She was offended. She asked him to wait and closed the door, turning the lock with a sharp snap.

She went to the parlor and took from the wall the photograph her parents had had framed of her cousin April's wedding party, taken the previous summer. They had all had to stand very still while the photographer, a tiny Greek with nervous hands, set fire to his heap of powder and clacked the shutter. April and her fat doctor looked like stuffed animals, April's parents smug, and Lucy's mother and father uncomfortable and pale, but Luke was striking in the suit she was mending for him upstairs, with his chin raised and his brows arched. Lucy herself looked pudding-faced and gawkish in her ridiculous ruffles. It was a faithful reproduction.

She lit a lamp from the candle and opened the door wide to shine it on the photograph. She pointed out her brother. "It's a good likeness," she said. "Though I wish he'd smiled."

"People rarely do in pictures. The result is usually unfortunate. Thank you. You don't know how much help this will be."

Once again she was forced to adjust her impression. Richard Connable was a study in contrasts.

"Your father seemed doubtful when I told him what had happened. Is it possible? Can you—restore him?"

"It's too early to tell. Good evening, Miss Brookside." He juggled the framed photograph under one arm, put on the laughable hat, and tipped it. When he turned away, he looked for all the world like an overstuffed scarecrow.

The following morning, Janus Connable received her in his courtly fashion and conducted her to the room with the pocket doors, which had been drawn aside. Nothing in his manner suggested either satisfaction or dejection.

The room showed no signs of the visitation that had taken place there the previous evening. It was wainscoted, with heavy curtains over the windows and a thick rug that muffled the stirring of the boards beneath her feet. Luke lay in a rosewood coffin with a white satin lining, his head and shoulders elevated slightly and his hands folded in white cotton gloves on the front of the blue military blouse she had not been privileged to see him wearing before. His fair hair was parted on one side the way he preferred, and he seemed to be smiling at some private joke. How often she'd been irritated by that smile, and in a flash she realized how much she had missed it. Now she would always have it.

The proprietor withdrew before the first tear, not to reappear until she had wiped away the last.

"It's he." She could barely hear herself. "I'd thought there might have been a mistake."

Janus Connable said nothing. He stood behind her and

to one side, his own hands folded before him in gray cotton gloves.

"They were wrong about the injury," she said. "His face is unmarked."

"With your permission, I'll tell Richard you said that. It's a father's responsibility to keep his son from becoming prideful, but his talent is so much greater than mine it would be a sin to let it pass without comment."

She knew then what she'd heard was true. She'd known it when Richard had asked for Luke's photograph, but looking at his unblemished face she could not encompass the fact.

"Is he not here, so that I can tell him myself?"

"He's sleeping. He retired only an hour ago. He would let no one assist him all night."

"Will he be present at the visitation?"

"It's doubtful. He's—eccentric about his gifts. He'd rather avoid contact with the family than be forced to accept a compliment. We've had discussions about it, but I despair of improving his etiquette." He permitted himself a faint smile. "I have the misfortune of having reared an artist."

As the elder Connable had predicted, Richard did not attend the visitation. Lucy's mother collapsed in front of the coffin and her father took her home, leaving Lucy to greet the friends and cousins who came with kisses and whispered platitudes. After the burial, she returned the photograph to the family parlor, and forgot about Richard Connable during the year of mourning that followed.

Some three weeks after she packed her veils in moth powder, she accepted a girlfriend's invitation to attend a ball at a pavilion on Lake Erie to raise money for the Union Army, which was regrouping after the defeat at Fredericksburg. Her father disapproved strongly, but exhausted and aged beyond his years by concern for his wife, who would never regain even the tenuous health she'd known before the death of her son, he could put up no protest that would dissuade her. Lucy had grown sick of grief.

The event was subdued, as befitted a war that was now in its second year, with no clear victory in sight. The colors were not gay, the music was dirgeful, and the dancing decorous. Lucy spared herself the humiliation of an unfilled dance card by taking up a station near the refreshment table, where she could greet friends she hadn't seen in months.

"Good evening, Miss Brookside."

She knew who belonged to the voice before she turned; they were the very last words she had heard from him on the doorstep of her father's house. He wore the same suit, or one identical, but had traded the Byronic collar for a low one of rounded linen, and the fussy stock for a simple cravat of becoming gray satin that brought out the color in his fine eyes. She was surprised to see him; but not as surprised as she was to realize that she was glad.

He asked her to dance. She refused, for unspoken reasons that seemed to satisfy them both. She asked him if he'd come with his father.

"I came in his place. He supports the war against rebellion, but thinks it doesn't look well for an undertaker to advertise the fact."

"Are you not also an undertaker?"

"Not yet. According to my father."

They talked of the war. He had not been drafted yet, but in the event had foresworn his father from purchasing his release. They spoke of mutual acquaintances and the inadequacy of the musicians. Suddenly the evening was over; the revelers were donning their wraps and drifting toward their carriages. She asked the question that had been on her mind all evening.

"Wherever did you find Luke's smile? It was his; but it wasn't in the photograph."

His expression was sober. "I found it on his sister's face."

"I didn't smile that day."

"Oh, but you did. The moment my father introduced us. I remembered it."

She knew then they would marry.

CHAPTER 7

The ceremony took place in St. Patrick's Episcopal Church, three months after their reunion at the pavilion and within sight of Luke's grave in the churchyard. They engaged the little Greek to take the portrait, after which her parents left, with hearty handshakes for the bridegroom and Janus Connable from Lucy's father; no scandals adhered to her new family, and he'd been spared the burden of supporting her in her spinsterhood. This rally from her sickbed was her mother's last. She would die in the spring.

Janus's wedding present to Lucy was like him, proper and filled with kindness: her grandmother's cameo brooch, nestled in a velvet-lined rosewood box.

The couple spent a week in Detroit, staying at the National Hotel, strolling the riverfront, guarded heavily by federal troops anticipating Confederate invasion from Canada, attending military concerts in the open air of the Campus Martius downtown. Flags fluttered everywhere and mourning was the dominant fashion; Luke's old First Michigan had been badly used at Bull Run, and heavy losses at Fredericksburg had decimated the Twenty-Fourth. The atmosphere was somber. In later years Lucy would concentrate on remembering the wedding and forgetting the honeymoon. But she and Richard were contented with each other's company.

Janus Connable took charge of her mother's funeral. By then, Richard's name had come up in the lottery and he was serving in Maryland, and once again Lucy greeted all visitors, her father having become frail and forgetful. Shortly afterward, he mistakenly sold a purgative to a customer suffering from scabies, and closed the pharmacy. He put the family home on the market and moved in with Lucy in the house she and Richard had rented two streets over from the funeral parlor.

In Baltimore, Richard became gravely ill after eating fish. A waiter was arrested on suspicion of being a Copperhead, but he was released when evidence of poisoning failed to surface. The regimental surgeon concluded that a parasite was the culprit. When Richard was strong enough to travel, he was sent home by rail, and thus missed participating in the Battle of Gettysburg, where rebel grapeshot tore his regiment to pieces. Lucy fed him and gave him cold compresses for his fever and made periodic excursions outside to find her wandering father and bring him back home.

Richard was silent in later years about his military service, but in his fevered dreams he said much. The War Department, in a rare exhibition of empirical reasoning, had assigned him to a graves unit, where he'd hoped to secure funerary experience that in peacetime conditions would require years to obtain; but if she interpreted his mutterings accurately, the detail had been an endless round of shoveling shattered limbs and torsos into crates and loading them aboard boxcars. She formed the opinion that if the shipments had been withheld a week, and sent all at once on open cars through any major city, the public outcry would force both sides to sue for peace. More than ever she admired what Richard had accomplished in her brother's case. When three decades later the *U.S.S. Maine* blew up in Havana Harbor and Buffalo crowded the sidewalks to shout encouragement to its young men on parade, she cut back her social intercourse to an occasional game of cards at home with neighbors.

Richard recovered and went back to work in the parlor. Most of his "clients" were soldiers, and all too often they arrived in a condition that even he could not repair. Every service conducted with coffin closed was to him an admission of failure. He became irritable and roared at her for every little thing. Her first miscarriage occurred under these circumstances. He became contrite and begged her forgiveness. For a time after she returned from the hospital, he was gentle and understanding, and took over most of her father's care until her strength returned. But the corpses kept coming. A gin bottle took up residency in the sitting room; he would drink, say hateful, cutting things to her, and have no memory the next day of what he'd said. She went to her father-in-law for counsel. Janus Connable listened without interruption and promised to speak with him. She never knew what passed between them at the parlor, but the gin bottle disappeared that night, and would not return for many years and to a different house in a different city. The creature who had drunk so heavily from it never did.

In December 1864, the last winter of the war, Lucy's father wandered outside during a bitter night. Neither she nor Richard were aware he'd gone until a city policeman knocked on their door just before dawn. An old man had been found frozen to death in the Lake Shore rail yard. A label she had sewn inside her father's coat had led the officer to their address.

Richard scraped away the frostbitten skin, filled in the sunken cheeks with wads of paper torn from the *Monroe Evening News* (Janus Connable's cotton stores were depleted, with no more coming from the Southern plantations), bleached away the brown spots on his forehead and the backs of his hands with peroxide of hydrogen, and transformed his thin hair from strawy white to silken silver with a solution of antimony. He replaced the lost skin with wax, melted and mixed with vegetable dye, blending it with powder and rouge. In his morning coat, with a starched shirtboard disguising his hollow chest, the old man (he was scarcely fifty) looked as he had in the prime of his middle age. His friends, none of whom had visited him since he'd come to live with Lucy, all agreed that the misfortunes of his life had failed to leave their mark. Richard could not be absent, but remained out of earshot of these unintended compliments to his skill.

The immediate effect of her father's passing was to free Lucy from the imprisonment of her house. Although her mourning excluded her from public social functions, on those evenings when Richard was not engaged with clients she rode with him in their carriage through snowy streets and along the frozen shoreline, wrapped in robes and blankets and watching the low profiles of lake freighters, darker than the sky, crawling through the open water on the horizon, the plumes from their smokestacks blacking out the stars. They carried iron from the mines in the Upper Peninsula to foundries in Cleveland where it was made into cannons and bayonets, and Studebaker wagons assembled in Detroit from lumber milled up north to carry ammunition and wounded. The war was very much with them and always had been.

And then it wasn't. In April, Lucy and Richard and Janus Connable attended a service at St. Patrick's to give thanks for peace and hear the bells toll for a slain generation and the martyred President Lincoln. "Nearer, My God, to Thee" was not Lucy's favorite hymn, had not been since before she'd sung it for her brother and her mother and her father, and she would not acknowledge it as the song she shared with Richard before all others. She was pregnant again and would never sing it to her child.

Nor *for* him, if it turned out to be a boy. He would know war only through Homer and Virgil.

Her father-in-law was a frequent guest in their home. Long hours in his back room had drawn him thin and he'd increased his wine consumption in response to his rheumatism, but he clung to the gentle manners and mode of dress of the postcolonial period of his courtship—buried along with his wife, who'd died giving birth to Richard. Wine and his affection for Lucy tempered his natural reticence: When the son was absent, gone to the kitchen for another bottle or working late in the parlor, the father became candid in her presence.

"His genius is in aesthetics," he said, more than once. "He hasn't much patience with embalming, not with the traditional methods. Youth is always searching for a better way; better meaning faster. I'm sure there is one, but he's going about it all wrong. He thinks he'll find it in modern chemistry, that the answer will be revealed in the future, when in fact it's concealed in the past. The first Egyptians used something called the Balm of Gilead. It's lost to us now, but when the Nile delta blossomed with flora we shall never know, the embalmers of the pharaohs stumbled upon this elixir, or this compound, or this method, that preserved the body better than this wine. And it held for an age."

"I've seen pictures of mummies in books," she said. "They look like dried figs."

"In thirty centuries, you and I will look like dust. Stories on the walls of the tombs tell of grave robbers apprehended while prying the lids off hundred-year-old sarcophagi whose occupants appeared as if they'd been buried that morning. Their skin was pliant to the touch." He refilled his glass. "Embalmers in those days were regarded on a level with the high priests. We've fallen from grace, and so shall we remain until one of us rediscovers the Balm of Gilead."

She smiled. "Perhaps Richard will be that one."

"Poor Richard. He lacks grace. I would no sooner leave him alone with a bereaved family than I would cage a crow and expect it to sing. I beg your forgiveness, Lucy. I forget he's your husband, and no longer mine to bear witness against." His kind face saddened. "What's your opinion of his decision to leave the parlor?"

She felt a chill in her stomach; she thought of the baby. Janus did not usually drink so much that he confused his ancient fables with current reality.

He read her thoughts. "He hasn't discussed it with you. I spoke outside my place." He was mortified.

"Richard and I have no secrets," she lied. "How much has he told you?"

He appeared relieved. "Only of his plans to go West and bring the wonders of nineteenth-century mortuary practice to the savages."

"Indians?" Her hand crept to her abdomen.

"Not *those* savages. I've read fearsome stories in the telegraph columns about the brigands of Barbary."

"Where is Barbary?"

"San Francisco." He was silent for a moment. Then he shook his head. "My concern isn't for myself. I shall hire an apprentice, and they tell me there will be a train all the way across the continent before the end of the decade, which even an old man may ride to visit his grandchildren. However, it is no city in which to have a child."

Richard was furious, and for the first time it had nothing to do with overwork or drink.

"That old meddler. I went to him for advice, to ask if he knew of any partnerships available in San Francisco. I swore him to secrecy."

"He remembered no such oath," she said.

"He's lost his resistance to spirits. It's a wonder he can find his way back to the parlor."

"When were you going to tell me we were moving West?"

"We aren't. Not you. Not right away. This is no time for you to travel. I was thinking of going out there in September, to find lodging and a position. Rooming houses are for bachelors, and there are few enough of those. I was going to send for you and the baby in the spring."

"You won't be here for the birth of our child?"

"We'll have ten children. I'll be there for all the others, and each will have his own nursery. That's where the future is. The East is all dried up from the war. The economy will take twenty years to rebuild. Meanwhile, we'll have worked our way up to the top of Nob Hill."

"I don't know where Nob Hill is."

"I'll remind you you said that in five years."

She smacked shut the book she'd been holding open in her lap. It had been a stage property, selected to keep her hands from shaking when he let himself into their tiny parlor. He'd been surprised to find her up past midnight; he'd spent the evening with a fourteen-year-old girl found floating facedown in the River Raisin.

"Who else did you confide in?" she asked. "Did you expect me to read about it in the *Evening News*, or were you planning to wire me from San Francisco?"

"I haven't even made up my mind I'm going. I didn't want to take the chance of upsetting you until I knew for sure. The baby—"

"Stop. Before you use our baby to excuse your cowardice."

Two days later she miscarried again. Another round began of apologies and coddling on Richard's part, but she
didn't blame him for the loss of the baby, nor did she tell
him what she'd learned from the doctor who treated her at
the hospital: her pelvis was too narrow, she probably would
never carry a child full term and was advised not to try,
because another pregnancy could destroy her health and
possibly end her life. She wept bitterly, more than she had
since the news had come of Luke's death. Richard concluded that this second disappointment had affected her
more than the first; he assured her there would be other
babies and reminded her of his plans to have ten children.
She had never been more courageous in her life than when
she managed not to become hysterical in response.

And so she resigned herself against motherhood, and
against telling Richard the truth, for instinct told her it
would wound him even more deeply than it had her. The
doctor would not elaborate on what steps she should take to
avoid pregnancy short of abstinence. A nurse was more
helpful. And if after she'd regained her strength Richard
took notice that the pattern of their relations had changed,
he never mentioned it. Similarly, he didn't bring up the
subject of San Francisco again. He'd quite obviously abandoned the idea.

It fell to Lucy to revive it.

With the grim chain of torn and blasted corpses from
the battlefields broken, Richard's hours at the parlor became almost predictable. He rarely reported to work before eight o'clock, and in the first six months after Lee's
surrender he failed to return home before dark only once,
when a Union veteran and a Michigan Central brakeman
fell out over the ex-soldier's wife behind a saloon on Sandy
Creek Road and Richard had to extract seventeen pieces
of shot from the brakeman's face and neck before begin-

ning restoration. This lack of challenge was taking its toll. He grew listless, complained that the meals she served him were without taste, and found fault with the behavior of his elected representatives in Lansing and Washington as they were reported in the newspaper. He'd never taken an interest in politics before except to cast his vote, which he never discussed even with his father. Lucy thought it was only a matter of time before the gin bottle reappeared in the kitchen cabinet.

"How does one get to California?" she asked one night, interrupting his judgment of the boiled turnips she'd placed before him. "Would we have to join a wagon train? Fight Indians? I heard a hideous story about pioneers trapped in the snow in the mountains."

"What does it matter? We're not going." He wobbled a turnip around the inside of his mouth.

"If we were, how far could we travel by rail? Or do we take the train to Philadelphia and sail around South America?"

"Nothing so adventurous. The Kansas Pacific is expected to reach Denver next year. From there you can take a series of stagecoaches and riverboats, hire private transportation, ride a number of short lines, and board the Central Pacific in Sacramento. The rest is like walking across the street. If we were walking across the street," he added.

She felt disheartened. She still thought twice before climbing the stairs to retrieve something she'd left in their bedroom.

But he was warming to the subject. He emptied his plate and scooped a second helping onto it. "If we wait a few years, we'll be able to ride the same train from Detroit to San Francisco, if the politicians quit pettifogging. By then, of course, ten thousand others will have preceded us. I doubt the frontier will wait for late opportunists."

"All this hopping about sounds expensive. Can we afford it?"

"Father has promised us a gift of money on the arrival of our first child. I think I could persuade him to part with some of it. And I'm a full partner in the parlor. I can borrow against it from the bank." He did not appear to have noticed when the tenses changed from *could* to *can*. She knew then that he'd never truly deserted the dream.

"He'll never stand still for that," she said. "He'll advance you the entire sum before he'd accept the bank as his partner."

"We may never see him again."

She smiled.

"We will if the politicians quit pettifogging."

"San Francisco may not be the end of it," he said. "There are mining camps and cattle towns all over the West, filled with charlatans who will empty a man's purse, then scratch out a hole and dump his friend or his wife into it with nothing so much as a flour sack to slow down the vermin. A proper parlor could drive them all out of business."

"A *proper* parlor, Richard. I'll not live in a tent and blow with the wind."

He set down his fork. For the first time in weeks she saw life in his eyes, but also doubt. "What's happened to change your opinion?"

She could not tell him the truth even then. Her own great inadequacy was burden enough. She could not bear his knowing it as well. He would say nothing—until the next fallow period steered him back to the bottle. And if he said nothing at all it would be worse.

"When we spoke of this before, I could not travel with you, and I would not have my baby when his father was two thousand miles away. Now I can go with you."

"It will be spring, and more likely summer, before we can make the journey. What if you're expecting again?"

Too late, she saw she'd backed herself into a corner. The only way out was to lie by omitting the truth. She reached across the table and laid her hand on his.

"You have my word that I will be with you in San Francisco or wherever the trade takes you," she said.

CHAPTER 8

That two-faced city," Lucy would always say, whenever the subject of San Francisco came up in conversation. It would become so much a habit that she would say it without thinking, and when their hearts were gayer than they ever would be again, Richard would chime in and say it with her, as if it were a beloved old verse. If it happened in the company of people who didn't know the tale, the uninitiated would watch them blankly while they laughed, or join in with a hollow chuckle, not wanting to be left out.

Lucy and Richard could not know it at the time, but the hypocrisy of the place was in evidence that first day. A strong wind had cleared the harbor of its chronic morning fog, allowing the sun to paint the bay a benign blue and glitter off the semaphore tower on Telegraph Hill. The station platform boiled with men in morning coats and tall shimmering hats and women in swaying skirts and cartwheel brims, parasols on their shoulders; there to greet new arrivals and accept catalogue shipments of dresses, rugs, bathroom fixtures, mining equipment, barber chairs, bolts of fabric, parlor stoves, bicycles, and perfumes and elixirs from Chicago, New York City, London, and Paris. Colored porters bustled about, tipping their smart caps and pushing wheeled carts piled high with trunks and portmanteaux. Slavery to them was only a grim dream. In fact, four years of Civil War, the ashes of which continued to smolder in Kansas and points east, had touched this city no more than a famine in China or a mutiny in India. The sight through the window of their day coach promised an auspicious end to torturous weeks spent in hot, cinder-laden chair cars, jouncing mud wagons, and paddle wheelers crowded with cargo and pickpockets.

"Civilization, Lucy." Richard was ebullient. "I told you we didn't leave it behind in Michigan."

"Thank the Lord." As recently as Denver, the newspaper boys had been shouting of duels and dismemberments. Richard had bought a copy out of purely professional interest.

It was the last sunshine either of them would see for a week and the delighted grin their porter gave them when Richard handed him a fifty-cent piece was the last smile that did not mask an un-Christian heart.

"Mr. and Mrs. Connable?"

They were watching their cabman load their trunk and bags into the back of his four-wheeler when the shout came, from a man striding their way across the platform. He carried a silver-headed stick—raised, as if to bludgeon his way through the crowd—and wore a gray cutaway over checked trousers stuffed into the tops of elastic-sided boots and a tall hat that matched the coat, angled over one ear to expose the curls plastered to his forehead. Lucy was sure his black Louis-Napoleon whiskers were dyed, and she suspected he wore a corset under his tight waistcoat. She remembered what her father had said about men who used cosmetics and cocked their hats, and distrusted him on sight.

His card introduced him as Pembroke Benjamin, with the real property firm of Benjamin and Harms, which Richard had engaged to find a place in a respectable neighborhood for him to open his business, and a residence he and Lucy could rent until they found something permanent. He had a broad English accent that reminded her of the speech affected by stage actors posing as members of the British upper class. She'd read Dickens and formed the opinion that the stinking alleys of Stepney were as close as he had ever come to the fashionable West End.

Some time would pass before she learned she'd been charitable in her assumption. Pembroke Benjamin's real name was Stanley Snave, and he was under a Queen's order of execution in Sydney, Australia, for the brutal murder of a harlot named Agnes Muck. He'd taken the name under which he was known in America from a character in a music-hall farce. His partner, N.O. Harms, was a fiction. Hard experience had taught him to spread his guilt over two or more parties while avoiding partnerships of any kind. Richard had selected the firm at random from the tombstone advertisements in the *San Francisco Call*, to which he'd subscribed for a year.

Benjamin/Snave was, in short, a Sydney Duck; one of the pestiferous mass of immigrants from England's oldest penal colony who had seized control of the brothels and deadfalls of San Francisco within months of the fabled gold rush of '49. Some seasoned and anonymous sailor had been moved to dub that region the Barbary Coast, after the murderous sinkhole of West Africa.

"I've met every train since yesterday morning, knowing you'd be on one," he said, pumping Richard's hand. "You're only the second couple I've seen who answered your description. The other turned out to be a bank manager from Boston and his sister."

Richard introduced Lucy. Benjamin swept off his hat and bowed deeply over her hand. "Our city is known for its great beauties," he said. "They shall have to lower their flags to half-mast."

She decided to let that pass as a compliment.

Benjamin climbed into the cab beside them and tapped the driver's shoulder with his stick. "The Oriental, my good fellow. I took the liberty of arranging a suite," he told Richard. "I'm sure Mrs. Connable will want a bath after her journey. Each suite comes with its own. Fresh hot water for every guest, and they change the sheets twice a week. You won't find that at the Palmer House in Chicago."

Richard said, "I hope it's not too expensive. The trip cost more than expected."

"Everything costs more than expected since the war. San Francisco is no exception; one might call it the capital. It's the birthplace of the five-dollar egg. That's bad news for customers, but good news for businessmen. You won't be staying there long. I've lined up some houses for you to look at, all with sound roofs, and a fine location for your parlor. It's two streets off Washington, just a hop down from the Bella Union." He appeared to remember something he'd forgotten. He drew a bloated wallet from an inside breast pocket, pulled out one of the folded slips of paper that stuck out from it at every angle, and gave the slip to Richard. "This is an accounting of the expenses I've incurred thus far."

Richard unfolded it. "Just how much does a cab ride cost in this city?"

"Those figures represent finders' fees. In addition to a number of cabmen, I employ agents at cartage companies and among the serving class to inform me of vacant properties. If you wait till they're listed, you haven't a Chinaman's chance of obtaining them. It's the price of doing business here since the railroads."

"I'm surprised they don't go to work for you full time. Back home, a cook or a teamster doesn't make this much in a week."

"In that event, they'd have nothing to sell. A good agent keeps his eyes and ears open, even when he's mucking out a drain. When you see the parlor and the houses I've picked out for your inspection, I think you'll agree it's a bargain."

"I've wired money to the Wells Fargo office in my name. You'll have to wait until I can draw a draft." Richard pocketed the sheet.

"Most certainly. Ours is a gentleman's arrangement."

"What is the Bella Union?" Lucy asked.

"A melodeon, Mrs. Connable. A place of refreshment and entertainment—and, I may add, no place for a lady such as yourself. However, it's the finest in California. It's gone six months without a shooting, and there hasn't been a fatal stabbing since Election Day."

"Hold on," said Richard. "I wrote you I wanted a place in a respectable neighborhood."

Benjamin looked uncomfortable.

"Well, now, there you're on a slick grade. Colonel Kendrick's got his pickle hooks—your pardon, I mean his hands—deep into Nob Hill, and the swells there don't encourage an undertaker's district; chaps from out of town might think there's too much business in that direction and take their galleries and operas up the road to Sacramento. It ain't, it isn't Murder Point I'm talking about; you're practically in Portsmouth Square. You can pitch a dead cat out your back door and hit any of the best hotels in town."

They passed a group of young men in bowlers and loud waistcoats gathered on a street corner, smoking cigarettes and passing around a hammered flask. Lucy grasped Richard's hand. He patted hers. "Who's Colonel Kendrick?"

"He pleases to call himself an officer in the National Guard, what we call the Pick Handle Brigade, after how they arm themselves when the public peace is threatened, which it hasn't been since they lynched Jim Casey in fifty-six. He *says* his family buried Edinburgh's finest citizens for three hundred years until he got tired of planting them standing up and split out for territory where property isn't so dear. My own best guess is the authorities tipped him out for pinching rings and watches off the horizontal customers. I know for a fact he gambles more than the wealthy bereaved pay him playing rondo at the Adelphi."

"Why is such a creature allowed to stay in business?" Lucy asked.

"He knows his Latin and don't, doesn't wipe his nose on his cuffs, so the gents and ladies took him in as one of their own. He wouldn't pass inspection in New York City or London, but the breeding stock's older there. Out here they're all of them no more than an uncle or a cousin removed from the rats that burrowed the hills roundabout for yellow metal, and for all their airs they wouldn't know a lord from a lobster. Here's the hotel."

The Oriental managed to impress, but only because it was the only substantial construction in a neighborhood of houses built from piecework elsewhere, brought in by rail or boat, and assembled on-site. It was three stories of pillared porches, and painted rather than whitewashed, with a liveried groom stationed in front to hold the horses while the guests went inside to sign the register. The common railroad hotels in Detroit and Monroe were no less noteworthy in appearance. Benjamin had taken heed of their financial situation, if only to leave them solvent to pay his fee and expenses. She wondered if he'd made an arrangement with the owner to steer business his way.

"I'll let you settle in," he said in the lobby. "Be back in an hour to show you your parlor. The beefsteak in the restaurant's as good as you'll find anywhere, but I don't recommend the chowder. Colonel Kendrick took two customers out of there last year." He lifted his hat and left.

"Curious fellow." Richard looked at his watch, a gift from Janus Connable at parting. Lucy was relieved to see he still had it.

* * *

Their steward was a young Mexican, smooth and brown in the uniform of a page, who showed them how to operate the fixtures and registered no reaction at all when Richard gave him twenty-five cents.

She bathed first. The plumbing rattled alarmingly, but the water was hot and the soap white, sharp but pleasing to the nose. She had had to make do with rusty brine and sandpapery cakes of lye for so long, she'd forgotten the feel of lather on her skin. And for days on end there had been no washing at all.

They were both hungry, but decided to wait until after their appointment with Pembroke Benjamin and go to a restaurant outside the hotel. They didn't know him well enough to decide if he was being humorous when he warned them away from the chowder. She finished dressing while Richard was in the bath, then sat down at the writing table and started a letter to her father-in-law. Then it was time to go downstairs.

The building Benjamin had found contained a single story on Commercial Street—an optimistic name on the part of some early booster, but beginning to show promise with a cigar store, a Chinese laundry, and a business that made and sold barrels to a number of distilleries doing good business at the base of Telegraph Hill, all within walking distance of the address. To the north sprawled wicked Barbary, whose chimneys spewed bituminous smoke into the fog that had come planing across the rooftops when the wind shifted from the bay, but other than that the place appeared no worse than the less savory regions of Detroit and Monroe; the eastern press had been known to exaggerate the poor conditions of the frontier in order to slow down emigration. The shops and rooming houses to the south bore fresh paint and their porches were swept, and the crest of Nob Hill was visible to the west, even if its mansions and well-kept stables were not. The site existed on the cusp of respectability, as did the mortuary business. Richard considered this an augury of good fortune.

Benjamin explained that the great fire of 1851 had claimed the building's second story, but assured them that the roof had been replaced twice since the disaster and declared sound. In an earlier incarnation it had operated as a saloon. He showed them the ramp by which the kegs and barrels had been rolled into the cellar from the street, and the ingenious mechanism whereby a platform could be loaded with inventory in the center and raised with ropes and pulleys to ground level in the open area where the bar had stood; it was in disrepair, not having been used since the police had shut down the business for various practices the city preferred to restrict to Barbary proper, but Benjamin felt it could be put right in short order, or eliminated just as easily if Mr. Connable found the arrangement inconvenient.

"What about rats?" Richard leaned over the square hole left open by the lowered platform. The cellar was impenetrably black but gave forth a potatoey odor of stale earth.

"They're smart for vermin," the salesman said. "They don't stay where there's no food, and six months have come and gone since there was sour mash stored down there. You'll want to take steps to keep them out, but you won't have to evict them."

"You said property doesn't last long here. Why has no one come forward to claim it in six months?"

"City ordinance. Once the police close a place, it can't reopen for a year, even if the business has nothing to do with the preceding type of establishment. They tacked that on after Perce Grapnel was caught selling Old Pepper in geranium pots out of the old Grizzly Bear."

"That's another six months. I need only six weeks to put

the place in shape. What if someone dies between then and December?"

"I wouldn't worry about that." Benjamin stroked his whiskers. "I know someone at the Hall of Justice."

"He must be pretty high up, if he can declare a moratorium on death."

"If he was that high, he'd be out of my reach any day but Sunday. Things work differently out here. A man in an appointed position is expected to show a little Yankee ingenuity. He's a reasonable gent and doesn't like to discourage respectable enterprise in the city. No ordinance is cast in stone where honest traders are concerned."

Lucy saw resignation on Richard's face. "What's the charge for this demonstration of progress?"

Benjamin raised and resettled his hat. Lucy would remember that pumping motion years later, the first time she saw Richard work the handle of an adding machine.

"Well, there's a fee to apply for a variance, and wire expenses to Sacramento to confirm you're not wanted for a felony in the State of California, and a fee paid there; it ain't precisely against the law to let a crook open up a legitimate business, but it don't look well when it involves reinterpreting a statute." His careful grammar seemed to elude him whenever money was the issue. "I think I can get him to waive the mandatory inspection, seeing as how the place hasn't been shut up so long the structure would deteriorate. Fifty dollars ought to cover it."

"And would I tender this amount directly to him, or through you as my agent?"

"Oh, through me. The other's bribery. The charter's specific on that point."

"For which service you receive a fee as well." It wasn't a question.

"Five percent, taken out of the consideration. It won't cost you another cent."

Richard said nothing, but resumed his examination of the building.

Lucy, who had never been inside a saloon, even a defunct one, held a handkerchief to her nose and mouth much of the time to lessen the stench of stale ferment that seemed to permeate the walls to their timbers. Spilled beer, rotten barley, expectorated tobacco, old cigars, and vomit haunted the place like disreputable phantoms. She would need another bath after they left.

Dust and soot caked the windows, reducing the interior to twilight, and smoke from coal-oil lamps and untrimmed wicks had begrimed the ceiling. Richard would want to replace the tin panels with lath and plaster in any case, and she did not think that anything short of demolishing the walls and replastering them would eradicate the smell. The rooms adjoining the former barroom were small and cramped; she refused to speculate on what sort of activity had taken place in them. Walls would have to come down to make room for visitations, and others erected in the big room if visitors were not to be reminded of its original function. No association of any kind with commerce in entertainment and debauchery must adhere to an establishment operated by Janus Connable's son. Then came fixtures, furnishing, and decoration. Six weeks seemed a sunny estimate for so much work. The very thought of the investment made her light-headed. But she knew Richard would commit to the building. She had seen his mind was made up the moment he saw the mechanism that raised heavy burdens from the cellar to the ground floor.

CHAPTER 9

Janus R. Connable, Esq.
79 Monroe Street
Monroe, Mich.

July 6, 1867

Dearest Father,

By now you will certainly have received my wire of yesterday's date, asking to borrow money, and responded. I promised that I would write with an explanation, and I pray that your regard for Richard and me, and the record of our past behavior, are sufficient for you to have complied, with absolute conviction that the debt will be repaid.

Please believe me when I state that only bleakest need would persuade me to have taken this step. Richard has no knowledge of it, and when he learns of it I have no doubt that he will be angry, as he has sworn to build a life for us independent of assistance from anyone. I am equally certain he will accept the loan; for our situation is desperate.

I have written you of Mr. Pembroke Benjamin, who has been privileged to act upon our behalf in the acquisition of the parlor on Commercial Street and this house, both of which we are leasing through his company. He is a grasping mountebank, incapable of performing the smallest service that does not involve his personal enrichment, but in this he is by no means alone here. Each day brings another of the horde of private and public parties offering some assistance without which it is impossible for a man to conduct business in San Francisco, and which can only be obtained with a cash outlay. It seems the city itself is nothing more than one of those ancient fountains in Europe, into which one casts a coin, makes a wish, and retires, uncertain as to whether the boon will be granted, but certain that one's purse is lighter for the attempt.

Just last week, in the midst of construction, a gentleman arrived at the parlor, resplendent in a uniform of blue serge trimmed with gold braid, but fat in the extreme, with the remains of several food-courses evident on the front of his blouse, introducing himself as a captain in the city fire brigade and demanding a five-dollar "tax" to cover the cost of a fire safety inspection. Richard, who at the time was in conference with the carpenter, replied irritably that he hadn't cash on his person, had not the time to conduct the captain on a tour of the ground floor and basement, and furthermore had no intention of paying anyone to perform a service that had already been paid for by the city taxpayers.

The next morning, the carpenter came to our house and explained that he was unable to begin work at the parlor because there was a padlock on the door and a policeman posted in front. Richard went to the parlor to confirm this account, and was handed a citation by the policeman, demanding that the building's occupant forfeit a fine of $100 "for gross violations of the Fire Code of the City of San Francisco."

There was nothing for it but for Richard to report to the Hall of Justice and pay the fine. The padlock was removed, and when the fat fire captain returned the next day, Richard handed him a five-dollar note, which promptly went into the lining of his uniform cap. He then took his leave, and you will perhaps not be surprised to learn that he inspected nothing on his way out. Richard complained to Pembroke Benjamin, who merely ran his fingers through his preposterous whiskers and remarked that this was "the price of doing business out here." Then he reminded Richard that he still owed the second half of Benjamin's fee for arranging the lease.

The incident of the fire captain was not unique, and to provide you with details of others would only be to repeat myself with few variations, and keep you from your clients. Suffice to say the money changers have got hold of this place, and by nickels, dimes, and dollars have bled dry our resources. The money we set aside to support ourselves until the parlor showed profit is nearly gone.

I would not have burdened you with the foregoing, or beseeched you for funds, if I did not suspect that Richard is considering approaching certain individuals who reside in Barbary, and who lend money without question, in the expectation that the sums will be repaid at high interest, and if they are not repaid, or at least the amount of the interest provided when called for, will injure or murder the debtor and point to his example when the next unfortunate hesitates. My husband, your son, is determined to make his way in this alien country. I have faith that he will, in the end. It is the immediate future I fear.

Please forgive the beggaring tone of this letter. My regard for you would be in no wise less should you choose to decline my entreaty and cast us, the Prodigal and his errant wife, back upon our own devices. I can neither remain silent nor scribble a chirrupy missive upon the capital weather in northern California. I remain, no matter what,

Your loving daughter-in-law,
Lucy

P.S. The weather is *not* capital; it is cold and vile and filled with damp. Whatever does not grow mold attracts meal-bugs and centipedes.

This first great test revealed Janus Connable to be as kind as the first impression he'd made on Lucy six years before. Long before her letter reached him, and within twenty-four hours of her telegram requesting money, he wired back:

DAUGHTER
WIRING TWO THOUSAND YOUR BANK TODAY STOP
TELL RICHARD VENTILATION CELLAR CRUCIAL
LOVE
FATHER CONNABLE

"He must think it's still the first day of my apprenticeship," Richard said, when she showed him the telegram. "When he comes to visit I'll have to show him the shaft I designed. A grown man could crawl through it."

"Did you read the first part?"

"I did."

"You're not angry?" She hadn't been able to sit still since the telegram was delivered. She'd gone to the parlor, just to get the worst over with, but the painter told her Richard had left on business. From there she'd gone to Pembroke Benjamin's flyblown little office on Clay Street, only to learn he hadn't been there. She'd come home hoping to find him waiting for her. She hadn't, but he came in almost on her heels.

"You're not angry?"

"This morning, I might have been." He spiked the yellow flimsy on the desk that came with the house. "That was before I went to see Spurling, on Pacific Street."

"Who is Spurling?"

"He pleases to call himself a gambler, though if he ever took a chance on anything besides a man's ability to re-pay him I'll put a flowerpot on my head and go to live in Chinatown. He has scars all over his face and the most enormous mole. I thought at first he had two noses."

"You didn't borrow money from him!" She sat down at the desk. Her legs wouldn't support her.

"No. I don't know what made me more nervous, that mole or his Burmese manservant. Whoever buries that fel-low will have to use a piano crate. I apologized to Spurl-ing for taking his time and came back here. It's on the way to the post office or I'd have stopped and wired Father myself."

They'd been counting their pennies for weeks, dining on sausage and sauerkraut when they went out and on bis-cuits and gravy at home. That night they went to the Parker House and ordered the salmon, with plover's eggs and oys-ters, and ate strawberries for dessert while a Russian vio-linist dressed as a cossack exerted himself to drown out a profane game of monte taking place in the gaming room next door. They had wine, went home, and made love. They both felt their fortunes had turned.

They had. San Francisco, for all its bumptious growth, was a small town in spirit, and although Richard and Lucy were satisfied of their bankers' discretion, sudden faith in their solvency gripped the laborers at work on the parlor. The improvements progressed at an accelerated rate. Old plaster fell from the walls in sheets, the rubble was flung into the street for fill, new plaster went up. Partitions van-ished, to reappear elsewhere. Richard bought an iron-and-crystal chandelier secondhand from a hotel undergoing similar sweeping reconstruction and ordered it strung overhead in the new foyer. Lucy selected soothing green wallpaper with green fleurs-de-lis from a book in the back room of a shop on Washington Street, and while she was in the parlor measuring the windows for curtains, a boy in patched knickerbockers and a dirty cap came to the door, offering to sell a rug he said he'd rescued from a trash bin. Richard tried to send him away before he unrolled it, but Lucy insisted on seeing it. At her prodding, Richard relented and gave the boy ten dollars; the rug complemented the wallpaper perfectly.

The next day, Lucy hid the newspaper announcing a burglary at a mansion on Nob Hill and including a description of the rug among the items reported missing.

Guilt overcame her at the end of a week. She confessed to Richard across the breakfast table.

"I'd wondered why the paper didn't come that day," he said when she'd finished.

"We must return that rug to its owner."

"Why? We paid for it."

"It wasn't the boy's to sell."

"We didn't know that."

"What difference does that make?" she asked. "We cannot benefit from someone else's misfortune."

"Back in Monroe, I'd have agreed with you. Out here, that's the standard coin, as that millionaire who lost the rug surely knows. He's replaced it by now, and wouldn't thank us for making the trouble and expense unnecessary. He'd probably have us arrested for receiving stolen property."

"But what if someday he comes to the parlor to bury a relative and sees the rug?"

"Rubbish. He'll go to Colonel Kendrick." He picked up his fork and resumed his assault on his boiled egg.

She never brought up the subject again. Instead, she remained alert for other indications that the two-faced city had got its pickle hooks into Richard.

* * *

The hammering and sawing continued through July, minor notes in the wheezing, clattering symphony of a city that was constantly reclaiming itself from sodden ash. They ate from crockery selected by someone else, at a table that was not Lucy's taste, and slept in a rented bed in a house that offered every inconvenience but a rate they could not afford, and from which Richard was absent most of the time, supervising the progress at the parlor. He left directly after breakfast, agitated and preoccupied, and returned long after dark, his soles dragging and sawdust in his hair. After two weeks it seemed that things had always been this way and always would be.

Then, on the last day of the month, the last of the workmen packed his tools into his six-foot hinged case and departed for his next assignment, a gambling hall going up on the foundations of its predecessor, a casualty of yet another fire. Lucy dressed up as if she were attending the theater, in hat, gloves, and her last pair of undarned hose, and accompanied Richard in a cab to the parlor, an indulgence he thought appropriate to the occasion; for weeks now he had walked the six blocks to and from the canvas sheets and scaffolding twice a day, saving the fare for joints and rabbets. The cabman, impressed by his silk hat and ebony stick, tipped his own shabby bowler, helped Lucy up the step, and registered surprise at the Commercial Street address Richard gave him. Evidently he'd expected nothing less than the opera house.

Nothing about the building's exterior suggested it was a place where liquor had been sold and consumed or other entertainment provided those who could afford it. In appearance it was a private house, painted white with gray trim, with lace curtains tied back from the windows with ribbon, fashioned by Lucy with material from a dress shop on Stockton. The windows sparkled. A bricked path led from the sidewalk to the porch, where a professionally painted sign swung from chains stapled to the roof:

RICHARD J. CONNABLE
UNDERTAKER

The business cards he'd had printed carried the same legend, with the building's address in one corner. Lucy had protested in favor of Janus Connable's more elegant terminology, but Richard was unmoved.

"My father is a colonial figure, hopelessly stuck in the eighteenth century. Up until ten years ago, he was still keeping his records in Latin. I'm not so certain even the new millionaires on Nob Hill know what 'obsequies' are. They'll think I sell French perfume."

"Imagine their disappointment when they crossed the threshold."

He'd frowned. His sense of humor had never extended to his profession, and the experience of San Francisco had decreased its limits withal.

The original door of oaken planks bound with iron had been replaced by paneled mahogany, with an oval of beveled glass in the center and a bellpull with a handle of painted china. The new management had little to fear from police battering rams. He opened the door and stood aside for her to enter.

The foyer with its papered walls and troubling rug was dignified, not intimidating, the chandelier hung high so as not to shout out its presence. A door marked PRIVATE led into Richard's office to the right, containing a desk and a glazed book press purchased from an attorney of Pembroke Benjamin's acquaintance, recently barred from practice in the State of California. The press awaited an appropriate selection of books, but the daguerreotype Richard had brought from Michigan of his father at age twenty hung in a silver frame on the wall opposite the desk. He indeed looked every inch the Georgian gentleman in his longish hair and ruffles.

Richard drew aside a curtain in an opening at the back of the foyer, in one of the walls that had been erected to eradicate all memory of the barroom. Lucy went through. She felt as if she were entering a salon rather than a saloon.

He had set up the room as if for a private service, with four rows of folding chairs and a rectangular pedestal built of smooth stained walnut near the back wall, designed in conference with the carpenter, who had constructed it to the proportions of the mobile platform that had once carried kegs of beer and cases of wine from the storage room in the cellar to the area behind the bar. It lacked only a coffin and its occupant. Part of the original musicians' stage, carpeted now in leaf tapestry, had been preserved in one corner for a minister or a eulogist to stand when addressing mourners. Services outside church, a fashion slowly gaining ground in the East and Middle West, had by no means taken hold in largely Catholic San Francisco; but the future was never far from Richard's thoughts. (*He thinks . . . the answer will be revealed in the future, when in fact it's concealed in the past.*) Tall windows draped in burgundy velvet pierced the walls, with bronze candle sconces pointing toward a sky-blue ceiling—painted from memory in that foggy town. Everything smelled of turpentine and freshly sawn wood.

Lucy knew there was more she would not see. The ladder to the basement had given way to a flight of steps leading into a mortared and whitewashed chamber, plumbed for running water and furnished with benches and equipment for the preparation of what he called his clients, a pretty conceit inherited from his father, whose old-world ways were not entirely lost on the present generation. She had seen some of it delivered, but she knew that for her there would be no unveiling. In four years of marriage, she'd never been invited into the back room on Monroe Street.

"What about the organ?" she asked suddenly.

"Ordered from Denver. By the time it arrives I hope to have found someone who can play. That piano man who punishes 'Sally in Our Alley' every night at the Olympic doesn't answer."

"Richard, it's wonderful. Nothing here can compare with it."

"That's untrue. It's handsome, I agree, but quite ordinary. I'm told Kendrick has marble Cupids carved by artisans in Greece and shipped round the Horn. I haven't his deep pockets. But I have something he hasn't." He raised his stick and thumped the floor twice. "I paid one of the men to stay an extra day. I wish now I'd brought a bottle of champagne for a proper launching."

The pedestal shuddered. They stood back to watch it descend. Something twanged. The pedestal stayed put.

Richard raised his voice. "Crank it down, McCabe! Did you miss the signal?"

A hoarse baritone drifted up from below. "Can't, sir. Rope broke."

Richard replaced the unreliable ropes with belts from a harness shop on Russian Hill, and amused himself one entire afternoon raising and lowering the pedestal, lubricating the pulleys with axle grease until they operated noiselessly. The next order of business was to arrange for a reliable coffin maker. He hardly hoped for an alliance as fruitful as the one his father had enjoyed with Aaron Steinmetz in Toledo for twenty years, but he assumed he could find a decent cabinetmaker in a city of busy carpenters.

In this he was disappointed.

Of the three shops in the city that specialized in making coffins for the carriage trade he hoped to attract, one was under exclusive contract to Colonel Kendrick, and its proprietor would not even meet with Richard to discuss terms. Richard was unsatisfied with the workmanship in the second, where a paper-thin veneer of mahogany enabled the owner to charge a premium price for cheap pine with brass-plated iron handles and, he suspected, minimal reinforcement on the bottom; one careless or clumsy pallbearer was all that was required for it to fall and split open on the way to or from the hearse and spill the client out into the street. Many a reputable undertaker had lost his city license through overthrift in this one area.

The third place he visited presented a network of barely

navigable narrow aisles between precarious stacks of lumber and bolts of lining material, with tools strewn all about, and a pair of Macedonian brothers named Stavros, who apologized and explained in broken English that they were behind on all their orders: Business was too good locally, with the Mother Loders of '49 all approaching fifty years of age on top of nearly two decades of imported cognac, young mistresses, and goose livers swimming in butter, and dying by the dozen—"dropping like horse apples" was the description they used. They asked him to come back in six months, after the first wave had finished expiring.

Once again, Pembroke Benjamin came to Richard's rescue. There was, of course, a fee for his services, and a stipend to cover his army of informants, to which Richard agreed with more resolution now than resignation. He had come to think of this fellow in his preposterous whiskers and corset as something less than a genuine real property agent but more than a handyman, adept at odd jobs of every description and a dependable sort of crook. His cramped office above one of the city's proliferating Chinese laundries, with its sweaty walls and rickety Wooten desk stuffed with paperwork belonging to a previous tenant, hosted a steady traffic of pimps, pickpockets, ticket-of-leave men, and minor politicians, all seeking or offering favors, and Richard considered himself lucky whenever he made it up the narrow stairwell without colliding with someone on his way down. Benjamin hoisted you by your ankles and shook out your pockets and laughed at you as he was doing it, but he always came through. Richard had been dealt with far less honorably by men who considered themselves honest.

Benjamin came around to the parlor early the next morning. He took a tour of the premises, admired the pulley mechanism ("Our nineteenth century, I'd live in no other"), and gave Richard a slip of paper plucked from his porcupine of a wallet. "There's the address, and I wish you luck finding it. He's the only man in Barbary not beholden to anyone, not even Kendrick. My gent there says he can make a block of wood stand up and sing 'John Brown's Body,' and he should know; he's an expert on eternity-boxes."

"He's in *Barbary*?"

"Well, they're not all spivs and murderers. Who'd they have to feed on if they was?"

His name was Massimo Victor Crespo. Richard and Lucy called him Max.

His shop was as hard to find as Benjamin had predicted. It was built onto the back of a rooming house that fronted on Pacific Street, of timbers salvaged from old sailing craft by a carpenter whose skills weren't a patch on Crespo's; but its address belonged to an alley whose name was unknown even to the natives, who used it as a latrine on their way between saloon and brothel. Neither the alley nor the establishment had a sign at present; any it might have had had long since gone into a stove or been nailed over a rat hole, as if that had ever been a barrier against the least determined rat. Richard told Lucy he'd passed the alley three times before he happened to spot a smooth brown-skinned young man in a knee-length apron made of ticking washing his sole window with a rag and a bucket. It had to be the only clean window in Barbary.

"I need sun," was the explanation Crespo gave. "Candles cost money."

When they met, Richard had no idea the man he'd asked for directions was the man he sought. The young man—it turned out he was born the same month as Richard—snatched the piece of paper from Richard's hand, looked at what was written on it, said, "*Sì*. Is me," and in one motion crumpled it into a tiny pellet and threw it into the alley.

This impressed Richard more than anything else about their first encounter, and there was much to impress. Most people, he told Lucy, would have handed back the paper. Crespo seemed bent on destroying every scrap of evidence that he'd ever existed.

He was Richard's height, but wiry, with glossy black hair brushed straight back from a profile that belonged on a Roman coin. He was clean-shaven, but the blue shadow on his chin bore witness that daily attention was necessary to maintain the condition. He applied the same close attention to his teeth, of which he had perhaps the only complete set in Barbary—straight, white, and hidden from view except when he smiled, which he did only when sufficiently amused by the depths of cruelty to which modern man could sink. He wore a white shirt under the apron with the sleeves rolled up to his elbows and a black necktie. He was quite the most dignified thing for blocks.

"I'm told you make coffins," Richard said.

"I make nothing."

The building behind Crespo seemed to have started out as a livery stable, with two wide doors flayed open at present. Augers, bits, and braces covered the interior walls and an oblong box lay across two sawhorses. It was unmistakably a coffin, lacking only a lid and handles.

"What's that you're working on?"

"Is not for sale."

"I wasn't offering to buy it." Richard gave him one of his cards.

Crespo looked at it, gave it back.

"I'm an undertaker." He didn't know if the man read English any better than he spoke it.

"Colonel Kendrick?"

"No, I'm Richard Connable."

"I know Kendrick. You are with him?"

"No. I've never met him."

Crespo said nothing. His eyes were ash-colored beneath heavy lids. Richard thought that if he raised the lids, the embers would blaze.

"Who's making the coffin?"

"Me."

"You said you make nothing."

"I make this. Then nothing."

"Who are you making it for?"

"Me. Is my coffin."

It would be a long time, and Crespo's English a little better, before his story came out in detail. When Colonel Kendrick had first opened shop, Massimo Victor Crespo had made all his coffins, eventually hiring an apprentice to help fill the orders that started coming in after his first efforts were unveiled in visitations and services. At that time, both his cabinetmaking shop and Kendrick's undertaking parlor were located on Battery Street, a respectable although not fashionable section of town; but increasing business from the gentlefolk had enabled Kendrick to move to Nob Hill, after which his orders to Crespo fell off. Two weeks of silence passed before the Italian learned that Kendrick had struck an arrangement with the firm whose owner had refused to meet with Richard. An item in the *Call* announced that Kendrick had been inducted into the Ancient and Honorable Fraternity of Free and Accepted Masons, in the eyes of San Francisco society a good business move, but hardly conducive to any association with a practicing Roman Catholic like Crespo.

The high train had passed him by, but he might still have fared middling well with his other projects and the occasional order from other undertakers had he not become drunk and made a number of indiscreet remarks that found their way back to the colonel. Shortly thereafter, Crespo received a visit from a fat man in a stained uniform who introduced himself as a captain in the city fire brigade.

At this point in the story, Richard saw in a flash the circumstances that had forced the craftsman to relocate to a place no ward heeler would bother to take away from him, and led him eventually to the decision to end his life—but not before he'd fashioned for himself a suitable vessel in which to spend eternity.

The means he'd selected for his suicide were as methodical as his work ethic. He'd determined to drink himself to death. The opportunities in his neighborhood were certainly plentiful, and if at the beginning he saved his pennies by ordering cheap grog and bedpan gin in places like the Boar's Head, the Fierce Grizzly, and the Cobweb Palace, he could afford to finish himself off with good Pisco brandy at the Bella Union. He calculated it would take six weeks, if he stopped eating and invested as many continuous hours as he put into any other project.

He told the suicide part of the story to Richard, placing as he did so the lid on the unfinished coffin and planing its top with long, graceful sweeps of his knotted forearms, removing wood in two-foot curls.

"Who will put you and your fine coffin in the ground?" Richard asked.

"I not decide. I keep money out from the drinking fund to pay for it."

"What if you're too drunk to make the choice? You might go to Kendrick in your confusion."

"I not start until coffin is finish. I wish to kill myself, not disgrace my work." He bent and blew away some loose curls.

"It seems a shame to bury work like this."

"You bury yours, no?"

Richard took out his wallet and laid a number of banknotes one by one on the lid of the coffin. He hesitated, then placed the rest of the notes he had with him on the pile.

"That is what?" Crespo asked.

"Money. I can't imagine it's changed that much since you saw any. I'm buying this coffin."

"I said is not for sale."

Richard unhooked the heavy gold chain from the watch his father had given him and placed the chain on top of the notes. "Twenty-two karats. You'll dig a long time in the hills to match it."

"No coffin is worth."

"Everything costs more than expected in San Francisco."

Crespo shook his head. "Three coffins, this. Four."

"Then that's three you owe me. Do you think you can postpone your drinking plan long enough to deliver?"

"Why?"

"I've never cared a great deal for secret societies, Masons and such. They're a waste of time I could be spending studying new methods of embalming."

"Colonel Kendrick, he won't like."

"Well, I'll see you two Kendricks and raise you a Pembroke Benjamin."

"Pembroke Benjamin is who?"

"What does it matter? They all look the same when you get them on the bench." He took out the card the Italian had returned to him and poked it under the pile of gold chain.

" 'Richard J. Connable, Undertaker.' " Crespo nodded, looking at him. "I remember."

Richard found an ambulance at a wagonwright's shop on Front Street, unclaimed and unpaid for by the U.S. Army at Fort Alcatraz after the need to house military prisoners on the island had vanished with the war. He thought it would make a decent hearse, but the wagonwright wanted too much for it. He still had horses to buy and stable, advertisements to place, and the rent on the house and parlor, and his only assets were what remained of the two thousand dollars he'd borrowed from his father. The wright, a white-whiskered seventy with a bald head as red as a cherry, poked a plug of tobacco into the hole in his beard and said, "You an undertaker?"

"I am, hence my interest in a hearse." His patience with the average fellow's tenuous grasp on the obvious was shallow in the best of circumstances, and he'd been all day looking at vehicles that were either unsuitable or outside his budget.

"What you charge for burial and such?"

His intolerance began to fade. "That would depend on the *such*."

"My ma's ailing. I promised her a minister and a plot."

"What about visitation?"

"I don't know what that is."

"The lying in state, when her friends and family come to say good-bye."

"I'm her family. All her friends are dead. She's ninety-six."

Richard said, "I think we can come to an arrangement."

He had a hearse, and his first client.

There wasn't much time. The old woman could barely swallow thin broth; her doctor said a healthier person would have given up weeks ago. Working without a break, Massimo Crespo trimmed the ambulance with gingerbread panels, lacquered it an even glossy black, and helped the glazier he'd recommended install the windows in the sides. Richard had it fitted with brass lanterns and replaced the iron falloes with rubber tires. Lucy balked at black satin for ninety-three cents the yard, bought bedsheets instead and dyed them black to make curtains for the interior. Richard found a pair of gray mares in a livery on Sacramento Street; one had a milky eye, and in horse terms their combined age was a hundred and fifty. The stable hand said they were good for three more years if no one whipped them up above a trot. Lucy called them the Sisters. It was true that they got on like two ancient spinsters who'd been living in the same house for decades, quarrelsome and mutually devoted.

The old woman died at last. Crespo had built a sturdy coffin of simple pine with polished iron handles and lined it with linen stuffed with horsehair. The old woman was emaciated and nearly bald, but cotton in her cheeks, an application of Imperial Persian powder, a suggestion of rouge, and a snood disguised the worst ravages. White cotton gloves covered gnarled fingers and red swollen knuckles.

Lucy found a pin of amethyst-colored glass in a Drumm Street jumble shop and clasped the old woman's black burial dress at the neck as she lay in the visitation room. It brought color to her cheeks and filled a hollow in her throat.

When the wagonwright saw her he lowered his head and his shoulders shook.

"That pin's good for a hundred dollars," Richard whispered to Lucy.

"It cost ten cents."

Richard drove the hearse from the parlor to a cemetery in the old Yerba Buena section, where plots were available for reasonable rates if the bereaved were willing to stand the risk of losing the departed to a mudslide; it was on the steep side of Telegraph Hill. The minister, a Methodist and a veteran of Alpine rituals, dug in his heels at graveside and read from First Corinthians. Richard gave him two dollars. Lucy and Crespo attended, to fill out the party, and the wagonwright shook hands with them all, wringing

Richard's at the last. Tears followed the furrows in his cheeks and dripped off the end of his beard.

The next day, the following advertisement appeared in a black border among the inside columns of the *Call, Bulletin*, and *Times:*

All Your Needs Foreseen and Considered.
A Gentle and Caring Place.
All Services Provided.
All Faiths Welcome.

R. J. CONNABLE
UNDERTAKER

Reasonable Rates and a Serene Setting

116 Commercial Street San Francisco

This do in remembrance of me.
Luke 22:19

Lucy had contributed the Bible verse. It had been read at the ceremony for her brother Luke.

She was seated in the kitchen when Richard came home with a copy of each paper under his arm. His expression changed when he saw her. She knew she was pale. She'd been vomiting all morning.

The doctor, a cheerful young man with a bright set of unopened medical books on the shelf behind his desk, examined her and confirmed her suspicions. If there were no complications, she would give birth in the spring.

n Episcopal service, Richard. And don't bury me on the side of a hill."

"Yes, of course," he said. "In forty or fifty years, when our grandchildren are old enough to attend."

He was jovial, overly so in response to her somber instructions. The young doctor, to whom she'd confided the warning she'd received in Monroe, had prescribed confinement to her bed for the period of her pregnancy, and in deference to her request had assured Richard this was just a precaution in view of her history. In private he told her he thought the original prognosis was unnecessarily dismal; but his forehead furrowed and he said he'd consult with a colleague at St. Francis' Hospital. Meanwhile he'd visit her regularly during her confinement.

"If I carry this child into labor," she said, "and if it's a question of its life or mine, I want you to promise me you'll choose the child."

"It won't come to that."

"Please promise me."

He promised.

People, she knew, lost spouses and went on. When they lost children, they never recovered.

Richard engaged a nurse to stay with Lucy while he was

at the parlor. She was a wan thing, much frightened of life, who when she found her patient reading the volume of Plutarch that Richard had bought for her in a secondhand bookshop, scolded her and took it away, lest her child be born a pagan. She gave her instead a book of stories from the Bible, and Lucy read of fratricide and human sacrifices and royal fornication. She drank eight glasses of milk a day, which added to her nausea. She begged Richard to bring her tomato juice, for which she had a raging thirst. He asked the nurse, who said, "Certainly not. Tomatoes are deadly poison."

Massimo Crespo came to visit, with flowers. He wore a tight black coat and a stiff-brimmed hat he didn't know what to do with once he took it off. He made no reply to Lucy's whispered entreaty, but returned the next day with another bouquet, and hidden inside it a jar filled with bloodred liquid he'd squeezed himself, being careful to strain out the seeds with cheesecloth. She drank half of it straight from the jar, and when she heard the nurse coming, instructed him to hide it. He unbuttoned his coat quickly and stuck it underneath. With the nurse in the room, she thanked him for his visit and asked him to come back the next day. He knew what was meant.

One day he surprised her with a dish of tomato slices fried in olive oil and perched on thick slices of warm bread. She ate all of it and used the last morsel of bread to scoop the oil off the plate. She asked him if his mother had taught him how to prepare it.

"My father. He was cook in Messina."

"Is he still there?"

"He is dead."

"I'm sorry. Have you any other family?"

"My mother, three brothers. All dead. Cholera. My wife."

"Cholera also?" She could not encompass it.

"She kill herself." He twirled a finger next to his head. *"Insensato."*

"I'm very sorry."

He believed her. He told her he'd joined a crew of merchant sailors as a ship's carpenter, sailed around Cape Horn, and jumped ship in San Francisco. He told her a little about his experiences with Colonel Kendrick; but his English failed him finally and he grew silent. He was bitter about many things. But he had the kindest eyes she had seen since Janus Connable's, when the lids were lowered, and when she spoke, he listened. Richard did not always, and even when she felt he would, she could not tell him how deeply she loathed San Francisco and missed Monroe. These things she confided to Massimo, not that day but later, after his visits had become a daily event. She knew instinctively that he would share their conversations with no one, especially her husband. He offered no solutions, made no responses at all, except to meet her gaze as she spoke, assuring understanding. He was the only friend she'd made since her wedding, and that he should be a man seemed to occur to neither of them as unusual.

Richard, aware of the visits but not knowing what passed between them, was not suspicious of the relationship. He was, in fact, grateful that she was not lonely while he tended to business at the parlor. And he was drawn to Max as well. He was a gifted cabinetmaker, too good to be making coffins only, and as a man who took pride in his own work Richard respected that quality in another; furthermore, he liked the Italian for many of the same reasons Lucy did. When Richard placed an order, Max heard what he wanted, and delivered satisfaction, along with improvements the undertaker had not thought of, and for which no extra charge was made. He listened, too, to Richard's complaints about the price of doing business in San Francisco, the open palms that had to be filled, the self-satisfied expressions on the faces of both public servant and underworld extortionist that he longed to smash but could not, and he sympathized. If Max was Lucy's first friend outside her marriage, he was Richard's first ever; the sons of undertakers were not considered prime material for easy intimacy, and acquaintance with undertakers themselves was something to be put off as long as possible. The situation with coffin makers was much the same. When the hours dragged at the parlor, or work finished early, Richard formed the habit of strolling around to Max's new shop on Clay Street and visiting with him as he glued and sanded and varnished and released the spirits he professed to believe were trapped in the wood.

However, the hours did not drag often, and work seldom finished early. The wagonwright had a great many more customers than friends, and he told them all what Richard Connable had done for his mother and what a shame it was she had to be put into the ground just when she was looking better than she had in years. People listen to such stories out of politeness, only to remember them in detail when they have need for the same services; they do not like to shop. Within a month of the old woman's burial, Richard had embalmed and restored a failed Forty-Niner, dead of an infection of the blood, a young railroad worker, crushed to death between coupling cars in the rail yard, and a three-year-old girl who had fallen into the harbor and drowned. The little girl was the greatest challenge, for her body had not been found for three days and the stricken parents pleaded for an open coffin so that her four-year-old brother could see her and understand. Richard was close to satisfied with the results.

Commerce in death was unpredictable, more so there than in Michigan. A heat wave could be counted upon to deliver the aged as well as some physical laborers who carried hods and loaded heavy feed sacks into the beds of wagons, red-faced and streaming, until they collapsed, but even the most experienced in Richard's trade could not prepare for a sudden fire in a crowded hotel, a pitched battle between Chinese tong hatchetmen and white street toughs in Barbary, and the city's murder rate seemed to rise and fall both with the tide and against it. The Chinese remained aloof, boxing the bones of their dead and shipping them to the land of their ancestors, and many of those whose throats were slit in alleys for the coppers in their pockets were fodder for potter's field; but the number of victims with middle-class families was sufficient to provide experience plugging bullet holes and replacing severed ears and noses with new ones fashioned from wax. When a popular East Street madam was brought to his parlor by three harlots powdered and buttoned for their sojourn outside Barbary, Richard managed to reattach her jaw, stitch up the gash that had nearly decapitated her, and disguise the repairs even before her slayer, a notorious Shanghai agent known as Singapore Jack, was dragged from the police station by a mob fortified with whiskey and hanged from a lamppost at the base of Telegraph Hill.

As luck had it, Singapore Jack himself became a client when his brother, who owned the saloon where Jack had "recruited" most of his charges in return for the bounty paid by the owners of understaffed ships, cut him down and brought him to Commercial Street in the back of a buckboard. Jack had dangled for the better part of a day, and with his neck broken and nothing to hold his head on his shoulders but sinew and skin, the neck had stretched nearly three feet. In order to make him presentable for a last visit by his elderly mother, a housemaid in the employ of a Washington Street attorney, Richard removed the head and sewed it back on after discarding the excess material, concealing the clamp that prevented the head from lolling left or right beneath the satin pillow that supported it. He poked the tongue back inside the mouth, closed the bulging eyes, and used paste and powder to turn the purple face a natural shade of pink. Jack's brother was grateful and paid him a bonus, which Richard divided with Max Crespo, whose simple suggestion had solved the problem with the neck. Max was reluctant, but accepted finally, rewarding Richard with one of his rare broad smiles. He really had abnormally fine teeth.

None of the practical details made its way back to Lucy at the time. She would learn of them many years later, when all the secrets in Richard's back room had been revealed.

The Connable Undertaking Parlor became known in Barbary as the place to go when your loved one took a pick handle in the back of his skull or fell down a flight of stairs with a bellyful of tanglefoot or dragged too much opium into his lungs in Chinatown. Most of his clients were respectable, but very few months passed without a consumptive on his bench who faced his first bath in a year or a pimp who had mistaken a bottle of spirits of ammonia for Old Gideon. The people who brought them in—purse snatchers, women of ill fame, and the occasional honest laborer or seamstress—paid him with filthy banknotes and jars filled with greasy coins; one gave him a goat, which he accepted because he'd heard the milk was good for infants. Max explained it was, in fact, a billy, not a nanny, and could not be expected to give milk of any sort. He took it off Richard's hands to manage the grass growing in the strip between his shop and the sidewalk. This story Richard shared with Lucy, who laughed so hard the doctor had to be summoned to make sure she hadn't miscarried.

"I promised you Nob Hill," Richard said when the crisis had passed. "We may not get there on the back of a goat."

She hoped they never would. It might mean they would never leave.

Aloud she said, "This town's full of hills. I can't imagine one's any different from all the others."

As it happened, Richard's reputation for good work at an honest price climbed Nob Hill before he did. It spread much more slowly in respectable San Francisco than in the deadfalls and bagnios where its citizens never trod. Undertaking was not a subject commonly discussed in drawing rooms, and the conversation in the Forty-Niners' Club concerned itself far more often with the price of gold than the price of a funeral. But Colonel Kendrick, the millionaires' undertaker, had a keen nose for competing establishments, and when the wind blew from the direction of Commercial Street, he decided to pay his colleague a visit.

Elsinore Kendrick had operated a successful parlor in Chicago before coming west in 1855; not to dig for gold, but to dig holes to lower men into who had found it, and charge a premium for his services, tailored as they were to the carriage trade. With the money he'd received from selling his share in the Chicago business to his junior partner, he'd taken a year's lease on a sixteen-room Queen Anne mansion on Nob Hill, established living quarters for himself and what became a succession of mistresses on the second and third floors, and converted the ground floor for embalming and visitation, with fixtures and furnishings he'd bought in New York and brought with him around the Horn. His predecessors were mere diggers, working out of shabby houses with antiquated equipment; their hearses rattled like shop wagons behind spavined teams and the coffins they sold were of uniformly poor quality.

Coffins, in fact, had posed a problem throughout his first ten years in California. The first wave of fortune seekers seldom included genuine craftsmen; he cringed when he thought of the well-dressed cadavers he'd been forced to bury in boxes thrown together by hammer hacks who were better left framing saloons and outhouses. Massimo Victor Crespo had come late, and it was Kendrick's good fortune to have struck an arrangement with the Italian before he was sufficiently familiar with the language, and the place, to determine what his skills were worth. However, Kendrick considered that Crespo would have fared far worse at the hands of Kendrick's slipshod, unscrupulous competitors. The colonel had owed him nothing when he severed relations with the papist to become a Mason and conduct business with brothers of the order. By then, other good cabinetmakers had settled in the city, and if their work was not quite equal to Crespo's, they worked faster, and their rates were reasonable based on volume—they employed apprentices and pieceworkers, and operated more like a factory than an old-fashioned shop—and in any case elaborate hardware and a shiny finish made up for all the imperfections his unsophisticated customers would ever notice. In the meantime he had prospered well enough to purchase the Queen Anne house outright from the Forty-Niner who had leased it to him in order to take up residence in a rambling monstrosity of brick and stone nearer the hill's crest.

Kendrick was five feet seven and weighed 210 pounds, most of them solidly gathered around his middle. At that point in the century, a healthy stoutness such as his connoted distinction and position, and the governor in Sacramento, who was built along similar lines, hesitated not at all before commissioning him a colonel with the National Guard, with the responsibility of containing mob rule in the City of San Francisco. Kendrick immediately placed an order with his tailor for a splendid uniform, piped with gold and cinched with a sword belt, and topped off by a plumed bicorne hat he wore in parades and to monthly meetings where he joined with his fellow guardsmen to inspect their buttons and the polished pick handles issued them as weapons. There as with the Masons, membership broadened his base of potential customers. Since Barbary was by and large peaceful at present, the likelihood of his having to wade into a riotous gang with only a stick in his scabbard was beneath consideration. In the event, he could always resign his commission for reasons of health; he suffered from gout.

For all its swelling population, the community remained a small town in temperament. All of this was known or suspected by others in his circle and by their servants, who spread the intelligence among delivery boys and shopkeepers, some of whom sweetened their income with gratuities offered by members of the press in return for titbits of human interest. Colonel E. Kendrick, the millionaires' undertaker, became a figure of entertainment in the "City Items" columns. They reported with enthusiasm his every pronouncement on the political situation in faraway Washington and described gleefully the color-blind combinations of dress he wore to balls. San Francisco worshipped its characters: Joshua A. Norton, a deranged derelict who fancied himself Emperor of the United States, was no less a public fixture than the mayor. An undertaker who mixed with society and scorned to drape himself in the drab weeds of his calling was bound for notoriety even in a city of eccentrics.

In her confinement, Lucy read of Kendrick's exploits and reported them to Richard, who disapproved of his expectant wife exposing herself to troubling current events. He told her nurse, who banned newspapers from the household. Lucy put away her resentment behind Richard's good intentions—and asked Max to bring the *Call* with him on his next visit.

On the day he presented himself in the foyer of Richard Connable's parlor, Colonel Kendrick wore a plum-colored coat over a green waistcoat with a ruby pin in a cravat whose shade Richard could best describe to Lucy as mulberry. The cuffs of striped trousers broke at his patent-leather insteps and he removed a soft-crowned tan hat with a yellow feather in the band. His face was shiny pink, with a light dusting of talcum where he shaved, and he combed out his gray side-whiskers so that his head formed a triangle with a rounded peak. Richard, forewarned of the visit by the colonel's card in a servant's hand, greeted him in the frock coat and necktie he wore for customers. They exchanged small talk, one professional to another, and Richard conducted him on a tour.

Kendrick approved of the fixtures in the basement, made some suggestions, and was impressed by the rope-and-pulley arrangement that removed most of the physical labor from conveying the client to the visitation room. In the room itself, he inspected closely the child who lay in state in the miniature coffin Max Crespo had tailored for her. She clutched a rosary in her white-gloved hands and appeared truly to be asleep.

"This is not the girl from the harbor," said the colonel, straightening.

"It is."

"There is no sign of swelling."

"It's an evaporating process. I used a lamp and reflectors and attended throughout. I had to stuff two fingers of the right glove with cotton to replace what was missing. Fish," he added.

"You did all this yourself?"

"I can't afford an apprentice just yet."

Kendrick stroked the coffin's walnut finish. "I recognize this cabinetry. Crespo takes his time."

"So do I."

They repaired to Richard's office, whose bookshelves now bore poetry in good bindings. Richard regretted he had nothing to offer in the way of refreshment. He declined a cigar from Kendrick's leather case, and watched as he lit one for himself. Kendrick's own family coat of arms, an emblem that appeared on his hearse and business card, glittered on the band.

"You're very young to have acquired so much knowledge and skill." This was phrased as a statement, but it seemed to require an answer.

"I apprenticed for my father, Janus Connable. He's the best undertaker in Monroe."

"I prefer the term *mortician,* regardless of the title the newspapers have hung upon me. I rather think *undertaker* suits a grave digger better."

Richard said nothing.

"I'll come to the point, Mr. Connable. I'm considering opening another parlor in this neighborhood. I've accomplished all I can up on the hill. When that happens, an entrepreneur must expand or perish. You'll find that to be true in your own case, and probably a great deal sooner than I. Things are moving so much faster than when I came here a dozen years ago. They will move faster still once the Transcontinental is finished."

"In that case, there will be more than business enough for us both. I don't care to overextend myself before I'm even established."

"The difference between expansion and spreading oneself too thin is purely a question of finances. I can help in that regard."

"Are you proposing to invest in this parlor?"

"In a matter of speaking. I'm considering purchasing it outright."

Richard had been expecting this. Kendrick was too fat to have come all this way just to talk shop.

"I'm young, as you said. Too young to retire."

Kendrick blew a jet of smoke toward the picture of Janus Connable on the wall. "It would be a crime, not to say a sin, to deprive the local bereaved of talent such as yours. In addition to offering you twice what you've invested in this parlor, I'm offering you a position as manager, at a salary of six thousand per annum. I very much doubt even your estimable father ever managed to clear that much his best year."

"I'll wire him and ask," Richard said. "He's still in business."

"Can I take that as an expression of interest?"

"Curiosity only. Thank you, Colonel. I prefer to work for myself."

"You needn't decide now."

"I'm afraid I must. I have a visitation in one hour, and another client in the cellar, as you saw. I don't know when I'll find time for another pleasant conversation such as this."

Kendrick scowled at his cigar, which seemed to have turned quite acrid. He put it out in the ashtray Richard had provided.

"You have a wife," he said, "and a child on the way. I myself am a widower, without progeny, but it would seem to me you should be thinking of their welfare instead of your own independence."

Richard rose and extended his hand. "Thank you for your visit."

The other remained seated. "I'm careful in my ventures. It's less costly to buy an existing business than to start one from the ground, and to interview prospective managers. If I can avoid the extra expense and bring benefit to a respected colleague into the bargain, so much the better; but it is not absolutely necessary, especially when that colleague is ungrateful. I intend to operate a parlor in this neighborhood, with or without your cooperation. If it's to be without, we'll soon see whether there is business enough for us both."

With a little effort, he pushed himself up from his chair

and pulled down the tabs of his preposterous waistcoat. "Thank you for showing me your charming parlor. I shall remember what you said about a lamp and reflectors. It's crude, but I'm sure I can come up with a refinement."

"I'll get your hat."

Richard forestalled telling Lucy about Kendrick's visit, to avoid upsetting her during the last month of her pregnancy. He told Max, swearing him to secrecy. The Italian listened without interruption, as always. It was the best way to improve his English.

"He do you what he did me," he said afterward. "But you don't drink yourself to death. Who would bury you?"

"Not Kendrick. Those clothes of his would shock me awake."

CHAPTER 12

When Lucy went into labor, ten days before the date predicted, Richard was attending a funeral at the mission of San Francisco de Asís, and her doctor was setting a broken leg. The nurse delivered the baby. Max, arriving for his daily visit, cast aside his flowers and contraband newspapers and held Lucy's hand, the nails of which drew blood from his palm. Her narrow pelvis proved only a momentary obstruction for the six-pound, seven-ounce girl. By the time Richard got there, Lucy had already named her Victoria, after Massimo Victor Crespo. She had her mother's slender bone structure and her father's cool gray eyes.

The birth confirmed Lucy's love—as a sister for a heroic older brother—for Max, even as it eroded Max's friendship with Richard. Richard was mortified that he'd missed the event, and unrealistic about not having been summoned. There had not been a spare moment, and even if a messenger could have been sent, Richard could not have responded in time. Yet the man who'd felt no jealousy about his wife's friendship with a male business associate now formed a cold resentment: They shared the memory of the arrival of Richard's first child, and Richard was excluded.

The two men retained their respect for each other as

craftsmen and honest traders, but Richard's visits to the cabinetmaking shop ceased except when there was a specific detail to be discussed. Lucy saw the change and was saddened, but she knew from some instinct that nothing she could do or say would restore what had been lost. She suffered for herself as well. When she recovered from the physical ordeal, Max stopped coming around; and because in her world and Victoria's women did not go out unescorted to visit men who were not their husbands, Lucy did not see him again until the christening. There, as arranged months earlier, Max stood up as Victoria's godfather. No words passed between him and Richard in the church, and Lucy only encountered him thereafter when he happened to be in the parlor on business when she stopped by while wheeling her daughter about.

Weeks went by before she learned of Colonel Kendrick's call upon Richard. He told her of it when he could bear the secret no longer; when, in fact, the colonel's orchestrations had begun to affect business at the parlor.

Kendrick was a man entirely without integrity, and could not be relied upon even to carry out a threat in the form in which he'd made it. He did not open a second parlor in competition with Richard's. Instead, his influence took the form of a new round of city inspections at the Commercial Street address, conducted by officials in and out of uniform, with hats off and the crowns overturned, the better for the proprietor to drop banknotes inside. The building, which had stood undisturbed on the same spot for six years, was found to have been constructed too close to the street, trespassing upon public property; the drains in the cellar were constructed incorrectly, contaminating the groundwater with offal discarded during embalmings; the mechanism that lifted coffins and clients from the cellar to the visitation room was unsafe, and might bring its load crashing down upon the unfortunate who worked the crank—Richard, in fact, was charged with endangering himself. There were numerous other malfeasances, all spelled out quite properly in the statutes, and all of which were commonly waived as pork-barrel items introduced by long-departed aldermen in the interest of earning their honoraria whilst filling their own upturned hats with undocumented booty; but not in Richard's case. He was being bled dry by the torture of a thousand cuts.

Fewer clients came to his door, and this, too, found its source in Kendrick. Recreating in the Forty-Niners' Club, attending meetings at the Masonic Lodge, reporting for National Guard inspection, he let slip that he hated to speak ill of a colleague: however . . . Rumors of coffins used more than once, plated-iron hardware represented as solid brass, darker hints still of boxes buried empty and their intended cargoes sold to the medical school for dissection. *Mind you, I do not place any store whatsoever in unsubstantiated tales, but when one hears of them so frequently, and from so many quarters* . . . It didn't matter if his listeners didn't believe him—they were businessmen themselves, and had to recognize what was happening even if they considered themselves to be above such transparent practices—the stories were too good not to repeat. They rode the currents of whispered conversation like coal smoke from Barbary, spread down the hill and across the harbor, and settled like soot over the Connable name. Processions that a few weeks ago would have commenced at his parlor passed by, led by rattletrap hearses operated by black-nailed diggers from Barbary in their shabby beaver hats. Richard stood on the sidewalk with his hands in his pockets and watched them pass.

"You should bring suit for slander." Lucy was nursing Victoria when Richard had poured forth his concerns, and was careful to keep her tone even. The girl's appetite was never robust; when she fed, it was important not to distract her with a sudden sharp word.

"Kendrick knows all the lawyers, and lunches with a judge of the Superior Court. To bring those lies out in open testimony would be to give them a gravity they don't deserve. Most of the people I do business with read the columns, or have them read to them, and believe every word. I could win my case and still lose the parlor. More likely I would lose both."

"What will you do?"

"Wait out the situation. Some other scandal is bound to come along and wipe out all memory of Kendrick's calumnies. That's one thing you can depend upon here."

"Do you ever miss home?" She stroked Victoria's head, covered now with golden down. She could not bring herself to look him in the eye.

"I miss the way people tell you to your face whether they approve of you," he said, "and of course I miss my father. I don't miss working for him. He wouldn't pay me a compliment if I brought back change."

"He said you have genius."

"I imagine he was drinking wine when he said that," Richard said after a moment. "Come to think of it, he seldom disparaged my restoration work."

"He thought you too impatient for a better method of embalming."

"Well, we won't speak of that. Father should not have. He's begun to lose that discretion you value so much. Obsequies." He shook his head.

Lucy raised hers. "What is the Balm of Gilead?"

He frowned. "Nothing at all. A fable."

"I don't know if you'll find it in San Francisco," she said. "If that's what you're looking for."

* * *

Victoria's delicate appetite bothered the doctor at first, and he stopped by twice a week with a portable set of scales to weigh her and note her progress. At length he declared her healthy; "A lady in the dining room. She may marry a president."

"I hope she won't," said Lucy. "I hope she marries a man without a worry in his head."

Richard was drinking again. He didn't stagger or slur his words, but she smelled gin when he came home from the parlor, and he never spoke to her in the evenings except to respond in surly monosyllables when addressed. But his anger this time seemed to be directed inward. She did not fear for herself or her child, but at the time of her pregnancy Max had told her the full story of his own despair at the hands of Colonel Kendrick, and she worried that Richard's silence masked a growing despondency over the situation on Commercial Street. She wished she could discuss her fears with Max, but she had not seen him in weeks, and in any case Richard's rift with him would prevent him from offering comfort in masculine friendship. Richard did not make friends easily. The opportunity to do so was limited in his profession, and his own insularity prevented him from seeking a confidant. There would be no other Maxes.

Victoria learned to walk. Richard began hiring his hearse out to other undertakers, all of whom seemed to prosper in reverse ratio to the firm of Connable. With fewer orders for coffins coming into Max's shop, the Italian began to make and sell fine furniture. Richard bought a beautiful spindle rocker that converted into a high chair simply by pulling out a pair of pegs and fitting them into other holes. Max had offered it as a gift, but Richard paid him for it without comment.

In April 1869, Richard and Lucy celebrated Victoria's
first birthday. For Lucy, the highlight of the occasion was
a brief visit from Max, his first in nearly a year; he set before the toddler a beautiful box made from eight different
kinds of hardwood with a hinged lid, into which a young
girl could place baubles and ribbons, bowed gently over
her mother's outstretched hand, shook hands stiffly with
Richard, and left without a word passing between the men.
Richard for his part did not insist on paying for the gift.

Three weeks later, at a place called Promontory Point
in the territory of Utah, the Union and Central Pacific railroads joined, girdling the North American continent with
stays made of steel. The newsboys were shouting the head-
lines in the street when Richard came in and announced
he'd sold the parlor to Colonel Kendrick. They were leaving the two-faced city.

Richard had rehearsed the transaction. As he did, he'd
brushed his coat and hat carefully, blacked his boots,
boarded a cable car, and presented himself in the foyer of
Kendrick's gabled and turreted home and parlor, its par-
quet floor buffed to a mirror finish and the headless marble trunk of some unidentifiable Greek deity balanced on
a pedestal. A young swallowtailed apprentice led him upstairs to the colonel's study, where more antiquities reposed
on shelves in glass cases and Kendrick received him in a
silk dressing gown of Oriental design that made him look
like a fat madam in charge of a brothel in Chinatown. His
host offered him brandy, which he declined; he had that
morning, he explained to Lucy, put the cork back into the
bottle for good.

Facing each other in leather wingback chairs, the men
negotiated.

"The offer to purchase your establishment stands at the

original price," Kendrick said. "However, I have made other plans for management. Young Gardener, whom you just met, has shown a great deal of promise. To be frank, your name has become a liability."

"I'm aware of that." Richard spoke without emotion. "I want your assurance in writing that the parlor will retain exclusive use of Massimo Crespo to construct its coffins."

"We refer to them as *caskets* now; repositories for valuables. I'm quite satisfied with the firm I employ at present. Crespo works too slowly for a volume business."

"With a guaranteed retainer, he'll be in a position to hire an apprentice, and thereby double his output."

"I cannot agree to that."

Richard slid a long envelope from his inside breast pocket, leaned forward, and balanced it on the arm of Kendrick's chair.

Kendrick left it there. "What is it?"

"A letter composed and signed by James Alonzo Werner, an estate attorney with an office on Washington Street."

"I've done business with Werner," the colonel said. "Upon occasion my services are paid for by the estates of the deceased."

"One of my first clients was his housemaid's son. Werner values her highly. This is a letter of intention to bring action against you for slander, defamation of character, and restraint of trade. The circumstances are explained in the document."

Kendrick smiled. "I know a few lawyers myself, as well as some other officers of the court. Are you prepared to ruin yourself over some idle conversation?"

"Are you?"

"Mr. Connable, this is most transparent. Unlike certain of your customers, I don't quake at the mere mention of an attorney. I deal with them regularly on both a professional and a casual basis."

"I'm already ruined. You saw to that. You were too thorough for your own good. Once you've taken away a man's income and reputation, he has nothing to lose by going after yours. That letter names several officials of the City of San Francisco as witnesses Werner intends to subpoena on behalf of his case. I suppose it all swings upon the amount of your faith in the relationship you share with these men, and in how they will answer certain questions put to them in open court. My own acquaintance with them was brief and superficial, but it's my observation they'd follow a banknote out a second-story window."

"Bribing witnesses is a serious offence." Kendrick's face approached the crimson in his dressing gown.

"I agree. The problem with buying loyalty at auction is the transaction lasts only as long as the time between bids." Richard sat back. "You're very wealthy, and can draw this out until my own poverty forces me to withdraw the complaint. You're the better judge of how your customers on the hill will regard you by then."

"This is extortion."

Richard looked at him quizzically. "Most morticians would hardly need to be extorted into association with a master craftsman like Crespo."

Kendrick picked up the envelope, fumbled in a side pocket of his gown, and straddled his nose with a pair of spectacles. He stuck a thumb under the flap, paused, then returned the spectacles to his pocket and thrust the envelope across the space that separated them. "I assume you can return this to Werner as undeliverable. I'll have the papers drawn up."

Richard pocketed the envelope and withdrew another.

"I took the liberty of asking Werner to put our agreement in writing," he said. "I know how busy you are now that there is no one else to take up the slack."

The colonel took it at last. "I erred, Connable. I should have offered you a partnership."

"I should not have accepted it," said Richard, "and here we'd be anyway."

The money was more than sufficient to carry them back to Michigan, buy a house, and invest in a new parlor. Lucy had the evidence of the bank draught signed by Elsinore Kendrick and Richard's eyes, the whites of which were clear for the first time in weeks, and still she could not believe it. Leaving San Francisco! With difficulty she suppressed a sudden urge to wake up Victoria in her crib and shout out the words. She asked if he intended to buy out his father's interest in Monroe or set himself up someplace like Toledo or Detroit. "It wouldn't look well for two undertakers named Connable to compete," she said.

"We're not going back to Michigan."

Her heart plummeted.

"That would be failure," he said. "We didn't come all this way to let a rotter like Kendrick send us slinking back."

"Where, then, Sacramento?" There were no other cities in the region large enough to support a business such as his, and what she'd seen of the capital on their way down suggested a place with all the charms of San Francisco minus the ocean view.

"No, I'm quit of this cursed El Dorado, and you and Victoria will be soon. A few months ago I sent out inquiries. At the time it seemed in the way of a last resort, so I said nothing about it. I was wrong. New towns are blossoming all over since the railroads came through, and old ones raised nearly from the dead. They're raw, and attract brutes; their cemeteries tend to grow faster than their commercial districts. That's why I'm going out there first, to find a safe place for you both before I send for you. I'd as soon drop you in the middle of Barbary otherwise."

He slid a dirty, wrinkled envelope from the same pocket that had contained the others. "You have no idea how many undertakers are seeking partners to answer the increased demand," he said. "This is the best response I've received by far."

She took the envelope and studied it before lifting the flap. The return address was written in a slovenly hand, smeared by the many other hands through which it had passed in mail cars and on the Overland, and almost illegible. The postmark read *Hays, Kansas.* She'd never heard of the town.

III

The Undertaker's Friend

Whiskey and business do not go
well together; it should be avoided
(the whiskey, I mean).

> —Henry F. Cate,
>   "Funeral Etiquette,"
>   *Preserving the Dead: The Art
>   and Science of Embalming*

CHAPTER 13

The letter was signed, *Sergei Rubyoff, Prop. Rubyoff & Rubyoff Mortuary Specialists, Hays City, Kansas, U.S.A.*

In elaborate but imprecise language, Rubyoff greeted "Mr. Richard J. Connable, Esq.," thanked him for his timely communication, and set out the sad tale of his brother Gregori's recent death from complications of the liver and Sergei's subsequent efforts to serve the bereaved of Hays City with only the assistance of an inexperienced apprentice. The city's status as a supply base and freight-storage depot for wagon trains serving the Eastern states from New Mexico, and the near proximity of Fort Hays, had packed it with merchants and their families in the scant two years since its founding, and with overflow cattle trade expected with the approach of the Kansas Pacific Railroad, the surviving Rubyoff was forced to seek help from a seasoned source. He offered a junior partnership and temporary quarters in his own home, with meals included, until such time as Richard found suitable accommodations elsewhere for himself and his family.

"I beg you, Mr. Connable," the letter concluded, "to give ample consideration to these overtures, as I am in competition with the Rooney brothers, who are four and determined to make theirs the only undertaking firm in the city."

Lucy finished reading the letter and laid it in her lap. "I don't like this mention of the Rooney brothers," she said. "It sounds as if you're trading one Colonel Kendrick for four."

"I didn't say there wouldn't be challenges. The other offers I've received are for employment only. Rubyoff wants a partner, with no investment required."

"He has a drunkard's hand." The script was uneven and blotched from spilled liquor, she suspected. "He admits his own brother succumbed to the condition."

"All the more reason for me to remain sober, if true. Inactivity is my downfall. It looks as if I'll find more than enough to keep me occupied in Hays."

"But how will you keep from happening what happened here?"

He retrieved the letter from her lap and slipped it back into his pocket. "I was a babe in the woods when I came here; I expected the frontier to be a more open place than the wicked East. I know now that when it's a case of Connable *versus* Kendrick, it's better to be Kendrick."

Victoria cried, interrupting Lucy before she could ask what he meant.

She packed Richard's bags, slipping Janus Connable's picture in its glass frame inside a folded shirt to protect it. The collections of Tennyson and Browning he'd bought for his office went into storage in a trunk. Everything else in the parlor had gone to Kendrick in the sale. She was bitterly disappointed to have to remain in San Francisco until Richard sent for her and Victoria—she found the city harder to bear now that escape was possible, and she and Richard had not been separated since his army service—but she knew his reasons were sound; reading between the lines of Sergei Rubyoff's letter told her that much of his green, uncured city was like Barbary, and would require intimate study in order to isolate its better neighborhoods. She feared for his safety, but she would not use this as an excuse to talk him out of the venture. It was the first sign of hope he'd shown in months. She would not pour him back into the bottle a few hours after he'd crawled out.

He deposited enough money in the bank to sustain Lucy and Victoria for three months, and showed her how to make withdrawals—something her mother had never learned, and which she suspected was rare even in her own circle. She felt herself her husband's equal. More gratifying—and a fill to her heart—Richard invited Max to their home, explained the situation, and entreated his former friend to look after his wife and daughter while he was away. Max, who had come intending to thank him for the concession Richard had wrung out of Kendrick to continue the parlor's association with the cabinetmaker, was stunned into silence by the request; but he nodded briskly and the two clasped hands. Of a sudden, the Italian pulled Richard in close and embraced him briefly. Then he bowed to Lucy and walked out.

On the day of Richard's departure, one hour before his train was due, Pembroke Benjamin rang at their front door. When he saw Lucy standing behind Richard holding Victoria, the real property man swept off his tall hat, bowed deeply and theatrically from the waist, and handed Richard one of his cards, on the back of which he'd scribbled a name.

Richard looked at it. "Who is Isaac Shindle?"

"He's in the way of being me," said Benjamin, "or as close as you'll find in that part of Kansas. We've done business in the past. Give him my name if you need assistance you can't find nowhere, anywhere else."

"How did you know I'm going to Kansas?"

He smiled in his stiff whiskers. "How'd I know you shivvied old Kendrick and made him say thanks for the lesson? You can stand on any hill in this town and hear the chinks jabbering in Hong Kong if you hold your head just so."

"Is Shindle in real property?"

"He sells cigars."

"I don't smoke." Richard made to return the card.

Benjamin kept his hands on his hat. "It don't, it doesn't signify. Just about everyone else does, and goes to Shindle's store to sample his stock and confess their sins. He's got the biggest ears and the smallest mouth in town. Show him my card and watch him switch."

"What's the charge for this service?"

"This one's on P. Benjamin. When a chicken eats a hawk, it's entertaining, and good for business. No gaming place ever drew new customers by winning all the time. I don't expect the colonel to appreciate it up there on the hill, but down here it means more pilgrims and money from the East. Ma'am." He bowed again, clamped on his hat, and left, swinging his stick.

"Curious fellow," Richard said.

Lucy said, "Don't lose that card."

They said good-bye at the station. Richard kissed Lucy and bent to kiss Victoria, who was more interested in looking at the huge smoking locomotive than responding, and waved at them from the platform of his car as it slid down the track. He looked handsome in his new black bowler and the oilcloth cape he wore to protect his clothes from cinders. Lucy hugged her daughter tight.

Richard's letters arrived in packets. He wrote them daily, but they were held at the post office until the next wagon train left for the railhead at Abilene, where they were put aboard a car and shipped west. For Lucy, his account of his first weeks in Hays read like serial adventures in the fiction section of the *Call,* complete with cliffhanger endings and an anxious wait for the next installment. There were details he left out as unsuitable reading for a young wife and mother, and that would reveal themselves in years to come, when these descriptions no longer applied to her.

Hays, on first sight, had a temporary quality unmatched even in San Francisco, which burned over every few years and rebuilt itself on thrice-used foundations with new lumber carved from the forests farther inland. Richard would later learn that the town itself had been dismantled on another site after it was bypassed by the Kansas Pacific and reassembled here under a new name. It was walled with saloons on both sides of the broad main street, with false fronts belonging to fictitious third stories and balconies where the town's harlots gathered with fluttering scarves, twirling parasols, and other devices designed to attract the attention of new arrivals in trousers. Troopers on leave from the fort two miles away loafed on porches and watered their mounts from troughs in front of the buildings, and freighters bucket-brigaded heavy sacks and bales of paper from the backs of wagons into storage buildings covering city blocks. The place looked prosperous, and its newest visitor, who had seen Detroit pop up out of the ground like mushrooms around the Fort Wayne barracks, and San Francisco fling wide its golden gate to hordes of immigrants from Europe, Asia, and the eastern United States, detected the accelerating hum of a community preparing for yet more growth. With freight and passenger cars rattling into Abilene, ninety miles to the east, it was only a question of time before the rest of America made its way to Hays: excursionists and entrepreneurs from New York and Chicago, congressmen from Washington, and gaunt herds of cattle from Texas, trailed by thirsty cowboys with pokes in their pockets and hell to raise. The stagecoach Richard rode into town passed a sprawling cemetery on the approach to town (identified, inexplicably, by a sign over the gate reading BOOT HILL) that had all of Kansas in which to expand; forward thinking on the part of some city planner with experience of other such places. Sergei Rubyoff had not exaggerated in his letter, it seemed.

His parlor was an unprepossessing house on Prairie Street, a whitewashed saltbox that Richard might have mistaken for a schoolhouse or a church but for the sign pegged into the overgrown front yard:

RUBYOFF & RUBYOFF
MORTUARY SPECIALISTS

Sergei I. Rubyoff
Prop .

A line had been painted out beneath Sergei's name and there was a space between the second *p* in "Prop" and the period. Someone had removed an *s*.

Something long and reddish-brown streaked out of the weeds that bordered the path to the front door, stopped halfway across to squat on its haunches and crane its neck, blinking at Richard, then darted into the weeds on the other side. It was his first glimpse of one of the several thousand prairie dogs locked in combat with surveyors and carpenters for possession of Hays City.

"Mr. Cunnable! Velcome!"

The man who hurled open the door resembled a prairie dog himself. He was no taller than Richard, but appeared to be, with his round head spiked atop a long neck sloping without benefit of shoulders into his narrow trunk. His hips stuck out on either side, like riding breeches, and from there on down to his paper slippers he was chubby. It was as if photographs of two distinctly different body types had been torn in half horizontally and the top half of one pasted onto the bottom half of another. The effect was in no way diminished by his choice of costume: black waistcoat buttoned tightly above fawn-colored trousers and stripes on his shirtsleeves. He parted his prairie dog–colored hair in the center, plastered it down, and cultivated bristly moustaches that twitched with every shift in expression. He was about thirty, five or six years older than Richard, but looked older yet with his black, bright eyes glittering behind rimless spectacles.

"Mr. Rubyoff?" Richard put down his bag to shake hands. Rubyoff's was marbled all over with old acid stains, like Janus Connable's.

"I knew you would come today. I looked at the sky this morning and I said, 'Today comes Mr. Cunnable.' And you see I was right. *Entre-yous, s'il yous plait.*"

Sergei Ivonovich Rubyoff and his younger brother, Gregori, had fled Russia at the height of the pogrom season, intending to homestead in Kansas and grow wheat. In Leavenworth they were set upon by deserters from the fort and robbed of all their possessions, including their trousers and boots. The only employment they could find was with a local taxidermist, who hired them to clean and dress the carcasses of the creatures he restored for the sporting officers and trainloads of tourists who came through from Europe and the East, shooting the indigenous game and having specimens stuffed and mounted to ship home. The brothers hollowed out dozens of hawks, flayed hundreds of prairie dogs, and spent an entire week skinning a bull buffalo and curing the hide for a standing mount that wound up greeting visitors to a castle in Scotland. The taxidermist approved of their thorough work habits, and soon they were assisting him in the studio. There Gregori displayed a talent for casting beaks and claws in plaster in cases where the original features had been damaged or obliterated by slugs or buckshot, and mixing paints to match the natural colors; their grandfather had painted miniatures modeled by members of the imperial court in St. Petersburg, and Sergei's brother had inherited his artistry. Sergei, more methodical, proved useful in such mechanical operations as tanning, stuffing, and mounting, as the condition of his hands bore witness from their contact with the corrosive agents involved.

Then the taxidermist contracted a parasite from the diseased carcass of a prairie hen and closed the shop to move back East for treatment, taking with him his forms and instruments and volumes of Audubon. The brothers went to work for the mortician at Fort Leavenworth. The principle was the same, and Sergei, who had developed a severe allergic reaction to feathers, stopped sneezing. He did the embalming, Gregori the restoration. At the end of a year, they'd saved enough to continue their journey, but they had lost their enthusiasm for farming, and so opened their own parlor—first in Rome, Kansas, then in Hays after the railroad spurned Rome and that city was pulled down, put back together near Fort Hays, and christened after the fort. They'd been in business there two months when the four Rooney brothers arrived from Milwaukee, along with a Studebaker wagon packed to the sheet with the latest equipment, balms, and cosmetics, and set themselves up in a house they built on First Street.

Richard understood only parts of this story the first time through. Sergei spoke without stopping as they toured the visitation room, to which the door opened directly from the street; the morgue, where no plumbing was installed because there was as yet no running water in Hays; and the little hall bedroom upstairs, where Richard deposited his bag. Sergei's French and Yiddish were better than his English and, the visitor suspected, his Russian. Richard had grown up in Michigan and knew a child of rural peasants when he saw one, notwithstanding his pretty fable about an artistic ancestor in the court of Alexander I. His speech was sprinkled with foreign words and phrases and his accent was unique to himself: His new partner would always be "Mr. Cunnable," and he transposed his *v*'s and *w*'s and showed an even less scrupulous regard for all the other consonants. It was a little like attending the opera: Richard picked up two words out of five and managed to find meaning in the rest by way of context.

The visitation room was garish, a Jew's interpretation of Eastern Orthodox grandeur with materials available from the catalogue at the local mercantile. The walls were flocked, vulgar imitation Turkish throw rugs scattered the broad plank floor, swags of crimson and green and mustard choked off light from the windows. Eggplant velvet cloaked the pedestal where the coffin would sit, and there was a sickly sweet odor of incense. Amidst all this, angels and cherubim might be expected but, grotesquely, the round tables and corner shelves where they might have stood supported prairie dogs skinned and stuffed, enough to populate a town, all striking the same characteristic pose Richard had observed in their living counterpart on the path outside, upright on their haunches with their paws drawn into their chests and heads turned as if to sniff the air for the scent of predators. They were mounted in the morgue as well, taking up space among the basins and pumps, observing with frozen curiosity the sheet-draped figure on the bench, and on the aprons of the staircase and in the room where Richard would sleep—Gregori's old room, he supposed—and all over the large sitting room that connected it with Sergei's, where they sat to visit.

His host noticed his reaction. "The fauna here"—he said *pauna,* forcing Richard to reflect on the meaning, then hurry to catch up—"is more limited than around Fort Leavenworth. I've found reason to be grateful we did not open a taxidermy shop."

"Based on what you wrote in your letter, I'm surprised you've found time for a hobby of any sort."

Sergei looked uncomfortable. He adjusted his spectacles.

"Gregori was a disappointment," he said. "He told me he drank as he did for worry of the Rooney brothers. But the drinking began long before either of us had ever heard the name Rooney. Before we left Russia, if I may speak ill of the dead. Gregori drank because he drank. And now he is gone."

The teapot whistled in the little kitchen downstairs: a lean-to built out back. The building had been a schoolhouse in Rome, but the Rubyoffs had claimed it before the community could attract a teacher. He went down, and returned fifteen minutes later carrying a squat brown crockery pot and two homely cups on a platter. He described the elaborate silver set that had been their parents' wedding gift, stolen from them in Fort Leavenworth. Richard in charity chose to believe him.

"I think I can supply the rest," he told Sergei. "The Rooneys tried to buy you out. You refused, and rumors started to circulate."

Sergei's brows rose above the rims of his spectacles. Then he shook his head slowly. "The story of evil is old, that you can tell it with such precision. The citizens of Hays were disturbed to learn that their gone beloved would be stuffed, dressed in the raiments of dead kings and highwaymen, and exhibited in Madame Tussaud's wax museum in Paris, while sandbags stood in for them in their graves. I doubt two in ten had in their lives heard of *la* Tussaud. But a lie with a name attached travels so much farther than a lie with none."

"City officials came to visit. Your establishment was found wanting in several particulars."

"Once again, you are a seer." Sergei returned his cup to his saucer untasted. "Hays City is less than two years old, and yet it has managed to amass so many ordinances; too many to set on paper, if I may be so bold."

Richard slid a hand into a pocket, reassuring himself that the card Pembroke Benjamin had given him was where he had put it.

"The Rooneys have done nothing that has not been done before," he said; "and what one man—or four men, for that matter—can do, another can undo."

"I bless the devil that taught you this wisdom, and the God that brought you to this place. However, I should warn you that if there is an antichrist, his name is Fergus Rooney, the elder of the clan. He worships Mammon, and would sacrifice even his brothers upon that altar."

"A businessman. You can reason with him on those terms. Surely there is business enough for two undertaking parlors in Hays."

The uncomfortable look returned. "I may not have been entirely truthful in my letter. There have been only two deaths here this year. We divided them between us."

"Hays is booming; anyone can see that." Richard was alarmed. "In the midst of life, we are in death. I've seen it in San Francisco: Too many people fighting over too little gold, and tragedy the consequence. You have a client right now in your morgue."

Sergei's tea seemed to have turned; he pulled a face and set down the cup and saucer. "Please come with me."

He rose, and went to the stairs. Richard followed him down past ranks of prairie dogs posed like members of the Imperial Guard. In the morgue, Sergei paused with his hand on a corner of the sheet that covered the shapeless figure on the bench.

"I was quite excited when it came in," he said. "One tires so much of posing prairie dogs."

He twitched off the sheet in one motion. The gaunt gray timberwolf thus exposed seemed to grin at him with lips drawn back from its fangs.

CHAPTER 14

. . . And so Rubyoff confesses that he misled me about the facts of the situation in Hays City. Although the population here is clearly on the ascendant, the mean age of the immigrants is between twenty and thirty, and there is little of the fighting and gun play that has made the Abilene cattle town the subject of national attention. Rubyoff supports himself by growing corn, green beans, and tomatoes behind his house for his table, selling some to one of the hotels in town, and from occasional taxidermy, such as the wolf he is stuffing and mounting at present for Philip Sheridan, the Fort Hays commander, who shot the animal from horseback while on patrol recently. At present it represents the only income on the horizon.

I hasten to say that Rubyoff is not a schemer, merely a man fighting for survival by desperate measures. It is the old story. Even the Rooneys sustain themselves and their enterprise through a part interest in the Cheyenne Hotel, a place popular with speculators and the owners of the various cartage firms that stop here for storage and supplies. Its accommodations are superior to the Freighters' Retreat, where the teamsters stay.

Rubyoff is genuinely uneasy with the pressure that has been applied against him by the Rooneys, whose acquaintance I have not yet made, although one sees one or all of them daily, crossing First from their parlor to the Cheyenne Hotel, and dining at their table in the window on the ground floor. They are a truculent-looking quartet of Irish roughnecks, despite their close shaves and tight waistcoats, and are somewhat feared as leaders of the local citizens' vigilance committee. The feeling in Hays is that when the K.P. tracks reach this far, they will bring the cattle trade from Abilene and Ellsworth, and with it the rowdy behavior that prevents undertakers in such places from starvation. It is therefore in the brothers' best interest to control the enterprise without interference from outside. Since the untimely death of his own brother Gregori, Rubyoff feels that a partnership will stand firmer than one man alone against four and their influence.

In spite of his duplicitous letter, my sympathies lie with Rubyoff, and I agree with him that Hays City offers great opportunity, especially for the businessman who has established himself before the first wave of entrepreneurs sweeps in from East and West. However, the situation until then is lean. Do you and Victoria be patient . . .

Lucy stopped reading Richard's letter. Victoria had fallen asleep in her arms in the convertible rocking chair Max had made, and she herself had stopped listening to the words when she knew where they were headed. They meant many more months before Victoria would join her father in Hays, and Lucy her husband. The clatter of dray wagons in the street outside and clangor of the cable cars crawling up and down Telegraph Hill morning till night would remain part of their experience for a long time yet. Lucy rocked, hated the rented house and rented furniture, and missed Richard and Michigan.

Someone rapped softly on the screen door. The front door stood open, and the strong sunlight sliding under the lifting fog was behind the visitor, but she recognized Max's posture, the peculiar way he cradled his bowler with his forearm, as if posing for a photograph. She got up, transferring Victoria from her lap to the chair without disturbing the sleeping child, and went to the door, pausing to glance at her hair in the mirror opposite the staircase.

"I come at a bad time," Max said, when she let him inside. "You are resting, yes?"

"I just finished reading a letter from Richard." She took back her hand. "We won't be joining him before fall."

"I am sorry. But I am happy." He shrugged, supplying something his English could not. He took a package from under his arm and gave it to her.

She untied the cord and removed the brown wrapping. It was a book of photographs, ten inches wide and six inches high, mounted between stiff boards with mottled endpapers. The pictures were of Rome, Italy: the Coliseum, the Pantheon, the dome of the Vatican, printed in sepia on heavy stock. The captions were written in Italian.

"It's beautiful," she said, turning the pages. "Did you bring it with you to this country?"

"No. It is in a shop on Market Street. I see it and I think of you. I say to myself, 'Perhaps she is finish with the Bible stories.'"

She laughed. Then she felt a twinge of shame. "It must have been expensive. You shouldn't be spending your money on gifts."

"I read first. Is what is best about books. You take, and still you can give."

"But what is the occasion?"

"My birthday. Today I am thirty."

She laughed again, and had to stop herself before she woke Victoria. "I should be giving *you* a gift. That's how we celebrate birthdays in this country."

"In mine, too."

He tipped a hand toward the screen door. Through it, she saw a brougham drawn up before the porch, with ivory side panels and a two-horse team.

"It's handsome! Is it yours?"

"*Sì*, today. Is a waste on me."

She looked at him. He'd had his hair cut very recently—a question mark–shaped swath of lighter skin showed where it had been sheared around each ear—and a tiny dot of sticking plaster marked where he'd scraped his chin too close.

"Max, I can't go out riding with you. I'm a married woman."

He hoisted his brows.

"Oh, you want to come? I take out my goddaughter." He smiled at her confusion, showing his beautiful teeth. "In my country is a tradition. Is very bad to refuse."

"It is?"

His brows slid back down. "*Sì*. Today."

She put down the book and went to get shawls for herself and Victoria.

Gregori Rubyoff's ghost was very much in residence in his room.

In preparation for Richard's stay, Sergei had emptied the walnut wardrobe and nicked rosewood bureau of his brother's personal effects, but he'd overlooked an empty brown whiskey bottle that had rolled under the painted iron bed and come to rest against a baseboard, and a collar in its box, yellowed beyond laundering and crosshatched inside with old dirt. Atop the bureau, under mourning crepe, stood a framed *cart de visite* photograph of two young men standing in an overdecorated parlor, bearing the name of a Fort Leavenworth studio in gold copperplate on the mat.

One was Sergei, the other a year or two younger and built more expansively, with a suggestion of baby fat in a face bordered by curly dark hair and the sort of encircling whiskers Richard associated with Quakers and mariners from Massachusetts. It may have been Richard's imagination, influenced by what Sergei had told him of his brother's behavior, but he thought he detected signs of dissipation in the somewhat sullen features more suitable to a man of forty, with self-indulgent habits.

Less open to interpretation was the fug that had settled in the room, of unwashed linen and stale liquor and the neglect that came with surrender. He had noticed that same malaise in Massimo Crespo's workshop during the early days of their association, and more lately in his old office in San Francisco, after it had become clear that Colonel Kendrick had won. A man could air out a room, scrub it with spirits of ammonia, repaper the walls, and apply fresh varnish to the floors and furniture, but nothing short of a complete reversal of fortune could make the smell go away entirely.

He spent a troubling night, aching in all his muscles from the journey in a springless stagecoach and before that a succession of chair cars, unrefined even by George Pullman's nascent vision of passenger comfort, and disturbed by snatches of dreams in which Gregori's face featured prominently, used up at twenty-four; rose at dawn, washed and shaved from his predecessor's basin with a pitcher of water provided by Sergei the night before, and went down to find his host unrisen and Hays City just beginning to stir for another day of bullwhacking, profanity, loafing, drinking, philandering, and prairie dogs, prairie dogs, prairie dogs.

Crossing a street, he put his foot through an inch of crust on top of a burrow, painfully twisting his ankle and drawing a sympathetic snort from a bushy-browed sergeant in blue wool and yellow galluses knocking out his pipe on a porch post.

"You need a stick to get around in this town," he said. "It's all quicksand and varmint shit."

"Where's yours?" Richard sat on the edge of the boardwalk and kneaded his ankle.

"I don't walk. I'm cavalry. Only I stopped riding good horseflesh into this town. Best mount I ever had shattered its cannon in one of them holes. I'd druther shot my cousin Harold." He stuffed the pipe with what looked like pencil shavings from a pouch made from some creature's scrotum, possibly belonging to the horse with the shattered cannon.

"Someone ought to do something."

"That's the sheriff's job. City pays him ten cents for every rat, stray dog, and prairie dog he shoots on top of his county salary."

"Then why isn't he busy? He could make a fortune here."

"This ain't his hour. Mr. J.B. Hickok don't turn out before noon nor go back to ground much before sunup. He's a gambling man, and hell on Old Gideon."

The name meant nothing to Richard, who stood and tested his weight on the ankle. It hurt, but was sound. "What's a cardsharp and a drunkard doing keeping the peace?"

"I expect no good Baptist come forward to put his name on the ballot." The sergeant struck a match on the porch post and watched the flame burn down to the wood. "You a preaching man?"

"I'm an undertaker." Richard brushed sawdust off the tail of his frock coat.

"Which Rooney are you?"

"My name is Richard Connable. I work with Sergei Rubyoff."

The sergeant set the match to his tobacco. A yellow flame shot up and burned half of it before settling into an orange glow. "The taxidermist?"

"No. Do you know where I can find a man named Isaac Shindle?" He fingered the card in his pocket.

"The seegar man?" The sergeant pointed the stem of his pipe at a building on the opposite corner. "Got him a counter in Tommy Drumm's saloon yonder. Tommy don't open till ten."

Richard thanked him and asked where he could get breakfast.

"Town's got more places to eat than drink; almost, anyways. Cheyenne Hotel's the best if you want to avoid prairie-dog steak boiled in prairie-dog piss with prairie-dog balls on the side. It's on First Street. On second thought, though, you're better off taking your chances in any of the other places."

"Why?"

"Cheyenne's just across the street from the Rooneys'. They eat there every day. I don't know Mr. Overland or Mr. Wells Fargo, but I don't bet they eat in the same place."

"Maybe they do," Richard said. "Maybe they should. Everyone needs transportation."

"Vertical transportation's another thing, I reckon." The sergeant pushed himself away from the post. "Pleased to make your acquaintance, Mr. Constable. Watch where you step."

"Connable." But the man was too far down the boardwalk to hear.

The Cheyenne Hotel restaurant was located on the ground floor of a building that showed some aspirations of permanency: a stone-and-mortar foundation, fretwork and gingerbread on the front porch, iron horse-head sconces picketed along the side facing the street to illuminate the boardwalk in front at night. The dining room was appointed as well as any Richard had seen in Detroit and San Francisco, with linen and silver on the tables, a well-swept Brussels carpet, and waiters in starched aprons and neckties. When he asked for the table in the bay window looking out on the street, the headwaiter apologized, explaining that it was reserved.

Richard looked around. At that hour, fewer than a half-dozen diners were eating breakfast. But he didn't cross-examine the headwaiter, who led him to a corner table and handed him a menu bound in green cloth boards.

When the first man arrived to claim the table in the bay window, he guessed what his last name might be, and confirmed it by asking his waiter.

"That, sir, is Mr. Rooney. He dines here with one or more of his brothers every morning and evening. They own the funerary establishment across the street."

He'd seen the parlor on his way there, a white colonial with fluted pillars supporting the front porch and a plaque mounted next to the door:

Fergus O. Rooney,

Argus F.X. Rooney,

Adlar M'G. Rooney,

Oscar F. Rooney,

UNDERTAKERS

"And which one is that?" Richard asked.

"To tell you the truth, sir, I don't know. One Rooney looks pretty much like all the rest."

This Rooney resembled a typical Irish tough, scrubbed up, dressed up, and sobered up for an appearance before a magistrate. His thick black hair was pasted back from a low forehead as with shellac, his handlebars waxed, and his blue chin perched atop a guillotine collar. It was a belligerent chin and his eyes were as small as buckshot. He wore a tight black coat over a black waistcoat, both carefully brushed, but Richard, with his experience of churls and farmers forced into suits for mourning, intuited that he spent much of his time in private in his shirtsleeves. He sat with his back to the window and tucked his napkin under his collar.

Richard ordered coffee, poached eggs, and ham. By the time his meal arrived, so had two more Rooneys, dressed as the first and each possessing the same out-thrust chin and tiny eyes with handlebars in between. They were all as wiry as prizefighters, but the first man the waiter had pointed out was thicker through the chest and looked older than either of the others. Richard guessed he was Fergus, the oldest; and since no fourth had showed up well into the meal, it was the youngest and last-listed, Oscar, who had stayed behind to look after the parlor. There were subtle differences between the remaining two, but as to which was Argus and which Adlar, he couldn't say.

Nor did it matter. They all looked like schoolyard bullies.

Isaac Shindle wore a soft black hat on the back of a leonine head of red hair and whiskers as coarse as copper wire. He weighed at least three hundred pounds and draped himself in a striped smock like an Arab tent that covered the stool he sat on behind his counter and made him look as if he were floating in space. He reminded Richard of an observation balloon he'd seen demonstrated at Fort Wayne.

Shindle glanced at Pembroke Benjamin's card with his own name scribbled on the back, put it aside, and resumed rolling a cigar. "I ordered some Turkish tobacco through him last year," he said. "I rolled it and sold a case to General Sheridan. He sent a box to Grant. I could use more."

"You'll have to communicate with him," Richard said. "He said you're the man to come to in Hays City when you need something."

Shindle continued rolling. Rows of cigars filled his oak-and-glass counter and open boxes on top. The rest of Drumm's Saloon had begun to fill with freighters and troopers from the fort. They were interrupted from time to time by customers buying cigars, usually by the fistful: He charged between a penny and a nickel, according to length and girth.

"I work with Rubyoff, the undertaker," Richard said.

"I wouldn't close my eyes around him. You might wake up stuffed." Shindle's smock shook from his chuckling.

"Then you know what the Rooneys have been saying about him."

"If you don't want to hear what people say about people, Tommy Drumm's isn't the place not to do it."

He thought about that, then decided it wasn't worth working out the meaning. "Rubyoff says it doesn't stop with talking. The Rooneys have bribed the authorities to pester him with inspections and fines."

"Fines are how Hays makes money, outside of warehouses and supplies. I pay my share to avoid paying the tax on tobacco."

"No one's trying to run you out of business."

"If they did, who'd pay the fines?" He cut the end off the cigar with a contraption that looked like a hay knife attached to a board and laid it atop a stack in one of the boxes. "Hickok's the man you want to talk to."

"The sheriff? Can he stop it?"

"If he wants. He's the man stands behind the men collecting the fines." Shindle pointed a tobacco-stained finger toward the bar, behind which an assortment of pistols, rifles, knives, and shotguns lay on shelves under a sign calling for customers to check their weapons. "Everybody's armed in Hays. Why'd they pay a fine if it wasn't Wild Bill doing the collecting?"

At dusk, Pembroke Benjamin strolled down Commercial Street toward the house he'd rented Richard and Lucy Connable, six blocks down from the mortuary parlor now owned by Colonel Kendrick. A buyer was interested in acquiring the house, tearing it down, and building a hotel in its place, he said; Benjamin suspected a brothel was what he had in mind. The rest of San Francisco was growing, why not Barbary? But the fellow wanted to open for business before winter. If Mrs. Connable wasn't planning to join her husband soon, Benjamin felt he might interest her in a smaller place for less rent.

An ivory-paneled brougham with a good team was drawn up before the house, where lamps burned in two windows. Benjamin didn't recognize the rig, but married ladies of good quality didn't entertain visitors past dark, so he smoked a ready-made cigarette and leaned against a lamppost to wait. There was a fat fee coming from the owner of the house if he made a good sale, and some money too from the owner of the smaller house if he could talk Mrs. Connable into moving. He didn't want to finish out his day without the prospect, and he didn't want to have to come back.

He finished his last cigarette, then took out the cardboard stiffener with the picture of Lotta Crabtree for a keepsake and threw away the empty foil package. He'd been waiting half an hour. When the front door opened, he moved out of the circle of lamplight and watched Crespo the coffin maker come out and climb onto the driver's seat of the brougham. He untied the reins and rattled off without looking around.

Benjamin stood there until the house went dark a minute later. Then he went home.

That was the account he wrote in his letter to Richard Connable in Hays City.

CHAPTER 15

The jailhouse, built solidly of logs with square iron bars sunk deep into the sills, looked as if it had been designed to outlast every other building in town, a telling indicator of things to come. A printed sign stuck in the window of the door read: J.B. HICKOK, SHERIFF. *Then why "Wild Bill?"*

Hickok wasn't in. A deputy named Ranahan or Lanahan told Richard through a gumload of snuff that the sheriff was in Ellsworth and wasn't expected back before the end of the week. Richard went back to Rubyoff's.

He found Sergei in the morgue, poking a postmortem knife at the vitals of the wolf carcass on his bench. Richard held up one of the stiff hind legs to give him room to work, but after sawing through tough membrane for less than two minutes the Russian put down the knife and sat on a low stool with his elbows on his knees and his head in his hands. His face was gray.

"I have an anemic condition," he explained. "It comes and it goes. It is the heat that brings it on."

It *was* hot; the sopping heat of southern Michigan in August had nothing on Kansas. But Richard recognized the symptoms. Once during his restless night he'd smelled the sharp sting of liquor, but since that was part of the permanent atmosphere in Gregori's old room, he'd attributed it to its late occupant. Now he remembered Lucy saying Sergei's letter was stained with alcohol.

"I have the same condition," Richard said. "It goes away when I stop drinking."

Sergei lifted his head from his hands. His expression was so much like a child's who had wet himself that Richard was sorry he'd said anything.

"I am worse than Gregori, much worse. He at least wore his shame in the open."

"It's only a shame if you give in to it. I saw the Rooneys today. Believe me when I tell you they're not worth following your brother to the grave."

"You spoke to them?"

"No. I saw three of them having breakfast in the Cheyenne Hotel. But I know their methods well enough, and I see their weakness."

"What is that?"

Richard shook his head.

"We'll discuss it after I've had a chance to speak with Sheriff Hickok. He's out of town at present."

"What has Wild Bill to do with undertakers?"

"Everything, if even half of what Isaac Shindle says is true. He's murdered for the army, the United States marshal's office, and himself. He killed a man in Springfield, Missouri, in a fight over a prostitute, and in some place called Rock Creek he shot down a man and his young son simply for calling him a name he didn't like. San Francisco has more than its share of pimps and killers, but it's resisted pinning badges on them so far."

"I know Shindle. He is a bad Jew. He celebrates Easter and trades on Saturday. You should not be spending time with the likes of him."

"*Not* spending time with the likes of him has been what's put you in this tight," Richard said. "If you expect to win against the Rooneys, you must become more like them. You must become them."

"It is too late for that." He put his head back in his hands. "I am sorry I have brought you all this way just to fail."

"That's how one talks from inside a bottle. Do you miss your brother so much you'd join him before your time?"

"It is not so easy as that. You do not know."

"I do know," said Richard.

And to prove it he went upstairs, searched Sergei's room, and found a collection of squat amber bottles behind the doors of the commode. They were empty, and their labels all read INDIAN SACHEM'S ELECTRIC HEALTH RESTORER, FOR TREATMENT OF CHILLS, FEVER, TOOTHACHE, ASTHMA, AND WHOOPING COUGH; but a sniff of one told the story. At length he discovered a bottle three-quarters full on the nightstand, inside a ring of erect prairie dogs standing sentry, and brought it downstairs. He found two glass tumblers, dragged a chair from the visitation room into the morgue, sat down, filled both glasses, and handed one to Sergei, who sat on his stool with his eyebrows lifted to his hairline. Richard touched them together with a dull clank. "To the Union."

"L'Chaim." Sergei lifted his automatically and drank deeply.

Richard drained his glass without lowering it, then topped off the Russian's and refilled his. He drank more slowly this time, without toasting.

"Gregori did not drink like that." Sergei sounded out of breath.

"Gregori did not grow up around poisonous chemicals. Drinking is an expensive pastime for me. I need half a bottle just to pierce the crust." He poured again.

He didn't remember finishing the bottle, but when he woke, still sitting on the chair and as stiff as anything he was likely to find in a morgue, the Indian Sachem lay empty in his lap, so he assumed the last drink had been his. The stool Sergei had been sitting on was empty.

The sun was setting; they had drunk away the rest of the morning and all of the afternoon, taking brief naps between swigs, then picking up the conversation where it had left off. Richard had learned that Sergei still wrote to a young lady of his acquaintance in Russia, but since she had not answered in more than two years he feared that she had married, or fallen victim to a purge. Richard had a foggy recollection that he had told his host something of his wife and daughter, and possibly of his life in Michigan, before the final blackness. He got up, found a lamp and a box of matches, and lit the wick. Then he found Sergei, huddled on his side on the workbench next to the wolf with one arm flung across the carcass, breathing contentedly. Richard covered both with the sheet.

The snake-oil tonic, with fusel oil added to give it a medicinal whang, was slower to leave his system than gin; he was still slightly drunk, and something banged spongily inside his head, like a hammer striking the hull of a ship sunken in deep water. But with the aid of the lamp, he made a more thorough inspection of the morgue's shelves than he had the day before.

Not surprisingly in view of his background, Sergei Rubyoff's cabinets contained agents as well suited to the preservation of animal hides as human cadavers: arsenic, alum, saltpeter, chloride of lime, and mercury bichloride filled bottles with cork and rubber stoppers, among others with unfamiliar labels in Latin and strange characters he thought at first were Aramaic, but decided were Hebrew based on his knowledge of the Russian's origins. When he pulled out the drawers of an apothecary chest, assorted glass eyes stared up at him from the recesses.

Sergei's pumps were barely functional. Someone had

patched the bellowses and bulbs with squares of oilcloth and sticky tree sap; they wheezed asthmatically when compressed, and little air came out the nozzles. Most of his instruments were more appropriate to a blacksmith's shop. There was also the problem of irrigation and drainage: Water was brought in buckets from the town well, and a glance out the back door revealed where the brothers had dumped the offal of evisceration, then shoveled lime on top of it from an open sack beside the door to hinder the spread of disease. It was medieval. But then Richard had begun his inquiries in San Francisco with the expectation of making an investment.

He just hadn't expected it to involve exorcism.

A sharp gasp turned him around. The sheet flew off the bench, Sergei leapt to the floor, lost his balance, caught it against the edge of the bench, and stared at the dead wolf. "Not again," he said.

Richard lectured him without preamble. "Anyone who came in here would believe what the Rooneys have been saying about you. There isn't a thing in this room I wouldn't expect to find in a taxidermist's studio." *Including you,* he almost added; and promised himself never to drink again, even to demonstrate a point. He did not like himself when he was cruel.

"It is the frontier." Sergei ran a hand through his hair, which pomade and his sleeping posture had forced into a hedgehog bristle on one side. "One learns to make do with the materials available."

"Hays City is not the Sahara. This morning I watched a pair of teamsters unloading a stove from Detroit. We have only to order what we need from Chicago."

"What shall we use for money?"

Richard blinked. "Did you think I would accept a partnership without intending to make a contribution?"

"I cannot allow you to throw good money after bad."

"There is no bad money. It's what you do with it that's bad or good. We're going to start by bringing this parlor into the nineteenth century: That's good. Then we're going to spend some money the way the Rooneys spend it, which is bad. But it will be good in the end."

"Is that what you meant about becoming the Rooneys?"

"Actually, we're going to do them one better," Richard said. "At breakfast this morning, they drank four bottles of wine between them, and they were missing one brother. I hardly assume they're any more temperate at dinner. That's their weakness, or one of them. It won't be ours. From now on, the only alcohol under this roof will be the mythyanol we pump into our clients' arteries. You must agree to that. If not, I'll take the next train back to California."

"I will not be giving up anything you are not." Sergei fingered his rodentlike moustaches. "I see what you were about now, although you might have found a less dramatic way to make the impression."

"As you said, it's the frontier. And there must be no more dead animals in this parlor."

Sergei cringed as from a blow. "I must finish the wolf. General Sheridan gave me twenty dollars on account."

"Finish it. When it's gone, get rid of the prairie dogs as well. They're hardly diverting with so many live ones about, and stiff creatures are the last thing we want people to think of when they visit an undertaker."

"Mortician," Sergei corrected.

"We'll let the Rooneys be morticians. They look the part."

"What shall I do when the hours hang heavy?"

"Embalm and restore. This bout of good health won't last forever. Sheriff Hickok will see to that, if no one else will."

"I *am* weary of waking up on that bench. It is not always an animal I share it with."

"What about the other?"

Sergei thrust out his hand. "You have my word, Mr. Cunnable. No more drinking, and no more dead animals."

"Richard." He grasped it.

That night in Gregori's old room, Richard wrote a long letter to Lucy, finishing with the news that he was likely to be in Hays quite a bit longer before he could send for her and Victoria; he was wiring funds to see them through. He felt guilty, for he knew Lucy would be upset, and because he missed them both. But he had no doubts about the wisdom of the decision. He'd traded one Colonel Kendrick for four, as she'd predicted, and war with the Rooney brothers would leave little time for nest-feathering. He consoled himself further by picturing the reaction when he introduced his wife and daughter to their comfortable new life. By then the railroad would surely have come, and brought with it a mortal population sufficient to support the finest undertaking parlor on the prairie. On that thought he went to sleep, and dreamed no more of Gregori Rubyoff's sad ghost.

The next morning he breakfasted in the sitting room with Sergei, who was still gray from yesterday's excesses and not inclined to be adventurous beyond tea and toast. Richard himself was famished. After recording an inventory of what was needed to make their morgue competitive with whatever First Street had to offer, he went out to post his letter and order a pile of scrambled eggs and a thick slab of ham at the Cheyenne Hotel, washed down with a pot of coffee. Sergei stayed behind to make a fresh start on the general's wolf, which would not wait another day; one sniff revealed that it had passed from rigor mortis into the beginning stages of putrefaction.

All four Rooneys were at table that morning. As he'd

suspected, yesterday's absentee was younger than the others. The chin wasn't as prominent and the eyes less inclined toward beady, but he had the same low forehead and dressed identically, in a tight coat that looked as if it came off directly when he wasn't in public. Richard was taking his seat at a table near the kitchen—the restaurant was more crowded at that hour and the waiters distracted—when Fergus, the eldest, drained his glass of wine and rose to leave. The others stood up in a body and followed him out. That was encouraging; Richard had been concerned that he might have to deal with four independent spirits instead of just one. He ate at a leisurely place and when his waiter came with the bill he asked him where he could find a druggist.

"I'm sorry, sir. Was one of the eggs bad?"

As anticipated, the druggist, a red-cheeked German missing a little finger, didn't stock most of the items on his list, but he bought mythylic alcohol and plaster of paris. The druggist, intrigued by the items and by Richard's careful dress, asked if he was a doctor.

"No, I work with Sergei Rubyoff."

The druggist wrapped his order and tied it with cord. "I didn't reckon he needed anybody's help to stuff those prairie dogs."

"We're undertakers." Richard paid him and left.

Because time indeed hung heavy, he helped Sergei dress and skin the wolf. Removing the hide was a tedious process, as the Russian cautioned him that any stretching would show on the finished specimen and affect the nap of the fur. They split the skull with care, removed the brains and scraped the bone, cut away the tongue to cure separately, tarred the gums to arrest decay and keep the fangs from falling out, then resealed the skull with plaster. Sergei saved the brains in a basin, soaked them in tannic acid and a solution of alum and arsenic, and used them as a sponge to treat the inside of the hide, which together they staked out behind the parlor to dry in the sun. When Sergei tied a bandanna around his nose and mouth to strip the skeleton of its rotting meat, Richard excused himself to step outside and retch.

"Mind the hide." Sergei pared a long section off the spine and swished his knife around in a basin filled with cloudy water.

The hide, the Russian said, would require three days to cure, unless rain forced them to bring it inside to start all over again when the sun came out. There seemed to be more to taxidermy than undertaking, Richard said, and Sergei agreed. "Undertakers bury their mistakes," he said. "Taxidermists exhibit theirs for all to see."

The Russian tarred the skeleton, arranging it into the pose it was to maintain once the tar stiffened, and sculpted a counterfeit of meat and muscle out of twisted horsehair bound in place with string. During this process he paused frequently to study a photograph he'd tacked to a cabinet door, taken by a naturalist of another of the species in the attitude of stalking prey, with jaws wide open as if poised to strike. He said the naturalist had been killed and eaten by his model shortly after squeezing the bulb. Richard asked if that was true.

"I am teasing. Wolves are the gentlest creatures on the planet, so long as you are not a field mouse or a lame deer. However, hunters prefer their game fierce; if not when they shoot it, at least when they display it, to impress the pilgrims."

"Pilgrims?"

"You and me, my friend. The ones whose English is either too good, or not good enough. You see how much I have learned about this country of yours."

Richard watched him molding scraps torn from the *Kansas State Record* sodden with paste over the makeshift muscles. "Where did you learn your anatomy?"

"Cossacks razed my village when I was small. I helped sort out the body parts for burial."

"More teasing?"

"I never tease where Cossacks are concerned." He pulled a knot tight with the string between his teeth and cut off the extra length with scissors.

Richard wrote a letter that night to the mortuary supply company he'd done business with in Chicago to request prices on the equipment he needed, and posted it the next day on his way to breakfast. He'd gotten an early start, and finished just as the Rooneys took their table.

This time, Fergus Rooney looked straight at him. He crooked a finger at his waiter, who leaned down, listened, glanced toward Richard, and said something in reply. Then he handed around the menus. Fergus interested himself in the bill of fare then and didn't look up as Richard walked out.

Richard wondered if he'd been talking to the druggist, or possibly Isaac Shindle. The fellow was Pembroke Benjamin's creature after all, and not to be trusted not to peddle information wherever it had value.

Outside, he heard gunshots. He asked a young trooper strolling past on the arm of a woman in ruffles and paint if there was some kind of trouble.

"Just the usual sort," the trooper said. "Wild Bill's back in town."

L ife near Barbary had made Richard a kind of connoisseur of gunfire. The sudden crash that awakened one in the dead of night, the double crack of two weapons discharged almost simultaneously, the report, long pause, then report again of a half-finished job laid to rest—these sounds meant a man killed or seriously wounded. The pulse, release, pulse, release, pulse behind the announcement of Hickok's return was target practice.

Richard followed the sound of the gunshots, prodding the earth before him with his ebony stick, around the corner to the log jail. There he paused before the sight that greeted him, and had to scramble out of the path of a stopped freight wagon whose driver cleared his throat to get his attention.

A split-bottom chair had been set up in front of the sheriff's office, and the man who occupied it had it tipped back, with his heels propped against the hitching rail that ran past the boardwalk. Those heels, small and narrow as a woman's, were shod in soft moccasins dyed a shade of rose that made them resemble dancing slippers. With them, the man wore a bright yellow coat, whose skirt brushed the boards, over a silk, rose-embroidered waistcoat and checked trousers, and an incongruous gray bowler on the back of a head full of auburn curls to the shoulders. The effect was girlish, and Richard might have taken him for one of the balcony harlots but for the star on his chest and moustaches trailing from an upper lip that stuck out like a duck's bill.

He cut a figure as ridiculous as Colonel Kendrick's; and now Richard knew him for a dangerous man.

The sheriff's knees were spread, and just as the undertaker started his way, flame spurt from between them and something struck two yards to Richard's right with a noise like a pebble striking a clay pot. A headless prairie dog quivered on its haunches in the sandy street, then tipped over on its side, kicked one muscular hind leg in a bicycling motion, and was still.

Another shot, and a prairie dog nearer the opposite end of the street lost its head. Hickok changed pistols and shot a third just as it popped up through a hole in the street. Richard noticed then that a bench had been erected beside the chair with an assortment of firearms laid out side by side on top: the ivory-handled Colt Navy revolver he'd just emptied, an over-and-under derringer, a pistol of the squat-nosed variety referred to as a Bulldog, and a double-barreled Stephens ten-gauge shotgun sawed off to just three feet.

When Hickok paused to fan away the smoke with his hat, Richard took advantage of the recess to finish crossing the street. He mounted the boardwalk just as the sheriff drew aim with his second weapon, a Colt Navy matched to the first, and fired. This time he missed. The rodent ducked down on all fours at the last half second and darted for the cover of the opposite boardwalk. Hickok cursed, flung down the revolver, snatched up the shotgun, and emptied one barrel. A cloud of dust and splinters flew up from the boardwalk across the street, leaving behind a half crater in the planks as if some huge creature had taken a bite out of them.

"Shit! Town expects me to pay for that." He plunked the shotgun back on the bench.

"You can make up for it by shooting two dozen more prairie dogs," Richard said by way of greeting.

The sheriff looked up at him, measuring him from head to foot. He had a large, thick nose, sunburned and peeling, and mean little eyes like the Rooneys'.

"Tell that to the county," he said. "They ain't paid me for the last eight dozen. I'll be a rich man if they don't cheat me and the prairie dogs hold out."

"Whose idea was it to build Hays City on top of a prairie-dog town?"

"No time for ideas. They slap up buildings like white-wash and don't care if they're atop rattlesnakes or cow flop. Two years ago, all this you see belonged to another town in another place with another name, and I'll warrant it'll be in another place two years from this day. My old pard Will Cody lost his drawers on this enterprise when it was called Rome. Now he's back to shooting buffler for the K.P. Life's a sudden thing here on the border, Preacher."

"I'm not a preacher."

"Schoolteacher then. You here on county business, or is it you're soft on small critters and carpentry?"

"I have business, though I can't say whether it has to do with the county. I'm not a schoolteacher, either. I'm an undertaker. My name is Connable."

The front legs of the chair struck the boardwalk with a bang. Hickok scooped a handful of brass cartridges out of an open box on the bench and reloaded the second revolver. His upper lip stuck out in a pout. "There goes my afternoon. I was fixed to sit in on a game at Drumm's."

"My business won't take that long."

"It don't signify, Connable. When I see a black cat or an undertaker, I got to go out and find a white horse before sundown or my luck turns toes-up. A white horse in a town full of freighters is a scarce thing, so it means a ride out in country."

"That's just superstition."

"Be it so, but I've fought Indians and white men and the whole Southern Confederacy, and I never went seeing a black cat or an undertaking man without I seen a white horse before dark, and here I am at thirty-two. How you think I come to miss that last varmint twice?"

"Surely you've missed before."

"Not with no scattergun." He spun the Colt's cylinder, which buzzed like a rattlesnake.

"If that's your policy, you ought to stay away from the Cheyenne Hotel. Four white horses in one day must pose a challenge."

"You work with the Rooneys?"

"No, I'm Sergei Rubyoff's partner."

Hickok blew out a lungful of air in a chuckle and laid the revolver on the bench. He sat back again, hooking his thumbs inside his long coat. "Oh, hell, why'd you tell me you're an undertaker? I don't need to see no white horse after passing the time of day with no taxidermist."

"He's put that aside. We're going to run the finest embalming parlor in the State of Kansas."

"You might want to check with Fergus Rooney first."

"I was under the impression I'm checking with him now."

The sheriff stood. He towered over Richard by five inches and had gone pale under his sunburn. "Men have got themselves kilt for less than that, you damn blackbird."

"I meant nothing by it."

"Out here you say what you mean or nothing. State your business or walk on."

A crowd had begun to gather at the end of the boardwalk, trooper blue among the freighters' flannel and canvas. Richard couldn't decide whether they'd come out from cover because the shooting had stopped or they'd been drawn by some kind of scent.

"I'd rather not discuss it here in the open," he said.

Hickok chewed the end of a moustache. At length he picked up the Colts and stuck the barrels under the yellow sash he wore knotted around his waist. He put the Bulldog in a coat pocket, nestled the derringer in his waistcoat in place of a fob, and cradled the shotgun. He used the end of it to summon a Negro from the crowd.

"There's a penny for every dead prairie dog you find in the street," Hickok said. "Bring them into the office when you're through."

"Yes, sir, Wild Bill." The man put his hat back on his head and stepped off the boardwalk.

"Don't call me Wild Bill," Hickok called after him.

"Yes, sir, Mr. Hickok."

They went inside. The deputy sheriff Richard had spoken to a few days earlier was seated behind the desk, reading the *Record*. He lowered the newspaper to aim a question with his face.

"Go get breakfast, Pete." Hickok leaned the shotgun into a wall rack with shotguns and rifles on either side.

The deputy folded his newspaper and got up for his hat. Snuff bulged his lower lip. "Someone's coming out from the fort, don't forget. You might want to get them two cleaned up before they get here."

"They can lick themselves like a cat. What am I, the house nigger?"

"Tom Custer don't like you already, Jim. Why you want to go out of your way?"

Hickok grinned. "If I had his brother, I'd be colonel by now. I never did admire a shirker."

Later, Richard found out the sheriff had broken up a brawl in Drumm's Saloon the night before, beating up two troopers with his fists and throwing them in a cell. Hickok had just ridden in from Ellsworth and was too tired to reason them out of their high spirits. There was a history of bad relations between the administration in Fort Hays and officials of the city and county.

Hickok plunked himself into the deputy's late seat and started opening and closing drawers. "Lanihan keeps hiding it," he said. "He plans to run against me on the Prohibition ticket next election."

He came up finally with a bottle of Old Gideon, sloshed the contents around speculatively, then drew the cork and tossed it over his shoulder. "I'd offer you a pull, only I don't drink with blackbirds. There ain't enough white horses in Kansas." He swigged from the bottle.

"I don't drink." Richard remained standing. "Your Christian name is James, is it not?"

"That's what it says in the Bible back in Illinois. Where do you hail from?"

"Michigan. Why do they call you Wild Bill?"

"That's a mistake, which the journals and ten-cent shockers don't mind repeating. I only accept it from joshing friends. I'm Jim to most that know me. You'll call me Sheriff Hickok."

"Forgive me if I'm forward. It doesn't seem to me a man of your reputation should earn his living shooting prairie dogs in the street."

"Prairie dogs, mongrels, rats, and all other kinds of vermin. I've wolfed and shot buffler too, but not from no chair. I was told it was a perquisite of the job when I put my name on the ballot. You know what a perquisite is, Connable?"

"An incidental emolument. An inducement apart from one's salary."

"Emolument." Hickok rolled the word around his mouth, working his long upper lip, then washed it down with rye. "I taken a Cheyenne lance through the thigh last year. Rot

set in and I had to fight to keep the leg. I used the lance for a crutch while I needed it and sold it to a fellow in Julesburg. I sold it again in Ellsworth last month. I reckon that's what you'd call an emolument." He stroked his thigh. "I still get the miseries when I'm too long in the saddle. No, Mr. Connable, I can't say I think about shooting prairie dogs one way or the other."

"There's more to the office, of course," Richard said after a moment.

"That there is. There's two sorry troopers on the other side of that wall will swear to it."

"I meant ordinary enforcement. A town comprised almost entirely of frame buildings is dangerously combustible. Businesses must be inspected for fire safety. Then there is the matter of the unstable infrastructure. The firmest foundation is only as sound as the earth beneath. Proprietors who fail to maintain their structures against collapse must face fines or condemnation. How you manage to look after all that and still find time to keep the peace and shoot vermin and travel out of town is a mystery."

"I go to Ellsworth for entertainment, if you're curious about that." Hickok leveled his mean gaze over the top of the bottle. "I make it a practice never to get drunk where I work."

Just then the door opened and the Negro came in, working the latch with an elbow. The bodies of several prairie dogs dangled by their legs from each hand, held straight out from his body and dripping on the floor.

The sheriff shoved the newspaper across the desk and told Richard to make himself useful. He opened the sections and spread them on the floor in a corner. The Negro laid out the carcasses side by side.

"Amazing," Richard said. "Every one hit in the head."

"How many?"

"Dozen even, Mr. Hickok."

Hickok took a coin from a waistcoat pocket and snapped it off his thumb. The Negro caught it in his hat. "That's two cents I owe you. Come around tomorrow."

The man thanked him and left.

"Prairie dog's head's about the size of a man's heart," Hickok told Richard. "It ain't just the bounty. I'm a peace officer, not a county clerk. There's people who look after ordinances and such."

"But they have no authority without a recognized representative of the law to enforce it. In Monroe, Michigan, the local constable receives a percentage of the fines and penalties he collects from those found to be in violation of the township charter. I assume some arrangement of the sort is in place in Hays City."

"Monroe, is it? I knew a cavalryman hailed from there. Tight with a dollar and a kind word." Hickok drank. "It ain't strictly the same. Things are different out here. Some rules you make up as you go along."

"That's been my observation."

Richard unbuttoned his coat, spread it slowly to one side to show he wore no weapon, and drew a stiff brown paper parcel bound with a tie from the inside pocket. He laid the parcel on the desk.

Hickok stood the bottle on the blotter, picked up a letter opener with a pewter handle shaped like a naked woman, and twitched loose the bow with the point, which he then used to lift the flap and expose part of the banknote that lay atop the stack inside. He withdrew the opener and let the flap fall shut.

"That's a sight of cash to be carrying around, Connable. I can't speak for a citizen's safety with so much bushwhacking scum floating around here since the war."

"In that case, I'd be grateful if you'd deposit it in your office safe. I'm new to the community. I assume there are fees and taxes to be paid. Having been warned by you of the danger, I could hardly justify offering robbery as an excuse for delinquency."

Hickok shaved a callus on his shooting hand with the edge of the letter opener. "I never made it to Michigan. I didn't know this was how things was done that far East."

"It's how things are done everywhere, with varying degrees of subtlety. However, for the past two years, I've been doing business in San Francisco."

"That explains it, then. Except what you expected to find here you couldn't out there."

"Pioneering is largely a matter of timing. I got too late a start."

"Six weeks more and you could say the same thing about Hays. Them four Irish ain't the kind to let the grass grow. Folks don't call it the race West for nothing."

"You ought to consider buying a white horse of your own, Sheriff. With six undertakers in town, the investment would pay for itself in a month."

Hickok rocked his chair once. He appeared to have forgotten all about the parcel on the desk.

"I didn't think of that," he said. "I expect the railroad'll bring more yet, and business for all. It's the buzzards that lose."

"The Rooneys should bear no grudges when that comes to pass."

"I wouldn't draw to that hand. Four of a kind still beats a pair."

"I'm calling it anyway," Richard said.

Hickok laughed.

"I like the way you blackbirds talk when it ain't about coffins and wreaths and such." He slid open the top drawer of the desk and used the letter opener to drag the parcel across and into it, as if he were scraping crumbs off a table.

He clapped the drawer shut and sat back with the bottle. "Now that I think on it, the Rooneys ain't been inspected since I took office."

Richard prepared to leave. Hickok cleared his throat. The undertaker waited.

"If Rubyoff's clearing out of the taxidermy business, what's he fixed to do with all them prairie dogs he's got stuffed?"

"Throw them out, I suppose. There can't be much demand for them locally."

"Well, now, you're wrong there. There's a dime apiece in them for me, once I knock off the heads and shake out the sawdust. How's fifty-fifty sound?"

"My partner and I would be honored if you'd accept them as a gift."

"I will, and thank you. I'll send that nigger around for them tomorrow. He can look for his own white horse."

Lanihan, the deputy sheriff, came in as Richard was heading for the door. He looked at the carcasses laid out on the newspaper and took the toothpick out of his mouth.

"I wasn't through reading that," he said.

Richard found Sergei apronless and in his shirtsleeves, brushing the mounted wolf with a curry comb strapped to his hand.

The animal stood on the floor of the morgue, frozen in mid-stride with its hackles on end and its head turned slightly, lips peeled back from its fangs and its snout wrinkled in a savage snarl. The Russian had painted the gums pink, limning the fangs in black, fashioned a realistic tongue from the end of a leather belt (the genuine article had cured less convincingly), and dyed it a dusty shade of red. The yellow glass eyes gleamed as from fires within.

"Gregori was not the only artist in his family," Richard said.

Sergei went down on one knee to pluck a shred of newspaper from between a pair of clawed toes. "All beasts look alike, except perhaps to one another. Gregori's great genius was to make a man look like himself. You pay a mortician— forgive me, my friend, an *undertaker*—no compliment when you praise his work. Ours is an invisible art."

"I never thought about it that way, but of course you're right. Why, then, do we work so hard?"

The Russian straightened and smiled his shy smile.

"I have thought about this. If the situation were reversed, we would wish someone to make us look like ourselves as well. It is a Christian thought, I confess; but Jesus was a Jew. The common wisdom is that funerals are for the living, but that is the same as saying that weddings are not for the bride. If you are fortunate, you have three times to shine during your brief passage through this life: when you are born, when you marry, and when you are committed to earth. Those are the only times when pride is no sin, and they should not be squandered. Even if no one attends the events."

His smile evaporated at the end of this address. Richard guessed the source of his sudden sadness.

"Did you embalm and restore your brother?"

"Yes, and I made a poor job of it. He was jaundiced, you see, and I did not know that in such cases the fluid turns the tissues green. He went green to his grave, though no one saw it but I." He fingered his moustaches. "I never tasted liquor in my life before that night."

"I'm sorry."

"I should have put aside my resentment and gone to the Rooneys. They are scoundrels, but good undertakers." He placed a hand on Richard's shoulder. His face was grim. "You must promise me never to embalm one of your own."

"I hope never to have to make that choice."

"That is not an answer. Place them in the ground as they fell if necessary, but under no circumstances must you pierce their flesh."

"I promise."

Sergei patted him gently and withdrew his hand. He beamed down at the wolf. "It is good, is it not? Let us hope the general doesn't put it in the billiard room, where the officers will hang their coats upon it."

An hour later, they received the same party from Fort Hays that had come to collect the two troopers from Hickok's jail. Richard saw the unfortunate pair slumped in the ambulance, their faces bruised and swollen and gray from inner misery, when Sergei opened the door to admit Captain Tom Custer, a lieutenant named Anderson, and two thick-shouldered troopers with the map of Ireland on their broad, burned faces.

The captain was young for his rank, fair-haired and freshly barbered, with a center part, corn-silk moustaches, and more than a small amount of self-satisfaction in his blue eyes. Richard understood he was the brother of a brevet general and a holder of the Congressional Medal of Honor for service in the war. He had the chin of a Rooney and the squared-off posture of a born bully.

His face was flushed, and his manner with Sergei more abrupt than seemed warranted by a simple errand the captain was performing on behalf of his commanding officer; but then Richard remembered he had come there straight from the sheriff's office, where Hickok had not been disposed to welcome him tenderly. He interrupted Sergei's greeting to direct the troopers to go to the back room and fetch forth the wolf. They went without eagerness, one of them crossing himself out of unconscious habit. Doubtless they expected to have to sort through an inventory of human cadavers.

They came back presently bearing the specimen between them, hunched a little and grunting from the burden. Custer looked it over quickly, made no comment, and barked at them to strap it to the boot of the ambulance. He exchanged a pair of banknotes for a receipt signed by Sergei and presently the partners were alone.

"Cossack," spat the Russian.

Richard was distracted. "What could make a thing of horsehair and sawdust so heavy? Or were they shamming for a bonus?"

Sergei looked embarrassed.

"I put sacks filled with the lead shot I used to weight the prairie dogs in the cavity. People do not believe they are getting their fair account if the purchase lacks substance." He shrugged. "Perhaps, if the savages lay siege, they can fire it from a cannon."

"*That* would be a final sight to carry to the happy hunting ground."

The Russian laughed. Richard had not heard him laugh before. The youthful sound reminded him that only a few years separated them.

But Sergei's explanation had caused him to notice something in retrospect. None of the mounted specimens occupied its accustomed place in the visitation room. He remarked upon it.

"I removed those upstairs as well," said the other. "I put them in the woodshed. This winter we can use them to start fires."

Richard told him of the arrangement he'd made with the sheriff. Again the Russian laughed.

"Only you, my friend, could sell prairie dogs in Hays City. You make me glad I am not a Rooney."

That evening, the partners went over the ledgers and discussed the equipment Richard wanted to buy.

"I do not know these pastes," Sergei said, peering at Richard's handwriting. "The undertaker in Fort Leavenworth stocked nothing of the kind."

"Had you done so, you could have repaired your mistake with your brother. They're metal-based, like arsenic, but for external use, and cover all manner of flaws and discolorations."

"I am a primitive. I cannot read half these names."

"You could hold your own against the diggers in Barbary even as you are. But we're not interested in holding our own. I'll show you how to use them all. If you can make a wolf seem to live again, you can do this. An artist is not his paint."

Sergei turned over a page and stared at the rough diagram his partner had drawn. "What good are plumbing fixtures with no running water? It's too far to the Smokey Hill and Big Creek to lay pipe."

"We'll build a reservoir and elevate it. Gravity will provide the pressure we need, and rain the water."

"I am no carpenter."

"Who builds your coffins?"

"Adolf Armundsen, when I can persuade him. But he works for the Rooneys as well, and will be certain to inform them."

"They'll find it all out eventually. Meanwhile they'll let us alone." Richard had told him the rest of his conversation with Hickok.

"Can we trust Wild Bill?"

"At least until we are outbid. By then we should have had sufficient time to place ourselves on an equal footing with the Rooneys."

"If someone had told us in Russia that the trade in death here was so competitive, we should not have left. Or perhaps it would have made no difference. We did not know then we would be trading in it."

"It's often this way after a war. My father told me it was the same when the fighting ended in Mexico. The grave units turn out diggers in number, and they imagine themselves to be expert." Richard popped open the face of his watch. "What time is the Overland due tomorrow?"

"Noon, if there is no rain. Are you meeting someone?"

"Merely the mail. I expect a letter from my wife any time."

. . . Believe me, friend Connable, when I repeat that it grieves me to write of this, and that I do so only in the assumption that you have deposited funds to your wife's account and in the suspicion that the man Crespo is an opportunist, exploiting her lonely humor to his own aggrandizement.

It is possible—nay, probable—that Crespo's own character is as fine as Mrs. Connable's, and that I malign him unjustifiably, and her by association. No doubt the affair is innocent after all. The experience of this city alone has caused me to place a dark interpretation upon the evidence.

I am, I earnestly hope you will agree,

Your friend,
Pembroke Benjamin

Richard read the letter five times, the fifth while leaning on his elbows at the end of the bar in Drumm's Saloon over a glass of gin, his first since before leaving San Francisco and his first spirits of any kind since his first full day in Hays. He wasn't taken in by Benjamin's oily reassurances any more than by his protestations of friendship. If he wasn't angling to be paid to spy on Max and Lucy, he hoped to spur Richard into sending for her and Victoria early to retrieve her from the coffin maker's clutches and prosper by finding another renter for the house; that, in fact, was the reason he'd given for loitering there that night, whatever respectable terminology he festooned upon it. The man never drew breath without calculating how it could be turned to his profit.

At first, Richard had taken heart from that knowledge; the man was lying. But he had not lied before, merely obfuscated, which was an art in itself, elevated by those who practiced it as altogether a finer thing than base prevarication. An honest man may slip, but a dishonest one would never change his lay, to borrow from the language of Barbary. He'd seen what he'd reported. Lucy knew the dangers of allowing a male acquaintance to leave his horses and rig in front of her house for an hour past dark. Whatever had taken place inside had made her forget or cease to care.

He knew it to be his fault. He'd spent too much time at the parlor, had been a beast when he drank, had placed half the continent between himself and his family to chase the flimsiest guidon of opportunity without regard to their feelings in the matter. At the stroke of a pen, he'd added arbitrary months to the separation, again without consent, and assumed he was acting on their behalf when in fact he was revenging himself against the Colonel Kendricks of the world.

A great interplanetary body placed itself between him and the sunlight streaming through the front windows, eclipsing it. He smelled cigars.

"Brandy, Tommy, if you please," rumbled Isaac Shindle's voice, deep in the mounds of flesh beneath his tentlike smock. "Another gin for Mr. Connable."

"Thank you, I'll buy my own." Richard stared at his reflection in the gold-chased mirror behind the bar, dwarfed beside the cigar maker's.

"No one buys his own liquor in this town. You gather together as many friends as you can find, then hook the owner of a freight company and get him to buy for the lot. They're making money too fast to spend it on their own. It's railroad fever."

"But it will end when the railroad comes through." He didn't know why he was having the conversation.

"That's what makes it fever. Did you ever see a deer mesmerized by the lamps of a locomotive? He can't move off the tracks, just stands there until it runs him over."

Tommy Drumm, the lanky owner of the establishment, poured their drinks two-handed. Shindle paid him and

drank without proposing a toast. He uncurled his little
finger from his glass to point it at the letter lying open on
the bar. "Bad news from home?"

"I have no home." Richard folded it and put it inside his
coat.

"There's a deal of that going around. Your wife?"

Richard said nothing. He regretted accepting the drink.

"I've a wife in Albany, New York. I imagine she's taken
a lover by now. At least I hope so. A woman needs watering or she withers."

Richard turned and threw a fist. Shindle caught it with
a palm the size of a shovel. His hand closed, compressing
muscle and bone. When he let go, Richard clamped his
hand under his arm. It felt as if he'd caught it in a door.

Drumm came over and laid a bung starter on the bar.
"It's too early for that, fellows."

"Thanks, Tommy," Shindle said. "You'll let me know
when it's time?"

"You ought to stay behind your counter." He picked up
the long-handled mallet and returned to the other end of
the bar.

Shindle worked his fingers and took another drink. "I'm
sorry for my manners."

"It was a filthy thing to say." Richard shook circulation
back into his fingers.

"I'm not popular. Someone would've run me out of town
months ago if I didn't sell cigars cheaper than anyone else.
But I was talking about my wife."

Richard's face burned with humiliation. He poured gin
down his throat.

"I am not a gossip," Shindle said, and changed the subject. "Did you meet up with Wild Bill?"

"I did. You're not the least popular man in town."

"He's an acquired taste. He's the kind of man you need

when you need him, but is hard to get rid of when you don't. However, they never last long. There's always another town with a fresh need. So you are here to stay." It wasn't a question.

"It looks that way."

The big man emptied his glass in a long draught and patted dry his beard with the back of a hand. "You should send for her."

Richard said nothing. Shindle pushed his bulk away from the bar.

"Why don't you send for yours?" Richard asked.

"I did. I sent her a ticket. The trains only came as far as Kansas City then. It might not still be good."

"How long ago was that?"

"Two years ago, when the prairie-dog town was bigger than Hays. I'll wait another two years, then go on to Denver. Life is too short to spend more than four years waiting for a woman to make her choice." He lumbered away and took his seat on the stool behind the cigar counter.

When Richard returned to the parlor, Sergei was seated in one of the upholstered chairs in the upstairs sitting room, reading a Hebrew newspaper from the stack he received once a month from New York City. The Russian raised his head and twitched his nose. Richard knew he stank of gin.

"I'm sorry, Sergei."

"Is it talk?" asked the other.

He shook his head and went into his room, drawing the door shut. He set the lamp he'd brought from downstairs on the edge of the washstand, took out Pembroke Benjamin's letter, raised the smudged glass chimney, and poked one corner into the flame. When it caught, he held it for a moment, then dropped it into the basin to finish burning.

He took the lamp over to the little writing table, sat down, slid over a sheet of foolscap, dipped a pen, and began his letter without waiting for the words to come.

Decades would pass before he told Lucy the circumstances behind his decision to plead with her and Victoria to join him in Hays City before the end of summer. She told him then she'd suspected it the moment she read his letter, although Pembroke Benjamin's role was a revelation. By then Benjamin had been dead for years, a victim of a vigilante lynching committee pledged to reform Barbary.

CHAPTER 18

Adolf Armundsen was built like an ape, which was a distinct advantage in the highly competitive occupation of carpentry in Hays City. His legs were stunted from multiple fractures suffered in a childhood plunge down a flight of stairs in his native Norway, but his arms were long and corded with muscle, and the sight of him swinging from one timber to another high in the frames of his buildings, with a hammer thrust under his belt and nails clamped between his teeth, was a local attraction, no more to be missed than Wild Bill strutting about in all his coxcomb finery.

Residents and visitors who wanted to witness Armundsen's acrobatics throughout August and September 1869 had to drop by either the Rubyoff-Connable mortuary parlor where he was constructing a water reservoir atop a scaffolding as elaborate and solid as a railroad trestle, or the lot on Second Street where he was building a house for Richard Connable, his wife, Lucy, and their twenty-month-old daughter, Victoria. Richard had bought the lot from Isaac Shindle, who had intended to grow tobacco on it until he'd learned that the changeable Kansas climate was inhospitable to the crop. Pending completion of the house, a suite of rooms had been arranged for the family in the Pioneer Hotel; Richard's bedroom above the parlor was barely adequate for one occupant.

Early in construction, Armundsen descended at sundown and took up a plane to finish the coffin he was building for one Bill Mulvey, dead of a gullible nature. Mulvey, a sometime prizefighter and full-time troublemaker from St. Joseph, Missouri, had been in residence approximately four hours when Sheriff Hickok invited him to stop throwing his empties through windows. When Mulvey, armed at the time with a revolver (or two, depending upon who told the story), refused, Hickok looked past his shoulder and said, "Don't shoot, he's only having fun." When Mulvey turned his head to see who he was talking to, Hickok lifted one of his Navy Colts and shot him through both temples.

Richard, who was still living the bachelor's life across from his partner's room, got the commission from Hickok himself, whose knock brought him in his stocking feet to the front door. He'd been preparing for bed.

The sheriff was soberly attired that evening, in black Prince Albert coat, striped trousers, stovepipe boots, and broad-brimmed hat with a ribbon band. He smelled of whiskey and brimstone and looked worn out.

"Got one for you around the corner," he greeted. "He's got no friends, so there won't be any frippery needed. County pays ten bucks for the box and burial. His weapons will cover it. He drunk away most of what he brought to town." He turned away.

"Why us and not the Rooneys?" Richard called after him.

"Too far to walk."

Sergei kept his pair, an old gray and an older piebald, at the livery down the street. Richard woke him up and went to get them while the Russian removed the canvas tarpaulin from the hearse behind the parlor. This was a former depot hack, painted black, with the original leather curtains in the windows to protect passengers and cargo from dust. They hitched up the pair and drove to the scene, where a crowd had gathered in the light spilling out of the saloon on the corner, pacing off the length of Wild Bill's shot and describing the event with exaggerated gestures for newcomers. The body lay where it had fallen, minus its boots and material torn away from the clothing for souvenirs.

"It is like home," Sergei said. "The winters are a little better."

They embalmed anyway, although no services were planned or visitors expected; Richard felt he needed the practice after months of inactivity, and he wanted to observe his partner with a human subject. The arsenic and bichlorides were sufficient for a body destined for swift burial. Sergei went about the evisceration efficiently, tarred the cavity, and filled it with newspapers and sawdust. They made no attempt to repair the damage made by the bullet, which had entered two inches above the left ear and exited a half inch above the right.

Sergei said, "A man must shoot many prairie dogs to shoot like that."

"He didn't start with prairie dogs," Richard said.

The journey to Boot Hill was a procession of sorts. Sheriff Hickok followed the hearse on foot as part of his official duties, and some idle townsmen trailed behind to make up for not being present to witness the actual shooting. At graveside the Methodist minister read from Psalms in the singsong voice of an auctioneer—joined, somewhat surprisingly, by two or three harlots, fidgeting a little in the dowd they reserved for appearances in court and shielding their eyes against the unaccustomed sunlight. Richard gave the Negro grave digger a dollar to unprop himself from his shovel and rode back to town with Sergei at the reins.

"That's the saddest funeral I ever attended," Richard said. "Even a drunken lout deserves someone's tears."

That evening, he dined at the Cheyenne Hotel. He'd invited Sergei, but the Russian, who really did suffer from anemia, retired early. Richard was tired of taking his meals alone. Lucy had written that she and Victoria would be aboard a train as soon as she'd settled their affairs in San Francisco. He was more involved in calculating how long that would take than he was in reading the menu when he realized it wasn't the waiter standing next to his table.

"Fergus Rooney. And you're Richard Connable. High time we met, sir."

He stared at the hand that was outthrust toward him; a strong hand, accustomed to physical labor, and stained all over in the badge of the profession. He grasped it out of polite habit, and found himself engaged in a contest of strength. The man's grip was as tight as a wooden clamp.

The eldest of the brothers wore his daily uniform of tight black coat, matching waistcoat, white shirt, and high cruel collar, notched as if to make room for the pugnacious Rooney chin. The tracks of the comb showed plainly in his slicked-back black hair and he showed two gold eye-teeth in an iron smile. His eyes were smaller and meaner than Hickok's, totally without warmth.

"Don't get up, sir," he commanded, when Richard made an overture in that direction. "I'll be sitting for a moment, with your permission, and not take up any more of your time than that."

"Be my guest. Have you eaten?"

"My order's in." Rooney flipped up his swallowtails and dropped into the chair opposite. When he rested his forearms on the table, his cuffs rode up to expose a matting of thick black hair. "You buried Wild Bill's latest. That will get you a line in history if you do nothing else."

"I was convenient. One more corner and he'd have deposited Mulvey at my door."

"A gentleman's answer. I hear you're tighter than that."
Richard made no response.

"Connable, that's English, ain't it?"

There was something defiant about that *ain't*; an old
weapon, taken down from the wall and given a new edge.

"So I'm told. My father was born in Boston, and I in
Detroit."

"Well, it don't signify, as they say out here. I left old
fights back home with my grandmother's lace. How's partners with the Jew?"

The waiter appeared then, as if he'd been hovering in
watch for his moment. Richard ordered sliced duck and a
cup of coffee and surrendered the menu.

"Rubyoff is a good man to work with," he said when
they were alone again.

"It ain't the Rooshian I'm meaning. I'm meaning Kike
Shindle. He's got his thumb in everything shady in this
town. The cigar stand's just a blind. He had one in Ellsworth and used it to sell lots on the railroad right-of-way
to pilgrims till the K.P. got wind of it and sent out a track
gang to tell him how the cow ate the cabbage. Only reason they didn't bust every bone in his body is they couldn't
get to them through all that tallow. But they busted enough
to make him light a shuck to Hays."

"I wonder why the Kansas Pacific bothered. It seems to
me it was the pilgrims who were cheated."

"He done it by wire. They was all of them back East,
with nobody to bark at but the policeman on the corner.
His mistake was to sell a string of lots to a big shareholder
in the railroad; 'twas him found out from the surveyors and
set the track gang on him."

"He doesn't strike me as foolish enough to try the same
thing here."

"Here he's a pimp, got him a string of hoors in a house

at the end of Prairie. That's where the well is, and you can't draw water without them hulloing to you from the balcony."

"That seems harmless enough." Richard couldn't see Rooney's purpose.

"Jews don't stop at just one enterprise. Once a month he's out back of Tommy Drumm's after dark, helping load crates off a wagon into the storeroom. Now, why do you figure a big tub of goo like him would exert himself to help out a couple of dusty freighters?"

"It's my guess you know the answer."

"Opium." The Irishman leaned forward across the table, bringing his leer within six inches of Richard's face and dropping his voice to a murmur. "Raw busthead dope, imported straight from wicked China and waiting for the first chink graders to get to Hays City and make him a rich man out of what the K.P. pays them, probably in that same house on Prairie: harlots upstairs, black dreams on the ground. He always goes back to the railroad. That's where the money is now."

"How do you know this?"

"Who you think keeps Wild Bill in them pimps' clothes, or did before you fell in? He's the one tries all the doors in all the alleys. Shindle told him it was Turkish tobacco, and paid him not to ask any more questions. But the sheriff's been around. He knows the smell, and that tobacco don't come in no crates stamped HONG KONG TO SAN FRANCISCO. Turks and chinks don't get on. Talk is Shindle's got him an agent on the Barbary Coast."

Richard knew then the story was true. Shindle had said he'd bought only one shipment of Turkish tobacco from Pembroke Benjamin, and one innocent transaction wasn't a satisfactory explanation for the bond that seemed to exist between them.

"It seems Sheriff Hickok is no less determined than Mr. Shindle to become rich," he said.

"Why you think he plays cards at Drumm's every night? Tommy's in too, got to be, and he and Shindle pay him to show his face there and bend back ideas anyone might have to stick up the place and make off with them crates. That old injun baiter learned a thing or two requisitioning for the army."

"Why are you telling me this?"

Rooney sat back to give the waiter room to set Richard's meal before him. When the waiter asked if he required anything else, it was the Irishman who spoke up, impatiently sending him away. Then he leaned forward again.

"It wasn't in my plans to tell you a damn thing, till you went and got yourself in tight with Wild Bill. My parlor's as sound as Wells Fargo, but suddenly I'm paying fines left, right, and center to keep from getting condemned. You was seen twice talking with Shindle, so I thought I'd come over here, tell you what I knew, and see by how you took it whether you was in on the opium. I see you ain't. I played a hand or two of poker myself."

"If you're satisfied, my food is getting cold."

"Go ahead and eat, if you can chew and listen at the same time. You can end up eating prime rib and champagne for breakfast."

Richard ate. In his experience, when an enemy made a pitch, it was never brief.

"Jews got the Midas gift, but they think too small," Rooney said. "Shindle's looking to make a tidy bit off celestials, who do like their pipe, but they ain't got much to spend, and anyway they'll be moving on with the railroad. By then he'll probably have something else lined up, but he'll never get out from behind that cigar stand. Meanwhile, with the tracks coming through, he could expand his operation, ship to every railhead on the frontier, and retire at thirty, rich as Pharaoh."

"That would mean getting the railroad to cooperate,"

Richard said. "They have strict rules against transporting contraband."

"I wasn't suggesting taking on the railroad as a partner. They gobble 'em up same as they gobble up land. They ship coffins all the time, and I never met a conductor or a porter who'd pry up the lids to see what's inside."

"You're forgetting we don't ship that many coffins. Rubyoff and I have had one client since I came, and he went only as far as Boot Hill."

"See, that's what working with Jews does to a man. It makes him think small and too short. Once the tracks come through, we'll be crammed to the top of the Presbyterian Church steeple with drunk cowboys, fresh off the trail and nothing to bugger for two months but the cows and each other, and one hoor to six of them. They'll be throwing lead by the bushel, and who's to question three or four extra pounds in the losers' coffins? That's two thousand in gold by the time it's cut up and smoked."

Rooney sat back again, his golden eyeteeth showing. "You don't have to come in. If you don't, it'll just take twice as long to show profit, and I won't have to split with anyone but my brothers and Shindle. But from the way you handled yourself since you came to town, I don't expect you're dumb enough to pass it by."

"What makes you think Shindle will cooperate?"

"He's a Jew, ain't he? Jews worship money and Jehovah, in that order. And if he don't, someone may just go to the governor and ask him what kind of sinful Sodom he's got fixed right here in the God-fearing State of Kansas."

Richard tore open a roll. "I'm an undertaker, not an industrialist."

"Don't decide now. Talk it over with Rubyoff. Only don't think on going to the governor or anyone else yourself. Back in Limerick me mum and da' sold me into indenture to a Croom undertaker. Before that, the Rooney brothers had a rough reputation I can't say we didn't earn, and the magistrate don't know half of it. Talk is you're expecting your wife and wee child anytime."

He stopped buttering the roll. "What's that to do with what you were talking about?"

Fergus Rooney slid back his chair and stood. He seemed to be operated by a system of springs, like the experienced fighters Richard had seen battering one another on wagers behind the Fort Wayne barracks. "I like my trade," Rooney said. "It kept me out of the dock, and Black King Charles never saw a worse hell than an Irish prison. But the money's slow to come, and you got to squeeze out tears for folks you'd laugh at another time. I ain't looking to make it my life's work, but it has its points. Ask yourself who really counts the crosses in Boot Hill, and would make note of two more in the forest?"

He waited until the Rooneys finished their meal and left, striding four abreast across the street to their parlor. Then he paid his bill, went to the post office, and sent a telegram to San Francisco:

LUCY DEAR
STORM DAMAGE SLOWING HOUSE CONSTRUCTION STOP
DELAY COMING UNTIL FURTHER WORD STOP PLEASE
UNDERSTAND I MISS AND LOVE YOU AND VICTORIA
BUT WILL NOT HAVE YOU LIVING LIKE INDIANS

LOVE
RICHARD

The telegrapher counted the words and pursed his lips. "What storm damage? Weather's been fair for a week."

Richard asked him how much for the wire, and paid him to send it.

He went from there to the parlor, where Sergei went on mopping the floor in the morgue as Richard spoke. Finally he wrung the mop out into the bucket and stood them both in a corner.

"What can we do?" he asked. "We are not opium smugglers. In Russia they would cut off our hands."

"Here they'd just hang us. I embalmed a hanged corpse in San Francisco. I shouldn't want to be one. On the other hand, if we turn him down, he'll suspect us of going to the governor."

"Perhaps we should."

Richard shook his head.

"He wasn't bluffing when he threatened the lives of my wife and daughter. I can't keep them away forever, and I've invested everything I have in Hays City. I couldn't afford to run away even if I were to let an Irish hooligan bully me into it."

"This is all my fault, my friend. I should never have written you."

"It's the frontier. I hardly expected to make silk from burlap."

"We cannot make even burlap of this."

"Certainly not by ourselves."

"Who can we go to, if not the governor?"

"I don't know," said Richard.

But he knew.

Within the starry stillness of a Kansas late-summer night, Tommy Drumm's saloon fed off its own atmosphere, like some remote planet. The lamps strung from the tin ceiling on iron falloes squandered most of their light atop the pall of smoke and whiskey fumes that hung six feet above the floor, and what light strained through it reduced white cuffs, spotted playing cards, the liquor in the glasses, and the green baize on the gaming tables to a monochrome dirty ocher. In all that brown-green mulch, only James Butler Hickok stood out, in a coat of crushed red velvet with shining brass buttons and a yellow silk cravat transfixed by a garnet pin that glittered like a drop of blood. He studied his cards with his head tilted to keep the smoke from his cheroot out of his eyes and hair, and didn't see who had come up beside him until his gaze shifted to the man's face.

"Oh, shit." He flung down his hand.

The other men seated around the table—all except the one who had just raised the stakes—jumped when Wild Bill folded, and threw in their hands as well. With a surprised grin, the man who had just bet laid his cards facedown and raked in the heap of chips with his forearm.

"They looked like perfectly good cards to me," Richard said.

"You'd turn a royal flush into a handful of pig shit." The sheriff pushed back his chair and stood, swaying a little. "I'm through, boys."

One of the men who'd folded, an obvious freighter with black beard growing down a neck as big around as a venison haunch, topped off his glass from a bottle that had been reused so many times its label hung in tatters. "Bill, I never knowed you to walk away from a game while you still had a jingle in your pocket."

"I wouldn't, if you'd a white horse in yours." He wobbled toward the bar. Richard followed.

Hickok spun suddenly and snatched a fistful of the undertaker's shirt. He was drunker than Richard himself had ever managed; the whites of his eyes were as red as his coat and his breath was 100-percent ferment. Half an inch separated Richard's left cornea from the glowing coal at the end of his cheroot. "Blackbird, if you're trailing me with measuring tape I'll embalm you myself."

"I have something to discuss," croaked Richard.

Tommy Drumm drifted their way and filled a glass from a bottle. "Have one on me, Bill."

Hickok didn't move. "It's four months till Christmas."

"Let's agree it came early this year. If you're planning on staying in town, we need all the undertakers we got."

Richard felt as if steam were rolling off his eyeball.

Suddenly the sheriff opened his mouth wide and belched laughter in his face. He let go of his shirt and cuffed him on the shoulder. It felt like a log glancing off.

"It ain't as bad as that, Tommy." Hickok turned toward the bar and hiked up the glass. "I always leave a few for seed."

Drumm gritted his teeth in a grin and drew a beer for a freighter.

"What you cussing to discuss?" Hickok watched Richard's reflection in the mirror behind the bar.

Richard glanced toward Isaac Shindle's counter. The cigar maker appeared to be dozing on his stool, hands folded across his great belly. Richard turned back.

"Fergus Rooney told me what's in the storeroom."

Hickok's throat muscles constricted noisily in mid-swallow. He relaxed them, releasing fresh whiskey into his system. He said nothing, watching Richard's reflection.

"Rooney's holding out on you. He means to strike a partnership with Shindle to sell opium all down the railroad."

"What opium's that?"

"He offered me a partnership, to pack the merchandise in coffins and let the Kansas Pacific do the rest."

Hickok set his glass on the bar without making a sound. "I'm supposed to fill the rest of the space in the boxes, I reckon."

"He's an ambitious man."

"And you ain't."

"I just want to be let alone to do my work. My wife and child are coming to join me from San Francisco. If I thought Hays City was going to turn into another Barbary, I'd tell them to stay where they are. I did, actually, until this opium business is put to rest."

"I smoked a pipe or two in my time. I like whiskey better, especially when the other fellow's drinking it. Dope makes him feel as tall, but don't dull the eye. Chinamen don't drag iron as a rule, so them I can just buffalo and throw 'em in a cell till it burns off. I figure to earn my living sheriffing where it's needed. The living won't last where there's dope."

"You must get rid of the opium."

"Yeah, well, there's one thing wrong with that only. It ain't against the law."

"Not everything Shindle's engaged in isn't illegal," Richard said.

Hickok paused in the midst of lifting the stub of his cheroot to his lips for one last puff. He turned it sideways and studied it.

A week later, Sergei finally accepted an invitation to join Richard for breakfast at the Cheyenne Hotel; the Russian disliked eating in restaurants, but the mercantile that stocked the salted herrings he ate every morning had missed a shipment and he was out. The Rooneys, all except Adlar, the third brother, were at their usual table when the pair entered. Fergus looked up from what appeared to be his first glass of wine and nodded at Richard, then turned to engage his youngest brother in conversation.

"Do they serve nothing with the eggs besides sausage, ham, and bacon?" asked Sergei, peering through his spectacles at the menu.

"Potatoes," said his companion.

"Fried, no doubt, in pork fat."

"If you don't ask, you can't go to hell."

"There is no heaven and no hell. There is only Hays." He folded his menu with a sigh. "I shall have toast and jam."

Richard didn't respond. Adlar Rooney, lankier than his brothers but dressed identically, with the same simian forehead, pointed handlebars, and prowlike chin, had come in and leaned down to whisper in his oldest brother's ear. Fergus snatched his napkin from his collar, threw it onto his plate, got up, and strode from the room, leaving Adlar still half-bent and his other brothers confusedly in mid-rise.

"What is that, do you suppose?" The scraping of Fergus' chair had captured Sergei's attention.

"Bad news, evidently."

"What bad news can there be in undertaking, apart from discovering the secret of eternal life?"

"Another enterprise, perhaps." Richard returned to his own menu, which he had memorized long since. He'd said nothing to his partner about his conversation with Sheriff Hickok.

Sergei shook his head and filled their cups from the silver coffeepot the waiter had brought. "Why a man should want more than one business or more than one woman mystifies me. He has but one head, and one *schmuck*."

The next day, the *Kansas State Record,* in its city column, reported that Sheriff J.B. Hickok of Ellis County had arrested Isaac Shindle in the city of Hays for the illegal manufacture and sale of cigars. Shindle's merchandise and equipment had been confiscated and transported to a cell in the county jail, along with several crates that had been removed from the storeroom of Drumm's Saloon.

"Why should Wild Bill arrest Shindle after all this time?" Sergei asked. "He himself has bought cigars from him."

Richard busied himself with the contents of the crate that had arrived that morning from Chicago. GEOGHEGAN MORTUARY SUPPLIES was stenciled on the lid he'd prised off with the edge of the shovel Sergei used to hurl quicklime onto the offal he dumped behind the building, and would never use for that purpose again once the new drainage system was installed. Richard tested the pump's compression, examined the trocar, and removed the bottles of glycerine and formaldehyde from the straw packing. He felt his partner's gaze.

"Did you talk to Hickok?" Sergei asked.

"I did." One of the bottles was moist on the outside. He wiped it with his palm and sniffed. He decided condensation was the culprit, and not a hairline crack.

"Why did you not discuss it with me?"

"I felt certain you'd have advised me against it."

"I would have; but that is not the point."

Richard looked up at him. The Russian appeared as if he were about to cry. His partner recognized it as an expression of anger. "You're too gentle," Richard said. "You would have agonized over it, and your agony would have infected me. Some things that need to be done never are for fear of the consequences."

To his surprise, Sergei rose from his stool and stared down at him. His eyes were huge in his pale face.

"You know nothing of consequences until you stake your own flesh and blood."

He went upstairs, and did not come down again until the following morning, when he declined Richard's invitation to join him again for breakfast at the hotel, even though he was still out of herring.

Richard arrived there later than usual to find a waiter removing china and cutlery from the Rooneys' table. Neither the dishes nor the utensils had been used and the cloth was unstained. He asked his waiter about it.

"They didn't come this morning," the man said. "They've always finished and left by now."

Richard waved away the menu and went out without ordering. He had an idea where the brothers had gone.

He saw he was right when he had to step off the boardwalk on the way to the jail to avoid a collision with the four abreast coming his direction. Their heels clomped the boards like war drums and they strode with their heads sunk between their shoulders and their fists balled at their sides. Eight eyes looked straight through him unseeing. He smelled raw whiskey in their wake.

"I ain't seen so many blackbirds all in one spot since the cholera come through Topeka," greeted Hickok, when Richard opened the door to the office. "Come ahead in. Day's shot to hell already. I will be, too, if that gang of micks get their way."

The sheriff was seated behind his desk with his feet crossed on top in a pair of yellow boots with cruelly pointed toes, peering at his visitor through the side-by-side barrels of a shotgun, the rest of which lay in parts on the blotter. Hickok was in his shirtsleeves, gathered with pink garters to match the stripes on his green waistcoat. His trousers were green poplin.

"They threatened you?"

"Not so's I could stick them in the tin for the judge, but I've had my hide hunted by the best. You get a sense for it."

"Is it because of the Shindle business?"

"Well, what else? Hand me that stick, will you? Lanihan's went and took the cleaning rod home with him again. I swear I'll fire him if he don't beat me out for sheriff in December."

A bamboo cane as narrow as a toothbrush stood in a blue-enamel spittoon in the corner near the door. Richard drew it out and passed it across the desk. He watched Hickok tie a rag onto the ferrule end and poke it through one of the barrels. "Fergus is a hothead, but I shouldn't think he'd forget it entirely and challenge you."

"If an Irishman was ever made King of England, he'd declare war on Jupiter. But he wouldn't fight it himself. He'd pour Old Gideon into some fellow dumb as a box frame to do it for him. I ain't so much against hiring out as I am the quality of the help. That's how come you never heard of any King Paddy the First."

"I never would have approached you if I thought it would come to the Rooneys hiring a killer."

Hickok swabbed the other barrel. "You knowed they'd blow when you lit the fuse, so let's have no more on that. Anyway, it's been too quiet since Mulvey. You can shoot only so many prairie dogs before it gets to be like plowing furrows. I left Illinois to spare myself that kind of work."

"What will happen to Shindle?"

"A fine, with some jail, if the judge don't use tobacco. He'll pay his debt and start up again somewheres else. The merchandise will be federal property after the verdict. Little Phil Sheridan will clear him some space with Sam Grant by way of a couple of cases of cigars sent to the White House, and I reckon the army'll burn the dope, what don't get smoked by troopers or sold through the post trader. John Jake Astor's lucky you wasn't around when he traded in beaver. You'd have had him up for poaching and stomped on a fine fambly fortune at the start." He began putting the shotgun back together. "Speaking of famblies, when you taking delivery on yours?"

"I am not, until this Rooney business is settled."

"It's settled, where you sit. My part in the transaction's just started, but I'll be quit of it soon enough, one way or the other. Fergus never let an itch go unscratched for long."

"You talk as if you don't care which way it goes."

"Oh, I like living. It's a habit I enjoy." Hickok finished reassembling the shotgun and slammed shut the breech. His eyes were red-rimmed but clear. "I like money, too. Not so much for the having, but for what comes with it: good cigars, sipping whiskey, duds what fit, and women you don't have to strike a match in the dark to see she's alone in her drawers. But I don't consider any of it when I'm playing cards. The minute you think them chips you're betting is anything other than just plain clay, you start losing. And shooting is just playing cards standing up."

He leaned back in his chair and notched the gun into the wall rack. "That's wisdom I'll thank you not to spread all over town, Connable. I am a sore loser."

The man's name was Strawhan (or Strawhim, Straughn, Stringham, Strawborn, or Strawhun, depending upon to whom you spoke or which newspaper you read—and the name might change between the morning and evening editions). To complicate things further, he answered to both "Sam" and "Jack." Richard Connable saw him twice only: in a bowler and duster carrying a leather valise from the Ellsworth stage into Drumm's Saloon, and three days later, stripped on Sergei Rubyoff's bench with a bullet hole between his eyes.

He was an angular man in his middle twenties, clean-shaven, with dark hair curling over his collar, although by no means as long as Hickok's, and had the kind of pale blue eyes that disappeared in a photographer's magnesium flash. The owner of the local studio, who paid Tommy Drumm for the privilege of setting up his camera in the saloon and taking the man's picture propped up against a gaming table tipped on its side, had to draw irises on the negative with a pen before anyone would buy the *cartes de visites* he offered for sale.

Strawhan and Hickok were old acquaintances. The sheriff, it was said, had helped the Ellsworth city marshal arrest him on several occasions for breach of the peace, with all the broken ribs and bruises that entailed, and had assumed some role in the man's recent incarceration in Fort Hays for a similar violation. Shortly after midnight on the morning of September 27, Strawhan, in the company of friends, boasted that he'd come to Hays for the purpose of "cleaning out" Wild Bill, who when the news reached him at his table in Drumm's, paused to read his watch, then resumed playing. When, nearly an hour later, a roaring in the street announced that the "cleaning committee" had arrived, the sheriff cashed in, stepped outside, and shot Strawhan through the head, slick as a prairie dog. The dead man's friends scattered.

Later that morning, a coroner's inquest was convened, mainly on the strength of the contentious history between the two principals. The jury heard eyewitness accounts that Strawhan had drawn a revolver, listened without emotion to the testimony of his former companions that his hands were empty at the time of the encounter, conferred briefly, and announced that the deceased "came to his death from a pistol wound at the hands of J.B. Hickok, and that the shooting of said Stringham was justifiable."

There was no debate as to which mortuary parlor the body would be remanded to for preparation and burial. The brothers Rooney were unavailable, having packed their bags and a trunk and left on the noon stage for Abilene and the train station there. No one could account specifically for the sheriff's time between the shooting and his appearance at the inquest hours later, conservatively dressed and sober, but there were those in Drumm's who said they knew someone who swore he'd seen a flamboyantly attired figure pounding on the Rooneys' door in the small hours with the butt of a pistol.

Hays City was left with two undertakers only, and the Kansas Pacific only months away from completing the leg between there and Abilene. But for Richard, heating a lump of wax in a spoon over a candle to plug the hole in Strawhan's angular brow, the prospects were far away from his thoughts. He'd received a telegram that morning from Lucy, announcing that she and Victoria were leaving San Francisco on the afternoon train, bound east toward Kansas.

IV

The Undertaker's Wife

O You who see whom you bring who
came forth from the house of
Min. I have not misbehaved.
O Demolisher who came forth from
Xois, I have not transgressed.
O Disturber who came forth from
Weryt, I have not been hot-
tempered.
O Youth who came forth from the
Heliolitan nome, I have not been
deaf to words of truth.

—Declaration of Innocence
Before the Gods of the Tribunal,
The Ancient Egyptian Book of the Dead

Small, confident Victoria, dressed similarly to her mother in a bonnet and tightly woven dark wool cape to keep cinders out of her hair and clothing, stood on the seat with her fingers curled over the edge of the pull-down window to watch America rumble by at forty miles per hour. When a joint in the tracks jarred her off her feet, Lucy was waiting and caught her in her arms.

"That's a lesson, little Queen," her mother said. "From now on, I'll warn you once and let you suffer the consequences when you don't listen."

But Victoria wasn't frightened. She squealed with laughter and squirmed for freedom and her late perch at the window. Lucy smacked her bottom, sat her firmly on the seat, and held her close until the crying stopped.

Victoria thought she was named for Britain's Queen. She'd gotten this idea from a salesgirl on Commercial Street who'd asked her name and when she gave it said, "And how is the empire, Your Majesty?" Lucy's explanation of the question had had Victoria pushing her court of three sawdust-stuffed dolls into bows whenever she entered her bedroom.

Her mother never corrected the assumption. She had not seen Max since the night of her Great Mistake; propriety kept her away from his shop as always, and Massimo

Victor Crespo had not been to visit. She knew why, and was grateful, for her shame was as great as his. She'd told herself that nothing would have happened had she not that day received Richard's letter informing her that they must remain separated for several more months; but she could not blame it on Richard, and certainly not on Max, who was a lonely man, a deeply sad man, and a man so accustomed to hardship and loss that he accepted the small pleasures that came his way with two thousand years of Roman Catholic guilt. That it had been well placed this time had made no difference; his shame burned as hotly when the pleasure was sanctioned and earned. She knew who was to blame.

When Richard's next letter had come, canceling the earlier message and begging her and Victoria to join him at their first opportunity, she felt certain in her heart that he knew; she could not have said why, but the letter had seemed more desperate than warm, and although all the endearments she expected had been in place, they seemed to have been edited in, as if to forestall questions he wasn't prepared to answer. No amount of self-convincing would shake her from this belief. No restless nights of needing to hear the truth from Richard would in the glare of day overcome her lack of courage to expose her guilt in his presence. Her strongest emotion, which washed over her in a crested wave each time she read the letter, was infinite relief. A second chance she did not deserve had been extended her.

When the telegram came, claiming construction problems with the new house and advising her to delay coming yet again, she knew the reasons to be a lie. Richard, she thought, had had second thoughts, and like her was unequal to the necessity of candor. She did not hesitate, but burned the flimsy in the stove and hastened her packing. When she saw Richard, if he mentioned the wire, she would feign ignorance and let him assume that she'd left San Francisco before it arrived. If she delayed even a week, she feared more letters, each one distancing them further. If things came to an accusation and a confession, they must do so in person. And if, despite her certainty, the house was far from ready, she would take a room for her daughter and herself and work in the kitchen to pay for it if Richard refused to put them up.

The hideous worst was better than staying where she was. For the rest of her life, Lucy would hate the two-faced city with the increasing potency of a physic that turns ever more poisonous after its beneficial properties have expired.

The last part of their journey was the hardest. They shared a succession of ramshackle coaches, mud wagons, and at one point a delivery hack, barely converted to passenger use with crates bolted to the bed for sitting and a canvas sheet that leaked, allowing the rain to run down their collars and pool inside their shoes as thoroughly as if they'd ridden exposed. During one three-mile stretch of washboard road, Lucy, Victoria, and their fellow travelers spent as much time on the floor as on their makeshift seats, and the little girl threw up three times. At no point did they experience the comfort or even the sight of the legendary red Concord, whose gentle leather straps absorbed the bumps and jars of the West's raw topography, and whose side curtains sealed the occupants away from mud and dust. Brief stops for rest and sustenance offered a respite only from constant movement. The meals in the way stations consisted mostly of boiled beef, hard biscuits, and tarry coffee—Victoria refused to drink the curdled milk without a splash of coffee added to disguise the taste—and the cots were only a slight improvement over the floor. In some cases the floors were cleaner.

At the last stop before Hays City, Lucy and Victoria chose the water closet over eating, monopolizing it while mother washed her face, hands, and bosom, scrubbed her protesting daughter to a red glow, applied powder to herself, and dressed them both in clothes she'd been saving at the bottom of their portmanteau under a fold of clean muslin. They emerged badly creased but appearing fresh and clean, their hair dressed and caught with combs. Lucy ignored the glares of the other passengers waiting in line for the facility and hoisted Victoria and herself back aboard the coach without the assistance of the driver, who stood beside the vehicle with his watch balanced on his palm as if it were a compass.

In contrast to sooty, fog-dripping San Francisco, Hays sprawled, all yellow wood and whitewash, beneath a golden haze of sawdust. It appeared to be building itself straight up from the prairie even as the coach rolled down through the wagon ruts, locked into them as securely as a train to its rails, past the cemetery and along the main street. Even the horse manure smelled fresh, indicating that street crews removed each day's accumulation before evening, as opposed to the strata and substrata of Barbary's two decades of offal, both human and equine. The city looked and smelled and sounded of hope, with its hammers and saws banging and wheezing gaily, building anew instead of rebuilding from fire and destruction. Victoria, clinging to the bottom of the window, watched a pair of bull-necked teamsters lowering a medieval-looking arrangement of white enamel, iron fretwork, and mohair upholstery from the back of a wagon onto the boardwalk in front of a barber shop; she insisted it was a throne and asked if her namesake the Queen had come for a visit. Lucy was still thinking of a reply when one of the men put his foot in the street for leverage and stepped into a prairie dog hole, almost losing his grip on the chair, and cursed in a mixture of English and German. She put her hands over her daughter's ears. The entire State of Kansas seemed to be one vast prairie-dog town. She couldn't believe only two days had passed since she'd spotted her first one and asked a fellow passenger what kind of squirrel it was.

As the coach slowed nearing the Wells Fargo office, she felt her pulse in her throat. Would Richard respond to her wire by refusing to meet her, or, more drastically, leaving town completely, abandoning his wife and child in a city filled with strangers and surrounded by empty grassland? For the first time since she left California she realized the rashness of her decision, felt that instead of running toward her husband she was running away from Max Crespo, and from herself and her horrid mistake. All she had were the clothes on her back and Victoria's, three pieces of luggage, and the little over two hundred dollars that remained from the amount Richard had left for her in the bank, some of it in her reticule and the rest pinned inside the hem of one of her petticoats. Life in San Francisco had shown her how small a sum it was, and everything she'd heard of these upstart towns that anticipated the railroad pointed to a swift drain and beyond that scrubwork to survive.

Or worse. She had, as was the custom, always cast her eyes down or to the side whenever she passed a harlot on the street, but out the corners she'd seen their pinned and mended finery and layers of paint and powder and wondered at the lives that had led to the present pass. When one had a loyal and responsible husband and a child for extra security, it was easy to blame poverty and immorality for such wretches. But she, too, was guilty of an immoral act, and two hundred dollars was a thin bulwark against the penniless state, with two lives to maintain and only a frayed thread connecting her to Richard, betrayed Richard. Her eyes searched the crowd of greeters, curious loafers, and eager and desperate souls hoping for mail from home for the only familiar face between California and Michigan. Only a shrill "Mummy!" from Victoria told her

how tightly she was gripping her daughter's hand. She relaxed her grip; but then the girl squealed again and she let
go in alarm. Her heart stalled in the moment before she
saw what Victoria had seen: Richard, in his new bowler
and best morning coat, pushing his way through the crowd
to get to the coach.

The house stood a hundred yards from its nearest neighbor, with another lot between, which Richard had bought
also from Isaac Shindle. "It's a good investment for later,"
he explained. "Until then, even the best neighbors are best
kept at arm's length." The roof sloped steeply to prevent it
from collapsing beneath the Great Plains' infamous heavy
snowfalls, and the stairs to the second floor slanted up the
outside of the building, a carpenter's shortcut common on
the frontier, allowing him to stack the upper story atop the
lower like children's blocks, thus cutting weeks off construction time; Richard promised the stairs would be enclosed before winter, so Lucy and Victoria wouldn't have
to put on outerwear just to go up to bed. The rooms,
sparsely furnished in anticipation of Lucy's homemaking
choices, were small except for the kitchen and dining
room, with low ceilings to trap heat in winter and ventilation ducts installed to allow air to travel freely in summer,
and two heating stoves, a homely one set between oak
uprights in their bedroom near a connecting door to Victoria's and a handsome parlor model in the downstairs sitting room with colored quartz panels and fittings of solid
nickel. There was a Dutch oven in the kitchen and a space
waiting to be filled by a cookstove on order from Detroit;
until then, Lucy would have to prepare their meals in the
brick oven.

Conducting the tour, Richard had hurried ahead of his

wife and daughter, pulling down canvas drop cloths and kicking fumy rags into corners, meanwhile keeping up a running account of his meeting the stage every day for the week past, never knowing which one they would be on and hurrying the laborers along. The last of them was still at work outside, three-quarters through a second coat of paint. The man of the house was as nervous as a bird, showing a side of his character Lucy had never seen. She could not imagine that she'd felt panic only twenty minutes before. She was reassured—and with reassurance came a stab of fresh shame—that he knew nothing of what had taken place in San Francisco. In a rush of desperation she pounced on his arm as he made to retrieve an abandoned putty knife from a windowsill. "Richard, the house is beautiful. It's so open and cheerful, and it's ours. I was afraid to hang even a picture in the house in California."

"You can hang them from the ceiling if you like. You haven't seen the basement yet. We can store potatoes and preserves to last the winter and still have room to butcher a steer."

"I want to see the steer!" said Victoria.

"Papa was only joking, little Queen. We don't have a steer."

"Is it coming from Detroit?"

Richard laughed and hoisted her off the floor. Lucy saw new creases in his cheeks when he smiled at his daughter. He seemed to squint often, and blink rapidly when he came in from outside or moved from a dim room to a bright one, and during their first embrace she'd become aware of the clamshell eyeglass case in his breast pocket, a new addition to his wardrobe accessories. He'd put on weight, and this she attributed to the heavy breakfasts at the Cheyenne Hotel, dutifully reported to her in his letters. She decided her first order of business upon reinstating herself as the woman of the house would be to put him on a program of brisk daily walks and more meals at home, where the bill of fare was under her control.

Face close to her father's, Victoria appraised him with her cool eyes, then put out a chubby hand to touch the dent at the bridge of his nose, made by his new spectacles. She seemed on the point of asking a question when another voice interjected itself.

"May an uninvited visitor pay his respects?"

They turned toward the open front door, where a man holding a soft hat impressed Lucy as if he had stepped out of an editorial cartoon. He was oilcan-shaped, broad at the base and narrow at the top, with a round head stuck on top of his neck and corrective lenses shining like freshly polished windows. His black morning coat and tan trousers were worn but ruthlessly well brushed. She knew who he was immediately.

Sergei Rubyoff bowed from the waist when Richard introduced them and produced a bouquet of cut flowers tied with a periwinkle ribbon from behind his hat. Victoria giggled and clapped her hands. "Are you a magic-man?"

"He's a magician in his parlor." Richard sent her out into the backyard, enclosed by a whitewashed fence.

Lucy accepted the flowers and put her hand in Sergei's. "I feel we're friends already, from Richard's letters."

"I know I am yours." He adjusted his spectacles. "I am sorry that my purpose for coming here is not entirely social."

"Hickok again?" Richard said.

"Not this time. A freighter dropped dead in John Bitter's. A heart attack, the doctor said. The man had just delivered a walnut desk and four glazed book presses to Judd, the loan agent. He carried them alone up a full flight of stairs."

"A big man?"

"Enormous. He drank two quarts of beer straight from the pitcher and ordered another before he collapsed. His partner, who is paying, said the man has a wife and children in Minnesota. He will freight the remains to Abilene and put them on the train there."

"Where was he while his partner was climbing all those stairs?"

"He said Big Ned liked to show off. My own opinion is he went to John Bitter's to hold his seat."

"Minnesota is three days by train. We'll need plenty of arsenite of lead." Richard touched Lucy's arm. "I'm very sorry. I'll be late. You'll find flour and preserves in the pantry. You mustn't wait up for me. I know you're exhausted."

"You'll be hungry when you get home." She kissed him while Sergei studied the plasterwork. "I may be rusty, but I haven't forgotten what it means to be a man's wife."

When the men had gone, she unpacked, with Victoria helping, dragging clothes on the floor, dropping things, and making the process take twice as long. Lucy's scolding lacked conviction. She was happy to be moving about on her own outside the confines of a coach or chair car, and relieved to be doing something other than waiting and thinking. Richard had bought quite a nice wardrobe, with room to hang her dresses next to his coats and suits, but the bureau didn't match and the drawers stuck; when she knew what their budget was in this new place she would order furniture, rugs, material to make curtains. Such thoughts were like unpacking, occupying her with harmless things.

She was unfamiliar with the Dutch oven, but managed to bake an apple pie with the flour and shortening and preserves, and used a knife to pare away the burned edges of the crust. The warm sweet smell made home of the house. It wasn't a balanced meal, but tomorrow she'd find out what the town had to offer in the way of meat and other staples. A sinister-looking device mounted on the kitchen wall with a crank turned out to be a coffee grinder; she hung the pot on a hook inside the oven and soon the raw smell of fresh paint and sawdust was part of the house's history.

Richard was late. Victoria had gotten hungry hours before, and she and Lucy had shared a slice of pie. Then daughter had curled up next to mother in the padded rocker in the parlor and fallen asleep while Lucy read one of the novels she'd brought. Then she, too, had slept, to wake up when Richard bent over her and kissed her on the forehead. He smelled of formaldehyde.

They put Lucy in the little bed Richard's coffin maker had built for her in the room adjoining theirs, and made love quietly and desperately in their own bed. She lay naked in his arms afterward. There was barking outside, a lot of it.

"Does everyone in Hays own a dog?" she asked.

"Those are prairie dogs."

"I had no idea they made so much noise."

"You'll get used to it. Just like the cable cars rattling all night."

"I don't want to think about San Francisco."

They were silent for a moment. A shivery tinkle of breaking glass drifted their way. Someone laughed, a booming deep *haw-haw*.

"You'll get used to that too," Richard said, when she stirred at the sound.

"First I'm going to get used to you." She snuggled tighter against him.

"Victoria's twice as big as I left her."

"Some days she eats as much as any man. Others she fasts. She's part bear."

"She has your eyes."

"She has not. They're yours."

He said nothing.

"What's wrong with your eyes, Richard?"

"It's those taxidermy chemicals of Sergei's. The fumes. We have an oculist in town now. I had these made." He fumbled his eyeglass case off the nightstand and opened it. Moonlight glittered blue through the lenses when he held up the spectacles. "I don't need them on cloudy days. However, Hays hasn't many."

"Why do you work so hard now that you have a partner?"

"Now that the railroad's so close, we're getting more cattlemen in town. They build up grudges they can't carry out on the trail, and they and the freighters don't get along. There are more gamblers, too. They don't have to cheat to clean those cowboys down to their boots, but some do, and when you've lost your whole season's wages it doesn't much matter whether you lost them honestly or not. That heart attack today was the first time I haven't had to plug a bullet hole or stitch up a scalp in weeks. There's work enough for more than two. If only the Rooneys had foreseen that, Hickok wouldn't have had to run them out of town."

"Is it safe for Victoria?"

"Safer than Barbary; but let's don't let her out of our sight."

"Are we settled?"

"Pound on the wall."

"What?"

"Make a fist and give it a good whack."

"I certainly will not. You don't know how rare it is for Victoria to sleep all night."

"You could pound it with a heel and not punch through the lath. I wouldn't have built the place that solid if I thought we weren't going to be here more than a few months."

She almost crawled inside him then. Everything was going to be all right.

CHAPTER 21

R ichard! You never told me the town has a theater."

They were walking along Prairie Street, taking the grand tour. Victoria, gloved and hatted like her mother, clung to Lucy's hand, and Richard carried his stick. The shop windows contained merchandise Lucy had not seen in San Francisco, including women's hats and dresses in styles she had seen only in *Harper's*; periodicals traveled faster than textiles, and what was fashionable in New York and Chicago was still chugging its way through the territories on locals. Fine buggies and carriages lined the street, hitched to fat, well-brushed mares and geldings. A pair of wooden spectacles swung from an iron rod above the door to the oculist's office where Richard had bought his tinted glasses, and there were striped awnings everywhere. It all reminded her of Monroe when the summer people were in town.

The prospect of Hays City having a theater came up when she turned away from a window lined entirely with buttons and ribbons and spotted a man dressed like Charles II in a history book she'd read, pausing by a corner post to strike a match on the wood and set fire to a long thin cigar, tilting his head to keep the smoke from gathering under the broad brim of his plumed hat. The pen-and-ink engraving she'd seen did no justice to the verdant green of his coat, the hem of which, trimmed with red fur to match the plume on his hat, swung to the tops of his boots, polished to a mirror finish with chamois-colored trousers stuffed into them. He wore a broad belt of the same shining black leather with a rectangular brass buckle the size of a hymnal and two pistols stuck inside it with their yellow handles twisted forward. He looked a prosperous buccaneer with copper ringlets to his shoulders.

"It hasn't, my dear," said Richard. "Not the kind with ropes and curtains and boxes for the gentry. However, Wild Bill is doing his best until one can be built."

She tightened her grip on his arm. All she knew about Sheriff Hickok was what Richard had written her, and from it she knew him for a corrupt and a killer.

"Let's cross the street," she said.

"Too late. He's seen us."

Hickok came their way. Mexican spurs, globbed all over with silver, jangled at his heels, and his cigar trailed smoke like a locomotive.

"It's a capital morning, Connable. I'll go out on the scaffold and say this is the missus."

"Lucy, this is our sheriff. Jim Hickok, Mrs. Connable."

He swept off his hat and made a courtly bow, exposing his hair parted in the middle and plastered to his skull. "One more respectable woman in Hays is always an occasion for celebration. It was too much to hope for that she would be so beautiful."

"Thank you."

"Are you a pirate?"

The ends of Hickok's moustaches lifted. He remained bent, his face within a foot of Victoria's. "Well, now, little lady, I never taken a ship, though I once stole a wagonload of whiskey out from under the U.S. Army. Does that count?"

"You smell like flowers," she said.

"I been to the barber. It'll pass." He straightened and tugged his hat back on. "Welcome to Kansas. I'll serve you at my pleasure." He strode away.

"That was short," Lucy said.

"He's off to the livery to find a white horse."

She bent her knees and gathered Victoria close. "I don't think he liked being told he smells like flowers."

"He does, though," Richard said. "Just like the ones in the visitation room."

On November 2, 1869, James Butler Hickok was defeated for reelection by Peter Lanihan, his former deputy, 114 to 89; the county population had grown wary of his ready gunwork and unpredictable binges, and had decided prairie dogs weren't so hard to coexist with after all. Wild Bill filled out his term playing poker in Drumm's Saloon and shooting buffalo for sport. Near the end of December he sent an entire buffalo to a friend who operated a hotel in Topeka, to supply his dining room with steaks and roasts. When he turned over the office, people thought he'd be moving on, but he continued to occupy his seat at the gaming table and increased his alcohol consumption, stumbling along the streets at all hours, taking potshots at prairie dogs, and missing them most of the time, to the detriment of signs, flowerpots, and plate-glass windows. In July 1870, he celebrated Independence Day for two weeks straight, culminating in a drunken argument with two troopers from Fort Hays, one of whom died of his wounds, while the other returned to duty after a brief convalescence. Captain Tom Custer, who'd shared bad blood with Hickok since the latter's scouting days with the Seventh Cavalry, threatened to declare martial law in Hays City unless and until the former sheriff was turned over to federal authority. But by then Wild Bill was gone, to resurface in

Abilene nine months later as its newly sworn city marshal. His predecessor, Bear River Tom Smith, had been lured into a trap by enemies and beheaded.

"Palmy days for the undertakers in Abilene," Richard told Lucy, over the top of the *Record*.

"You're busy enough." She wiped and stacked her new china in the cabinet Adolf Armundsen had made and Richard had given her on their anniversary. "You cannot follow such as Hickok around from town to town like a vulture."

"Blackbird. That's his term. He's as superstitious as an old woman." He folded the paper over. "Adolf's almost finished building the new school, it says here."

"I want to go to school." Two-year-old Victoria sat on the floor, plucking at the stitches on one of her dolls. A spill of sawdust had made a small heap on the braided rug. Lucy yelped, snatched the doll from her, and ignored her bawling as she swept up.

"That time's still a bit off, little Queen." Richard had fallen into the habit of calling her that. He and Lucy seemed to have established an unspoken agreement that she was named for the old dowager in Buckingham Palace. "They don't teach evisceration in kindergarten."

"Richard!" snapped Lucy.

"I'm sorry, dear. It was a slip."

It wasn't his first. Ever since their reunion, he'd made casual references to details of his work, something he hadn't done at home before, even when she'd asked curious questions. In every other way, he'd resumed being a family man almost without transition, and certainly without resentment for her own misstep, which now seemed so long ago. It was as if he needed to talk about what happened at the parlor, and it shamed her to have to discourage him for Victoria's sake. She'd tried to bring up the subject when they were in bed, with the little girl asleep in the next room, but by then he had been too tired to pay attention. He was tired most nights. The railroad gangs had moved within miles of town and came there every night after dark and on Sunday, Irish and Chinese, to brawl with each other, with cowboys and freighters and townsmen, and among themselves; when the knives and clubs came out, so did Richard, with his wax and paste and powders to mask the wounds and bruises for the survivors who came in answer to wires to claim their husbands and sons and brothers. When a Christian Chinese succumbed after one pipe too many in a basement on First Street—what the newspapers referred to as a "dive," shortened from the divans where the smokers sprawled to dream their black dreams—Richard and Sergei collaborated to invent a cosmetic to impersonate amber skin, mixing saffron from Lucy's kitchen with the flesh-tone base. The first experiment was unsuccessful, and the cadaver came out orange, but after scrubbing away the mistake, they blended the mixture with the aluminum paste designed to counteract the verdigris effect of embalming fluid upon jaundiced tissue, tried it out on a small spot on the palm of the man's hand, and pronounced it perfect.

"Not that we'll ever need to repeat it," he said during one of his indiscreet moments at home. "Christian Chinese are only a little more common than colored priests."

Shortly after the 1872 spring thaw, competition arrived in the person of one Hadrian Wanamaker, driving what looked like a medicine-show wagon with his name lettered on the side in Old English and beneath it the words MORTUARY SCIENTIST and, at the bottom, USING THE LATEST PARIS METHOD. He set himself up in a rented house on Second Street, a prime spot across from Hollander's florist shop, and patrolled the city from one end to the other, handing out his card. He stopped to pay a courtesy call on Sergei and Richard, who thought him a charlatan; first because he looked so much the part, tall and gaunt in silk hat, morning coat, and winged collar, second because he was peddling Falcony's slipshod process of salts and zinc sulphate as the latest advance from Europe. Richard knew the Falcony to leave the cadaver dessicated and sallow, like a mummy in a museum. But by that time there was business enough to go around. He was irritated, but not threatened, when Wanamaker placed a column notice in the *Record* extolling his method as the most modern of its kind west of Chicago. He told Lucy you knew a town was growing when the undertakers went head to head.

She said, "You're forgetting the Rooney brothers."

"Fergus Rooney was barely an undertaker. His brothers gave common diggers a bad name. Wanamaker will get half his business because he looks like a stage manager's idea of a mortician. Next to him I look like a hotel clerk."

"If you'd looked like an undertaker I shouldn't have married you."

"I'm not complaining. It's just human nature not to like surprises."

"You should place a notice of your own, the way you did in the *Call*."

"In San Francisco I was the challenger, taking on Colonel Kendrick. Here, I'm Kendrick to Wanamaker's Connable. I'm inclined to give him the same sort of consideration I gave myself under similar circumstances. But I won't give him the satisfaction of responding to a shot fired across my bow."

"That's because you're no one's Kendrick. I won't hear that said of you even if it's you saying it."

He looked up at her from the paper. He was seated at the kitchen table, pushed back from it to give her room to roll out a crust on its floured surface. Victoria was napping upstairs. "I can't imagine you're this upset about a little competition. I don't hold the patent."

She went on rolling for a moment, then put aside the pin,

wiped her hands on her apron, and went to the drawer in the sideboard where she kept her recipes written neatly on squares of butcher's wrap she cut out herself. She drew out a slit envelope and gave it to him.

"It came today from your father. I wasn't going to show it to you until after supper."

"Is he ill?" He folded his paper and took out the letter.

"I think he must be, though he wouldn't say. He's sold the parlor to young Wilson, his apprentice."

She watched him read the letter. Janus Connable's script was as fine and steady as ever, but the way the tails of the g's and y's tangled with the writing on the next line had told her his eyesight was suffering, probably from years closed in with many of the same fumes that had driven Richard to an oculist.

"He says he's saved enough to live comfortably for the rest of his life," Richard said. "I'm pleased for him. He's worked hard for as long as I can remember."

"But what will he do?"

"Read, I suppose. Attend the theater. He says here Detroit has a fine new opera house."

"He'll read morticians' guild bulletins and attend autopsies. You know he'd never retire as long as he had his health."

"Do you think we should go back for a visit?"

"I think he should come live with us."

"He'll never agree to that. He's been alone most of his life."

"No one his age wants to be alone."

"What difference does that make? You know how stubborn he is."

"It's a family characteristic," she said dryly. "You should wire him a ticket and invite him to visit. He's never seen his granddaughter. You can meet him in Abilene and bring him back here. Once he's here, it will be harder for him to refuse to stay."

He touched a corner of the letter to his lower lip. "You should send the wire. It will be harder for him to turn you down."

"I felt sure you'd say that. I wired him this afternoon."

She hadn't heard Richard laugh in months. The sound woke up Victoria and she went upstairs to settle her back to sleep. When she returned—carrying the girl, who was wide awake—she found him scribbling on the blank side of the envelope his father's letter had come in, using a corner of the table that was clear of dough.

"If you're answering his letter, it might not reach him before he leaves," Lucy said.

"I'm drafting a notice for the *Record*. If I don't, you'll just write it for me."

"Are you angry?"

"Only with myself, for forgetting I left you alone in San Francisco for months. I should have known you'd become independent."

"What's that?" Victoria asked.

"That's your mother."

"Am I indy—indy—?"

"Not yet, little Queen," Lucy said. "But you're going to take lessons from your grandfather."

Janus Connable sent back the tickets, explaining that an early heat wave had decimated Monroe's elderly population and that he'd volunteered to help out at the parlor until Wilson's own apprentice was sufficiently seasoned. Another invitation that fall was refused on grounds that he was recovering from pneumonia brought on by the long sweaty hours in the parlor with no opportunity to change out of the clammy clothes of the day before. A blizzard compelled him to turn down another in late December. But Lucy was persistent, and in April 1873, the old undertaker boarded a train west.

By then, the tracks had reached Hays, and Richard, Lucy, and Victoria Connable were standing on the new-sawn platform when Janus descended with help from a porter, carrying an old-fashioned carpetbag that smelled faintly of moth powder. He blinked behind a pair of green-tinted spectacles with sidepieces—they reminded Lucy of goggles—and searched for a familiar face with a quizzical smile on his lips.

Lucy was struck by his appearance. He was in his early fifties, but looked much older; he'd aged fifteen years in the six since she'd seen him. He held himself as erect as ever, but the effort was visible, giving him a stiffness he had not had before. Always slender, he was now absolutely a scarecrow, although a well-dressed one with his Georgian-era suit altered to his new frame; the bones of his skull stood out and when he recognized Lucy and snatched off his soft black hat, his scalp showed through his thinning hair, which still hung to his tall collar. A splinter of white bristle stuck out of creases in his neck where his razor had missed. He looked, in his Byronic stock, like a visiting lecturer on fossils, a living fossil himself.

He took Lucy's hand, as coolly gentle as if it were their first meeting; but she knew the subtle changes of his expressions and knew how much he was moved. He looked pale and tired, and more than from just the long journey, at least the one involving trains.

"I cannot decide whether you've grown more beautiful or I'd forgotten how beautiful you were to begin with," he said. "The first is impossible, and yet I see that lightning has struck again. Good afternoon, Victoria. Have your parents told you bogey tales of your old grandfather?"

Victoria, five now and attending school, looked to her mother for a translation. She wore a blue bonnet that brought out the color in her eyes, cool and patient like Richard's. Sometimes the child's flashes of maturity frightened Lucy. It was as if she were burning through her youth in surges.

"Kiss your grandfather, child," she said.

Janus presented his cheek, which the girl went up on tiptoe to brush with her lips. Slowly he drew himself back up and shook Richard's hand.

"You're working too much, son. You shouldn't be going blind faster than I."

"I learned at your knee. It isn't fair to change the rules now." He pried the carpetbag out of his father's grip.

The room Richard had intended for his study had stood vacant most nights while he worked, so they had moved the desk, chair, and book presses to the spare bedroom upstairs and put the bed, wardrobe, and nightstand in the study, to prevent Janus from having to climb stairs. The old man—neither Lucy nor Richard thought it odd how quickly they'd come to accept the phrase—seldom slept a night through, and they heard floorboards creaking and smelled the lamp in the parlor when he sat up to read. His preferences ran more toward Lucy's romantic novels than his son's collection of poetry and Dickens, but whenever an undertaker's trade publication came in the mail, it was Janus who read it first. However, he made no mention of the details of the profession when his daughter-in-law and grandchild were present, changing the subject gracefully whenever Richard brought it up; Lucy was certain he was sharply disapproving when father and son were alone, because Richard stopped bringing his work home. The elder Connable had the well-bred manners of a duke, and if he was growing deaf in one ear, he had the courtesy to ask the speaker's pardon when he required something to be repeated; no honking "Hah?" ever issued from his lips. Victoria tried to imitate the way he held his fork in the continental manner, with acrobatic results that made the others laugh and her cry. More than ever she was convinced she came from royal stock.

Richard reported that the old man approved of the establishment where his son and Sergei conducted business, and of the Russian as well. The morgue fixtures, more modern than his own, impressed him favorably, and the water reservoir that made Rubyoff & Connable independent of the town's antiquated fetch-and-carry system received his enthusiastic praise. He was less enamored with the wide array of embalming agents they kept in stock, pronouncing them unnecessary clutter as well as a fire hazard; Richard's obsession with experimentation had always irritated him, and now that he was retired, professional ethics bound him to silence no longer. "Rest assured that if you found the Balm of Gilead," he said, "you'd throw it over in search of something better. Any process that preserves a client more than a week is a useless extravagance, borne by the survivors. Cosmetics is the future of undertaking; concentrate on that, and clear space for it."

That night, Richard and Lucy heard a thud and went downstairs to find Janus stretched out in his robe and nightshirt across the threshold between his bedroom and the parlor. He was clutching Lucy's copy of *Fallen Among Thieves*. They managed to awaken him and get him into a chair. Richard went for the doctor, who examined the patient and suggested nervous collapse and possibly apoplexy. He counseled rest and as little agitation as possible.

For most of the next week, Lucy's routine remained unchanged: Dress Victoria, feed her and Richard and see them off to school and work, serve Janus his breakfast in bed, help him into the parlor, where he insisted on spending his day, and see he took the mild restorative the doctor had prescribed, a spoonful after each meal and before bed. In between she gave Victoria and her father supper—together, when he wasn't working late, separately when he did—slept, and rose in the morning to start again. She made no complaint, and felt no resentment; she had anticipated some life of the kind when she'd begun pressing Richard to invite his father to live with them.

Which in fact he had not. When Janus was strong enough to dress himself and walk without help, he announced that he'd taken enough time from their young lives and was going back to Monroe at the end of the week. When Richard and Lucy remonstrated, he became agitated, and they were forced to hold off. During the doctor's next visit, Lucy consulted with him in the kitchen, out of Janus's earshot. The doctor said the man was a patient, not a prisoner, that his life was his own to preserve or discard, and that upsetting him by demanding he stay was likely to bring on the debilitating or fatal attack they all feared.

Richard and Lucy conferred. "No one's ever been able to force him to do anything he didn't want to," he said. "He's lived stubborn, and that's how he'll die."

"I wish you hadn't discussed embalming."

"He brought it up. That's always been our chief difference. I didn't even argue the point. He worked himself into a fight all by himself."

"I never knew him to be so contentious back home."

"Some wines grow bitter with age."

"Don't you," she said.

Janus looked stronger and more fit getting ready to board the train than he had alighting from it. Richard commented on it later, but Lucy kept her opinion to herself: If the old man's body were as strong as his will, he'd live another fifty years. He leaned down for Victoria's kiss, which came this time with her arms around his neck, grasped Richard's hand, but instead of kissing Lucy, he murmured in her ear. "Hays has no permanence. Transience is contagious. If you don't take him to someplace solid, he'll be drifting and plugging bullet holes all his life."

"What did he say?" asked Richard as the train began to roll. Janus lifted his hat and smiled through his open window. Victoria waved energetically.

"He said not to let you work too hard."

"Sauce for someone else's gander. He never took a day off until he retired, and that was just a day."

Five months later, they received a telegram from Augustus Wilson, Janus' former apprentice, informing them that Janus had collapsed during a visit to his old parlor and had not regained consciousness. Richard, Lucy, and Victoria boarded an eastern train. At their first stop in Abilene, a porter handed them another wire from Wilson: Janus had died without rousing himself. They completed the journey to arrange for the funeral. Richard and Lucy had not been to Michigan in seven years. It was the beginning of the end of their time in Kansas.

Unlikely as it was, the common-law marriage of Big Esther Shrunk and Stan Peabody lacked those glamorous features that would inspire the romances Lucy Connable read to transport her far from her responsibilities as wife and mother. But it was one of Hays City's great love stories, even if its ending was more suited to the police column of the *Kansas City Record*, which reported it in grisly detail. Lucy banned the newspaper from the house after that to spare Victoria, who had discovered the diversions of reading.

Big Esther was the popular member of her family. Her two brothers, Ernest and Edgar, operated a beer saloon and boardinghouse on the undesirable side of the Kansas Pacific tracks, where they let the rooms by the half hour to independent prostitutes and their clients, who had gambled and drunk away their stakes in Tommy Drumm's and John Bitter's and could no longer afford the rates at the better bawdy houses in town. The Shrunks were widely believed to have started Big Esther in the Life, and when Hickok was in office he'd tried twice to connect them to mysterious disappearances, along with their chattle, of transients who'd been unwise enough to take advantage of their cheap lodgings. An extinct buffalo wallow known as Blackwell's Bog, five miles from the commercial district, was their suspected place of eternal rest, but energetic attempts to drag it had produced only sodden muskrat huts and the rib cage of a horse with a bad sense of direction.

The sister alone had made the transition across the tracks. Visitors to La Parisien Maison on Third Street swore they'd seen her lift the pump organ well clear of the parlor floor on her shoulders, and that she'd have managed to stand upright beneath the burden if the ceiling were only two feet higher; they encountered little skepticism. Esther stood six feet in her stockings and weighed three hundred pounds. She had a booming laugh to match, and demonstrated it frequently; there never was a joke so bad she couldn't find humor in it, and her own collection of off-color ticklers was legendary. She never forgot a joke or the customer who first told it to her. She was La Parisien's biggest draw, also its most successful resident. Clients struck breathless by the house rates migrated toward the one woman who promised the most for their money. They left with no complaints, as well as an unsteady tread.

Stan Peabody was a Texas drover. He ran well to the small side, all sinew and bone, which with his talent with a rope and capacity for hard work and long hours kept him employed with only brief periods of liberty between outfits; he seemed designed by God for the scrappy little mustangs that filled the strings. Stan met Big Esther on his first drive to Hays after the railroad came, and boasted that they would marry when he returned. He was back next spring, and surprised Big Esther and everybody else by taking her off the line, renting a small house a mile from town, and taking work behind the counter at Blevins' Mercantile to support them both. In ten months they never missed a Saturday night at Drumm's or a Sunday morning in church. Strangers found them an amusing couple on sight, the man half the size of the woman, but on the shortest acquaintance pronounced theirs a heavenly match. It was Stan's loudly proclaimed intention to celebrate their first anniversary with a proper wedding. When, quite unexpectedly even to Big Esther, a pair of fat and healthy twins popped out of her two months before the Big Day, their happiness was profound.

Big Esther was at home nursing a twin at each gargantuan breast when a friend from La Parisien told her that Stan was carousing at Drumm's with one of the three new girls who'd been hired to take Big Esther's place. She buttoned up and went to see for herself, packing her babies like pistols on her hips, and roared like a buffalo bull when she saw Stan undressing the girl in the corner near where Isaac Shindle's counter had once stood. She was a tiny thing, no bigger around than Esther's neck, and a consumptive into the bargain. Tommy Drumm expected a scene and reached for his bung starter, with little confidence it would be much use against a jealous woman who lifted pump organs for entertainment; but by the time he had it in hand, Esther had thundered out, leaving the batwing doors flapping. Stan hurried after her, adjusting his trousers.

By midnight, everyone in Hays City knew what he'd found when he got home: Big Esther and her twins sprawled in a pool of blood on the floor of their scantily furnished parlor, the big kitchen knife she'd used to slash the babies' throats and then hers still in her fist. By the time a coroner's jury heard the evidence and cleared Stan of suspicion in the deaths, all of Kansas knew the story from the *Record*. Stan himself did not appear. He was in jail for his own safety, trussed with manacles and rope and under twenty-four-hour guard. Sheriff Lanihan, arriving at the death scene moments behind him, had had to wrestle with him to keep possession of his own revolver, with which the distraught man announced he was going to kill himself.

After three days, Stan seemed to have calmed down enough to attend the triple funeral, and Lanihan released him, to his later regret. No one ever saw Stan again. When Blackwell's Bog was dragged, this time successfully, the common wisdom was Stan had thrown himself in. Then the coroner dug eleven pieces of buckshot out of his back, and someone remembered that Ernest and Edgar Shrunk had shown up late at Esther's funeral, out of breath and smeared with black muck, when her coffin was being loaded into Rubyoff & Connable's hearse.

While it was known that the Shrunks had never owned a watch between them and weren't much concerned with arriving anywhere on time had they ever had occasion to consider it, and that filth was pretty much their daily uniform, no one doubted their guilt. A community stricken with grief and horror, with no erring husband to act it out on, and for that matter no great regard for the Shrunks of this world in general, is prime material for a lynching party. Lanihan had just started for their establishment, arrest warrants in his pocket, when a mob of cowboys, freighters, and drifters with nothing better to do until the disorderly houses opened at dusk, battered through the door at Shrunk's, dragged Ernest and Edgar out of the cubbyholes they'd crawled into for concealment, slung ropes over the glass insulators of two telegraph poles along the K.P. tracks, and hauled them up by their scrawny necks. Three of the mob leaders were later arrested for conspiracy, but a local jury found them not guilty on both counts.

"Frisco justice," said Richard, when the bodies arrived at the parlor.

Big Esther, Stan Peabody, their twins, and the Shrunk brothers were all still alive when Richard and Lucy, each holding one of Victoria's white-gloved hands, visited Janus Connable for the last time in the parlor where Lucy had first met Janus more than a dozen years before. Nothing about the solid old house had changed, except that it seemed smaller, and the sign outside now read WILSON FUNERAL HOME and beneath it, in smaller letters, A.P. WILSON, PROP. Richard shook hands with Wilson, a man two years his junior, but with a complicated arrangement of moustaches and side-whiskers that would have added forty-five minutes to any man's morning toilet, and the family passed alone up the burgundy-carpeted aisle to the coffin, burnished maple with brass handles.

Janus lay propped up slightly with his arms crossed in the old Egyptian pharaoah manner, the stains on his hands concealed by gray cotton gloves. His gentle face was relaxed and his eyelids looked as if they might flutter open at any moment. Wilson had filled in the hollow cheeks and the furrows in his forehead. His up-slanted brows looked sympathetic, as if he were commiserating with the family in its sorrow. He looked a poet in his old-fashioned suit, high collar, and black silk neckstock.

Lucy's brother Luke had lain in this same spot, but the thought held no reality for her. In her responsibility as an undertaker's wife she had attended many visitations and services since, and each had been unique to the client. She felt Janus's kind spirit like a warm wind, and behind it the cold of approaching winter. A world without him in it must be less hospitable.

Wilson, or Janus, had added a carpeted step at the base of the pedestal for mourners to kneel upon. Richard lifted Victoria onto it so she could look down at her grandfather. Her face was still, her eyes watchful and—to Lucy, at least—eerily understanding. They had explained to her that she would see Janus one last time in a kind of sleep, and then not again for many years; but at this moment she seemed fully in command of the concept of death. Once again her mother felt the chill of too much wisdom too soon.

Richard bent over the coffin, and for a moment Lucy thought he meant to kiss his father. But their lips did not meet. She heard him sniff rapidly three times. Then he straightened.

Wilson waited for them at the curtained doorway.

"Aluminum chloride," said Richard.

The young undertaker started, then resumed his expression of detached sympathy; he was evidently unaccustomed to discussing details of his work in that part of the establishment. "It was your father's request. He wanted the minimum. Disinfection only."

"I was told he was stricken suddenly and never had the chance to speak."

"Oh, he made all the arrangements at the time he sold me the parlor. Your father wasn't one to leave anything in an untidy state."

"His final message," Richard said as they were leaving. "I told you he was stubborn."

Victoria said, "He isn't sleeping. He whistles when he sleeps."

Lucy was relieved. Her child thought like a child after all, with direct reason.

The services were brief, with a sermon delivered by a Lutheran pastor, new since Richard's time, but who obviously had known Janus from more than just his notes, and well attended; Janus had been a comforting common denominator among nearly all the members of the local community who had suffered losses during the last thirty years. Lucy thought it was the same as when a beloved old general practitioner died, after having brought several generations into the world, except that in Janus' case it was in the other direction. There was some weeping, and most of those present joined the procession to the churchyard. Lucy wept at the graveside, Richard swallowed frequently. Victoria watched the proceedings with quiet interest and asked no questions. She was an observant child but not a curious one in the usual sense.

Strangers approached the family on their way out to tell them of the old undertaker's acts of kindness well after their loved ones were in the ground. As they were leaving, Richard told Lucy he'd known nothing of his father's continued commitment in certain cases once his professional role was ended. He confided this in a tone of hurt.

"He was a private man," Lucy said. "To boast of his generosity would have spoiled it."

"Well, you knew him better than I did." Aboard their hired carriage, he picked up the reins and never said another word on the subject.

Janus' attorney, who had represented the interests of the parlor and overseen its change of ownership, read the will, which left all Janus' personal possessions to Richard except his extensive library of manuals and bound journals of the American Society of Morticians, which went to the local college, and his small private library; this touching collection of romantic novels had been set aside for Lucy after Janus' visit to Hays City. Richard had not known they existed. They were found shelved behind the professional publications in the study of the one-story house the old undertaker had leased after giving up his quarters at the parlor. Richard arranged to sell the furniture and donate his father's wardrobe to charity, but kept his watch and chain and shipped other items of sentimental interest West. Five thousand dollars, including Janus' savings and the proceeds from the parlor sale, were to be wired to their bank once the estate fees were paid. At the end of a week, during which the family visited Lucy's cousins and their

families, looked in on past acquaintances, surveyed familiar old places, and marveled at the growth and change
since the war, they went home. The cousins were polite
strangers, comfortably married to their doctors, devoted
to their children, and foreign to Lucy's life. Nothing in
Monroe compelled the Connables ever to return.

At the station in Hays, all the talk was of the tragedy in
the Shrunk-Peabody home. The coroner's jury had just
been dismissed and the bodies transported to Rubyoff &
Connable, who had a contract with Ellis County for the
burial of all deceased persons not claimed by relatives or
associates. Richard found Big Esther and her twins waiting when he reported to work.

She was larger and heavier than most of the men the
partners had embalmed, and both were grateful for their
new apprentice, a young man who had failed medical
school in Philadelphia and worked his way to Kansas as a
freighter; he'd intended to open a barbershop, only to find
four such establishments already in competition when he
reached Hays. His was a steady hand with scalpels and a
trocar, and the months of heavy labor proved useful when
they turned Big Esther over to drain.

The dead woman's friends had taken up a collection
worthy of the finest funeral yet seen in the city. Sergei and
Richard agreed that to lay the twins' tiny corpses in state
would be too heartbreaking, and that their small coffins
must remain closed; but they took care to embalm them
thoroughly, and invested the time and effort that would
have gone into their cosmetics on Big Esther, who must
look as if no wicked blade had ever touched her ample
flesh. That meant fine stitching and a high ruffled collar that
made her resemble a much younger version of the Queen
in London. Neither sawdust nor mortar must replace her

viscera, as no coffin would bear the weight, and no fewer than six pallbearers equal to the burden; a month's back numbers of the *Record* filled the cavity, as in the old days of Sergei's taxidermy. Her face, quite pretty, as unlined and unblemished as a child's, responded well to paste, powder, and paint, and a former fellow resident of La Parisien Maison volunteered to dress her hair, as she did for all her living colleagues, arranging it into elaborate waves and fixing them in place with ivory combs. With her prominent and tobacco-stained front teeth whitened with borax and bleach and a wedge of plaster inserted beneath her upper lip to suggest a faint smile, she proved the parlor's most attractive client to date.

Richard felt little satisfaction. The children's tragedy affected him deeply. Although he performed their embalming with no show of emotion before Sergei and the apprentice, that night in his and Lucy's bedroom he wept bitterly while Lucy held him. She knew this for a substitute for the display he had not made for Janus, and did not attempt to stop him until he slept from exhaustion. Then she cried for the small lives lost, and prayed for Victoria's safety. For the soul of Big Esther, who had been too cowardly to pass over alone, she found no words of salvation.

Adolf Armundsen, a stern family man who held fat whores and their bastards in small regard, took inspiration from his bonus, crafting the woman's coffin from sturdy elm reinforced with iron bands from a cooper's shop inside, where the satin lining concealed them, and corners weighted evenly to distribute the burden for the six burly freighters recruited to carry it and its mortal contents between parlor and hearse and cemetery. He reserved his imagination for the infants' coffins, which he made of basswood, a material popular for children's toys, whose lightness of weight complemented its cargo and whose satiny surface took an eggshell finish that bespoke innocence.

These boxes were identical, like the twins, and placed on covered trestles flanking Big Esther added an ethereal touch to the solemn services. An evangelical minister, well-known and -liked by the residents of La Parisien, with a rolling baritone and the head of a Roman emperor, presided, reading from Revelation and *Sonnets from the Portuguese,* a favorite of Esther's whenever he'd visited, and bowed to the "evening ladies" in their borrowed weeds and to their escorts—smooth-palmed gamblers, sunburned cowboys, and freight handlers with their beefy necks and broken knuckles—as they filed out behind the coffins. The minister directed an expression of mild rebuke at Ernest and Edgar Shrunk when they piled off their white mule, red-faced and filthy in their everyday overalls, just as the half-dozen brutes were heaving their sister into the hearse. Of the absence of the husband, Stan Peabody, he made no remark.

Rubyoff & Connable had reached detente with Wanamaker, hiring his hearse and his services as driver to follow theirs with the two tiny white coffins visible through the side windows; it was a fine conveyance, custom-built to replace the circus wagon he had used to gain attention his first year in business. The procession included a motley string of buckboards and hired buggies to transport the less able-bodied mourners, cowboys in crisp flannel and clean neckerchiefs aboard curried horses with black ribbons tied to their manes, and men and women on foot, dragging clouds of prairie-dog dust behind their heels and hems. Uninvolved pedestrians and shopkeepers watched it pass from the boardwalks, the ladies lowering their heads and the men removing their hats for a woman they would not have spoken to on the street and children whose existence they would have refused to acknowledge because they were illegitimate. A reporter covered the event for the *Record*. The story went out over the wires and appeared in Eastern newspapers as further evidence of the barbarous conditions on the frontier:

A Harlot's Obsequies.

Hays City, Kan.—Dozens of mourners attended last week when the Rev. A. Hazen Rice led services for Esther Shrunk, a "sporting lass" celebrated in this cattle camp, a place well known to these columns for its unbridled character, and her two children, all dead by her hand. . . .

Details were provided about the "gentility" of the corpse's appearance ("composed in her decomposition"), with credit paid to the messrs. Rubyoff and Connable (misrepresented as "R. J. Constable"). It was the first notice the national press had taken of Richard and his work; neither he nor Lucy could have predicted where it would lead.

Several days elapsed before Stan Peabody's corpse came to the parlor, minus the gunnysack it had worn to the bottom of Blackwell's Bog and the lead slugs the Shrunks (by popular declaration) had pumped into it. Since Stan was considered indirectly responsible for his family tragedy, no one came forward to pay for a service, and so he was consigned to the earth with minimal embalming and no restoration, as the county budget did not provide for anything more elaborate. Stan's fate, too, merited attention back East, as a sequel to the earlier story, and again Richard's name was mentioned, this time spelled correctly. It had been a busy homecoming, with more in store.

The Shrunks, upon whom the grief and rage of the community settled, did not survive Stan's discovery by more than two hours. They were cut down from their ropes and freighted to Rubyoff & Connable in the bed of a buckboard driven by Sheriff Lanihan's deputy. Ernest's neck was broken, leading to the elongation Richard had observed after the San Francisco lynching, but Edgar had strangled to death, empurpling his features, protruding his tongue, and starting his eyes from their sockets. Richard snapped the canvas tarpaulin back over them with an oath.

"Let Wanamaker have them," he said, turning away. "I quit."

CHAPTER 23

Six years ago, when Richard had sent out inquiries looking for a venue to replace San Francisco, the most cordial regrets had come from a man named Robert McLoughlin, proprietor of the Golden Pledge Funeral Chapel in Virginia City, Montana, complimenting Richard upon his credentials and explaining that as he hoped to persuade his son to come in with him as a partner, he had no need for his services, but asking him not to forget the establishment, as the population was growing steadily and the time may yet be near when the chapel would have to choose between expansion and stagnation. The old gentleman (as Richard then thought of any man who had a grown son) had seemed sincere, and his precise script indicative of the orderly mind Richard valued in an undertaker. He kept the letter and its envelope bearing the chapel's address and an engraving of a mission-style building in the corner. On the evening of the day he sent the Shrunk brothers' remains to Wanamaker, he stopped at Drumm's for a single drink, then went home, rifled through the humpback valise where he stored important documents, and retrieved the letter. He reread it and drafted a new letter of inquiry. This he showed to Lucy.

She'd been expecting something of the sort since the day they left Michigan after Janus' funeral. She knew the signs

of restlessness. Richard's breakdown after embalming Big
Esther's twins had confirmed it. And tonight his lips tasted
of gin.

She told him she'd abide by whatever decision he made.
She was afraid that if she showed too much enthusiasm,
he'd take it as a poor opinion of the entire Kansas venture.
Hays City was an unruly boy, too big for knickerbockers
and yet not mature enough for trousers. It was all rowdy,
brawling strength and no judgment. Drunken laughter had
long since drowned out the barking of the prairie dogs at
night; by day the clatter of racing horses sent pedestrians
scattering, not always in time to prevent injury, and day
and night gunfire snapped. In another ten years, perhaps,
if it still existed, the town would find its level. Until then
it was no place to raise a child.

She would never have suggested moving. For the first
time since he'd left his father's employ, Richard was independent and successful, living in a house all his own and
designed by him, and although she was certain he'd have
complied, she did not aspire to be one of those wives who
directed their husbands' actions through guilt. She knew
Richard to a point, beyond which he was as much a mystery as when they'd first met in Janus' parlor. She didn't
know if the deaths of Big Esther's children had brought
him around to her own fears for Victoria, or if the arrival
of Ernest and Edgar's bodies had suggested he'd made no
progress since sinful Barbary. *If you don't take him to
someplace solid, he'll be drifting and plugging bullet holes
all his life.* Janus's last words to her, murmured on the train
platform; whatever their differences about priorities in undertaking, father and son seemed to share the same fears
about the rootlessness of a craft based upon the imperma-
nence of a public ceremony.

She hoped Virginia City—if it was to be there—was a
solid place. It was the territorial capital, a distinction that

suggested the presence of courts, schools, churches, and established order; but it was younger than San Francisco, built on the same shifting promise of instant wealth through easy gold, and the Two-Faced City swayed and plunged like a craft at sea.

They had money, thanks to Richard's inheritance and Lucy's organization of their finances, a skill developed during the months of their separation. With the sale of the house, it would be sufficient for the move, a new home, a partnership in an existing parlor or the establishment of a new one, and to support them for such time as the enterprise required to show profit. She could not say how Victoria would react to their pulling up stakes yet again. She'd been too young to be anything but excited the first time, but most of her life had been spent in Hays, she'd been attending school there for two years, and presumably had made friends she'd be loath to leave. Lucy didn't know if the last was true. According to Victoria's teacher, the girl seemed to get on with her schoolmates, but as yet had shown no particular attachment to any of them. She was bright in her studies, always among the first to offer an answer to a question put to the class, but refused help whenever she appeared to have difficulty with a lesson. A child who kept her own counsel, the teacher seemed to be saying, was a puzzle, and although the young woman—for she was much younger than Lucy—would not presume so much as to inquire about Victoria's life at home, she would be aware of the father's employment, and Lucy could guess the rest. She wondered about it herself, often. The girl knew more of death than seemed healthy. An established city growing its second generation of children might provide the proper balance.

"That's a thoughtful face."

She stirred herself from her thoughts. She'd paused in her embroidering, and Richard, looking up from the

Tennyson volume he'd brought home from the parlor, had noticed.

She thought of prevaricating, then said, "I was thinking about Virginia City. I hope it's suitable for Victoria."

"I wouldn't trouble myself over it. It's been six weeks since I wrote McLoughlin. If he isn't dead, he's probably not interested."

"Have you heard from anyone else?"

"Denver and New Orleans came back undelivered. I think I told you Fort Worth turned me down. I'm still waiting on St. Louis and Tucson, but that's only been three weeks."

"Why did you not write to someplace East?"

"Only failures turn back." He returned to his reading.

Two days later, Robert McLoughlin wrote back, a long letter, apologizing for the delay and pleading business as the cause. His son had disappointed him by marrying and moving to Milwaukee, where he had opened a pharmacy, and the goldfields had claimed the series of apprentices McLoughlin had hired to take his place. He was more in need of a partner than ever, and named an investment figure that Richard and Lucy were convinced was a slip of the pen; an exchange of telegrams between Hays and Virginia City confirmed that it was not. The situation was so desperate, McLoughlin claimed, that he preferred to take a loss rather than risk pricing himself out of Richard's market. A second letter arrived, reiterating the offer and confessing that the description of Richard's labors on behalf of Big Esther Shrunk had appeared in the local *Montana Post,* fortuitously after Richard's query arrived, reminding McLoughlin of his letter and prompting him to take time from work to respond. The reason for his harried schedule, McLoughlin explained, was a recent devastating fire, which had taken nearly two dozen lives and required extensive reconstruction in those cases where the

clients could be lain in state at all. The wily old gentleman hinted there were things he could teach a partner
about restoring burned tissue, if he would but accept his
invitation.

"Oh, Richard, fire." Lucy glanced instinctively toward
the door, through which Victoria had departed for school
minutes earlier.

He made a dismissive gesture with the hand holding the
letter. "We'll build outside town, and order brick from San
Francisco, if we have to. I don't see how we can refuse his
price."

"We can afford to pay more."

"To whom? No one else has written. The West has been
settling itself while I've wasted my skills painting prostitutes and patching Hickok's targets. I've missed the demand. McLoughlin says there's a school, and a brand new
master who studied at the University of Chicago. You're
always saying Victoria's too smart for her lessons here."

She wished it *was* Chicago. But his mind was made up.

We the undersigned uniting ourselves for the laudi-
ble purpos of arresting thievs & murderers & recovering stollen propperty do pledge ourselvs & our sacred
honor each to all others & solemnly swear that we will
reveal no secrets, violate no laws of right & not desert
each other or our standerd of justice so help us God. As
witness our hand & seal this 23 of December A.D. 1863.

The placard, printed black on heavy gray stock, had
weathered into the plank door upon which it had been
tacked, becoming part of it, like an ancient rug trodden
into the floorboards it was intended to protect. The list of
names printed at the bottom had faded; others below it had
been swept away by some forgotten wind. It was the first
thing Lucy's eyes lit upon when she helped Victoria down

from the coach—a Concord at last, but far less comfortable than its reputation, and indeed less so than the Pullman cars they'd left in Dakota Territory. In between was a trail called the Bozeman, and even stoic Victoria had cried out at each bump and cavity in its broken spine.

Lucy pointed out the sign to Richard, who leaned forward to peer at it over his tinted spectacles. "It's twelve years old," he said; "a lifetime out here."

A dry, cold wind swept up a handful of snow and flipped it into Lucy's face, stinging like powdered glass. They had left Indian summer behind in the tablelands, where blossoms still bloomed, and plunged directly into winter. Snowcapped mountains, blue as bottles, reared above the false fronts on Main Street, near enough to touch. The air was so clear it gave her a headache, as if she'd stared too long through a powerful glass. Everything seemed as built of iron, even the log buildings in their civilizing jackets of board siding. Looking down the street, she picked out the saloons by the clusters of horses tethered in front of them, stamping their hooves and blowing thick clouds of steam. An unforgiving place, Virginia City. It would always be winter here.

Their leave-taking from Hays had been wistful but uncomplicated. One of the city's most successful land offices had been eager to offer their two lots for sale for far more than Richard had put into them, including the construction of the house, and Sergei had agreed upon Richard's price for his half of the parlor. The Russian had cried openly and unblushingly, pounding Richard's back when he embraced him, kissing Lucy's cheek, and tickling Victoria's when he leaned down to kiss her and give her a present: the last of his stuffed prairie dogs, that she and her parents might never forget their time in Kansas. Victoria had immediately sat on the railroad platform to introduce the rodent to the doll she was carrying. As the train rolled away, Hadrian Wanamaker, watering one of his matched blacks from the community trough next to the station, lifted his tall silk hat. He looked so much like a caricaturist's idea of an undertaker he made Lucy shudder.

A boy in a red uniform with brass buttons stacked their trunk and valises aboard a handcart and followed them into the lobby of the Golden Rule Hotel, paneled in cedar and presided over by an enormous buffalo head mounted above the stone fireplace. "Golden" and "Gold" seemed to be Virginia City's answer to "Open, Sesame"; there was, in addition to Robert McLoughlin's Golden Pledge Funeral Chapel, a Golden Gulch and Gold Nugget saloon, the Golden Crown Tonsorial Parlor, and even a land office operated by a man named Emmanuel Gold; but this last was likely happenstance. The advertising had had its effect. Pedestrians swarmed the boardwalks and their stagecoach had had to stand still for five minutes waiting for a jam of wagons, carriages, and buggies to clear before completing the last sixty feet of its journey.

A message was waiting for them from McLoughlin, apologizing for the press of work at the chapel that prevented him from greeting them in person but inviting all three Connables to join him that evening at a popular local restaurant, refreshingly named the Sugar Bowl, as his guests for dinner. The clerk who handed Richard the message, an old man with features like a crumpled banknote and an English accent, explained that the Sugar Bowl was formal. Lucy panicked, asked if the hotel had a board and iron she could borrow, but the old man explained that the Golden Rule offered valet service. Ten minutes after the family went upstairs, the boy who had brought in their luggage returned to collect Richard's evening suit, Lucy's best dress, and the outfit she'd made for Victoria to wear to church. They were ready in time to dress.

Robert McLoughlin—"Bob" from the moment they

met—spoke with a strong Scots burr and resembled the late Prince Albert, right down to the balding head, elaborate side-whiskers, and implausibly narrow waist. He was missing his right arm, and wore the empty black sleeve fixed to the shoulder with a diamond pin. With the easy cadence of one who has told the story often, he explained that his career as an army surgeon had ended when a Confederate four-pounder tore through the hospital tent at Shiloh, carrying away the arm and an ivory-handled scalpel belonging to a set of French manufacture that had been presented to him by his father on graduating medical school in Edinburgh. "Don't miss the flapper s'much's the scalpel," said he, when his guests murmured sympathy. "Factory burned down under the bloody Commune and I can't complete the set." He flushed and apologized to Lucy for his old soldier's language. She liked him immediately. Victoria was fascinated with his adept management of knife and fork. She tried to imitate it, slipped, and sprayed peas like grapeshot. Bob laughed boomingly.

The next day, Bob conducted Richard on a tour of the chapel facilities while Lucy and Victoria met with Lawrence Stripe, master of the one-room school a mile outside town. They were impressive experiences. The Golden Pledge offered a fully equipped morgue, with running water and anatomical charts on the walls, separate rooms for visitation and services, with seating for one hundred in the latter, and a library detailing the latest methods in embalming and reconstruction from America and Europe. Young Stripe, polite and composed, taught Greek and Latin as well as basic arithmetic and grammar, reeled off two thousand years of the history of Western civilization from memory, and kept the world rolled up above his blackboard, to be drawn down in sections like window shades; the city fathers had supported his plans for educating the miners' and merchants' children with generous contributions from the treasury. Victoria, prone to make snap judgments of character without expressing what they were, seemed to take to the young man, whom she'd impressed by finding Venezuela on the map. Three homes in three far-flung places in her first seven years had fueled her enthusiasm for geography.

Emmanuel Gold at the land office found a home they could rent or own, outside the city limits and only a brisk walk from the school, with a large kitchen, a parlor with a breathtaking view of the mountains, an indoor bath, and separate bedrooms for parents and child upstairs. Its isolation from the combustible buildings inside the city settled Lucy's fears of fire, along with the presence minutes away of a steam-powered pump wagon, pride of the volunteer fire brigade. They moved in at once and began adding new furniture from two shops the size of warehouses to the existing pieces.

When partnership negotiations were completed, McLoughlin revealed the truth behind the name Golden Pledge. Somewhat abashedly, the former army surgeon drew a long sheet of foolscap from a drawer of his desk and placed it before Richard. It was an agreement not to partake of strong drink on or off the premises, on pain of dissolving the partnership. McLoughlin, a man of lifelong temperance, confided that his son's bibulous habits had been the real reason for their parting of the ways, and had seen too many diseased livers to tolerate the practice. He stopped talking as with an effort, watched Richard anxiously as he read, and exhaled audibly when he chuckled and held out his hand for the pen. The news elated Lucy, although in truth she hadn't seen her husband drink to excess since the dark days in San Francisco. Her feelings of foreboding evaporated. Virginia City was in every sense the beginning of a new life for the Connables.

Richard had much to teach his partner about embalming

that wasn't available in his books and professional journals, and learned much in turn about restoration and cosmetic science. McLoughlin had assembled a collection of death masks, fashioned by him with plaster from the faces of cadavers of every physical type. His experience with burned flesh had led him to develop remarkably lifelike properties from muslin and cheesecloth, which when soaked in glycerine, molded in sections over the masks, allowed to dry, and applied to damaged features, replicated human tissue with the faithfulness of a graft; a bit of sanding, a coat of paint, and the client's own spouse would not know the difference. "Photographic portraits are necessary, of course," McLoughlin said. "I had to bury several promising prospects in closed coffins when none was available. Sitting should be required in every family that observes a burial fund."

His surgeon's fingers were sure and delicate, and although Richard knew his would never match them, he took to the process quickly and suggested refinements of his own. In cases where a hand was missing, McLoughlin made a cast of the existing hand and folded it atop the counterfeit to conceal the fact that the client now had two rights or two lefts.

"What if both hands are missing?" Richard asked.

"Then I make casts of my own, with the help of an apprentice. One hand looks very much like all the rest."

"What about a woman's?"

"That's what gloves are for."

"The man could teach Michelangelo how to sculpt," Richard told Lucy. "Some of those fire victims were 40 percent plaster of paris."

"Little pitchers have big ears," Lucy warned, setting a bowl of steaming turnips on the table.

Victoria said, "I know what that means."

"Clever girl," Richard said. "Maybe you'll marry an undertaker."

She munched her turnips thoughtfully. "I'm never going to marry anybody."

"Eat your supper," Lucy snapped, startling father and daughter with her shrill tone.

Winter in Montana was long and harsh, dumping carloads of snow to the windowsills and freezing the mercury. Spring was sudden. It started with reports in the mountains like cannon shot as the ice broke up, then there was flooding. Summer bleached the grass white and turned earth to powder, but failed to sodden the soul as it had in humid Kansas. McLoughlin, an expert fly fisherman despite his missing limb, taught Richard the basics standing up to their hips in the Madison River, and for the first time in his life Lucy's husband had a leisure activity besides reading. His inclination to stoutness ceased and they dined on trout three times a week.

Late in August, the *Montana Post* reported that James Butler Hickok, "the illustrious 'Wild Bill,'" had been slain by an assassin while playing poker in a gold camp in Dakota. Richard wondered aloud if he'd spoken with an undertaker that day and been unable to find a white horse to balance the account.

By then, he himself was too busy with work to fish. An epidemic of smallpox had kept the lights burning at the Golden Pledge throughout the night as he and McLoughlin decontaminated the clients with potash and arsenic and filled in the pustules with paste. For ten days he slept in the parlor—a mixed blessing for Lucy, who missed him and fretted for his health but was relieved not to have him bringing the miasma home. Lawrence Stripe closed the school, but three small corpses were delivered to McLoughlin and Connable. She wept for the young parents and dosed Victoria with sulphur, steeling herself against the child's loud complaints about the stench. Everything stank of rotten eggs.

The first chill snap of winter ended the emergency. School reopened, and horse-drawn sleighs replaced buggies and carriages in the streets of Virginia City. A thaw early in January brought false spring, but on the morning of the fifteenth the sky turned leaden and the iron smell of snow was in the air. Lucy layered Victoria in sweaters, wrapped her in an old fleece-lined coat of Richard's cut down for her, and was grateful when a neighbor whose son attended the school stopped by to drive the children to class in his phaeton. An hour later the snow started, first in flakes the size of saucers, then picking up speed as the cold ground them down to crystals. They accumulated on the ground at a frightening rate. When shortly before noon a parade of sleighs and carriages swept past the house, the horses plunging through drifts and the wheeled conveyances foundering, most of them eventually to be abandoned, Lucy donned coat and boots, wound a scarf around her head, and climbed aboard one of the runnered vehicles to help bring the children home. She was worried, but there was a festive air to the party; adventures were rare entertainment since the last citizens' vigilance committee had disbanded in favor of conventional law enforcement. Everyone looked forward to hunkering in with family around a fire while Old Man Winter gnawed at the shutters.

This first blizzard of 1877 took pity on Virginia City, as far as blizzards ever did. It claimed only one young life.

Tragedy must have its culprits, and as it had in Hays against the Shrunk brothers, emotion in Virginia City ran high against young Stripe. At one point he was placed in custody in a second-floor cell for his own protection, as vigilante talk resumed for the first time in years. Neither Richard nor Lucy held him responsible, however. Victoria had been a determined child, and impatient; with twenty-two excited children to look after until their parents could arrive to take them home through the blizzard, Stripe could be forgiven for looking another direction when she slipped out.

When it was established that Victoria was not in the schoolhouse, Lucy thought of the Chilsons, whose house and barn stood a little short of midway between the school and the Connable home. Wilbur and Elizabeth Chilson belonged to a strict Christian sect that prohibited public education, and schooled their own two children. They were not well known by their neighbors, since they didn't attend any of the local churches and kept in a tight group when they went to town for provisions, and they were suspicious of strangers. Minutes of frantic knocking passed before their door opened two inches, exposing Elizabeth's brown left eye and part of her nose. When she said no girl had come to her home, the neighbor who'd offered Lucy a seat in his sleigh forced the door and agreed to withdraw only when Wilbur Chilson took a shotgun down from the wall and palmed back both its hammers. Lucy glanced around the tiny parlor, at the boy and girl peeping out from behind their mother's skirts, and was satisfied Victoria wasn't there. A search of the barn found only a spavined mare and an indignant owl.

The party retraced the route to the school and started back again, leaning out over the runners and squinting through the driving ice splinters for some sign of a small figure in the snow. The man at the reins held the reassuring opinion that one of the other parents had taken up the girl and brought her home, and that when the storm blew itself out she'd be returned to hers. Nevertheless a search party was convened. Sleighs quartered the road and to a hundred yards on either side, and rugged former prospectors strapped on snowshoes and leaned into the wind holding hurricane lamps aloft and calling Victoria's name. Richard was notified, and with Bob McLoughlin's assistance replaced the wheels on the Golden Pledge hearse with runners and joined the search. Nearing dawn, Lucy, waiting sleepless at home, flung open the door at a noise and saw the black oblong looming her way. She experienced a new chill; but the two men had come merely to thaw out and rest before venturing forth again.

Another party found her. In the gray light sliding under the storm clouds, a shift in the wind had exposed an end of red scarf, and the men in the party waded up to it and pawed away the snow with gloved hands. At first they thought they'd discovered an old woman whose absence had gone unnoticed in the anxiety over the child. The face was gray-blue and pinched, its eyes open, with ice frosted on the lashes and eyebrows, white as with age. The body was less than sixty feet from the schoolhouse.

No flowers were to be had in Montana in January.

Neighbors tied ribbons and other bright scraps of cloth to the Connables' gate, and added to them their own children's toys, carved wooden trains and rag dolls and buttons on strings. Bob McLoughlin came for the body, but Richard insisted on riding back with him to the chapel. It was his turn to protest when Lucy came out in her cape and scarf and made to climb aboard. "I'll bathe my daughter," she said.

The small body was still blue, with purple patches where the blood had settled after it thawed. Lucy, alone with Victoria, crooned as she worked with soap and sponge, singing sentimental old love ballads, which Victoria had preferred to children's lullabies. She washed her hair, careful to tilt the head back to keep soap from the eyes, and dried her with a soft towel she'd brought from home. No one but Richard had seen her cry or ever would. When she finished, she covered the body with a sheet, tucking it in, and told Richard and Bob she'd return to dress her and arrange her hair. Their apprentice, a young miner named Appleton who had lost his stake on an empty shaft, took her home. Children sledding and building snowmen were the only dots of color on the drifted landscape.

Elizabeth Chilson came to keep her company, and that was the beginning of a change in the local attitude toward her family, as well as of a friendship that would continue through correspondence until Elizabeth died of peritonitis from a ruptured appendix in 1885; the Chilsons' denomination took the same dim view of medicine as it did of schools. When the news reached her, Lucy would experience all over again her loss.

During her stay, she gave Elizabeth those of Victoria's clothes that would fit her daughter, who was a little older; the church dress she kept out for the burial. She learned later, much later, that McLoughlin and Appleton had had to restrain Richard physically from attending the embalming, and that Richard had actually taken up the trocar before dissolving into a fit of anguish. He was exhausted, dozing fitfully on the leather sofa in McLoughlin's office and awakening from time to time to the smell of preservative agents. He identified each by its odor.

Lucy dressed Victoria with care, not pausing to dwell on McLoughlin's fine needlework closing the incisions, and seated the white cotton gloves between her fingers as she did when she put on her own. She dressed her hair with pins and a comb that had belonged to her mother and applied cosmetics, using her own rouge and powder, which she had always employed with subtlety, knowing Richard's opinions about women who painted their faces; if he'd ever noticed that she was one of them, he had kept the intelligence to himself. The fluids McLoughlin had used had restored some of the natural skin tone to the child's face, and Lucy enhanced them with a foundation and touched the cheeks and lips with high color, blending it with her fingertips. A special mouthpiece the former army surgeon had designed for the three children lost during the smallpox epidemic gave the merest hint of a smile, as if she were enjoying a dream.

Lucy fastened the collar with her grandmother's brooch. She'd intended to give it to Victoria when she turned eighteen.

Of the service she remembered little. The Methodist minister read from Psalms, she responded to the people who came up to her murmuring sympathy, and felt pity for those who wept. Richard drove their buggy behind the hearse. All of Virginia City seemed to have turned out for the procession. A path had been cleared through the churchyard, and the ashes removed from the fire the grave diggers had built to soften the ground for their spadework. The sun blazed cruelly off the fields of snow, a bitter wind reddened ears and made noses drip. For these reasons the graveside service was brief. The lumps of earth some of the mourners scooped off the pile to toss into the hole rang like rocks when they struck the coffin. Lucy and Richard were spared participation in this most painful of rituals.

When the last of those who were invited back to the house left, taking with them their covered dishes, Elizabeth Chilson stayed to clean up, and had practically to be ordered to leave. Lucy discovered the bottle of gin in the kitchen cupboard, missing two or three inches of its contents, two days later. She said nothing about it to Richard, and if he noticed that an additional inch was gone when he came home that evening, he made no mention of it. She was unused to spirits and diluted it with water, as much to soften its bite as to cover her theft. Elizabeth, detecting it on her breath during a visit, suggested she suck horehound candy. On her next visit she brought a Mason jar containing a clear, odorless liquid whose fumes nevertheless made Lucy's eyes fill. Wilbur, Elizabeth explained, kept a still in the barn loft—strictly to prevent illness. Richard need never notice a drain on his own reserves.

And so Lucy became a secret drinker. She never drank enough at one time to blur her speech or upset her balance, and even the mild headaches she sometimes experienced mornings were rare; nor did she drink with regularity. Days passed when the jar remained untouched behind the cleaning compounds on the floor of the pantry, and on those days she didn't miss its contents. Then something entirely unrelated to memories of Victoria would bring a flash of pain that was nearly physical, like a sudden blow that staggered her; then she would fill a water tumbler and empty it in a series of draughts, as if she were drinking a physic. It ignited a glow in her stomach and furred the pain, and she returned to her housework or errands. She never developed a taste for the harsh stuff, but when the jar was empty another took its place, and then another, without her ever having to broach the subject to Elizabeth Chilson; she would show up for her regular visit carrying a basket with a fresh jar inside, wrapped in a checked cloth, and exchange it for the empty one.

Richard's drinking was not clandestine. Most nights he fell into bed, snoring and tainting the air with the ferment on his breath; mornings he scrubbed his teeth and rinsed out his mouth with gin from a tumbler he kept in the bath. Nevertheless he remained relatively sober the first half of each day, performing his work as efficiently as ever and without drawing comment from Bob McLoughlin, who was no fool and could not have failed to note his breath or the red in his eyes and general air of dissipation in the crooked knot of his tie and yesterday's collar. The proprietor of the Golden Pledge was capable of great sympathy—a rarity in a profession that required its display but counseled against it in practice—and Lucy, if not Richard, guessed that he had granted his partner a grace period during which the pledge he'd signed was suspended. She didn't know how long it would last; when the glow was in her stomach, she hoped Richard would wean himself before it ended. When it wasn't, she knew things would not work out as tidily as that. She began to distrust the glow, and consciously to avoid it unless the pain was prolonged. The next time Elizabeth arrived with her basket, she had no empty jar to trade for it; the one in the pantry was nearly a third full.

McLoughlin fished alone these days, his invitations for Richard to join him having been declined since the beginning of spring. July fifteenth was a Sunday, and also the six-month anniversary of Victoria's death. McLoughlin came calling, in his rubber boots and the old tattered coat in whose many pockets he kept his flies and tobacco, leaned his willow pole in a corner inside the front door, and asked to speak with Richard. They were alone in the parlor for fifteen minutes while Lucy wiped off the stove and work spaces, thought about the jar in the pantry, and went on cleaning surfaces that shone already. When the visitor left and Richard did not emerge from the parlor, she untied her apron and went in to find him seated in his armchair holding a bank draught. His face was vacant; he was drunk to stupefaction. She slid the draught from between his fingers without resistance. It was signed by McLoughlin. The amount suggested a sum arrived at by adding half the chapel's profits of the past eighteen months to Richard's original half interest. He was no longer a partner in the Golden Pledge.

There were no scenes when they left Virginia City. On the morning their train left, Bob McLoughlin paid one more visit to the house, empty now of their portable possessions, shook Richard's hand, and bowed over Lucy's. Lucy had said her farewells to Wilbur and Elizabeth Chilson, promising to write when they reached Chicago, where they'd planned to stay for a month while Richard sent out inquiries for employment, and she and Richard had stopped at the churchyard to lay flowers on Victoria's grave. That was the hardest good-bye, nearly as hard as when they realized she was lost; but steaming away aboard the train, Lucy felt a lifting of the spirit, not unlike the one that came with the glow from Wilbur Chilson's liquor. For six months, Victoria had been in that place, beneath that marker, imprisoned by six feet of Montana; now she was everywhere. Lucy had never been able to speak to her in the house, or anywhere but in the churchyard. She knew how a telegrapher felt when the line was down and the key was dead beneath his hand. Here, and with increasing strength as the car rattled on, putting distance between her and that place of sorrow, she was aware that her whispered words were heard.

They'd planned to be in Chicago a month, less if the wires Richard intended to send out bore fruit earlier. They stayed four years. They checked into the Palmer House hotel, left after a week, and took a lease on an apartment on State Street, a brief commute by urban rail to the Craidlaw Funeral Home, a three-story building on North Clark, with visitation rooms and a morgue on the ground floor, a laboratory stocked with embalming agents, cosmetics, and mechanical equipment above, and classrooms under the roof, with enamel-topped tables, anatomical charts, and an articulated skeleton mounted on a stand. The establishment, which could be mistaken for a private medical school, had been founded by the late father of Dennis Craidlaw, its current proprietor, for the study of mortuary science. Its bills were paid by the students' tuition, and it offered middle-class funerary preparation to indigent clients for a fraction of the sum demanded by conventional undertakers. Richard, seeing a notice for it in the *Sun,* had come calling with his card, and was interviewed on the spot by Craidlaw, who maintained files of cuttings on subjects of interest to his trade and remembered his name from the *Sun*'s telegraph column at the time of Esther Shrunk's services. The salary he offered was princely by frontier standards, and Richard went to work as an instructor, performing embalmings before trainees and observing and criticizing their own efforts. Craidlaw, who had assisted his father after the Great Fire of 1871, was particularly impressed with his new instructor's skill at replacing burned flesh, and considered his ability to "heal" external wounds something close to sorcery; gunshot deaths were on the rise on Chicago's South Side.

Richard's daily drinking had ceased with the move from Montana, and Lucy's before that. From a savings account made more than healthy from the sales of Richard's partnership and the house in Virginia City, they furnished their comfortable rooms in good taste, had an enlargement made of Victoria's photograph, taken at age six in a Virginia City studio, had it hand-tinted, and hung it in an oval frame in the parlor. Richard engaged a maid and considered hiring a cook, but Lucy rejected that proposal, and after three weeks let the maid go, with an extra week's pay and a reference; shopping, embroidering, and reading novels lost their appeal very quickly. She reclaimed command of the household. More significantly, she became a hostess, serving tea and biscuits to the promising young men Richard invited home from Craidlaw's and letting it be known that she was At Home Wednesday afternoons to the other ladies of the Grand Army of the Republic, which she'd joined on her credentials as sister of a Union soldier slain early in the hostilities. In this way she filled the hours.

On the morning of the anniversary of Victoria's death, Lucy was unaware of the date. The next day was her At Home, and she fretted over the failure of the paperer to appear on time to finish the wall in the drawing room. It was mild for mid-January, with no strong wind blowing off the lake, and no snow; nothing, in fact, to remind her of a blizzard in Montana. When she was forced to confront the significance of the day later, the horror of having forgotten left her little room for grief. That came afterward, and with gale force.

What alerted her was a metallic scratching at the apartment door, as if some creature with steel claws were trying to get in. She opened it and found Richard, weaving and with his spectacles hanging off one ear, his key in his hand. She hadn't expected him home from Craidlaw's before evening, and not reeking of gin. In that moment she knew what day it was. The blow left her unable to react with anger or even disappointment. Instead she helped him into the bedroom, he leaning on her with most of his weight and not lifting his feet, and when he fell across the mattress, loosened his tie, unlaced and removed his shoes, and folded his spectacles on the nightstand. He spoke of his "little Queen" moaningly, then began to snore.

From then on, that would be his annual practice. Each time, Lucy feared he'd repeat it the next day and the next, for she knew the spiral from before, but each time, gray-faced and wincing at the tiniest noise, he would arise at his usual hour the following morning, dress with his usual care, sit down with her to breakfast, and leave for work, with no discussion of the previous day or the event it marked. Lucy was actually grateful for his condition. Helping him to bed and undressing him, bringing him coffee if he awakened in the night, kept her from dwelling on the dead and lent her someone childlike to look after in place of her child. They never spoke of Victoria on that date, and as the years went by they stopped speaking of her at all.

In the fall of 1880, the Palmer House hosted America's first-ever undertakers' convention, and Dennis Craidlaw, its organizer, persuaded Richard to speak at dinner. Richard was preparing a paper on various improvements he'd made on embalming processes popular in Europe for a trade journal, and read from it, receiving an enthusiastic response from his colleagues and a write-up in the *Sun*'s inside columns of the "Connable Method." The correspondent, bristling at the assignment, a punishment from his editor for missing a deadline while he lingered at a cockfight on Milwaukee Street, became determined to transform it into a coup. He excavated the Big Esther story from the newspaper's library, sent out wires, and assembled the responses into a Sunday feature under the headline WILD BILL'S UNDERTAKER, complete with steel-point engravings of the late "Prince of Pistoleers" and of Richard from the reporter's description ("He looks a bit like P.T. Barnum, but with more hair and cheaters"), and a sensational account of a Dismal Trader working day and night to prepare Hickok's victims for burial; the Shrunk episode was retold, and attention given Richard's labors during the smallpox epidemic in Virginia City, with some accuracy. The article mentioned the tragedy of young Victoria Connable, but the assertion that the father had been obliged by duty to embalm his own daughter was cut from the later editions after Richard paid a call upon the editorial offices accompanied by Craidlaw's attorney.

Following President Garfield's assassination in 1881, the same journalist visited Richard at work and inquired if he had considered offering his services to the nation's capital. He had, as a matter of fact; but only because Craidlaw had broached the subject, for the glory of the Craidlaw School of Mortuary Science, and had rejected the idea as undignified huckstering. He refused to answer the question and had the journalist removed by a pair of burly students.

The attention wore on the Connables, and before the onset of winter they took the first vacation of their married life. For two weeks they read, rested, and took long walks along the shore of Sturgeon Bay in Wisconsin, where they'd rented a bungalow. Stopping to change trains in Sheboygan on their way home, they learned that word of their arrival had reached the local press, and were themselves barraged by questions from reporters in derby hats and flowered bonnets:

"What does an undertaker do on holiday?"

Dig holes in the sand. (Laughter.)

"Is it true Wild Bill always aimed between the eyes to conserve ammunition?"

I don't know where he aimed, but that's usually where he hit. (Furious scribbling.)

"What's it like being married to an undertaker? All those dead bodies in the house."

Richard never brings unfinished work home. (Nervous titters.)

"Is it true you bury them in pasteboard shoes?"

Never in any establishment where I worked. I never used the same coffin more than once, either. (Embarrassed clearing of throats.)

"Do you plan to have any more children, and if so, would you encourage them to follow in their father's footsteps?"

No more questions.

Another party armed with writing blocks awaited them on the platform in Chicago. They looked enough like the ambushers in Sheboygan that Lucy thought at first they had all boarded an express specifically to finish the conference. The conductor, a gentleman, escorted them to another car, and instructed a group of porters to gather around them carrying luggage when they alighted, to escape notice. Richard tipped them all handsomely as soon as they were clear.

That evening in their parlor, Richard asked Lucy if she'd be very much disappointed if he gave Craidlaw notice and looked for new employment far from civilization. She began to cry, and it was several minutes before she could assure him her tears were from relief.

When she returned home from Connable & Haight, Lucy was tired—*desperately tired,* as the romantic novelists put it, and for the first time in her life she understood the phrase in all its implications; it was like reading about love all one's young life, and accepting it with only dim recognition until experiencing it firsthand. The three shallow steps to the front door of the house she had shared in Buffalo with Richard all these years each presented its own nearly insurmountable challenge, and she knew what it must be like for an insect to crawl over a pencil, as if it were a cliff to be scaled, for—what? The sensuous pleasure of a smooth tabletop. She pulled herself up the wooden railing hand over hand, as if climbing a rope, and thought for the first time in a while of Luke, her lost twin, and the fear he must have felt upon entering Fort Wayne after an unremarkable childhood in Monroe, and of the combat he would never live to experience. She would not let herself think of Victoria, small and alone and lost in a moving white wall of snow.

The key was heavy in her hand, the hole elusive. They connected finally, and she let herself in and uncoiled the strap of her reticule from her wrist—it left pink lacerations, she noticed, like the whip marks on the naked backs of captured buccaneers she had read about—and dropped it on the hall table where she and Richard put the mail they brought in from the box on the porch. She remembered the mail then, but hadn't the strength to go out and retrieve it. She would send Richard for it when he came home from his sinister business in Cleveland, and he would sigh and do as requested; the complaint would be in that irritating little release of breath she found so annoying. He had grown beyond giving it any more voice than that, and she beyond upbraiding him for it. Marriage was not so much accepting each other's shortcomings as knowing which ones merited a discussion that would enervate them both. At the moment she couldn't think of one that she would have the energy to address. She really was desperately tired. She dropped onto the settee in the parlor, still in her coat, too exhausted even to unfasten the toggles, much less traverse the remaining six feet to the padded rocker she preferred before all other seats. She couldn't remember the last time anyone had occupied the settee. Richard liked his old leather armchair, the neighbors they played cards with marched to the table in the dining room directly when they came in, and they entertained no other visitors. Lucy's brief brush with the social world had ended when they left Chicago.

From there they'd gone to St. Louis, where for the first time since San Francisco Richard established a parlor that was his alone, in the levee district. He bought it, equipment and all, from a dwarfish old Frenchman named De-Clerk, who nevertheless insisted upon visiting the parlor each day, climbing onto the chair in front of Richard's desk and gesturing with his gnarled two-foot stick as he recounted over and again his experiences in the fur trade, and how he'd made the natural progression from curing pelts to preserving human flesh for burial after beaver hats fell out of fashion, how he'd been his own grave digger until he found himself up to his knees in the Mississippi

River one time too many as the cemetery crept too close to its west bank, and how he'd be in the business still if every apprentice he trained didn't desert him after less than a year to head West and seek his fortune in cattle or mining; this last had been the complaint Richard had heard everywhere since he'd first left Michigan. The old man's presence was a help in translating entries in his ledgers and the hand-lettered labels on some of the jars and bottles on the shelves in the morgue, which were in French, in his spidery hand, but apart from that he was a bore and a nuisance, as well as a frightful old bigot. Richard was grateful when DeClerk's daughter and son-in-law came to fetch him back to live with them in Springfield.

St. Louis' large and cosmopolitan population offered Richard the variety he'd become accustomed to in Chicago: Natural causes, carriage accidents, mishaps in the rail yard, suicides, and gunshot wounds from across the river in grim East St. Louis sharpened his skills in many areas, but the preponderance of deaths by drowning, very common to cities whose commerce depended on river traffic, gave him the opportunity to refine the technique he'd experimented with on the little girl in San Francisco. Lucy, listening to him go on, thought it interesting, but not particularly disturbing, that he could make reference to the death of a female child without personal reflection. His professional disengagement was complete; he could feel and display sympathy short of sliding into paralyzing empathy, like a surgeon or a policeman. Nor was she upset by the graphic nature of some of his examples, the release of gases and the like. On a number of occasions before he finished staffing, she had volunteered to dress hair and apply cosmetics to female clients, and neither of them had brought up the first time she'd performed that service. The back room no longer held any mystery for her. Dear old gentle Janus would have been appalled.

In 1883, the steamboat *Silver Cloud* blew its boilers just below St. Charles, hurling the pilot's torn and broken body onto a bluff and corpses of mates and passengers as far as two hundred yards from the river. Twisted pieces of boiler decapitated a pedestrian ashore and collapsed part of a house, and two firemen went with the boat to the bottom. The mortician in St. Charles was short-staffed, and contracted with Richard, who rejoined the pedestrian's head to his body with braces and stitching, replaced the pilot's pulverized rib cage with fill not unlike what Sergei Rubyoff had used to mount his wolves and prairie dogs, evaporated moisture from the firemen's bloated tissue with a new electric heat lamp—a modern improvement upon the process he'd developed in San Francisco—and molded a new arm and hand for a female passenger crushed by a falling stack, as Bob McLoughlin had taught. He replaced burned tissue with cheesecloth, and as he often had, fell back upon his father's methods of grinding powders and blending pastes for the finish work; Janus had been far ahead of his colleagues in that area, if reluctant to pursue more efficient means of embalming. His son worked swiftly and without much thought, breaking only to eat and relieve himself and put drops in his sore and swollen eyes; the formaldehyde formula that preserved tissue so well continued its destruction of his ocular glands. There was nothing more anyone could teach him about his craft.

The disaster and its aftermath was, as Lucy had foreseen, an indication that their time in St. Louis was ending. Boiler explosions were not so common since the innovation of the safety valve, and not incidentally the decline in river travel since the railroads, and the story appeared in newspapers across the continent. The Connable connection had become a magnet for the morbid press. When reporters vaulted the iron fence around their home, rattling the knocker at all hours and trampling Lucy's flower bed, Richard advertised in the professional journals for the parlor's sale. His successor paid him a profit of 100 percent. They deposited the bulk of the money in their St. Louis bank, put the rest in a belt, and struck off West, always West.

Their stay in Creede, a log-and-canvas mining camp in Colorado, was over within weeks. Shortly after hard-rock mining commenced, a shaft collapsed, crushing sixteen men. Only seven of the bodies that were recovered offered any hope of restoration. The rest were sent on their way in closed coffins, and their closest relatives could not be sure if all the limbs and torsos wound up under the proper markers. Richard embalmed and restored the seven, deeded his wall-tent parlor over to his best apprentice, and he and Lucy went to Denver.

After that, she could seldom say with certainty whether this or that had happened in Cheyenne or Sheridan, or this friend or that rival had made their acquaintance in the oven of Tucson or the icebox of Bismarck. In North Platte, she stepped into a stairwell in the middle of the night, thinking it was the water closet in Billings, and ended up in a heap at the bottom with a broken leg. The only constant was Richard, drunk every January fifteenth, and Victoria, looking gravely out from her oval frame on the north wall of every downstairs parlor, her back to the storm.

The frontier closed. They'd seen it coming, if not in the houses and cities that sprang up where before only cottonwoods had stood perpendicular to the landscape, then in the number of clients who came to the Connable undertaking parlors dead of age or illness or falls from wagons as opposed to gunplay and hangings. One day—Lucy would remember the occasion with the joy of their wedding—Richard said that as long as the work was going to be the same West or East, they might as well go East, where a man could order fowl in a restaurant without risk of cracking a molar on a piece of lead shot. They chose Buffalo, for no other reason than that the climate in upstate New York was similar to Michigan's and that they'd never been there before, and whatever memories they made there would at least be free of the icy hands of the past. He bought into a partnership in a twenty-year-old firm, took the house Lucy had selected for its proximity to streetcars, and when the old founder retired, replaced the outdated facilities and hired Charles Haight, an eager young man with a delicate wife and a ten-year-old son, to assist him. Haight, it developed, was a graduate of the Craidlaw School of Mortuary Science in Chicago; although he'd enrolled long after Richard had left, the Connable legend had been established. But the apprentice was not so much in awe of the master that he hesitated to suggest improvements in the bookkeeping and billing procedure, and for that as much as his competence (not brilliance) in the morgue, Richard made him junior partner the year before he retired. Lucy had approved, despite Charles' tendency to be pompous, tolerable in a man of fifty but unseemly when there were no gray hairs to support it, and certain professional differences with the senior partner. She and Richard had discussed retirement, and they would not have to put up with Charles for long. In those circumstances, she'd almost have supported an unholy alliance with Colonel Kendrick.

And now little Charlie was in charge: or was, in any case, the one with whom she'd been forced to make arrangements. The receipt he'd given her was in her reticule. She must remember to put it away, in the bureau drawer where she kept her linens, where Richard would be sure to find it when he selected the items that were to be buried with her, to go with her best dress, recently cleaned by the new dry-process method and hanging in the wardrobe waiting for the smell of naphtha to dissipate; it was not much better than moth powder, and she wouldn't want a chemical odor to be the last impression she left. But perhaps he would know the details by then, from Charlie and his father. She couldn't imagine Richard approaching anyone else.

Certain other things would have to be destroyed, such as the letter she'd sent in 1885 to Max Crespo, which had been returned, creased and filthy and stamped all over with postmarks belonging to the cities and hamlets he'd stopped in after leaving San Francisco—the last, smudged and barely legible, from some place in Mexico. She supposed a good carpenter could find work anywhere; making coffins, perhaps, for revolutionaries and soldiers of the government in Mexico City. She'd written the letter and sent it in a fit of depression after her last letter to Elizabeth Chilson had been answered by Wilbur, with a brief summary of the circumstances of her death. She'd thrown out the stilted reply, but had been unable to part with her letter to Max, which had come closer to wherever he was than anything since San Francisco. It was upstairs in her glove box, under the gloves Richard would surely choose to cover the liver spots on her hands.

Richard knew about Lucy and Max. In the days following Victoria's death, they had spoken of things they would not have otherwise, and she'd learned then of the letter Richard had received in Hays City from that dreadful little man Pembroke Benjamin. Richard had been drunk when he told her, but she knew it was one conversation he'd never forget, although neither had brought up the subject since. He'd forgiven her. But she knew he would not understand the letter she'd written Max.

The clock struck the hour, the gears grinding between the chimes for lack of cleaning and oiling. She looked at the face, but she couldn't see the location of the hands. Her good eye was failing her, and that caused concern. She didn't really miss the use of the other. She fancied she could still see Victoria with it. Victoria would be almost thirty now, a shock. Lucy could picture her at that age, because she had always seemed so much older than she was, but she couldn't see her with a husband and children of her own. There had always been a distance between her and others, even her mother. Lucy could not imagine any young man putting up with it, and her children would be aware of it and resent her for it. It was as if Victoria knew she would not be here long, and from some sense of compassion so deep Lucy herself could not understand it, had set out from the beginning to spare all around her unnecessary grief by keeping them at arm's length. Children were wiser than adults were prepared to admit, and prescient to a degree that made perfectly reasonable people shudder and pick up their pace when they passed a cemetery at dusk.

Lucy really was desperately tired. It was only at such moments that she allowed herself to remember at such length—or, more precisely, could not prevent herself from doing so. She must not forget to put away that receipt, and destroy that letter, and soon.

A racking chill shook her. Her heart hesitated, like a gas flame sputtering, then resumed its rhythm. She thought suddenly of the coin-operated fixture in their hotel room the first night in Portland. Bad decision, that; the local morticians' association had formed a bloc that stifled free trade, denying newcomers access to goods and services essential to practice, and swinging the old club of obscure city ordinances to wear away at capital with fines and costs to comply. By then, Richard had the funds to fight them, but not the will; the chill damp climate permeated everything, including the personality of the residents. That mean greedy fixture in the hotel room was typical of the place. They'd left after eighteen days.

She sat absolutely still, one hand resting on the arm of the settee, the other on the cushion next to her. Her heart was beating normally, but she was still cold, and the day was warm, sunlight butting in through the west windows at an angle, solid as a girder. Just that morning, she'd been alarmed by Richard's sudden announcement that they would go West with the money that man Broughty had promised him. She hadn't known he'd been thinking along those lines, had thought he was contented to finish out his days in Buffalo. But the old transience was still there below the surface, like his taste for gin. Janus had warned her against it, but had given her no advice on how to prevent it. And now it didn't matter. He'd be making the journey without her.

She could barely see the clock now. She knew then the receipt from Connable & Haight would stay in her reticule until Richard found it, and that the letter to Max would wait for his discovery in her glove box and not among the ashes of the hearth. She could no more manage that flight of stairs than crawl up a sheer wall. She could not even stand. She hoped he'd forgive her as he had the first time.

She thought of Luke, seventeen forever and looking much younger in his coffin, her first experience with Richard's work, buttoned up tight in his uniform, a costume in a children's play. She thought of her mother and father, and in an arc of mutual loss, of little Charlie's poor mother, Madeleine, thin and pale as lace, no match for the Buffalo winter; of the Rooney brothers, roughnecks in morning coats, as vivid to her as if they'd met. She thought of Big Esther and the old woman in San Francisco, the client that had brought Richard into serious competition with Kendrick; of Janus' kind face above his old-fashioned high collar and stock that first time in the foyer of his parlor in Monroe; of Pembroke Benjamin's sly face and satanic, black-dyed whiskers; of Richard's face, beaming and proud, the first time he demonstrated the mechanism engineered to lift his clients from the basement morgue to the ground-floor visitation room on Commercial Street (the first time it worked, anyway); of ugly Creede, piled all around with red raw earth like discarded viscera, taller than the tents. Wild Bill, the killer, in his preposterous pirate's costume. Max's dark eyes, soft as a woman's in the virile olive face, his white even teeth. She smiled when she thought of their conspiracy to smuggle tomato juice past her thin-faced nurse. Richard's description of Isaac Shindle, like a tethered balloon. The brick buildings of Chicago. Virginia City, made of ice and iron.

Wherever did you find Luke's smile?

I found it in his sister's face.

There was another shuddering chill, and the pause in her heartbeat. She waited unmoving for it to start up again. And then she saw Victoria with both eyes.

Gordon Lindsey, John C. Broughty's secretary, stepped down from the Pullman to grasp Richard Connable's hand.

"It's been a privilege," Lindsey said. "I've spent most of my life in the company of famous men. They're usually a disappointment. You should be better known."

"What is that? Hordes of scribblers pestering you at train stations and knocking at your door. Why do you think your employer exiled himself to Long Island?" He was weary of this fellow, and aware of the time. If he missed the next streetcar he'd have to wait fifteen minutes for another.

"I wish you'd let me take you home. The cabs here are cheap compared to New York."

"The car goes right past my house. You don't want Warrick arriving in Chicago before you."

"They have to transfer him to the westbound. Mr. Broughty didn't intend for me to sit on the coffin."

Richard wasn't so sure he didn't. The telegram the secretary had received in reply to the progress report he'd wired was lengthy, but all he'd told the undertaker was he had orders to accompany Elihu Warrick's remains to Chicago, where Broughty's agents would claim them. On second thought, sitting on the coffin the whole way would be just what a man like Broughty would insist upon. Lindsey's offer to desert his post was flattering, but he'd been flattered enough for one day. He'd never much liked it.

Lindsey drew an envelope from an inside pocket. "He signed this bank draught before I left. I wish you'd reconsider Chicago. Mr. Broughty doesn't often invite a man to name his own price."

"Thank you. You'll find Craidlaw's people more than satisfactory to handle the last-minute details." He slid the envelope into his side pocket without opening it. They shook hands again.

When he stepped off at his corner, his shoulders sagged and his legs ached; he hadn't been on his feet for so long in years. His eyes burned. He stopped to moisten them from the dropper he carried everywhere now, then screwed it back into the little bottle, dropped it into his pocket, where it rustled against the envelope, and climbed to his front door. A house out West. He wondered what Lucy would say to Carson City. The dry heat would cure her rheumatism. She had trouble climbing stairs lately. And there would be no snowstorms to remind her of anything. He couldn't remember what had made them choose Buffalo.

There might be a parlor in Carson City where he could work one or two days a week. Warrick's case had reminded him how much he missed it. It was better than playing canasta with the cadavers from next door.

The house felt cold. The sun had set. He wondered if he ought to fire up the furnace, despite the date. No lamps burned, and it struck him that Lucy had gone back to sleep, and without him to wake her had not stirred. She'd seemed tired for some time. He'd noticed she favored her left eye when she read; he was sensitive to eyes. And she'd lost weight. He'd insist she make an appointment with her doctor, and make it himself if she refused. She never missed appointments.

He saw her reticule on the hall table then, and realized she'd been out. He didn't see her until he lit the gas pipe above the settee. And he knew without looking closer. It was the work.

Read on for a preview of

CAPE HELL

· **LOREN D. ESTLEMAN** ·

*Available from Tom Doherty Associates
in May 2016*

FORGE®

A FORGE BOOK

CHAPTER 1

Halfway back to civilization, Lefty Dugan began to smell.

It was my own fault, partly; I'd stopped on the north bank of the Milk River like some tenderheel fresh out of Boston instead of crossing and pitching camp on the other side. I was worn down to my ankles, and the sorry buckskin I was riding sprouted roots on the spot and refused to swim. The pack horse was game enough; either that, or it was too old to care if it was lugging a dead man or a month's worth of Arbuckle's. But it couldn't carry two, especially when one was as limp as a sack of stove-bolts and just as heavy. I was getting on myself and in no mood to argue, so I unpacked my bedroll.

A gully-washer square out of Genesis soaked my slicker clear through and swelled the river overnight. I rode three days upstream before I found a place to ford, by which time even the plucky pack horse was breathing through its mouth. In Chinook I hired a buckboard and put in to the mercantile for salt to pack the carcass, but the pirate who owned the store mistook me for Vanderbilt, and then the Swede who ran the livery refused to refund the deposit I'd made on the wagon. So I buried Lefty in the shadow of the Bearpaws and rode away from five hundred cartwheel dollars on a mount I should have shot and left to feed what the locals call Montana swallows: magpies, buzzards, and carrion crows.

The thing was, I'd liked Lefty. We'd ridden together for Ford Harper before herding cattle lost its charm, and he was always good for the latest joke from the bawdy houses in St. Louis; back then he wasn't Lefty, just plain Tom. Then he took a part-time job in the off-season blasting a tunnel through the Bitterroots for the Northern Pacific, and incidentally two fingers off his right hand.

Drunk, he was a different man. He'd had a bellyful of Old Rocking Chair when he stuck up a mail train outside Butte and was still on the same extended drunk when he drew down on me not six miles away from the spot. I aimed low, but the fool fell on his face and took the slug through the top of his skull.

Making friends has seldom worked to my advantage. They always seem to wind up on the other side of my best interests.

It was a filthy shame. Judge Blackthorne had a rule against letting his deputies claim rewards—something about keeping the body count inside respectable limits—but made an exception in some cases in return for past loyalty and present reliability, and I was one. It served me right for not allowing for Lefty's unsteady condition when I tried for his kneecap instead of his hat rack. The money was the same, vertical or horizontal.

To cut my losses, I lopped off his mutilated right hand so I could at least claim the pittance the U.S. Marshal's office paid for delivering fugitives from federal justice. I packed it in my last half-pound of bacon, making do for breakfast with a scrawny prairie hen I shot east of Sulphur Springs. I picked gristle out of my teeth for fifty miles.

The money from Washington would almost cover what I'd spent to feed that bag of hay I was using for transportation. After I sold it back to the rancher I'd bought it from just outside Helena, I was a nickel to the good. I rode the pack horse in town until it rolled over and died. I wished I'd known the beast when it was a two-year-old, and that's as much good as I've ever had to say about anything with four legs that didn't bark and fetch birds.

I spent the nickel and a lot more in Chicago Joe's Saloon, picked a fight with the faro dealer—won that one—and another with the city marshal—lost that one—and would have slept out my time in peace if the Judge himself hadn't come down personally to spring me.

"You'd better still be alive," he greeted me from the other side of the bars. "This establishment doesn't give refunds for bailing out damaged goods."

I pushed back my hat to take him in. He had on his judicial robes, but the sober official black only heightened his resemblance to Lucifer in a children's book illustration. I think he tacked the tearsheet up beside his shaving mirror so he could get the chin-whiskers just right. His dentures were in place. They'd been carved from the keyboard of a piano abandoned along the Oregon Trail, and he wore the uncomfortable things only when required by the dignity of the office. It was unlike him to go anywhere straight from session without stopping to change, especially the hoosegow. I was in for either a promotion or the sack.

"How's Ed?" I asked. The city marshal's name was Edgar Whitsunday, but only part of his first name ever made it off the door of his office. He'd been named after a dead poet, but being illiterate he sloughed off the accusation whenever it arose. He was a Pentecostal, and amused his acquaintances with his imperfect memorization of Scripture as drilled into him by a spinster aunt: I think my favorite was "I am the excrement of the Lord."

"He's two teeth short of a full house," Blackthorne said. "I told his dentist to bill Grover Cleveland."

"That's extravagant. What did you do with the rest of the piano?"

He scowled. The Judge had a sense of his own humor, but no one else's. "You realize I could declare court in session right here and find you in contempt."

"And what, put me in jail?" I looked at my swollen right hand. "At least I used my fists. Ed took the top off my head with the butt of his ten-gauge."

"You should be grateful he didn't use the other end." He sighed down to his belt buckle; it was fashioned from a medal of valor. Just what he'd done to earn it, I never knew. Even scraping forty years off his hide I couldn't picture him scaling a stockade or leading a charge up any but Capitol Hill. Probably he'd helped deliver the Democratic vote in Baltimore. "You cost me more trouble than half the men who ride for me. A wise man would let you rot."

"You make rotting sound bad." I slid my hat back down over my eyes. "Find somewhere else to distribute your largesse. This ticky cot is the closest thing I've had to a hotel bed since I rode out after Lefty."

"You can't refuse bail. Marshal Whitsunday needs this cell. The Montana Stock-Growers Association is in town, and you know as well as I those carpetbaggers will drink the place dry and shoot it to pieces."

"Good. I was getting lonesome."

"Shake a leg, Deputy. You're needed."

That made me sit up and push back my hat. He wouldn't admit needing a drink of water in the desert.

He said, "I'm short-handed. Jack Sweeney, your immediate superior, went over my head to Washington and commandeered all my best men to bring the rest of Sitting Bull's band back from Canada to face justice for Custer."

"They gave that bloody dandy justice at the Little Big Horn nine years ago. What's the rush?"

"Sweeney's contract runs out in September, and there's a Democrat in the White House." He held up a key ring the size of Tom Thumb's head and stuck one in the lock. "Go back to your hotel, clean up, and report to my chambers at six sharp."

"Since when do you adjourn before dark?"

"I swung the gavel on the Bohannen Brothers at four. You've got forty-five minutes to clean up and shave. You look like the Wild Man of Borneo and smell like a pile of uncured hides."

"How'd you convict the Bohannens without my testimony? I brought them in."

"They tried to break jail and killed the captain of the guard. That bought them fifty feet of good North Carolina hemp without your help."

"Bill Greene's dead?"

"I'm sorry. I didn't know you were close."

"He owed me ten dollars on the Fitzgerald fight. I don't guess he mentioned me in his will."

His big silver watch popped open and snapped shut. "Forty-four minutes. If I catch so much as a whiff of stallion sweat in my chambers, I'll fine you twenty-five dollars for contempt of court."

"Collect it from the stallion."

"That's twenty-five dollars you owe the United States."

I swung my feet to the floor, stood, wrestled for balance, and found it with my fists around the bars. "What's so urgent? Did we declare war on Mexico again?"

He looked as grim as ever he had during damning evidence. "What have you heard?"

Forge

Award-winning authors
Compelling stories

. . . .

Please join us at the website
below for more information
about this author and other great
Forge selections, and to sign up for
our monthly newsletter!

. . . . 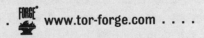 www.tor-forge.com . . . .